Praise for Caleb Quinn...

For the western adventure fans who read the L'Amour novels again and again comes a fresh story teller, vividly recreating the nineteenth century. From a manor house in Ireland to the brawling American West, Coryell takes his characters on an exciting journey of hope and redemption by way of enough "near misses" to assure that the pages keep turning. *When the Night Bird Calls* is an odyssey of quiet and deceptive style with surprises at every turn.

Ann Golias
Writer

America was a land of opportunity and adventure for the great masses of underprivileged and downtrodden Irish in the 19th century. Bruce Coryell tells the epic story of a one of these Irishmen named Caleb Quinn who killed a brutal British landlord while still a teenager.

His escape from Ireland and his coming of age in an American circus makes for a remarkable tale. In manhood, during the Civil War, he was the first of a kind, a sniper; the prototype of our modern Navy Seal or Army Ranger.

The epic story ends in Texas with a life or death struggle with a fierce and feared Comanche warrior. Of course along the way, our hero, Caleb has not one, but two "love of your life" great love stories.

No first book author has done a better job telling his story. The reader is there for all the action, suspense, pain and love that quickly flow and sometimes dramatically change from page to page. You won't want to put this book down!

If you like to read Louis L'Amour, you will love this book. The author just might be the next great American adventure writer.

Tipton Golias
President & Founder, Helena Laboratories,
ETOCO, Inc., and a history buff

D. BRUCE CORYELL

WHEN THE NIGHT BIRD CALLS

THE SAGA OF CALEB QUINN

dccoryell@yahoo.com

TO PURCHASE COPIES OF THE NOVEL WRITE OR
EMAIL:

15 HAVANOGOTTA ROAD
MINERAL BLUFF, GA 30559

dccoryell@yahoo.com

ISBN-1:978-0-578-05201-4

FIRST PRINTING APRIL 2010
PRINTED IN THE UNITED STATES OF AMERICA

ROBIN,

Thanks for coming to the Focus Group; I hope you enjoy the book-

Bruce Crippel

Acknowledgement

This novel is dedicated to my family and friends whose names I shamelessly borrowed with some trepidation but no apology. I can only trust they enjoy finding glimpses of themselves within its pages.

It is also dedicated to my wife, Chris, who shares our home with me in northern Georgia, and who is the driving force and inspiration for all that I have written.

A special thanks to a dear friend, Mary Stanley, and my mother, Evelyn Bevill, for the editing work they so generously provided.

A heartfelt thanks to Helena Laboratories, especially T.G. and Ann, Carrie F., John F., John T., Reg W., and all my other friends at the "flying H" who made this first publication necessary.

Respectfully

D. Bruce Coryell

"Better to pass boldly into that other world, in the full glory of some passion, than fade and wither dismally with age."

~James Joyce, an Irishman

Part 1

I am the inferior of any man whose rights I trample underfoot.
~Horace Greeley, a printer

Chapter 1 The Conflict

Under cover of late night darkness the group of six men emerged from the thick stand of ash trees growing just a short stone's throw from the house of their intended victim. They were hard men living in hard times and not above bending the law if, by doing so, it put a few precious pounds in their pockets. They were neither bad nor evil men at heart, but years of poverty and deprivation at the hands of their English rulers had turned them into desperate men willing to accept whatever work they could in order to provide for themselves and their impoverished families. In that they were not much different from the people living in the mud and stone house they were approaching.

A seventh man, an Englishman, was the only one among them carrying a firearm. The others, all Irish born and bred, were forbidden by English law to own or carry firearms. As a result the other men were armed with belt knives and crude hardwood clubs the thickness of a man's wrist and the length of a man's arm. These were especially lethal weapons in the hands of a strong man, and all of the six Irishmen had a good measure of strength and the willingness to use it if necessity dictated.

The silent house standing before them was, like most of the homes of the Irish peasant, windowless, making it fairly easy to approach unseen and unheard by anyone within. Still, the men made their way to the house with great caution, moving as silently as stalking wolves. They were all well aware the man inside was extremely dangerous. Throughout County Antrim, Michael O'Connell was known as a man of courage, of superb fighting skills and a great strength inherited from his father and honed by years of back-breaking labor and harsh living. He was also a man of the outdoors known to have a sharp instinct for survival and the eyes and ears of both predator and prey. A man who had proven his ability to overcome great adversity on more than one occasion.

The men approaching the house knew blood would be spilled this night, and if careless, it might well be their own. Added to their concern was the prospect of also dealing with his two sons, both young, but also known to be staunch fighters when provoked. As the men silently made their way forward, only a solitary field mouse, foraging in the predawn for a few seeds left over from the summer, observed their stealthy passing.

Sweating slightly despite the coolness of the night air, the nervous men eased themselves silently over the short stone wall bordering the property, and moved in unison toward the front of the house. Coming within a few feet of the door they paused, collecting their breath and listening for any noise coming from within, any sign indicating their approach had been detected. Hearing none and making none themselves, two of the largest men moved forward and stopped in front of the entry. Following a silent nod from their leader they lowered their shoulders and charged hard into the door before them. The door, made from ships' timbers washed up on the nearby shore, was more solidly built than the flimsy ones more common to poor Irish households. The portal withstood their assault, but only barely. Hastily backing away, the two men once again threw themselves forward. Their second charge ripped the door from its leather hinges and sent it crashing onto the dirt floor of the darkened room.

The sound of the first attempt to break down the door instantly awoke Michael O'Connell, the lone man sleeping on the straw covered floor. Rolling away from the thin mat used as a bed and throwing off the heavy wool blanket covering him, he reached for a polished hardwood cane, crafted by his own hand, and always kept within easy reach. The cane was normally used to aid the walking of the long ago crippled man, but when needed could be used as a fearsome weapon. This was a time of such need, and Michael, with a calmness learned by a lifetime of conflict, determined to put it to good use. Bracing himself on the cane, he was half-way to his feet as the door shattered from the impact of the second blow and the first two assailants, framed in the light of a half moon, poured inside. Michael, cane in hand, moved forward to meet them knowing his attackers most likely intended murder, or at the least to cause him serious injury.

Caught partially off balance by the sudden collapse of the door and unable to see clearly in the dark room, the first intruder was barely able to raise an arm in time to protect himself from the cane slashing out of the dark. Michael could hear a satisfying muted crack as the cane struck the intruder on his raised elbow, shattering muscle and bone. The man fell back, groaning from the pain caused by the broken elbow.

Pushing his injured cohort ruthlessly aside, the second assailant charged headlong into the fray. An experienced fighter, he swung his club in front of him while staying low and bent at the waist as he hurled himself forward, intent on using his weight and momentum to bowl over his victim and bring him to the ground, thus enabling him and the others to bring a swift end to the fight.

Michael had seen and overcome similar attacks before, and rather than meet force with force, dropped the cane at his feet, ducked low, turned sideways, and used his straightened left arm to catch his assailant in the chest. At the same time with his right hand he grasped the charging man in the groin area, lifted the totally surprised man over his head, and tossed him nearly half-way across the room. With an audible thud the man hit the ground hard, landing on his back and shoulders, knocking the breath from his lungs, lucky not to have landed on his head and neck as Michael had intended. Michael, his back now to the door and the remaining men, without looking, threw back his right elbow as hard and fast as he could, catching a third man solidly in the center of his face, breaking the man's nose and collapsing the bones protecting the lower part of his right eye.

Spinning around quickly, Michael felt in the dark for the cane he had dropped at his feet, but before he could grasp it, a solid blow from an unseen assailant's club struck him across the right shoulder, breaking the collarbone and driving him down on one knee. Shocked by the blow and unable to lift his right arm, Michael kicked out with his right foot hoping to catch the fourth assailant in either the stomach or groin. His foot met only empty air. Before he could recover, he received a second blow from either a fist or club, for he could not tell which. The blow, striking him in his face, split his lower lip and left several of his upper front teeth loose and bleeding. Knocked back and dazed from his injuries, Michael tripped over the still prone figure of his second assailant and fell hard, striking the back of his head where the floor met the wall.

Realizing there was no one else in the house to come to Michael's defense, the remaining uninjured men, seizing their advantage, were on him before he could regain his feet. Michael felt his head pushed down by a strong hand while thick calloused fingers sought to gouge out his eyes. Opening his mouth as far as possible Michael clamped his teeth down hard on the man's hand, catching the soft flesh between the thumb and the forefinger. Violently twisting his head from the left and then back to the right, he tasted blood he knew was not his own. Despite the pain caused by his loosened teeth, he continued biting down through the flesh of the hand until he was struck another blow by a well-aimed club, splitting his forehead open half its length. A torrent of blood poured down into his eyes and over his face. Blinded, half unconscious, and unable to raise even his one remaining good arm in defense, he was unable to ward off any of the following blows to his head, neck and shoulders. In a final act of survival, he turned on his side and desperately curled his body into a ball and wrapped his left arm around his head hoping that even a moment's reprieve from his enemies' blows might give him enough time to regain his feet and go on the attack. Injured as he was, his thoughts were not on escape, only attack; to kill those who would kill him.

Had it been ten years or perhaps even five years before, he might have succeeded. But for a severely injured man of nearly forty-five, an age when many Irishmen had gone to their Maker, Michael had the will and the courage, but not the strength. As the blows from his assailants continued to rain down on him, he slowly slipped into blessed unconsciousness. As if looking at a dying candle, slowly and mercifully the bright lights swirling before his eyes faded away, to be replaced by total darkness. Michael neither heard nor felt the many blows that followed.

After witnessing the fight from just outside the open door, Lord Warington, the English leader of the attack, spoke into the darkened room, "Drag him outside, I want to see what we have left to deal with."

Quickly those men who had escaped injury grabbed the unconscious body of their victim by his feet, and dragged him over the broken door into the moonlit yard at the front of the house. There they spread eagled him face up on the ground.

A pail full of cold water struck Michael in the face, starting his return to consciousness and pain, a pain reaching to every part of his broken body. At first he was unable to open his eyes due to the bloodied dirt covering them, but even in that darkness it was evident to his slowly returning senses that something or someone was preventing the movement of his arms. A second pail of water thrown on him served to further clear his senses and wash away most of the blood and dirt covering his eyes. Now able to see, and with his mind clearing, he realized he was flat on his back in the yard, his arms stretched out on either side and held in place under the hob-nailed boots of several of his assailants.

Looking up from his helpless position on the damp ground he could see outlined against the faint glow of moonlight, the figure of a small man standing over him, holding a burning torch in one hand and a

4

riding quirt in the other. In a shrill voice filled with triumph and a hint of insanity, his enemy of many years spoke down to him.

"Michael O'Connell, it's good you are awake because I intend for you to feel even more pain. I want you to know that after all these years the Waringtons have won, and that you and your O'Connell trash will die this night. When I'm done with you, you will swallow your ignorant pride and beg me for a mercy that will not come!"

Then, filling his lungs with a deep breath and raising the thick black quirt high above his head, he began to thrash the helpless man lying at his feet, splitting his skin and drawing rivulets of blood with each swing.

Michael grimaced with each lash from the man's bloodied quirt. He felt the skin of his face, neck and shoulders being ripped into shreds, could feel his flesh being split apart to the bone. Still, he refused to give his hated tormentor the satisfaction of hearing him cry out. In his entire life Michael O'Connell had never begged, not to any man, not to the God he loved, and, of a certainty, not to an Englishman. Through his pain he could hear Warington, in an almost feminine voice, a voice filled with hatred, repeatedly scream at him, "Beg me for mercy. Beg, beg, beg!"

Warington's insane-like rage only grew in intensity with the continuing silence from his victim. Michael, summoning strength from his hatred for the Waringtons, had made not even a moan, nor did one word asking for mercy pass his tortured lips.

Warington, partially covered in Michael's blood, abruptly lowered the bloodied quirt to his side and stepped back to admire his terrible workmanship. After staring at Michael for a full minute, he then smiled and said to his men, "Finish him, and after you're done we'll deal with his missing whelps."

Warington turned toward the house and tossed the torch on to the sod roof as he departed and headed at a brisk walk in the direction of the horse he had left tethered in the woods. His men, three of them nursing wounds received during the fight, moved to follow their leader, but not before giving Michael several vicious kicks to the body and head, sure any man so badly beaten would die in a few minutes. Lord Warington, grimly determined to use any means to rid the countryside of all O'Connell men, young or old, proven poachers or not, mounted his horse. With his henchmen following on foot, he began the pursuit of the missing sons, determined to bring an end to the lives of the two remaining O'Connells, and an end to the shame which had gripped his thoughts for almost two decades.

Chapter 2 The Sons

"Irish twins" are two siblings born in the same year. Two such brothers, both born in the year 1842, one in early January and one in mid December, and both now sixteen years of age, found themselves shivering in the cold air of a foggy Irish morning. They had spent much of the early predawn hours running and hiding from a pack of determined pursuers led by Lord Warington. The brothers had fled for hours from the men, leading them first through the marshes and then the highlands and rolling hills that separated Ballycastle from Torr. It was only in the last hour before sunrise the exhausted brothers felt confident they had at last lost them.

Sean, the younger of the two by eleven months was of slight build, with pale green eyes hidden beneath a crop of mahogany-colored hair and a delicate smile, all gifts from the mother he had barely known. He was also fleet of foot, and despite being younger, the faster runner of the two boys. Like his mother he was by nature a daydreamer, both gentle and quiet, a lover of song and music, and in possession of a remarkable tenor voice. His was the voice that lent beauty to the songs of the Irish at Christmastime or during the secret gatherings of his fellow Catholics when they could find a priest devoted enough and brave enough to defy English law and conduct a Mass. Much like his father and elder brother, Sean could be stubborn, and once set on a goal or course of action seldom veered from it.

His brother, Liam, despite the many years of hunger brought on by the plague that had devastated the potato crop all over Ireland, was taller by several inches and much heavier. He stood an inch over six feet and weighing just under 170 pounds, much of it sinewy muscle, giving him the same extraordinary strength possessed by his father and his father before him. He was overly daring to a fault, often hot-tempered and unpredictable, but from a young age his courage and daring made him the acknowledged leader among his peers. When it came to a good fight or athletic contest, few grown men who knew young Liam would willingly challenge him to a test of bare knuckles or wrestling. Of those that did, none left the contest unscathed and only a few of the strongest and most experienced went away victorious. He was, like his father, a natural-born fighter.

Liam shared the dark brown eyes of his father, but where his father's eyes often seemed dull and filled with sadness, Liam's deep-set eyes were usually lively, as if a gleaming light burned within them, a light that seemed to get brighter when he became excited or angry, and, like his father, this could be often. Liam was his father's son in looks, temperament, and their insatiable passion for the outdoors. Both were proud, strong in their convictions, loyal almost to a fault, never shirked a responsibility or debt, were compassionate toward man and animal, never taking from nature more than was needed, and always quick to share with those of a greater need than their own.

The O'Connells were an example of the best men produced in this proud land of verdant hills, jagged wind-swept coast, and cold rushing streams.

Still cautious, Sean and Liam O'Connell lay hidden and motionless for another half hour, careful to make no movement that would betray their hiding place. They had known from the beginning of the pursuit that it was Lord Warington and his hired thugs who pursued them since no one else in County Antrim but Lord Warington possessed wealth enough to own such a fine steed or had the single-mindedness of purpose when it came to pursuing poachers. The brothers had chosen their hiding place well, for this was not the first time they have been hunted by Lord Simon Warington's hired men. Many of the hired men had once themselves been poachers, but now, usually out of desperation, worked for anyone willing to pay for their services. Many years back, English landowners had learned that if Irishmen would not be subjugated by force or the harsh laws imposed on them by the crown, they could often be bought off with only a few English pounds. The reality of starvation or even imprisonment had that affect on many an Irishman who otherwise would have staunchly resisted the hated English who had taken control of their county, a control of the land the Irish had endured for the past five hundred years.

For the pursuers, their failure to capture the young poachers would mean only a wasted night of searching followed by a return to the warmth of their own homes located near the Warington estate. For the ever elusive and somewhat desperate brothers failure to avoid capture would mean, at the least, becoming the main attraction at a flogging in the village square at Ballycastle or at Torr, or at the worst a public hanging designed to demonstrate to all who viewed it the penalty for opposing the edicts of English authority, however cruel and unreasonable those edicts might be.

The brothers, more than most boys their age, were well prepared to avoid falling into the hands of those wishing to do them harm. When they were barely out of infancy, their father began to teach his sons many of the skills needed in order to survive in a land of scarce resources, a land ruled by laws designed by their English masters to squelch the spirit, if not the life, of any Irish Catholic. He taught them how to find their way at night by the position of the stars, and when the skies were overcast with no stars to guide them, by the direction of the wind blowing in from the Irish Sea, the growth of moss on rocks and trees, or even the flight of birds heading for a known roost. On dark nights the brothers learned to recognize where they were by the different smells floating in from the sea or carried on the night breezes from the woods. In daylight they knew how to use hidden paths or camouflage to move unseen from their home to any hill, road, shoreline, river or stand of trees within their area of County Antrim. Thanks to the foresight of their father, in darkness or daylight, in even the most featureless terrain, they could always find their way to the safety of home, or when necessary disappear in the blink of an eye.

They became early masters of their environment learning full well how to make use of whatever nature provided. If hungry, they knew where to find berries, roots, and insects, even in the midst of winter. If cold, it took them only a few minutes to start a fire using the sparks from flint struck on a knife blade to ignite the dry grass which both carried at all times. By the time Liam and Sean reached their teens, few men in all of Ireland and fewer still boys of their own age, were more suited to endure the rigors of a poacher's life than the O'Connell brothers.

Perhaps the most valuable lessons learned from their father were those of patience, concealment, and the ways to outwit their English adversaries. Their father taught them from childhood that the best hiding place was often the most open, a place easily seen by their enemies, and therefore the place most unlikely to attract a searching eye. He called this strategy "taking the obvious and reversing it." It was a lesson that had never failed them.

Remembering their father's words they had chosen for their hiding place from their pursuers not the nearby wooded area cloaked in shadows and darkness, but a shallow depression in the open ground near the high grass growing at the base of a small and almost barren hill. Other than the grass, the only cover found there were several knee-high coarse bushes, the kind of cover few searchers would think to notice because of its shortness and the open location. These the brothers used to their further advantage by keeping their heads under the bushes so that any sign of their breathing was harmlessly dissipated by both the tightly knit branches and the hands the brothers held over their mouths. They were further aided in their concealment by the camouflage capes they wore over their bodies. The capes were made of small branches, grasses, mosses, leaves, and bits of dirt-colored strips of old cloth, all of which were interwoven into a net cut to lay out flat and sufficient in size to cover a large prone man. Even to an experienced eye such as other poachers, the boys in their capes were almost impossible to find if they chose to stay hidden and motionless, and that was something they were able to do for hours. Thanks to the lessons learned from their father, for several years now they were not only successful at trapping or catching game of all sorts, but they were equally successful at alluding detection or capture by vengeance-minded aristocratic English landowners.

Sean, his hand held an inch away from his mouth, cautiously whispered to Liam lying close by, "We must be about while the fog can still be used to hide our movement."

Liam, already thinking ahead of the need for them to put more distance between themselves and those hunting them replied in a low whisper, "Patience, Sean, it's better that we wait a few minutes and let the fog lessen."

Looking from left to right while barely moving his head he added, "You're right that the fog can hide us, but it might also cause us to walk blindly into the hands of our 'friendly' pursuers."

Liam's tone of voice was intentionally jovial, but his nervous stomach would have told a far different story. He knew full well how real was their danger, but he did not want his brother to feel his own apprehension, as it might fuel Sean's mounting anxiety. What Liam couldn't understand and that which worried him most was that although he and Sean had been hunted before, never had it been with the dogged determination shown by their pursuers this past night. Something had changed and Liam wanted to get home, not only for their own safety, but to ask his father **why** they were being so tenaciously pursued.

Without moving he whispered to Sean, "Do you suppose Lord Warington might be slightly upset by the dwindling number of his precious foxes running about on his property?"

Liam's question forced muted laughter to overcome both of them.

"You know how he loves to go fox hunting with his English

10

friends," said Sean, recalling that on the last hunt held, due to a shortage of foxes thanks to poaching, Lord Warington was forced to use previously trapped foxes in order to have a hunt suitable to his stature as Lord of the Manor.

Most of the poaching had come at the hands of the O'Connells. Once again the brothers shared a moment of silent laughter.

After waiting a few more minutes, Liam, judging it now safe enough to move, cautiously raised his head and looked out over the wide and nearly empty expanse before him. In no direction could he detect any movement save for a few wisps of lingering ground fog. Waiting a moment longer to take a final look, he whispered to his brother, "Time to go."

Sean, hungry, tired, and eager to end the night of running and hiding, and return home to a hot meal and warm blanket, promptly whispered back, "I'm ready."

With Liam taking the lead, as usual, they set out in the direction of the home they had left almost a day and a half before. After several hours of hard walking over broken and often slippery ground interrupted by only a few minutes of rest while they stopped to listen for any noise that didn't belong, they found themselves within sight of the only home they had ever known. Concealing themselves in the same woods that had previously hidden their father's attackers, they silently took in the frightening sight of their house smoldering beneath its burned thatched roof. The roof was almost completely burned away, but the walls of the house, due to their earthen and stone construction, still stood.

Although feeling a growing concern for their father's safety, the brothers remained concealed in the trees patiently looking for any sign of danger. After ten minutes of watching had passed, without detecting any movement near or in the house, they quickly crossed the open yard. Drawing the skinning knives they carried in their belts, the boys cautiously entered the house through the shattered doorway. Before them lay broken furniture and dishes, overturned boxes and baskets that had contained their small supply of food, and, laying on top of some scattered clothing, their father's walking cane.

All of this was disheartening to them, but what concerned the brothers most were the heavy blood stains in the dirt next to their father's sleeping place. Looking at the amount of blood on the floor it seemed certain to each of them that someone, most likely their father, had been severely injured or killed as the result of a violent struggle. By the barely visible marks etched into the hard-packed floor, both Liam and Sean suspected a body had been dragged outside the house. Exiting the house with a growing apprehension, Liam and Sean split up, desperately searching for their father or any sign of the people responsible for the destruction.

Liam, circling the area around the house found nothing and called loudly to Sean who was searching the woods. "Have you found anything?" In his urgency to find his father he little cared if anyone heard him.

"Da's not here," came the reply, "but I have found a horse's hoof marks and footprints of a number of men."

Joining Sean, Liam examined the tracks and footprints, now convinced the men who had been at the house were the same men who had been pursuing them. Moving back to the house for another look at the destruction, the brothers then decided to go to the only place their father would have gone if he was able to move. Fear for their father urging them on, they set out at a fast pace for the coast and the secret seaside cave the family had used for many years.

Chapter 3 The Passing

Michael O'Connell had drifted in and out of consciousness during the night and into the early day. Blood covered his face and caked in his dark hair and beard. His thinking was clouded by intense pain and the constant torment inflicted by the flies which had found the deep bloody cuts across his shoulders and face. His head throbbed, his body ached terribly, but worst of all was the thirst caused by exertion and the loss of blood. He needed water badly, both for his throat and to combat the rising temperature he felt throughout his battered body. Pushing with his left arm he twisted his body to the right and looked about the small cave. Barely able to open his swollen eyes he could see to his left stacks of small tin boxes which once contained tea leaves, but now held only a few dried or smoked fish and a handful of onions and other edible roots. To his right were several jute bags containing dried animal skins as well as a few snares, skinning knives, and stretching frames. Desperate for water he leaned over in an attempt to lick whatever moisture might have gathered on the tin boxes. There was none, and all he could do was run a dry tongue over his parched and split lips.

The enclosure sheltering Michael was little more than a large crevice cut into the cliffs by thousands of years of wind, wave action, and erosion. The cave was about twenty feet above the shoreline and slightly less than a mile from the O'Connell home. The opening to the cave was concealed by large, fallen pieces of rock that left only enough room for a grown man to crawl through. In addition to the rock the entrance was normally concealed by kelp woven into a covering similar to the capes worn by the O'Connells when poaching. Now it was uncovered. After enduring the torturous crawl on the obscure path leading to the cave almost a mile from his home, a trip made more torturous due to dragging himself over ground covered by rocks, shale, shell, and any number of low growing prickly thorn bushes which tore at his already tortured body, Michael could not summon the strength to return the cover to its proper place.

A few minutes after gaining consciousness, a series of severe convulsions racked his body while at the same time making him even more nauseous. Michael, although wanting with all his being to stay awake until his sons found him, for he knew they would, was nonetheless grateful for the darkness he felt closing in, a darkness where he knew there would be no pain, no excruciating agony. It was in this unconscious state that his sons were to find him.

As the brothers made for the nearby cave they took care to wipe out any sign of their father's passing while leaving none of their own. They warily approached the cave in case some of Lord Warington's hirelings, possibly under the command of his son William, could be lingering nearby to accost Michael's sons if they came looking for their Da. Nearing the edge of the cliff above the cave and still wearing their camouflage capes, the boys began to move slowly toward the cave dreading what they might find inside.

When they were within hearing distance of the cave, Liam, after listening for several minutes declared, "I'm sure it's clear," and tossing aside his cape, ran the remaining distance to the cave's entrance.

Crouching on one knee and looking in, Liam could barely make out what at first appeared to be only a pile of mud covered clothes lying on the cave's floor. As his eyes adjusted to the darkness, he quickly realized the clothes were covering a man's body, a body that could only be that of his father.

Moving to the lifeless form Liam knelt down and exclaimed, "Oh Da, what have they done to you?"

At that moment Sean squeezed through the entrance and collapsed at his father's feet. Looking at Liam he cried, "Is he dead?"

Bending down Liam placed his ear over his father's chest listening intently, hoping and praying for the sound of a beating heart. After a moment he detected just the faintest heartbeat. Straightening up he said to Sean, "He's alive, but only barely."

Thinking back to the destroyed house, he added, "Sean, we need fresh water, food, and warm blankets. Go back to the house, gather up what you can carry, and get back here as fast as you can, but be on the look out for the Waringtons or their men. They may still be looking for us."

Having by now observed his father's open wounds, he added, "I also need whatever tea leaves you can find. Hurry, Sean!"

Without further orders or hesitation, Sean, his heart racing, bolted from the cave, running as fast as he'd ever run in his life. He returned within a half-hour, carrying the things Liam had requested, along with a clean shirt he thought could be torn into bandages to cover his father's wounds. It had been a run that taxed his strength to its limits, and with the last of his energy, Sean handed Liam the bundle of things he had requested. He then knelt on the floor beside his father and, after taking several minutes to regain his breath, began tearing the shirt into bandages.

Liam tried to give water to his father but found it only possible to trickle a few drops between his cracked lips and broken teeth. Soaking part of the shirt in the cold water he bathed the wounds on his father's face and upper body, careful not to start them bleeding by rubbing too hard.

After several minutes cleaning the wounds, satisfied he had done all he could, he said to Sean, "That's done, and now I need the tea leaves."

Sean had been fortunate enough to find a half-full tin of tea in the ransacked house. Wetting a handful of the brittle leaves, Liam rolled them in his hands until they formed a moist, supple cigar shape, and then gently applied them to those deep wounds on his father's face and neck that were still oozing blood. Years before he had seen this treatment work and hoped it would prevent any further bleeding. He knew mosses could be used in the same way, but tea leaves, for reasons he didn't understand, seemed to work far better and faster at staunching a flow of blood. Completing the treatment, he then covered and wrapped the wounds with the make-shift bandages Sean had hastily prepared.

Following this, he carefully examined his father's body for possible undetected broken bones, but to his relief could neither see nor feel any. To his great dismay, he could see an enormous number of dark purple bruises covering Michael's upper body and back, a testimony to the viciousness his father's attackers had used when they administered what he had overheard Englishmen of noble birth jokingly refer to as "poacher's justice." As Liam looked at his father's wounds his hatred of the Waringtons and the English began to grow even larger than he could imagine. How could they so unjustly attack a man who was merely trying to sustain life for himself and his sons? Now he knew why certain men and women had risked and often given their lives to oppose English rule.

Michael O'Connell lingered in unconsciousness throughout the day and into the first hours of the evening. Twice during this time he seemed to struggle to speak, but to his sons' dismay only managed to push a weak gurgle through his torn lips. Although the brothers recognized their father's condition was critical, they remained optimistic that his great strength of body and will would overcome his injuries. It had always seemed to them that nothing; not the years of famine he endured, not the harsh life imposed on him by men or nature, nor even the severe beating inflicted by Warington and his men, could conquer his great strength. He was their father.

Hours later Sean and Liam, after carefully wrapping him in blankets, moved Michael a few feet from the cave entrance so that the added light might enable them to better attend his wounds, and in the hope the brisk sea breeze blowing against the cliffs might cool the fever gripping him. Despite their efforts and more than a few prayers, their father's condition only worsened as the day passed into night. Shortly past midnight, under a half moon, and penetrating through the sound of the ocean's waves lapping at the rocks below, the lilting call of a night bird could be heard. To the brothers, it seemed as if God was calling their father's soul, a thought that sent shivers through their bodies. Less than five minuets later, without having regained consciousness, Michael O'Connell passed away.

They buried their father on the top of the hill overlooking their home and the shallow, gentle stream running past it. Under a large and barren lightening-scarred tree and next to the wife he had lost twelve years earlier, Michael O'Connell came to his final resting place in the land he loved and was now forever a part of.

Chapter 4 Vengeance

The death of their father, and the manner of it, affected the brothers in different ways. For Sean the sadness was a complete thing. He felt drained of all energy, almost too heavy of body to move, his legs and arms leaden. He wished only to leave this now terrible part of the world, to go anywhere he could to escape the sorrow pervading his every thought.

Like Sean, Liam also felt a deep sadness, but unlike Sean, his sadness was mixed with a seething and unrelenting anger which filled his mind with thoughts of nothing but vengeance; the need to hunt those he knew beyond a doubt had brought about his father's gruesome death. Over his parents' graves, through clenched teeth and with fists and face raised to the sky, Liam swore to God above that for what the Waringtons had done to his family they would pay dearly. He would bring vengeance without mercy to the Waringtons by whatever means he could devise, at whatever price he must pay. Even with their father dead, Liam knew the Waringtons, who had hated the entire O'Connell family for over a decade, would not rest until they brought about the ruin of the two remaining O'Connells, Sean and himself. That he would not allow, and if moving to the attack first would prevent it, then move he would.

The Waringtons and the remaining O'Connells were now locked in a struggle to survive, and Liam was determined to strike them first, when and where they least expected. He would not wait for an attack to come to him and Sean. He would take the fight to them that very night. Liam planned nothing short of the total destruction of everything the Waringtons held dear. He would destroy their home, their possessions, and, if given the opportunity take their lives in exchange for the life taken from him. To this end he resolved to show no mercy to the Waringtons or any who stood with them.

After the burial, Liam and Sean returned one last time to the cottage to collect what supplies they could salvage from the burned out house, supplies they would need during the coming days, supplies needed for the long and dangerous journey Liam knew faced Sean and him after they exacted their revenge. He understood with certainty that whatever happened from this point on he and Sean would never again be safe in this ancient land they called home.

For an hour Sean and Liam carefully rummaged through their ransacked house, collecting extra clothes, a few cooking and eating utensils, fish hooks, a small roll of string, an extra skinning knife for each of them, extra flint, and three treasured tintypes, one of their parents' wedding, one of the O'Connell family, and the last of their father and mother taken just before her passing. Satisfied they had collected what was needed, the brothers placed their supplies in two bags, tied them closed, and left just as the sun dropped below the horizon. As they walked away neither Liam nor Sean dared look back at their home, both afraid that in the looking their hearts would break.

That night they made a cold camp within the deserted courtyard of St. Calum's Monastery, east of Ballycastle, and less than two miles from the Warington estate at Torr. The crumbling monastery sheltering the brothers had gone unused for over twenty years and was little visited by the inhabitants of the area. This was due in part to English law forbidding Catholics to gather in places to practice their "heathen" religion, but also due to the town inhabitants' ingrained fear of the ghosts of the dead rumored to frequent the monastery and the adjoining cemetery.

Sean, himself a staunch believer in the supernatural, in ghosts and spirits, in goblins, and witches and devils, turned to Liam, who sat in the dark only a few feet away. He said with a slight edge of fear to his voice, "Do you suppose there are ghosts here?"

Instead of replying and despite the fatigue overtaking him and the events of the day, Liam felt compelled to laugh, and did so. His loud, almost demonic, laughter swept through the broken walls of the monastery, past the rows of headstones facing the road, and out into the empty night. It was Liam's way of trying to empty himself of the heartache and sorrow he felt deep in his heart and mind. It was also his way of acknowledging to himself his hatred for the Waringtons. Hearing his brother's laughter, Sean feared that perhaps Liam was fey. To his great relief, Liam's laughter ended as abruptly as it started and a total silence returned to the courtyard.

Within minutes Liam said to Sean, "It's time to sleep for a few hours. After that we will have much to do before the sun rises."

Covering themselves with blankets the brothers immediately fell into much needed but troubled sleep. Liam, usually a heavy sleeper, was awakened several times during the night by the sound of muted crying coming from where Sean lay. He, himself, had cried in silence before he fell asleep.

Several hours before sunlight Liam awoke, revenge on the Waringtons foremost in his mind. It didn't take him long to formulate his plans. In a voice still hoarse from too little sleep he called to Sean. Sean, just barely awake and stiff from the cold night's sleep, sat partially up and looked at his brother. "We can't stay here, Sean. Lord Warington and his bunch will surely be searching for us and if we're caught it will be our end. Besides, it's time we called on the Waringtons."

Sean was giving his full attention to Liam, but could only reply in a thick voice, "After we do what I think you intend, where will we go?"

Sean knew they had no relatives in County Antrim or anywhere else in Ireland or beyond. Friends, yes, and good friends they were. People that would gladly help if asked, but their friends had families, and if caught aiding the O'Connells would be severely punished. This was a risk neither Liam nor Sean would ask of them unless it became an absolute question of living or dying.

"This past Christmastime," spoke Liam, "Da told me that if ever we were in serious danger, a danger which could take our lives, we should go to Belfast and find a man named Joshua Webster. From what father told me he's and old friend who owns a well known printing shop in town located just a few streets down from the docks."

"Joshua Webster," said Sean in a questioning voice, "I've not heard that name before, but it certainly sounds English. Why would you or Da trust an Englishman?"

Liam's reply was much the same as his father gave when asked the same question by a doubtful Liam.

"He's truly English, and that is cause for worry, but we have no choice but to find him and hope Da's trust in him was not misplaced. According to what Da told me, long ago he did Mr. Webster a great service, and because of this and the friendship that grew out of it he assured me that if any man, Irish or English, can be fully trusted, it is this Joshua Webster."

Sean, scarcely believing what he had heard, sat silently for several minutes while digesting this surprising information. "I had always thought it impossible our Da would make a friend of any Englishman."

In reply Liam said, "I know, but unless you can think of a better solution to our troubles, I think that we must follow Da's instructions and make our way to Belfast."

Liam, after waiting for a reply from Sean and failing to receive one, spoke again, "However, before we address that problem we must attend to Lord Warington and his bastard of a son. The two of them brought about our father's death, and I will not leave for Belfast until they have been made to suffer to the utmost for what they did."

Studying his brother's solemn face, Liam continued, "It's my intention to take the fight to them, to go to Lord Warington's estate and punish them in a way that even God would see fit. With luck, using what Da has taught us, and God willing, we shall find them and make them pay."

Before leaving the monastery to begin their assault on the Waringtons, Liam realized they had a serious issue to deal with. He knew the Warington estate was guarded by two great mastiffs. Although not trained to attack except on command, the dogs would surely set up a ruckus and rouse the inhabitants of the estate if they detected the presence of strangers. After discussing the problem with Sean, the brothers decided the solution lay in the backyard of Patrick Brannigan, a long time friend, fellow poacher, and a breeder of what many considered the finest fox hounds to be found in Northern Ireland. Leaving their supplies hidden in the dense brush overgrowing the monastery they headed at a fast pace to Patrick's.

Arriving at the home of the Brannigan's, they soon explained their circumstances to the sleepy couple. Patrick and his wife, after hearing the nature of Michael's death, eagerly gave them a dog, with the request, "Just let her go after she's done her job. She knows how to find her way home."

After the O'Connells left the two Brannigans could not help but laugh at the audacious plan Liam revealed to them.

"This," Patrick told his wife, "might well be a day the Waringtons never forget. I just wish to heaven I could be there to see it, but I can at least tell our grandchildren we played a hand in it."

One hour before sunrise, the brothers, approaching from the north, away from the main road and the danger of being seen by any early morning travelers, stopped several hundred yards short of their destination. Attached to Sean's wrist by a short rope was the young bitch given to them by Patrick. She was docile, quiet, and, as assured by

Patrick, in full heat. This was a temptation the brothers were sure would be irresistible to any male dogs guarding the estate, and both the Warington's mastiffs were male. Tying the nervous dog to the low-hanging branch of a tree, the brothers hid close by and waited. Less than half an hour later Warington's mastiffs, having caught the female scent carried to them on the wind, came out of the darkness and made straight for the bitch.

"Let her go," ordered Liam.

Sean quickly released the frightened dog, sure she would head for Patrick's. With one glance at the charging mastiffs, she took off at a fast run toward home followed by her ardent, drooling suitors. Totally satisfied the threat of discovery by the mastiffs was completely nullified, the brothers moved closer toward the Warington estate.

As planned, they snuck into the large stable standing in silence not far from the rear of the main house. Cautiously entering the stable they could see a cat sleeping on a hay bale and two horses in their stalls, but no people. If luck was with them, the Warington's servants would not yet have arrived at the manor to start the day's work.

"Remember," Liam said to Sean, "once I'm in the house it should take me no more than ten minutes to do what I have to do. If there's any trouble or if anyone approaches the house before the ten minutes are up, turn the horses loose and then set the barn on fire. If I get into trouble, I will need the distraction caused by the loose horses and the fire to draw attention from the house. If all goes well, I'll meet you here as soon as I've finished with our Lord Warington and William. If I fail to show up, or if we get separated, wait for me under the bridge on the road leading to Carnlough. If I'm not there within the hour you'll know I've run into a bit of a problem, and you should head for Belfast by way of Carnlough. I'll meet you there when and if I can."

"Whatever happens," Liam added, looking hard into his brother's eyes, "do not enter the house to help me."

Sean looked back into the face of the brother he knew he might never see again, knowing that what Liam was about to do to avenge their father was extremely dangerous. Liam was going up against two grown men, men who had guns, men who would not hesitate for a single second to kill him.

"I'll be ready, and only if necessary I'll meet you at the bridge," Sean replied, knowing, despite Liam's order to the contrary, he would wait nearby to give him any assistance he could, even if it meant disobeying Liam's orders.

With an assuring pat to Sean's shoulder, Liam said, "Good luck to us, brother," and moved to the front of the stables. As he was about to open the stable door a quirt lying on top of a ragged saddle blanket caught his attention.

"This I can use," he thought, believing such a quirt had been used on his father. Tucking the quirt under his loose-fitting shirt next to the razor sharp knife that had been his father's, Liam headed for the backdoor of the Warington's house.

He crossed the yard without event and casually entered the rear of the house through the unlocked door, pleased the Waringtons saw no need for security because they could not fathom anyone getting past the mastiffs who, if they detected any strangers, would alert the estate servants who lived on the grounds surrounding the house. He hoped if he were spotted by anyone, it would be thought he was just another young Irish lad newly hired to work on the estate.

Once in the house he slipped out of his boots and headed across the living room to the stairway leading to the second floor. After slowly and soundlessly climbing to the top of the stairs, he paused to look down the darkened hallway, trying to determine which room held Lord Warington and which held his son. As he moved forward a few steps he could see a faint light coming from underneath a door on the right. Hoping this was where he would find one of the Waringtons he moved toward it, removing the knife from his belt as he went. Holding the weapon to the side of his leg and bending low, he looked through the door's keyhole and could see a man sleeping in a four poster bed. A large candle burning on the nightstand next to bed was responsible for the light he had seen under the door.

"I have you now," thought Liam as he slowly opened the unlocked door, stepped inside, and softly closed the door behind him.

Moving slowly and taking shallow breaths, he reached the bed and pressed the point of the knife against the throat of what he now recognized as the older Warington. With some effort he resisted the urge to plunge the knife into the sleeping man's heart, just then realizing, with regret, he was not capable of cold-blooded murder. Instead he pressed the knife point against the exposed throat just hard enough to draw a drop of blood.

Lord Warington woke from his deep sleep, his eyes darting from left to right, unable to recognize who stood over him. Realizing he was caught at knifepoint and defenseless, he could only stammer in a shrill voice, "What…, what do you want?"

To his horror he heard, "I am Liam O'Connell, here to repay you for what you have done to my father."

Warington opened his mouth to deny any guilt, but before he could speak Liam struck him hard across the face with the quirt he had removed from inside his shirt.

Instantly blood spurted from his face. With a cry of pain Warington attempted to cover his face with a pillow, but Liam wrenched the pillow from his grasp and once more brought the quirt down upon him, a blow that was partially deflected by Warington's upraised arms as he tried to protect himself. It did no good against the resolute Liam. Over and over again Liam struck with the quirt, unable to control the growing fury which made him deaf to his enemy's cries for mercy.

To better observe the damage he had done he stepped back, not realizing he was mirroring the behavior Lord Warington had used when beating his father. Seeing the damage done to Warington's torn face Liam felt his rage suddenly subside. Despite his anger and the loss of his father he still retained an abiding sense of humanity, a humanity that would not allow him to strike even one more time. The cowering figure on the bed made Liam realize that nothing, not even the killing of a Warington, would bring back his father. The bleeding man before him was no longer a hated monster, only a cowering, pitiful, little man not worthy of further attention.

With a voice still shaking from the emotion of the moment, Liam looked down at the object of his spent rage, "You are a worthless coward not worth killing."

Returning the knife to his belt and tossing the quirt into Lord Warington's face, he lifted the candle from the bedside table and left the room hearing a great sobbing as he closed the door behind him. Having detected no sign of William, and knowing Lord Warington's screams would have roused his son had he been in the house, Liam, hastily descended the stairs. Reaching the lower floor he used the candle to ignite the curtains adorning the drawing room windows. The cloth burst into flames in an instant.

"I may not kill you with my hands," he muttered to himself as he observed the flames racing up the curtains to the ceiling, "but may you burn in hell for what you did."

Seeing that the fire from the curtains was going to spread rapidly throughout the room, Liam returned to where he'd left his boots and put them back on. He was about to go out the back door when a voice stopped him as suddenly as if he had walked into a stone wall.

"It's good of you to pay a morning call," said William Warington, standing in the doorway with a pistol in his hand, "and thoughtful of you to bring the hunt to us."

With the pistol pointed at his chest Liam felt the shock of total surprise run through his body. The sudden appearance of William rendered him paralyzed; he found it impossible to move. He was trapped. Before him stood the other of his family's tormentors, armed with a pistol, ready and wanting to kill him. Behind Liam was a smoke-filled room, now fully ablaze with a fire of his own making. He could not advance and could not retreat. There was no escape possible, only a few seconds to regret he'd allowed William's father to live, and that Sean would be left with neither a father nor a brother.

Chapter 5 Sean's Role

After Liam entered the house, Sean removed the flint from his pocket and holding it in one hand and his knife in the other, sat crouched behind the stable door, ready if need be to free the horses and set the stable on fire. Filled with both a sense of excitement and dread that caused his hands to quiver, he waited, intensely watching the house for any sign of Liam. Several times he thought he heard the faintest sound of a scream coming from the house. He knew a scream could not have come from Liam, for nothing his brother would have encountered could have brought such a sound from him, not at the hand of a Warington. Edging closer to the doorway, Sean was surprised to suddenly see the glow of a fire coming from the house.

"That has to be Liam's work," he thought, becoming even more concerned for his brother's safety.

As Sean continued to focus his attention on the house, he failed to see William Warington, astride a horse, returning from town after a full night of drinking to celebrate the demise of the man he had been taught to hate. His spirits were also bolstered by the preceding hours spent bedding a plump Irish tart.

Approaching the house William spotted the same fire seen by Sean. Although still feeling the effects of the whiskey he'd consumed, he quickly dismounted a short distance from the front of the house. Drawing his pistol from his waistband, and seeing that the fire blazing in the front drawing room would not allow him to enter from the main door, he made his way to the rear entrance of the manor.

Sean was moving from the stables toward the house when he spotted a man silhouetted against the blaze, moving toward the back door, a pistol held in his hand. He knew by the man's unruly yellow hair, his style of clothing, and the fact that only an Englishman would carry a pistol so openly that it was surely William Warington. He watched as the figure stepped away from the side of the house, paused before the open doorway, then took one step over the threshold. At the same moment, he could see by the light from the flames, Liam stepping into the hallway in full view of Warington. He realized at that moment that unless he acted instantly Liam would almost surely die at the hand of their hated enemy.

Knowing not to cry out a warning that would alert Liam and William, Sean gathered his legs under him and broke into a dead run toward the house, desperate to save the brother he loved, to prevent a death he could not live with. He covered fifteen, twenty-five, thirty yards, his heart racing in his chest, his feet churning in the loose gravel and dirt leading from the stable to the house.

As he got within twenty yards of the house he could see the younger Warington raise the revolver and point it at Liam, "Pease God," Liam prayed, "give me one more second."

The second came, and in that time Sean saw William turn in his direction and away from Liam. Summoning a final burst of energy Sean launched his body head first at the man pointing the deadly pistol at his brother.

In the instant before William was about to pull the trigger and send powder and lead into Liam's body, he heard the sound of dirt and gravel being crushed under running feet coming fast in his direction. Momentarily caught off guard by the sounds and realizing a threat was behind him, he spun to his left, bringing the pistol to bear on a figure hurling at him through the darkness. With the instinct of a feral animal he fired a single shot.

At the same moment, Sean, his body outstretched, buried his shoulder in Warington, knocking the breath from his lungs and sending him crashing to the floor at Liam's feet. Forgetting Liam, and seeing only the person who struck him, William raised the pistol and pointed it for a second time at Sean. Before his mind could command his finger to pull the trigger and send the second of the two shots it held into his attacker, William Warington, a man who, along with his father, had brought misery and agony to many an Irishman, felt an almost indescribable pain in his chest.

Knocked on his back and still partially dazed from Sean's impact he tried to understand what was happening. "Why can't I lift my pistol?" he thought. "What is happening to me?"

Before his mind could answer, a second surge of pain filled his stomach. With waning strength William bent forward at the waist trying to see through wide-opened eyes what was pressing down on him. What he saw was a hand holding a knife, a knife buried to the hilt in his stomach. The hand then moved away, leaving the knife embedded where it was. Now able to understand the pain, and comprehending that his own death must be only a few breaths away, Warington screamed. He screamed at the pain, at the outrage that he would die, that he would be put in the earth and forgotten before his time, but most of all that he would be unable to help his father finish killing all of the O'Connells whose deaths he had sought for so many years.

The last thing William Warington saw and heard was Liam standing over him proclaiming, "Yes, Warington, the hunt was brought to you, and now is over."

Making no attempt to remove the knife from the body, Liam stood up and gazed down at the dying William, feeling no remorse for what he had done.

"Killing a man such as that" he thought, "is a good thing to do."

Suddenly snapped back to reality by the growing heat from the flames and the smoke beginning to pour out of the open door, Liam recognized the need to begin his and Sean's escape.

Looking about for Sean he saw his brother lying crumpled just outside the doorway. Quickly moving to his assistance, he grabbed him by the arm and pulled him to his feet.

Walking calmly at first, the brothers broke into a run as they passed the barn and fled into the surrounding darkness, heading back in the direction of Saint Calum's. Arriving there shortly before sunrise, Liam, believing pursuers would surely be close behind, immediately set about gathering the provisions they had hidden away.

He had almost completed collecting their possessions when he noticed that Sean was not helping, and hadn't moved from where he sat down upon entering the monastery grounds. Wondering why, Liam suddenly remembered that twice while they were making their way back to the monastery Sean had stumbled, and Sean, even running in the dark, was not the stumbling kind. Suddenly alarmed, Liam moved to where Sean was sitting with his back against the stone wall which surrounded the church's grounds.

"Are you hurt?" he asked, hoping with all his might that Sean was merely tired from the night's work and his answer would be "No."

"I'm fine," answered Sean, but he still did not move, not even to touch Liam's hand as it reached for his shoulder.

"I just need a few minutes of rest to get my breath."

It was at that moment Liam recalled hearing the sound of a gunshot fired during the fight with William Warington. Kneeling down before his brother, he looked closely at Sean's face, seeing a grimace of pain Sean could neither hide nor deny with the smile he attempted to show.

Pulling Sean's coat open, Liam asked, "Where are you hurt?," only then seeing the large pattern of blood spreading down Sean's shirt front.

I'm not sure," Sean replied, "but I'll be..." Sean was unable to finish before a gush of bright blood filled his mouth, drowning out his words.

Liam began frantically tearing at Sean's shirt hoping somehow to stop the bleeding; hoping by some miracle to stop the flow of blood he knew was taking his brother's life.

Sean, after turning his head sideways to spit out some of the blood gathering in his mouth, was able to mutter while looking into his brother's eyes, "You know, you may have to go on to Belfast without me."

"No," Liam cried, "we're going together, but first you need a doctor."

Both brothers understood the lie. In this land long ruled by the English there was no doctor for the Irish. The only medical attention they might find would be that provided by Patrick who was known to care for animals, and when called upon, his fellow Irishmen.

Taking off his coat and wadding it up, Liam pressed it tight to Sean's chest, and placing Sean's hand on the coat told him, "Hold this firm against you until I return with help."

He started to move away only to have Sean grasp his wrist and pull him back.

"Don't go now," he pleaded in a whispered voice, "just stay with me for a while longer."

Sean's words ripped into Liam's heart, starting a flow of tears cascading down his face. Liam sat down beside his brother, wrapped him in his arms and put Sean's cheek against his shoulder. He was still holding him when the sun fully rose, a sun Sean could no longer see. Hours later beneath the red sky of Sean's last day, a desolate Liam buried him beside their father and mother.

Chapter 6 Flight

After saying a final "good-bye" to his brother, and nearly broken in spirit and body, Liam headed south intending to follow the coastline to Belfast, a journey he estimated would take more than the usual four and one-half days due to the almost assured necessity of eluding pursuers. By midday he reached the northeastern coast of County Antrim, and the strange rock formations that jutted straight out into the sea and then disappeared into the dark green churning waters. The road-like appearance of the rocks prompted the Irish to often call them the Giant's Causeway. Believing it would be near suicidal to travel during the day he sought shelter by squeezing his body down into a crevice formed by some of the large geometric-shaped rocks so orderly piled upon each other. There he spent the rest of the daylight hours afraid to move and as lonely and unhappy as he thought any person capable of being.

Little did he know that Lord Warington, the only witness to his attack, was gravely injured by the beating at Liam's hand and suffered from burns and smoke inhalation from the fire. He would be unable to speak to the authorities investigating the events at the Warington estate until half a day later. Because of this delay no organized pursuit would ensue until almost a full day had passed.

At dusk, an exhausted Liam set out to make his escape. In order to avoid being seen by anyone living along the shoreline and especially by British patrols, he headed inland until he was about a quarter of a mile from the road and high enough in the hills to look down upon any pursuers. He saw no one, but then reasoned the hard blowing wind from the sea and the cold air that came with it were probably keeping local people and pursuers alike inside their homes. As he looked down upon the shoreline he had just left his naturally inquisitive nature caused him to pause and wonder anew about what or who could have built the strange, seemingly hand-hewn rock formations which began on the shoreline. Like so many before him who had looked down upon these rocks, he could find no logical answer, but thought the tale of giants using the columns as stepping stones to Scotland was as good an explanation as any. He wished he could use the same stepping stones to escape his pursuers, but it was no time to take a swim in those cold waters, and he was no giant.

For almost a fortnight he traveled as rapidly as caution would allow, making no fire at night, traveling from dusk to dawn, and staying clear of the towns dotting the shoreline, preferring to stay about a half-mile inland of it. He skirted around the towns of Cushendun and Carnlough, Carncast and Ballygally, walking at night with only scant moonlight to see by, and when in rough country making such slow progress that several times he gave serious thought to using the road. But after seeing what looked like British troops manning a checkpoint by torch light, he realized that even at night the road might well lead him to a hangman's knot.

On two occasions from his vantage point in the hills above the road, he spotted other check points most likely set up for the sole purpose of capturing him. The second of these checkpoints was set up where the hills converged with the Irish Sea, squeezing the road between the two, and forcing the already exhausted Liam to go even wider to the west to get around them. He did so with little knowledge of the terrain, but using the stars as he was taught by his father, he unerringly returned to the southerly course that would take him to Belfast. When he reached Carrickfergus and the heavily traveled Belfast Road, he was able to make better time by mixing in with the large numbers of desperate men, women, and children heading for Belfast in the hope of finding work or food. At the end of the fourteenth day, a gaunt and hungry Liam crested the top of a hill overlooking the outskirts of the great port city.

Chapter 7 Belfast

After asking several people the whereabouts of a printing shop run by a Mr. Joshua Webster, a slightly tipsy tavern patron was able to direct Liam to the far end of Ravenhill Road near the Harland and Wolff Shipyard. Within minutes he had located the shop, a somewhat unassuming three story building set on a corner. Inscribed above the door frame he read the words *Webster's Printing Shoppe*.

The shop appeared closed, but having no money and no place other than the streets to stay at such a late hour, Liam gave three sharp raps with his knuckles on the oaken door. After several anxious minutes with no response, Liam was about to knock again when the door opened the width of a man's hand. Liam found himself staring at a short, somewhat portly, middle-aged man wearing a long night shirt. In one hand he carried a stout stick, presumably to defend himself while in the other hand he carried a burning candle. It was obvious to Liam from the man's sleepy eyes and disgruntled look he had been awakened from a deep sleep, and was none too happy about it. Squinting his eyes he slowly looked Liam up and down, warily noting the intruder's disheveled appearance.

"Young man," he said matter-of-factly, punctuating every other word with a wave of the stick, "I trust you have important business to conduct, elsewise you have disturbed me from a most appreciated sleep for no good cause."

"I do," said Liam, "if you are Joshua Webster."

A slight nod and a questioning "yes" from the shopkeeper confirmed that Liam had reached his destination.

"Go on, sir," spoke Mr. Webster, "what can I possibly do for you at this late hour?"

Standing as straight as he could and trying to ignore his fatigue, Liam replied, "I am Liam O'Connell, son of Michael O'Connell of Ballycastle."

Joshua Webster was startled by Liam's words. News of the young man's criminal actions and the subsequent manhunt had reached Belfast days earlier, and indeed, Webster's printing shop had made up the wanted posters distributed by the local authorities. The shocked proprietor, instantly aware that a great danger in the form of a wanted fugitive had arrived at his door, leaned his head out the open door and gazed about the street, fearful he might see someone, even a stranger, or worse yet, a uniformed officer looking their way. Seeing none, he reached out, grasped Liam by the arm, and with a quick tug pulled the unresisting youth into the shop, hastily locking the door behind them.

In the brief moment it took Mr. Webster to close and lock the door, Liam glanced about the shop noticing some unfamiliar machinery which he assumed was for printing, and many shelves filled with row upon row of books, more books than he had ever seen. Turning back to Mr. Webster, Liam was handed a candle the proprietor had lit for him after locking the door. In a quiet, almost apologetic voice, and now standing face to face with the proprietor, Liam spoke.

"Sir, I know I look like a common thief or laggard, but believe me, I am neither of those. I have endured a long and perilous two week's journey in order to reach you. I must also tell you I am being pursued by people wishing to do me great harm, even to the extent of taking my life."

Pausing to take a deep breath he continued in a slightly shaky voice, "Sir, I will leave if you ask it of me for I have no wish to endanger you due to my own troubles. I am here solely because my father once told me that if ever I was in the direst of straits, I should come to Belfast and turn to you, sir."

At first struck nearly speechless by this sudden late night event, Joshua, after a moment's contemplation, was quick to regain his composure.

Looking directly into eyes that could have only come from his father, Joshua's own best friend, he spoke.

"Your arrival here is not unwelcome, young man," said Joshua Webster in a kindly voice, "but please call me Joshua, and given my debt to your father, I am most happy to help you. I had even hoped to do so, for I knew already that you were being sought by the English the width and breadth of Northern Ireland."

"But before we discuss your problem at length," he continued after pausing to catch his breath, "I can tell from your appearance you must need food and rest."

Within the hour, Liam found himself fed, clothed in a fresh night shirt that barely reached his knees, and shown to a bed in the attic quarters provided by his host. He was to sleep for over ten hours.

When Liam awoke it took him a moment to realize where he was. After two weeks in the open Irish countryside, the room, the ceiling, and especially the bed, seemed out of place, so different from that which he had grown familiar, and so different from the house he was raised in. A soft bed, a mirror, a dresser, a glass filled window, all of these were things he had seen before, but was totally unaccustomed to. Looking about in the pale light coming through the window, Liam saw on the floor a brass slop bucket. Minutes later, having made use of the bucket, he examined the room more closely; looking with special interest for an avenue of escape should the authorities enter the shop in search of him.

"Unless I learn to fly," he thought, "there is no way out of here except by the stairs leading down to the shop."

It was not a comforting thought.

Liam could hardly believe how his fortune had changed in just a few short hours. On a dresser were towels, soap and a large china basin of water. On a chair against the wall hung a pair of pants, a shirt, a woolen cap, and a light-weight grey sweater, all of which surely were placed there by either Mr. Webster or one of his household. He immediately set about bathing and dressing in his new clothes. No sooner had he finished when Liam, still somewhat amazed by his good fortune, heard a soft tap at the attic door.

His "Yes," was followed by the cherubic face of Joshua peering into the room.

"Good afternoon, young man," said the shopkeeper with a wide smile showing through his short, brightly colored red beard and moustache.

"Good afternoon to you, sir, and again, I must thank you for your hospitality," Liam replied, while at the same time eyeing a large wooden tray carried by his host. On the tray was a plate heaped with a generous portion of meat smothered in steaming gravy, real chicken eggs, bread, honey, along with a steaming bowl of rich-looking pudding. Increasingly aware of his once again empty stomach, Liam eagerly accepted the plate handed him. While he ate, his host began to explain the full extent of the troubles faced by his guest.

Taking a seat in the empty chair, Joshua began, "News of what happened to your family and your subsequent actions regarding the Waringtons arrived here before you. You have unjustly suffered the loss of both father and brother, and for that my sorrow is nearly as great as your own. The authorities, at the urging of Lord Simon Warington have been searching in great earnest for you, and have posted reward notices throughout County Antrim offering a reward of three hundred pounds for your capture, dead or alive."

With a twinkle in his eye, Joshua smiled and added, "You have killed his son, done serious harm to Lord Warington himself, and for that I can only commend you. I firmly believe your father and brother, looking down from heaven as they must surely be, are extremely proud of the justice you rendered the most despicable father and son as ever was born."

Looking seriously into Liam's eyes, he continued, "However, consequently you are being sought the entire length of Northern Ireland. In an odd coincidence, I, myself, was commissioned to print the reward posters being put up in every village and town. A task I found somewhat amusing since if luck would have allowed, I would have been proud to have been the one responsible for the Warington's demise."

"However," he continued, "it doesn't lessen the seriousness of your situation. It is my feeling that should you stay here with me, or anywhere in this country, you will almost certainly be caught within weeks, if not sooner, and punished by hanging. There are too many men about, good men or not, Irish or otherwise, who would turn you in for the three hundred pound reward being offered. With this in mind, I have taken the liberty of making preparations for your speedy departure to the only place left to you - America. As such, it is my intention to book passage for you on the first ship I can find going there. To aid you on your journey, I am also preparing two travel bags which should be ready for you by the time of your departure."

Liam listened intently to all that Joshua said, pleased to hear of the help he would be given, but also wondering how he would be able to repay this man for his generosity. He fully agreed with Joshua's estimation of the danger facing him and hoped he could leave Belfast before his troubles brought ruin to this fine and brave man.

Now satisfied beyond any doubt that Joshua was indeed a friend, Liam, nevertheless said questioningly, "I have to know, why is it that you, an Englishman, are risking your life to aid me? Why, after so many years, did my father think of you, an Englishman, as such a trusted friend?"

After a moment of reflection, Joshua replied, "There are several reasons for my helping you, any of which would suffice on its own. The first has to do with Moira, the colleen to whom your parents introduced me, and who would shortly thereafter become my wife. She was from Ballypatrick, same as your mother, and perhaps as beautiful, too, or at least so it seemed to me. Why she chose me as her husband, me with my short stature and ordinary appearance, and English to boot, I've never completely understood. She was loving, kind and the sweetest person who ever took a breath. She was also Catholic, and as you can understand, it required a great deal of courage for her to marry an Anglican. But she did, and for that I have always been grateful. We had five years of a wonderful life when the blight wiped out all the potato crops throughout Ireland. Because potatoes were the only real source of food for the Irish, within months thousands upon thousands of people were dying of starvation...a starvation that was not visited upon the English households. When the starving people ran out of what little food they had stored, they ate their animals, and when the animals ran out they ate whatever they could find. Insects, rats, roots, kelp from the ocean, and finally even grass. They fought in the cities for garbage, for the scraps from the tables of the English, my table included. Death was everywhere, taking men, women, and children alike, including a large number of people from Ballypatrick. Moira was heartbroken, and angel that she was, could do no less than to go to Ballypatrick with all the food we could gather. After being gone for a month, she returned despondent and thin, only to immediately return with more food, but only enough to feed a few. To my everlasting sorrow she never came back to me. Whether she died of starvation or from a heart broken by the endless deaths she witnessed, or was accosted on the road by someone desperate for the food she had I have never been able to determine. I only know she was my first and only love, and she died as a result of English stupidity, greed, and an unforgiving prejudice."

Caught up in the memory of how he'd lost his wife, Joshua stopped briefly to clear his throat and wipe the moisture from his eyes. Continuing on he said, "You may ask, where was I? Why did I not go with her? I wanted to, but Moira insisted that while she was in Ballypatrick I should sail to London and use what little influence and connections I had to persuade the English Parliament to release to Ireland the huge amounts of surplus grain they were holding in England, most of it, I might add, imported from Ireland. Despite my most earnest pleadings those high and mighty pompous asses said 'no' to my request, arguing the grain was 'for emergencies,' and that the famine raging through Ireland was not all that serious. They knew differently, knew their own lie, but for years Charles Trevelyan, the Assistant Secretary of the British Treasury, had mismanaged his role as overseer of relief operations regarding the starving people in Ireland, a practice he refused to veer from. To my absolute disbelief he successfully promoted a hands-off policy saying the problem would 'take care of itself by natural means.' This man, utterly devoid of compassion for the Irish, also made great efforts to avoid any interference with private enterprise or the rights of English property owners. Unfortunately most Englishmen wholeheartedly agreed with his thinking and actions."

"I say it was not just the failure of the potato crop and subsequent famine, but greed and politics that cost millions of Irish lives, including that of my beloved Moira. For those reasons I will always oppose the English government; for its cruelty, its prejudice, and for being the indirect cause of Moira's death. "

As Joshua paused Liam could see an intense hatred of the English burning in the eyes of this short unassuming man.

Stopping to wipe his mouth on a handkerchief from his pocket, Joshua continued his story.

"Another reason for my willingness to help you is bound up with your father."

After taking several deep breaths he continued, "Years ago, when I was little older than yourself, my family took much of our summers in your beautiful part of County Antrim where we had a modest estate. It was run by a steward and tenant families who were honest, hard working, and usually turned a good profit if the weather cooperated. However, faced with overbearing financial hardships my father was forced to sell out to Lord Warington, a man that even then I thought to be cruel and lacking even the smallest compassion for the Irish. Unfortunately, I was correct. But I digress...back to your father's role in my life and this story."

Clearing his throat, Joshua continued, "During one of our summer holidays, while walking home from a friend's house late at night, I was surrounded by a group of young Irish lads, included among them was your father. All of them had suffered in one way or another at the hands of the English. Much into their drink, some of them were in a murderous state of mind, and before I realized my peril and could attempt to make an escape I was severely beaten and most probably would have been killed were it not for your father. He was, above all things, a good and fair man, so much so he could not stomach the senseless murder of even an Englishman. With no thought to his own safety he came to my rescue. When his words failed to stop their attack on my person, with fist and feet he fought off his own, and in the doing put his life at risk. Those he fought had no love for the English, and even less for an Irishman standing with one. From that time forth we became the best of friends, a friendship and a debt I feel to this day."

Staring about, Joshua went on, "We were an odd couple. I was a proper young English gentleman, a bit undersized, fairly well educated, and of a prosperous family. Michael had little education, was large and as strong as two ordinary men, and came from a proud, but impoverished family. I was a lover of books, whereas he loved the outdoors and although respectful of learning, had only the barest interest in reading or writing. For several years we visited each other, I traveled in the summer to the Ballycastle area and your father, on several occasions, stayed here in Belfast at my parents' home. I always found our time together to be the highlight of the year. And indeed, it was through your father's nimble mind and rough but charming personality, my very skeptical and deeply religious Anglican family gained a new found respect and understanding of Irish Catholics."

Joshua, having now told his story and beginning to sweat due to his heavy clothing and the heat coming from the two lower floors, drew out his handkerchief, and vigorously wiped his face. "Have you any other questions," he asked through the crumpled handkerchief?

Liam, finally understanding the mystery of his father and the Englishman's relationship, moved to solve one other mystery. "Sir, if it is not too much to ask, I do have one other question I'm hoping you can answer."

"Ask what you will," replied Joshua, "whatever knowledge I have is yours to hear."

Taking a moment to phrase the question, Liam asked, "Why is it that the Waringtons so hate my family? I admit to our poaching on their land, but so have many others, and they were never subjected to the hateful treatment the Waringtons seemed to delight in when it came to the O'Connells. As best I can remember we have never seriously wronged them."

For a moment Joshua seemed speechless, but in truth he was thinking back to the time just after that first meeting with Liam's father; back to the time when Michael and Simon Warington began the conflict that was to govern so much of the lives of the O'Connells, and the Waringtons, and eventually his own.

"When your father and Simon, who had yet to become Lord Warington, were young men," Joshua said, "both of them sought the hand of an exceptional young lady. That lady was your mother. She was beautiful, filled with laughter, wise beyond her years, and easily the most sought after lass in or around County Antrim, if not the whole of Ireland."

At this point Joshua caught himself thinking back to those days and the destiny of the people involved. Speaking to Liam as might a father to a son, he continued, "Your father loved her completely with his entire heart, soul and being. Of this I have no doubt. On the other hand, I believe Simon was incapable of feeling real love, and sought to marry your mother merely to satisfy his need to possess her as a trophy, to have and control what other men wanted, especially your father, who was both handsome and of a good heart, something the future Lord Warington was most decidedly not. To no one's surprise, save Simon's, she chose Michael to be her husband. Simon, small, selfish man that he was, found this intolerable, beyond his comprehension, but not beyond his far-reaching hatred."

Stopping for a moment to think about what transpired between Michael and Lord Warington, he then added, "I think that most men are born of a good and high nature, as was your father, and remain that way throughout their lives despite what cruel fate may be thrown at them. Others are born to the good, but are sometimes turned to evil ways by circumstances beyond their control. Life, I've learned, can be difficult, full of tragedies, sometimes forcing even good men to go against their nature."

Thinking of Simon Warington, Joshua continued, "A rare few others, and I would most assuredly count Lord Warington and his son among them, are born twisted and evil. They have no love of anyone or anything, unless it's power or cruelty, or both. From the day your parents announced their engagement Lord Warington began to wage a private vendetta against them. Warington, evil as he was, simply could not accept that your mother, coming from a humble Irish background, would choose to marry a nearly penniless man such as your father, as opposed to a man of property and social status such as himself. Even after the cholera epidemic of forty-nine took your mother from us, Simon never got over being rejected by her and continued to make life miserable for your family. His hatred ran so deep he passed it on to his son, it was almost as if William had been born with the same feelings as his father. Using the law he tormented your father unmercifully. The result was years of abuse heaped upon your family and the tragedy that has you standing before me."

Beginning to feel tears coming to his eyes from the memories of so long ago, and the treatment endured by his lost friends, Joshua added, "My opinion of Warington is so low that I am convinced beyond any doubt that shortly after your birth it was he who orchestrated the brutal attack by the men who crippled your father."

Tears had started to run down Liam's cheeks as he listened to the words of his father's friend. Joshua, seeing this, and in need of time to control his own emotions, excused himself in order to give this courageous but unfortunate young man some well needed privacy.

As the door closed behind him, he heard Liam's plaintive voice, "Oh Sean, how I miss you so."

Hearing Liam's words, Joshua wiped tears from his own eyes with the already wet handkerchief.

Chapter 8 – Escape

Late in the morning of his fifth day above the print shop Liam was summoned downstairs to the office of his benefactor. As he entered, Joshua said, "Please sit down and be comfortable, for we have much to discuss and little time to do so."

Getting directly to the point, he continued, "I have taken the liberty of booking your passage on the *Osprey* which sets sail for Baltimore on the morning tide. She is a converted cargo ship and won't offer the most comfortable of accommodations, but she was the first ship I could find sailing to Baltimore, a city I have reason to believe is best suited to your circumstances."

With all the seriousness he could put to face and voice, he continued, "The *Osprey* is called by some a death ship, and on more than one occasion has been known to arrive in port with fewer passengers than were logged on board. As such, I urge you once on board to trust no one, turn your back to no one, and protect yourself and your possessions at all times."

Liam, fully aware of the seriousness of Joshua's words sat quietly with a growing appreciation of the generosity and wisdom of his host.

After wiping his face with the ever-present handkerchief, Joshua continued, "The accommodations, as I have mentioned, may leave much to be desired, as you will most likely have only a small space to call your own. There may or may not be adequate food and water on board, depending on the number of passengers and the size of your purse. For that reason you will leave here with one hundred English pounds along with a goodly amount of provisions."

Rising from his seat, he moved to the two travel bags sitting in the corner of the office.

"In this bag," he said, pointing to the smaller of the two, I have gathered clothing, candles, two woolen blankets, gloves, eating utensils, an extra knife, one towel, and several bars of strong soap. You will also have your own sleeping hammock and a supply of rope. The other bag has a month's supply of food, including flour, sugar, salt pork, tins of tea, a small cooking pot, onions, a medicinal wine, pepper, ginger, honey, rolled oats, and as many limes as I could find. You should eat at least one lime every other day to ward off scurvy and gum disease."

Seeing an opportunity to interrupt Joshua, Liam said, "Thank you for all you've done. I'm only sorry I have no way to repay you."

"You owe me nothing and never will, for whatever I do it will never be enough to repay the debt I owe your father."

Reaching into his desk drawer he removed several sheets of papers. "But before we get too sentimental we have other urgent matters to discuss."

Leaning back and focusing on his young guest he said, "Using my humble skills as a printer, I have made up several documents which identify you as Caleb Quinn, an apprentice brick layer going to America in search of a better life. With luck and some acting on your part, any inquisitive authorities will think of you as a simple laborer, like many of the people in Belfast hoping to find a new and better life in America."

Having had his say, he handed the papers to Liam. Still not done, Joshua left his desk and removed a large grey coat hanging on a nearby coat rack. "The Atlantic can be very cold this time of year, and this coat will certainly serve to keep you warm, but it is not its warmth that makes it of great value to you."

Moving to place the full length wool coat in Liam's hands he said, "Sewn into the lining is one hundred and fifty dollars in American paper money along with a letter of introduction addressed to B. Carroll, Trader and Investor, Baltimore, Maryland. He is a great friend of mine and a man of integrity and considerable resources. I trust him as I trust myself to see to your safety and well-being."

Early the following morning, carrying the bags given to him by Joshua and wearing the fine grey coat with the rolled hammock slung on his back, Liam headed alone to the dock where the *Osprey* was berthed.

Joshua followed him at a discrete distance so that if Liam was apprehended by the authorities he could stay uninvolved at that point, but then work from behind the scene to somehow secure Liam's release or escape.

Fortunately no such incident occurred, partially due to the large number of people boarding the ship and to the 'gentleman's coat that masked his Irish heritage, but mostly due to the excellently forged identification papers Liam carried. As Liam walked up the gangplank, he gave one last look back, thanking Joshua by a meeting of their eyes, sorry to leave such a good friend, while also wondering what the imminent journey to America held in store for him.

Chapter 9 The *Osprey*

As the passengers boarded the ship, a pair of very interested eyes observed their every movement. Red Dugan, third officer aboard the *Osprey*, was not a man easily noticed, a characteristic he used to advance his criminal pursuits. He was of average height, weighed about 180 pounds, had a deeply pockmarked face, and squinty eyes that rarely made deliberate contact with the eyes of other people. He was a calculating man, bereft of visible emotions, and soft-spoken. He had made himself into the perfect unnoticed predator, ready to do whatever it took to relieve unsuspecting passengers of their valuables. He fully understood when patience or guile was needed, or when sudden violence would best serve his purpose. He had a keen mind which, combined with several years of experience preying on the ship's passengers, enabled him to unerringly spot the weak, the defenseless, and those people who might be carrying hidden valuables.

During the early days of the ship's voyages he used his position as a ship's officer to move freely among the passengers, to study their behavior, to look for any signs of wealth, to assess their vulnerability, or to judge the best time and means of attack.

On this morning he had spotted several people he marked in his mind as potential prey. First, there was a well-dressed couple in their early fifties accompanied by an elderly female servant. He also marked a younger couple, him with a wrenching cough, her looking lost and bewildered. Also of interest was one of the last passengers on board, a young man traveling by himself, somewhat thin and wearing clothes that seemed too new, too out of place on him. Of particular interest was the long, heavy woolen coat that would normally have been worn by a gentleman of some worth, yet here it was on the back of a boy that by all other evidence seemed nearly impoverished.

"Silly boy," thought Red. He had known more than one passenger who had come on board with money or valuables hidden in their clothing. Having selected Caleb as his best potential for profit Red would now wait until the perfect moment to strike. He knew it would be a long voyage with no need to hurry any action on his part. He would wait until his intended victim was at his most vulnerable.

Thanks to the documents given to him by Joshua and the large number of passengers boarding the *Osprey*, Liam, now officially Caleb Quinn, came aboard without incident. Following instructions from a crew member Caleb descended below deck and found himself staring with apprehension at his assigned quarters. Looking at this small dark area, no more than eight feet in length and five feet in height, he could not help thinking of Joshua's description of the ship's accommodations as 'uncomfortable.'

"How about nearly impossible," he said to himself.

It was beyond his imagination how the many people who boarded the ship could possibly be squeezed into such a small area. Even at that, the area assigned to him was slightly better than some due to the wooden bunk built into the side of the ship's wall. Most of the passengers had to contend with sleeping on bunks built in more open areas, with no walls on any side to provide privacy or protection.

After some thought Caleb, a name he still had trouble identifying with even after hours of practice, practice he intended to continue until the name fit, decided to use his bunk as a table and storage area. Stowing his bags under it, he then hung the hammock between two rafters on either side of the bunk. Using the empty bunk as a seat, Caleb sat down to observe the people settling in about him. Most of them appeared to be poor, looked frightened, and seemed even more appalled by their small quarters than he was. One of the exceptions was a young couple who took up residence directly in front of Caleb's bunk and only a short arm's reach away.

Although they had been among the last people on board they had already put away their possessions, and using several large blankets and ropes created a small enclosed area providing some degree of privacy. What also set them apart from the others was, whereas most passengers were seemingly dismayed by the prospect of living in such cramped conditions lacking even enough head room for an average-sized man to stand erect, these two were smiling, laughing at and with one another and seemingly enjoying the challenges facing them. Caleb could only sit and watch them, marveling at their joyful natures.

The first of them to speak to Caleb was the wife. She was tall, wore her brown hair to the waist, and had an infectious smile and pleasing laughter. Eyeing Caleb for just a second, she stepped toward him and announced in a sweet voice loaded with a heavy Scottish accent, "Hello, I'm Samantha Moore and the big ox trying not to break his skull on the rafters is my husband, Matthew."

Caleb rose to his feet, bumping the top of his head in the process, and stood before Samantha.

Pausing to rub his head before speaking, Caleb said, "Pleased to meet you. I'm Li- Caleb Quinn."

A moment later, following a second introduction by Samantha, he found his hand being painfully squeezed by her giant of a husband. Caleb was aware some men delighted in testing others with the strength of their handshake, and as Matthew increased the pressure on his hand, Caleb knew that this was one of those tests. Trying to show no emotion from the growing pain in his hand, Caleb stared into Matthew's face to see how serious he intended this contest would be. To his relief, he saw that Matthew had a full grin on his face and seemed bemused by Caleb's growing predicament. Caleb also realized, somewhat to his amazement, that the big man was using only part of his strength.

Trying to keep a calm face, Caleb, squeezing back as best he could, said, "Pleased to meet you, too; I hope I'm not hurting your hand."

The giant relaxed his grip, but still shaking hands laughingly replied, "Just funning you," and grinned even larger.

"This man," Caleb thought, "enjoys playing with his strength, but in a friendly way, and not the way of a bully. This is someone, I could learn to like."

Looking about at the other people who might have set up next to him, he felt fortunate to have such pleasant shipmates nearby. Caleb suspected that he and Moores would become good friends during the course of the journey.

Caleb's intuition proved to be accurate. Within days he and the Moores became close companions, spending many enjoyable hours discussing everything from politics to the condition of the ship, their plans for the future, and, of course, the weather.

There was one thing that proved very unpleasant and often interrupted their initial conversations, and that was seasickness. Caleb, often as not joined by Samantha, spent the better part of the first days at sea, leaning over the *Osprey's* railing, emptying their stomachs' contents over the side. To Caleb, the nausea and the constant weakness was unlike any misery he had ever known. More than once he wondered whether jumping overboard wouldn't be preferable to enduring even one more minute of the endless roll of the deck below him. To Caleb and Samantha, the only relief they could find came by staying above deck as much as possible in order to catch the fresh and cool breezes found there. By doing so they gained a small measure of relief, but opened themselves up to another sort of misery. Each time they staggered to the ship's rail they became targets for the playful taunting and seemingly unsympathetic teasing of Matthew.

Aside from the crew, the only person on board who seemed totally immune to the effect of the rolling ship was Matthew. Nothing, neither wind, nor cold, nor rough seas had any effect on his stomach or his enjoyment of being on the open Atlantic. On most occasions as Caleb, Samantha, and many of their fellow passengers were leaning over the side, Matthew would be there to laugh at their ongoing misery. This usually earned him a hard glare from his wife, one that promised a severe future act of retribution. For his part, Caleb could only issue a weak threat toward his oversized antagonist and then lean a little further over the rail.

Other than suffering Matthew's ever present humor, Caleb could have found no better friends on board the *Osprey* than the Moores. They were uncomplaining, easy to talk to, and helpful in any way they could be to Caleb or to any other passengers needing assistance or encouragement.

After only a few days, Caleb, Matthew and Samantha had, by mutual agreement, combined their food stores, an action much more to the benefit of Caleb than the Moores. He could barely boil water for tea, but Samantha was a cook of exceptional skill, making even the simplest of ingredients into delicious meals which she prepared each morning and evening. Caleb and Matthew, after only a few of her meals, became the envy of those passengers and crew fortunate enough to smell the mouth-watering aromas produced by her magical cooking.

Early on Caleb learned that his new friends shared his intense dislike of the English, and like himself, had their own reasons for wanting to get as far away from England and English law as they possibly could. In Scotland, Matthew was a builder of houses, boats, and almost anything that could be made from wood or stone. He built the houses and boats during the winter months but switched to working as a fisherman during the spring and summer months. Liam decided that Matthew's time spent fishing off the rough Scottish coast, and not just his natural toughness, was responsible for his tolerance of the rolling of the *Osprey* as she sailed in even the roughest of seas.

One evening Caleb casually asked Samantha why they wanted to go to America.

She replied in a tone that clearly showed her contempt for the English, "Matthew does not like to work for any man, much less an Englishman. We had a decent business in Ayr, one that earned us a good living, but the English wouldn't allow a business with ties to the Jacobites to exist, much less while earning a rather fair living. My father claimed distant kinship to the Stuarts, so that put Matthew in with my family even though he didn't have anything to do with the Jacobite uprising of '45. As our taxes were doubled and then tripled, the number of our clients, many of them frightened away from doing business with us by the English, went down. With no other recourse but to become penniless servants of the English, we came to Belfast to see if things would be better there. We soon found that being branded a Jacobite in Northern Ireland was no better than being one in Scotland. Somehow the word traveled to Belfast and the English wouldn't allow Matthew to work with any of the ship builders. Seeing no other way out, with the last of our money we booked passage to America."

Samantha paused to look at her sleeping husband and then said with a voice full of resolve, "I know this. Wherever we go neither Matthew nor me will ever stop trying to be free and independent. If it is humanly possible, neither of us will ever work for anyone but ourselves. For both of us, independence and the ability to live our lives on our own terms are the best freedoms we can imagine."

Caleb could see the determination in Samantha's eyes and hear it in her words. Knowing what he did of the Moores, he had little doubt they would persevere no matter what obstacles they had to overcome.

"I just wonder if I will show the same courage and resolve when I get to America," he thought.

By the end of the first week at sea, Caleb and Samantha had finally overcome their seasickness. For the rest of the voyage, when weather allowed, Matthew, Samantha and Caleb would spend as much time above deck during the day and at night as they could to escape the crowded and foul-smelling quarters below and to enjoy the simple pleasure of seeing the sun go down over the horizon, or to watch the blue water break over the bow of the ship. To each of them, even the cold wind off the open ocean was far better than the cramped and pungent conditions below deck.

Such was the case one night about three weeks out of port. After an hour standing together at the bow of the ship, Matthew and Samantha excused themselves and went below, knowing Caleb would remain topside and allow them an hour or more of privacy. Leaning his elbows on the rail after their departure, Caleb was suddenly aware of the presence of a man standing beside him. Glancing to the left he recognized the ship's third officer, a man Caleb had no liking for, and a man who seemed to enjoy the hardships imposed on his passengers by the living conditions on board. If what he and Matthew suspected was true, Dugan also used his position as a ship's officer to extort money from the more timid passengers when they were in need of food or fresh water.

Caleb could barely keep himself from flinching slightly as Dugan moved next to him and casually placed an arm over his shoulder.

"I think a lad such as you should be better friends with a man such as me, Mr. Quinn, don't you?"

Caleb's reply of "I have friends enough" didn't seem to discourage Dugan who made no attempt to remove his arm from Caleb's shoulder. It was an action Dugan often used to intimidate his intended victims.

Not seeming to have heard Caleb's reply, in a now more menacing voice Dugan continued speaking, "We being friends and all, I'm sure you wouldn't object to making ol' Red a gift of your pretty wool coat."

Dugan, for the past three weeks, had kept a watchful eye on Caleb, noting that he never went anywhere without the coat, wearing it even while he slept. To Dugan, this only confirmed his belief that the young man did indeed have money or other things of value hidden in the coat.

Before Caleb could respond, Dugan, using a bellaying pin hidden in his left hand, struck Caleb a vicious jab to the stomach. Caleb caught totally off-guard reeled back, hunched over in pain with the breath knocked from his lungs. Taking his time Dugan raised his arm and aimed a second blow at Caleb's lowered head, but just before the bellaying pin reached its target, his arm was stopped in midair, his wrist gripped in a strong hand. Surprised, but confident of his own strength, Dugan attempted to throw a fist into the face of the shadowy figure holding his wrist, but before his fist could strike he received a tremendous blow to the back of the head followed by two open-palmed slaps to his face and then a knee to his ribs. Suddenly devoid of strength and totally helpless, Dugan felt himself being lifted over the rail until he was looking face down into the dark water rushing past the ship's port side only a few feet from the bow.

Caleb, slow to recover his breath from Dugan's blow to his stomach, was able to look up just as Dugan was lifted off his feet and hung by his ankles over the side of the Osprey. The person dangling the frightened and screaming third mate was a grim-faced Matthew Moore. Caleb, just beginning to realize what was happening, was amazed by what Matthew was doing to Dugan. Although Dugan was a fairly large man, perhaps ten or more pounds heavier than himself, Matthew easily held him by his ankles while shaking him up and down as if shaking out a dirty blanket. Caleb knew Matthew was strong, certainly much stronger than the average man, but this was a demonstration of strength unlike any he had ever seen or imagined.

Over the sound of the wind in the sails and the water meeting the bow of the ship, Caleb could hear Dugan screaming at first, but then pleading to Matthew, "Don't, don't. For God's sake, pull me up!"

Matthew ignored him, causing Dugan to scream again in abject terror, knowing if he was dropped in the water by the bow he would be swept under the ship and cut to shreds by the thousands of razor sharp barnacles attached to the ship's underside. Dugan had seen men who were keelhauled until the barnacles left them nothing more than a bloody mess on a rope, and hell itself could not have been more horrifying. It was a hard bloody way to die. Those unfortunate men who did not get pulled back on board soon enough became victims of not only the razor-sharp barnacles attached to the wooden hull, but the ever present sharks swarming up from the deep to make a meal of them.

After a glance down at the helpless Dugan, Matthew looked directly into Caleb's eyes and asked, "Should I let him go, or do you want me to pull him back up?"

Matthew seemed to be testing Caleb's reasoning and his instinct for survival. Could he do what had to be done?

Caleb, knowing instinctively what must be done, hesitated for only a moment and then replied, "I believe it far better that you let him go."

Caleb felt no reservation about his decision. He had no doubt Dugan was a cold-blooded killer, the kind of killer who if allowed to live would never rest until he had exacted a deadly vengeance on Matthew, himself, and even Samantha. Dugan could not be allowed to live, not if they wanted to safely complete the remainder of the voyage without the threat of retribution, even to the point of death, looming over them. Matthew gave Caleb one more look to be sure, and then with a nod from Caleb, opened his hands. Dugan was screaming as he disappeared below the surface of the water, joining the many victims he had sent to the same watery fate. Matthew and Caleb then went below, speaking not a word to each other of what they had done.

Early the next morning, Caleb and Matthew were on deck mingling with passengers and crew, anxious to hear what was being said about the disappearance of the ship's third officer. To their relief and puzzlement hardly any words were spoken about his absence by either the crew or the passengers. It was as if no one, including the officers and the crew, cared that Red Dugan was gone.

"Maybe," said Caleb to Matthew, "everyone is glad he's gone and no one cares how or why."

Hours later they learned from a crewman that the captain had written in his log "Third officer Percy "Red" Dugan was lost at sea due to unknown circumstances."

After that, the only mention that Matthew and Caleb made to each other of the incident came later that day when Caleb asked Matthew, "How did you know Dugan meant me harm?"

Trying to look wise and serious, but unable to stop a small smile, Matthew replied, "Dugan was very sneaky and well-hidden, but I have eyes for such men, and when we were standing on deck I saw him lurking behind the ship's dingy, I figured he was up to no good, and as you would be the only person on deck after Samantha and me left, I figured you had to be the object of Dugan's attention. I then left Samantha below deck and went back to see what our Mr. Dugan was up to. You know the rest."

"Thank you for what you did," said Caleb with all the sincerity he could muster, "I owe you my life."

"That you do, but don't worry about it. Throwing that Englishman overboard was the most fun I've had since my wedding night."

Nothing else was ever spoken between the two of them about Dugan, but several times during the next week Caleb noticed Samantha giving him a look as if to say, "I know what happened, and you did right."

Chapter 10 Samantha's Enterprise

Dugan's disappearance did produce an unexpected opportunity for Matthew and Samantha. Matthew, a hard worker by nature and a man vexed by inactivity, was always looking for something to do, preferably something that would require the use of his hands while at the same time earning him money. Halfway through the trip he convinced the captain that he had a talent for carpentry and knew how to make any kind of ship's repairs. After the captain agreed to pay Matthew to work on repairs that were not completed in port, Caleb was surprised that at Samantha's suggestion, Matthew asked the Captain to pay him, not in money, but in food from the ship's stores. This proposal also puzzled the captain, but seeing no harm in it he agreed.

When Caleb heard of the agreement he couldn't resist asking Samantha, "What are you going to do with more food than you and Matthew could possibly eat, even with my help?"

Samantha just laughed and replied with a wicked grin, "Just you watch and see how a smart Scottish lass can earn a pound or two even in the middle of an ocean."

Caleb later found out Samantha had already gained permission from the captain to use the ship's galley whenever she wanted, day or night, as long as it didn't infringe on the normal operations of feeding the crew. This was only possible because Red Dugan was no longer the ship's third officer, and no longer in control of the ship's stores. It also helped that Samantha bribed the captain with a promise of "all the free apple pie and sugar cookies you can eat."

Using the food Matthew earned, Samantha immediately began to cook two hot meals a day for anyone willing to pay, charging the same nominal price to both crew and passengers. Within days she was making three times more money than Matthew would have earned for his carpentry work. Showing the soft heart of one who had known poverty and hunger as a girl, she gave free meals or reduced prices for those who had little or no money. To both hide her generosity and protect the pride of her poorer customers, she graciously made some of the women passengers her "assistant cooks."

As Samantha told Caleb when he asked about her generosity, "I know what it means to have an empty belly, and no one, especially women and children, will ever go hungry around me; not while I have one morsel of food to share."

Her answer only increased his conviction that Matthew was the luckiest of men to be her husband.

Feeling left out and rather useless, Caleb volunteered to help Samantha in the galley, but after a few hours of "helping" her, mostly in the way of sampling her sugar cookies, an exasperated Samantha pushed him out of the galley and told him in no uncertain terms, "If you really want to do me a favor, stay out of 'my kitchen' and go help Matthew...if he'll have you."

Caleb, feeling properly chastised, followed Samantha's suggestion and joined Matthew working below deck. Over the ensuing weeks, under Matthew's patient tutelage Caleb learned the basics of carpentry. He also learned from Matthew that good carpentry required a meticulous eye for detail, the need for common planning sense, and the ability to sometimes solve complex problems. It also helped to have a tolerance for blisters, punctures, and cuts on hands and fingers. Caleb's respect and affection for the Moores increased with each passing day.

Late one evening while counting her day's earnings, Samantha made a surprising announcement to Matthew and Caleb.

"By the time we get to Baltimore," she said in a business-like way, "I will have enough money for Matthew to start a business, with enough left over to build a small house for us and the baby."

She said it so quietly, with such calmness, that for several long seconds a slow to comprehend Matthew did not move or reply.

Then, with a loud "WHAT?," Matthew jumped up, and as he had done several times before, cracked the top of his head on a rafter, but this time the force of the impact was so hard it sent him crashing to the floor. Caleb and Samantha were still laughing when Matthew crawled over to Samantha and ever so gently wrapped his big arms around her.

Smothering her laughter with a big kiss he whispered to her, "Thank you, thank you,"

When they finally broke their embrace Caleb could see signs of tears in the eyes of both of them.

On March 15, after six long weeks crossing the Atlantic, the *Osprey*, under shortened sail and using the slight northeast wind, made her way up through the Patapsco River Valley and shortly thereafter docked in Baltimore. Her passengers, all 108 of them who had left Belfast, were on deck since the *Osprey* came into sight of Fells Point and then Fort McHenry. Matthew, Samantha, and Caleb were standing together at the rail as a crewman proudly informed them, while looking at the fort, "America's national anthem was written by Francis Scott Key during the Battle of Baltimore fought at Fort McHenry during the War of 1812."

Like Caleb and the Moores, all of the passengers were anxious to step foot on this new land, where the history seemed so young, and perhaps, ever more anxious to place their feet on an unmoving surface.

Part 2

"When the world says, "Give up," Hope whispers, "Try it one more time."

~Unknown Author

Chapter 11 America

After leaving the *Osprey* the passengers were herded into a large building used by the United States Customs Service authorities to process all new immigrants. Matthew, Samantha, and Caleb joined the other immigrants in a long, slow-moving line. All the passengers were subsequently examined by white-coated doctors looking for medical problems or infirmities. Those that failed the brief examination were sent to a quarantine area, while those that passed, including Caleb, Matthew, and Samantha, went to another line. After another endlessly long wait while their papers were examined for proper identification and their names were registered, they were turned loose to face their new world. Many of them, including Caleb, not understanding that in this new world life could often be made much more difficult if you were Irish.

After saying a long and reluctant goodbye to the Moores and making sure they had Beauregard Carroll's address, Caleb Quinn exited the immigration building prepared to walk into Baltimore proper and somehow find the office of the same Beauregard Carroll.

He had taken only a few steps when a large dark-skinned man stepped into his path and asked in a voice deeper than any he had ever heard, "Sir, would you be Caleb Quinn?"

Startled by the appearance of the first black man he had ever seen, and such a large man at that, Caleb, at first hesitated, then swallowing deeply answered, "Yes," not sure what else he could say.

"I am Phillip, sent by Mr. Carroll, "if you will follow me, sir." Then without waiting for a reply he took Caleb's baggage and started walking away.

Several minutes later Caleb found himself sitting on the open seat of the most elegant two-person carriage he had ever seen, much less ridden in.

"Before I take you to meet Mr. Carroll we have one very necessary stop to make," Phillip announced to his somewhat bewildered passenger.

"Where is that?" asked the puzzled Caleb.

"With your permission, Mr. Carroll has instructed me to take you to a bathhouse for a thorough delousing and bath."

Looking Caleb up and down and grimacing ever so slightly, he added, "By the look and smell of you, it is much needed."

Caleb could not tell whether the black man was truly being critical or just having a bit of fun at his expense. He also felt that having washed himself several times in buckets of seawater while on the *Osprey* he wasn't all that dirty or smelly.

Nevertheless, looking at Phillip and sensing this was not a man to argue with, Caleb replied, "Whatever Mr. Carroll says will be fine with me."

With a cluck of his tongue and a wave of the whip to the horse, Phillip then directed the horse and carriage through the crowded cobblestone streets and past countless stands and carts with vendors hawking what seemed to Caleb to be an endless variety of wares, all being offered by loud voices filled with promising words. Caleb was amazed to see endless numbers of both live and dead poultry, what seemed like arsenals of weapons, stacks of assorted clothing, endless trays of pastries, row upon row of vegetables, baskets filled with medicines, practically anything new immigrants, such as himself, could need or want. Caleb, accustomed to the meager offerings of Irish markets, could only stare in awe at the richness and quantity of the goods being offered.

Remembering the many times he'd had barely enough food to sustain him, he made himself a promise, "I will never go hungry in this land," while wishing that Sean was there to share in the bounty this new country offered.

Rounding a corner just off the market district, Phillip brought the carriage to a halt before a large, two-story, wooden building with a sign reading *Chesapeake Saloon and Bath House*.

Indicating the front door of the saloon, Phillip told Caleb, "Go inside and ask for Big Mamma. Then do as she says."

Phillip watched with a slight grin on his face as Caleb left the carriage and slowly entered the building. Two hours later Caleb emerged, vastly different in appearance than when he entered. His clothes had been brushed as clean as was possible, his hair had been cut short, washed and perfumed. The slight whiskers that had begun to cover his cheeks and chin were gone, and his skin, a ruddy brown when he went in had been scrubbed clean and pink by a trio of laughing ladies as Caleb enjoyed the first hot bath he had ever experienced. He had also been served a mug of beer, eaten a full meal of a wide variety of seafood and breads, and been embarrassed as never before. It was, he felt, altogether the best two hours of his life.

As he climbed into the carriage Phillip politely asked the grinning Caleb, "How was it, young man?"

Settling into the seat next to Phillip and feeling the exhilarating effect of a clean body and full stomach, a beaming Caleb could only reply, "It was wonderful and you were right. I truly needed a bath." Then rubbing his fingers over his shaven chin and cheeks, he said, "But I am wondering, why did no one ask me for payment?"

"I took care of the payment while you were upstairs," replied Phillip, not at all bothered by telling a small lie. What Phillip didn't tell his young passenger was that *The Chesapeake Saloon and Bath House* was owned by Mr. Carroll and a silent partner. He, Phillip Buckner, was that silent partner.

Relieved that he owed no debt to the kind ladies who had attended him, Caleb leaned back to get comfortable against the carriage's seat. As he did so he became aware that for the first time since shortly after boarding the *Osprey* his body and head weren't itching. As the carriage worked its way out of the port area Caleb was just beginning to fully relax when he noticed several store fronts with prominent signs posted on their windows and doors. Many of the signs read 'Help Wanted, No Irish Need Apply.' Seeing these signs, the feeling of pleasure gained at the bath house instantly faded away, replaced by the thought that someone, even God, must have surely cursed the Irish.

"Why else," he thought, "would we alone have to endure the potato plague, domination by the British, and now unwelcome signs in a country known for welcoming people from all corners of the earth."

A half hour later, lulled into drowsiness by the meal he had eaten and the steady rocking of the carriage as it made its way up Lombard Street, Caleb was startled fully awake as the carriage stopped in front of an imposing brick building.

"We're here," Phillip said, stepping out of the carriage and looping the reins around an ornate brass hitching post.

Leading Caleb to the front door, Phillip guided him inside, down a short well-lit hallway, and left him standing alone in front of a door with a plaque reading "B & C Trading and Investments." Underneath the name were the words, "Beauregard Carroll, Proprietor."

"Have a good visit," Phillip told him. "I'll be out front when you're ready."

Caleb's soft tapping on the door was followed by a "Come in, please" from a refined, cheerful sounding male voice that surprised

Caleb by its youthful tone. Caleb had expected Mr. Carroll to be an older man, much like Joshua Webster, but upon entering the office he could see he was grossly mistaken in his estimate. Carroll looked to be, at the most, thirty years of age. He had neatly trimmed dark brown hair, was slim, of average height, and dressed in an elegant-looking light grey suit appropriate for an English lord. Aside from having equally intelligent and kind eyes he was as different from Joshua as Caleb could imagine.

Rising from behind his desk, Carroll said in a sincere voice, "Welcome to America. I trust your trip went well and that your ride here was enjoyable."

"Yes sir, Mr. Carroll, very much so," replied Caleb wondering if by "enjoyable" Mr. Carroll was referring only to the carriage ride.

"Good" responded Carroll, "please, call me Beau, and by all means have a seat."

Caleb did so, sitting down in a heavily padded leather-covered chair, while Beau once more seated himself behind his desk. Leaning back in his chair and smiling, Beau said, "Perhaps you may be wondering how we knew at what time and day you would be arriving in Baltimore."

"I thought maybe it was some act of magic," said Caleb, mildly surprised that the man before him so accurately knew one of the very questions that had been on his mind since meeting Phillip.

"Not magic," said Beau, "but there are ships that sail much faster than the *Osprey*. The clipper ship, *Calypso*, left Belfast six days after the *Osprey* but arrived here four days ago. The captain of the *Calypso*, a friend of mine, delivered a letter to me from Joshua, one that told me in detail of your troubles in Ireland and your subsequent departure for America. After reading the letter I merely had Phillip wait each day at the dock for the arrival of your ship."

Hearing no response from his young guest, Beau continued, "Now that you're here, we need to attend to the important business of deciding what to do with you."

"That is something I've wondered about for many weeks," replied Caleb, thinking that perhaps he would be lucky enough to find work on the docks or in a mill.

"Well, you need wonder no more. If what Joshua said of you is even half the truth, and I'm quite sure it is, I have a plan I think will fit you perfectly."

During the next hour Beau laid out a plan that left Caleb amazed, somewhat bewildered, and was totally to his liking. During that time Beau impressed Caleb with his considerable knowledge of English and Irish politics. Caleb also came to realize that Joshua was being perfectly accurate when he described Beauregard Carroll as "a man of considerable resources."

After finishing their conversation, both men moved to the office door. Turning to Beau and extending his hand Caleb said, "I don't know how to thank you for all that you're doing for me, it doesn't seem possible that someone would do so much for a total stranger."

"At one time," replied Beau, "all of us who came to this country came as strangers."

He then added, "Perhaps there will come a day when I will call on you for a favor. All I wish for you at this time is that you, like I did, find a good life in this country."

Chapter 12 The Farm

The following morning, after a comfortable night's sleep in a nearby hotel courtesy of Mr. Carroll, a well-rested and exuberant Caleb once again climbed onto the carriage seat next to Phillip. They then began a two day trip to the northeast, their destination a place Beau had simply referred to as 'the farm.'

During the trip Caleb learned from Phillip that 'the farm' was the winter home of the *B and C Circus*, another enterprise owned by Beau.

"The *B and C*," Phillip told Caleb, "is a group of entertainers, show people and everyday workers, who travel throughout the northeastern states during the spring, summer, and early fall, but take up residence during the winter near Shenks Ferry, a small Pennsylvania town on the shores of the Susquehanna River."

"The farm," Phillip went on to explain, "is also the home of about a dozen retired circus people who live there year round and take care of the place during the months the *B & C* people are on the road."

Wishing to ease any concerns his young passenger might have about his new life on the farm, Phillip gave Caleb a reassuring pat on the back and said, "Caleb, the people living on the farm are good people, the best, but they are different from most folks. They are independent to the point that they don't easily fit into normal society. If you accept them and earn their respect, you will not only make trusted friends, but you will learn from them a lot about life and how to get by in this country.

Caleb, who had never seen a circus much less met any circus people, could only reply, "What makes them so independent, so different?"

He wanted to add, "So much like me," but didn't.

"I can only tell you they are from more countries than you can imagine, know more about hardships and living than any other people you will ever meet, and have some very exceptional talents and skills. Talents and skills Mr. Carroll hopes will be passed on to you."

Then with an amused look on his face, Phillip added, "I'll leave the rest for you to figure out on your own."

An hour before nightfall Philip pulled off the road and brought the carriage to a stop beneath a small group of trees sheltering a slow-running stream. "I've camped here before," said Phillip, "and it's as good a place as we'll find to spend the night."

Within minutes he had released the horse to graze and removed camping gear and a basket of food from the storage area at the back of the carriage.

Having seen several inns and taverns along the way, Caleb said, "I have money for an inn if you want to stay indoors," holding out to Phillip some of the money given to him by Joshua.

"Not a good idea," said Phillip, "not for a young Irishman just off the boat, and especially not for someone of my color."

Later, as the two of them ate a meal of cold chicken, cheese, coffee heated over the fire, and bread slavered with butter and honey, Phillip explained that Maryland was a slave state, and although he carried papers proving he was a "freedman" in the employ of B. Carroll, he still wanted to come into contact with as few people as possible, and that certainly included any nosy slavery-loving inn-keepers.

"More than one freedman with proper papers," he explained, "has disappeared and then been returned to a life of slavery."

It was at that moment Caleb became aware of the cruel reality of slavery in his new country. That night, as he lay awake looking across the fire at the sleeping Phillip, he wondered if maybe there was something worse than being Irish.

After traveling for most of the next day Phillip brought the carriage to a halt on the crest of a low hill, pointed down the dirt road before them and announced, "That my young Irish friend is the farm."

Caleb's eyes took in a piece of land as beautiful as any he had known in Ireland. Beau had simply described where Caleb was going as 'the farm,' but this was a farm unlike any of the family farms he had known in Ireland.

What he was looking at more closely resembled a small Irish village. Stretched out before him and running to the bank of a blue-green river were acres and acres of land. He could see several fenced pastures, some with cattle, some with horses, and some empty of livestock but filled with high stacks of hay. Caleb could see several barns, a row of a dozen or more modest houses, two large gardens, what looked like a blacksmith's shop, and seven or eight brightly colored wagons that resembled small rooms on wheels. They reminded him of the wagons used by gypsies who often traveled the roads of County Antrim. A small creek moved through the property toward the river and divided the land down the middle. A bridge sufficient in strength and width to carry the wagons spanned the creek. He could also see a few people moving busily about the property. Chickens, ducks, geese, and even a pair of peacocks roamed at will. A whisper of regret went through him as memories of the Ireland he left behind sifted through his mind. At the same time, he looked forward to beginning his new life in such a splendid looking place.

"There's your new home," said Phillip as he headed the carriage down the gently sloping road.

Minutes later they approached the first house, their arrival announced by the barking of a large brindle-colored dog. On the front porch Caleb saw a lanky, grey-haired man of about fifty, sitting in a rocking chair and dressed in what appeared to be clothes made from deerskin. Judging by the deep lines crisscrossing his tanned face, Caleb judged him to be a man who had spent much of his life living in the outdoors.

"Shut up, Al," hollered the man as he painstakingly unfolded his long legs and pushed himself out of the chair, "don't ya know friends when ya see 'em, even if one of 'em be double ugly?"

Still sitting in the stopped carriage, Phillip, pointing a finger at the old man, said to Caleb, "That cranky old flea-bitten fella' talking to his mangy dog is Uriah Cordell, your new boss."

It was instantly obvious to Caleb from the playful banter and the grins exchanged by the two men that they not only knew one another but were old friends and had a genuine liking for each other.

"It's good to meet you, Mr. Cordell," said Caleb as he climbed down from the carriage and extended his hand, his exuberant smile and bright eyes revealing the excitement he felt at being there.

"Young man, my friends call me Uriah, and as of now we're friends," said Cordell gripping Caleb's hand in his own calloused one, "it's good to have ya here even if it meant ya had to drag this worthless varmint into camp with ya."

Caleb replied with a smile and a short laugh, watching with interest as the two friends exchanged a brief hug and mutual slaps on the back. The three of them then joined a flea-scratching Al on the porch. After sitting down Phillip began explaining to Uriah the reason Caleb was brought to the farm.

After quietly listening to Phillip and glancing several times at Caleb, Uriah rose from his chair and told Phillip, "I think I can find somethin' for the youngster to do around here, but before we get to that I want to show 'im around while we still got some daylight to see by."

Phillip then stepped forward and offered his hand to Caleb, "In that case," he said, "I'll be getting back to Baltimore knowing I've left young Caleb in good hands."

"Thank you for everything," Caleb blurted, almost reluctant to let go of this gentle giant's hand. "I hope to see you again soon..."

"Shouldn't be too long," replied Phillip as he returned to the carriage. See y'all."

Leaving the porch, Caleb followed behind Cordell and Al, noting that Phillip, now back at the carriage, was unloading Caleb's possessions.

While trying to keep up with Cordell's long stride, Caleb said, "Sir, I was told by Mr. Carroll that I was going to be a roustabout. Can you tell me what a roustabout is?"

"Well, son, a roustabout is someone who usually has more muscle than brain, who does anythin' what needs doin', and works for anybody in this here circus that's needs somethin' done. It also means that on most days ya're gonna be the first one up in the mornin' and the last one asleep at night. And that's what a roustabout is."

"I think that's something I can handle," said a pleased Caleb.

Turning his gaze away from Caleb and toward the land making up the farm, Uriah said, "Ya're probably wonderin' what this here place is all about," and not waiting for an answer continued, "we can't work the circuit during the cold of winter so most of us come here, usually from late November 'til late April. We spend a lot of time gettin' ready for the next season, fixin' wagons and such, or just practicin' whatever it is we do. Other than that we try hard to force ourselfs to do a little bit of huntin', fishin' and relaxin'. It's a real dog's life, son."

Cordell paused just long enough to spit out a long stream of tobacco juice at a line of ants and then explained, "Most folks ya'll meet here go on the road come spring, but there's also them that stay permanent. Them're mostly old circus folks that got nowhere else to go, or elsewise no place else they'd rather be. They look out for the place when we're gone, take care of the animals and the gardens, put up vegetables and hay for the winter, and even keep us in meat and fresh fish the year 'round."

In a soft voice he added, "Some never leave," and pointed to a small area of carefully kept headstones enclosed by a short wrought iron fence.

During the next two hours Uriah took Caleb to all but a few of the wagons and houses, introducing him to every resident of the farm they could find. Afterwards, Uriah led Caleb to one of the larger wagons on the farm. Judging from the length of the grass growing under it, Caleb figured the wagon was seldom moved.

"This here guest wagon is where ya'll be beddin' down until I can find ya somethin' else," Uriah said to Caleb, knowing the wagon might at anytime be needed by Beau Carroll or his friends when they came to visit.

After thanking Uriah for the tour and the introductions, an excited Caleb entered the wagon through the Dutch door at the back. To his delight the wagon was comfortably furnished with a bed that folded down from one of the walls, a small pot-bellied stove, several shelves and cabinets, a water bucket, and a slop jar. He also found clean sheets, blankets, and towels, as well as his travel bag and a tray holding a plate of ham, cornbread and molasses, along with a mug of cool cream-laden milk. After slowly eating the meal, he folded down the bed, put the sheets and blankets on it, and lay down, his thoughts turning to the events of the day, the people he had met, and the thought that he had come a long way from County Antrim. Within minutes he fell into a deep dream-filled sleep.

Chapter 13 The Traveling Show

For the next year Caleb traveled with the circus throughout the eastern states, and in the process acquired a unique education which in many ways surpassed any learning found in a formal school and was certainly nothing like the clandestine hedgerow schools in Ireland. Those schools were held in secret places, often between thick rows of bushes, hidden from the English authorities who would have arrested any Irish caught being educated.

He was introduced to a way of living which again reminded him of the colorful gypsy bands that traveled through County Antrim and occasionally made camp near the O'Connell home. Much like the gypsies, the circus people were not always welcomed by the local town people, and much the same as gypsies often found themselves being forced into hurriedly breaking camp, sometimes as much as twice in one week.

True to Phillip's words, Caleb became a student of the performers in the circus, men and women from many countries and from many backgrounds. Within months of his arrival Caleb became their treasured "man-child," loved and cared for by all but never coddled. They were people who knew from experience the world could be a hard place and with that in mind went out of their way to teach Caleb what they thought he needed to learn to meet its difficulties head on. Caleb's new family challenged him at every opportunity, challenges that he not only gladly accepted but often reveled in. As the weeks and months passed he proved to be a fast learner. His strong young body and inquisitive mind soon enabled Caleb to achieve a degree of competence which sometimes matched, and on rare occasions even exceeded the talents of his beaming teachers.

His first teacher was the ever-talking, ever story-telling, former mountain man, Uriah Cordell. Born in the mountains of southern Tennessee and having spent most of his adult years in the western mountains trapping furs, living among the Indians, and leading settlers west made Cordell an expert with the knife and the rifle, and any other weapon that might be used in a fight. Under Uriah's watchful eye and sometimes gentle slap to the back of his head, Caleb learned to shoot Uriah's rifle, how to breath to improve shooting accuracy, to understand how wind and elevation could dictate aiming, how to hand-load ammunition to increase range and reliability, and perhaps most importantly when to shoot and when not to.

"Boy," Uriah would say, "if ya ain't sure of yur target just wait 'til ya are. Be patient and try not to get yurself caught with an empty gun when an enemy or a prime piece of game is close up. It would also help if ya didn't put a hole in another hunter, 'specially me."

Caleb proved to have an inborn talent for shooting the heavy long-barreled gun and quickly developed into an extraordinary shot. What Uriah taught him about the local wild animals combined with the knowledge of the outdoors gained during his childhood, enabled him to constantly grace the tables of his fellow circus workers with all kinds of game including deer, turkey, rabbit, and even an occasional black bear valued for its abundance of fat. Within a few months of firing his first rifle shot, Caleb's reputation among the circus people as a skilled shot and hunter almost equaled that of Cordell himself, and Uriah was someone they had never seen outshot with the long rifle.

One afternoon Caleb and Uriah were sitting around the fire after dressing out a large white-tailed doe when Uriah decided it was the right time to teach Caleb another lesson that might improve his chances of surviving a close up fight with whatever enemies he might someday face.

Uriah called to Caleb indicating with a gesture that he should take a seat nearer to him. Reaching behind his back Uriah removed a large knife from his belt and held it in front of Caleb, "See this here knife," he said, brandishing his long Bowie knife in Caleb's face. "It does one heck of a job on deer meat, but the time may come when ya need to use it to carve on a man who's tryin' to do the same to ya."

Hearing the words and looking at the large knife with the razor-sharp blade, Caleb's mind quickly developed an image of himself sticking a knife into the body of a man. That man was William Warington. It wasn't an image he liked to remember, but knowing he was about to get a knife lesson from Uriah whether he liked it or not, he asked, "You want to teach me how to kill a man with a knife?" Hoping as he spoke the words Uriah didn't know about what happened to Warington.

"Yep," replied Uriah, "but most importantly I want to teach ya how to keep someone else from slicin' into ya first. If'n it's an Injun' you might also have to worry about a war club or a hatchet. One other thing ya should remember, if ya ever git into it with Injuns, it ain't the

Injuns ya see that's likely to kill ya the quickest, it's the ones ya don't see."

Replacing the knife in the scabbard attached to the back of his belt, Uriah moved to the nearby fire and selected two foot-long slender sticks that were only partially burnt on one end. After beating the sparks out in the dirt, he walked back to Caleb holding out one of the two sticks with blackened tips.

"We'll start out with a little practice usin' these here sticks for knifes," he said to Caleb. "It's the same way I've seen Cheyenne daddies teach their younguns how to knife fight."

Handing one of the "knives" to Caleb, Uriah looked him up and down and said, "First off remember ya're kinda' tall and long in the arms, and that's an advantage ya'll have over most men. Most men, bein' shorter than ya will know they need to end the fight lickety-split, which most likely means they'll come in fast and stab for the stomach, tryin' for a quick kill. That wantin' to stab can git 'em killed quick if'n they're fightin' someone who knows how to take advantage of their impatience. Never forget that mistake and never make it yur own self. Be patient and use the natural advantages ya have with yur long arms."

Looking at Caleb he added, "Hell's bells, I've seen two idiots come together and with one stab kill each other at the same time. I can also tell ya I seen a man die 'cause he didn't have it in him to stick a knife into another man. That's not how I want ya to think. Ya need to be a cutter first, and a stabber second. Try to have a long fight, not a short one. If ya can, always go for the knife hand or arm. Cut and slice until the man can't hold his knife, and then cut and slice some more. It sounds ugly, but it's a winnin' way."

After taking another spit Uriah added, "One other thing. If'n ya ain't got it in ya to kill with a knife, ya better not carry one."

Caleb now knew Uriah had no knowledge of what had happened at the Warington estate. Before he could decide whether to say anything about his past experience with stabbing a man, Uriah's lesson was interrupted by the arrival of Jean Duval, a Frenchman who served as the circus' trick shot artist.

"Listen to the man," Duval said to Caleb, "Uriah's getting old and a bit creaky, but he is the last man anyone with a brain, including me, would want to face in a knife fight. If you ever get a look at that skinny body of his with all those scars all over it, you'd know he's been there and lived to talk about it."

"Well, thanky, Monsieur Duval," said Uriah, "comin' from a man whose been known to carry a hide-out pig sticker hangin' behind his neck and a two-shot Derringer up his sleeve, that's a mighty fine compliment."

Caleb looked closely at Duval's neck and could see a thin piece of rawhide around it. Caleb had noticed it before and thought it was strange that a man would wear a leather string for a necklace, but with Duval being French, he thought maybe it was just a "continental" fashion. Now he knew better.

"I got one more thing to add before we commence to stick fightin'," said Uriah. If ya can, always move to yur left, and when yur opponent stabs or slices try using yur left hand to swat or even hold the man's arm toward his body. That'll open up his knife arm to those cuts and slices while taking ya away from his blade. Cut 'im on his hand or fingers. Make 'im bleed to death or cripple 'im in his hands or even his legs, if that's what works."

Moving slightly away from Caleb and waving the burnt stick in front of him, Uriah said, "Now, let's ya and me give 'er a go."

Caleb gave Uriah a smile, thinking as he did that being younger and with his size and speed a bit better than the old man and despite Duval's words, he was about to give Uriah a lesson of his own.

"If that's what you want to do old man, but it'll be a shame to get that nice deer-skin shirt of yours all sooty."

The two men closely matched in size and reach, with the sticks in their right hands, now faced each other and assumed a fighting stance. They both started circling to the other's left. Caleb noticed Uriah's knife hand was held low, exposing his upper arm and shoulder. With a flick of his knife toward Uriah's knife hand, Caleb then raised his arm to chest level and made a lightening fast stab at Uriah's exposed shoulder. When Caleb's stick was half-way there his knife arm was suddenly knocked away, forcing it across his body. Before he could recover Uriah spun on the heel of his left foot bringing him fully to Caleb's right and slightly to his rear. Caleb's right side and back were now left completely exposed. With a casual upward swipe of the burnt stick Uriah slashed across Caleb's shoulder leaving a black streak. He then brought the stick up until the point of it stopped just below Caleb's right ear.

"I guess ya wasn't listenin' to what I told ya' about not stabbing," said Uriah.

Caleb was both embarrassed and annoyed at himself for being so easily and quickly bested. He had no idea Uriah could read him so accurately and then respond so quickly.

Jean Duval, watching with amused interest was not surprised because he had seen Uriah teach the same lesson before. He looked first at Caleb and then at Uriah, "I wondered if you could still do that little pirouette," he told Uriah. As Duval spoke, he couldn't help but break into a huge grin.

"Maybe you forgot you're an old man," he added, making reference to Caleb previously addressing Uriah as "old."

Caleb was forced to smile at Jean's comment, "I guess I also forgot how sneaky old men can be."

"Guess ya did," replied Uriah, "but I did bait ya into goin' for a stab by offerin' ya what looked to be a high open target."

"You did, and it's something I won't forget."

"Hope not," said Uriah, "but ya did do somethin' the right way. Ya were watchin' my knife and not my eyes, and that's good 'cause not too many men gonna stab ya with their eyes. That kind of fighin's usually done by womenfolk."

With that being said the lesson of the day was over.

What Uriah was to the long gun, Jean Duval, a semi-reclusive Frenchman reputed to have a military background in the French Foreign Legion, was to handguns. When performing his trick shot show, he could use a revolver or cap pistol with either hand, invariably hitting any target, large or small, still or moving. Duval was that peerless freak of hand and eye coordination that comes along once in a decade. After Caleb's knife fighting exhibition, it was at Duval's insistence that Caleb spent countless hours practicing with a variety of small arms, including the French LaMott pistol and the much smaller and less accurate Derringer. One talent Duval never displayed during his act, but taught to Caleb, was a fast draw technique using Duval's own self-designed shoulder rigged holster. The holster was small, made of very thin leather, and was almost impossible to detect under even a light-weight coat or vest. Jean was seldom seen not wearing one or the other. He was a man who had been taught by experience to always be ready for any unexpected threat.

"It also allows," Jean explained to Caleb, "the weapon to 'slip out' of the small holster easily and quickly, as opposed to a larger holster that requires the user to 'pull' or jerk the gun free. It is also a lot better and a lot faster than having to reach for a pistol in your pants or coat pocket."

While making Caleb practice with one of these special holsters, Duval often advised his young protégé that accuracy is of foremost importance, but accuracy combined with speed can be the difference between living and dying. You need to be able to employ both when facing an armed enemy.

Caleb took Duval's advice to heart, and after countless days of practice could draw, aim, and fire almost without thinking and almost as fast as Jean Duval himself. Caleb was quickly becoming much more than just competent with either pistols or the long rifle.

Perhaps the teacher Caleb most enjoyed learning from was Hung Fat, who, along with his wife, Mai Li, was acknowledged as the best cook in the circus or for that matter anywhere else. Invitations to join them at their table were eagerly accepted by those people fortunate enough to receive them. In addition to his culinary expertise Hung Fat was also a master of many other skills, most notably those of juggler, acrobat, tight rope walker, and when called for, a maker of the finest array of fireworks to be found on the Eastern seaboard. Hung Fat's fireworks displays were often used with great success to draw people to the circus show.

Caleb's training under Hung Fat began simply enough.

"Big, clumsy boy," Caleb was told, "hold this coin in the flat palm of your hand with your fingers outstretched."

When Caleb did so, Hung Fat said, "Now I will place the back of my hand on your open palm and attempt to turn my hand over and pluck the coin from your palm before you can prevent me from doing so by closing your fingers."

Over the next few minutes Hung Fat, time and time again, easily turned his hand over and plucked the coin from Caleb's hand before he could close it.

"There must be a trick to it," said an exasperated Caleb, "I may be slower than you but not that much slower."

"You are correct, there is a trick…one I know and you do not. It is now my wish to teach you many other things this humble Chinese man knows and you do not. Some of these teachings will involve tricks and others skills that must be learned through hard work."

With an impish smile he added, "You will have to think about what we did in order to understand which is one and which is the other."

During the following year Hung Fat's teaching enabled Caleb to achieve a degree of coordination and physical dexterity which amazed not only himself but also the other members of the circus troupe. Caleb could now juggle up to six objects at a time while talking and walking. He could do a series of body flips even while blindfolded. His peripheral vision improved to the point where he could clearly see something, especially movement, without looking directly at the object or person. He could also walk a tightrope forward or backward while casually catching objects tossed at him.

Early in their sessions Caleb came to understand that everything Hung Fat was teaching him was designed to train his mind as well as his body. Caleb's powers of concentration and memorization increased dramatically. He learned to notice almost everything around him. Movement, sound, color, shapes, and any number of objects that might have previously gone unnoticed or unremembered would register in his mind with little or no conscious effort. His ability to focus on his surroundings reached dramatic new heights.

To Caleb's surprise, easily the most unusual and unexpected of the circus people to act as his teacher was Lucinda Baker. Listed on the circus posters as Madame Dora, the Psychic Lady, it seemed to Caleb she could not have a talent which could be passed along to a young man. Such was not the case, not by a long shot! Lucinda had a lifetime of unique experiences, particularly when it came to gambling or understanding people. She also had a sharp tongue and an educated mind second to none, man or woman.

Caleb came to find out through talking to Uriah that even at an early age Lucinda was fiercely independent and rebelled both verbally and physically when her parents insisted she learn to be a 'proper young lady,' much like her older sister, Evelyn. Always competitive, Lucinda refused to be excluded from any activities she enjoyed, especially those so often reserved for boys. As a young girl, when her older brother and his friends played war in the nearby woods, she was there, crawling through the mud, climbing the trees, and firing make-believe guns. When they went swimming in the nude in the small secluded pond, she left her clothes hanging on the same bushes they did. Swimming, splashing, or swinging on the rope tied to a tree overhanging the pond, she was never mindful of the difference in her body and that of her male companions. In all things she refused to be excluded, refused to accept that there was anything she couldn't do.

Lucinda had a temper and was never one to timidly accept any insults from those same companions. More than once she returned home with bruised knuckles or a black eye, all joyfully earned while exacting revenge for any harsh words or disrespect directed her way. She accepted no boundaries on her behavior just because she was a girl, and she never failed to use her fists and feet to go where and when she wished.

Caleb, enthralled with the stories he'd heard of her younger years, and aware he knew very little about girls or women, often urged Lucinda to tell him her "life story." She finally acquiesced after assuring him that if he ever repeated any of what she told him his ears would end up being used as Christmas tree decorations.

She began her story by first confirming what Caleb had heard from Uriah. Then she skipped to her mid-teen years when much like Caleb, her life changed dramatically. Lucinda's father and his friends held a weekly game of card playing, and the night before her sixteenth birthday, as a special present, he invited Lucinda to observe. He enjoyed introducing his unorthodox daughter to novel experiences and felt that card playing would appeal to her inquisitive mind and sense of adventure. The game was private, played in their living room, and made up of some of Savannah's most successful business men. Their card playing skills ranged from poor to very good. Lucinda's father was among the poor.

Within the first hour Lucinda was hooked on every aspect of the game. She loved the verbal jousting that went on among the players. The clinking of silver and gold dollars, the drama of the gambling, and even the sight and smell of the cigar smoke that filled the room enthralled her. Most of all she liked the way one player could beat another using skill, wits, and not just the fortunate turn of the cards. Here was a game that entranced her. It was fun, exciting, competitive, and unlike the many games which favored the physical strength of men, the cards never favored any player over another, male or female.

At the end of the night's play Lucinda understood the rules of the game, and had begun to understand the mathematics involved. Later, in the middle of the night, she snuck out of bed quietly going to the secretary desk in the parlor where she removed the deck of cards her father kept there. She spent the next several hours shuffling and dealing out hands to herself and three or four imaginary players. These "nightly games" continued for several days and served to sharpen her hunger to play in a live game.

The next Thursday, after begging her father to take her along, she sat in on a second card playing session, this one held at the home of a county judge. She left the session with the knowledge that some players were inherently better or worse than others; that some men seemed to play to lose, while others were set on nothing but winning. Using her above average observational skills she noticed that the men often played as their personalities dictated. The strong, more successful men often played very aggressively, almost to the point of sheer foolishness. However, not surprisingly she observed this style of play often worked for them against players less inclined to take risks. Weaker men, unsure of themselves, could be manipulated or bullied into folding hands they should have played. Lucinda vowed that if she ever played she would be aggressive, but neither foolish nor timid. She would always go with the odds, and always, always play to win.

By the time Lucinda finished sitting in on a third session, one that lasted almost six hours, she understood a great deal about the strategies involved in the game. How skill and consistency were more important than luck because everyone's luck would invariably balance out over time. How betting patterns or players' actions and reactions, even the slightest twitch or hesitation, could reveal whether they were playing from strength or weakness. She learned to read the players to the extent that she could almost always tell who had a strong or weak hand, and who was bluffing and who was not. She also learned that those players who drank the most were most apt to make foolish wagers. She noticed that one of her father's opponents might pretend to be more "into his drink" than equated to the amount of drink he had consumed. She saw the ruse as a clever play that she would look for, or even emulate, when she began to play the game.

For the next year she was allowed to attend many more of her father's poker nights, using the sessions to hone her understanding of the game but always as a silent observer, never once being allowed to participate. She was forced to accept this exclusion but vowed that someday she would be a player, and a much better player than her father or any of his friends. More than a few of her dreams centered around sitting at the table with her father's friends and absolutely stripping them of their money and unwarranted masculine pride.

Being sent to finishing school in New Orleans at the age of seventeen finally afforded her the opportunity she so craved. With little trepidation, she snuck out after dark every chance she got, going into the

French Quarter of New Orleans to play cards at whatever gambling hall would permit entry to an unescorted female player. The time spent with her brothers while growing up gave her the climbing skills needed to leave the building through the second floor window in her room, returning the same way. Her "escape" was aided and abetted by one of the kitchen maids, Elizabeth. Elizabeth would clean up after dinner then take a carpet bag hidden in the pantry out to the bushes under Lucinda's private room window. Running up the stairs, Elizabeth would give Lucinda "the all clear." Lying down on Lucinda's soft mattress, she'd curl up in the down quilts sleeping comfortably as a decoy while Lucinda climbed down the trellis, retrieved the bag, changed clothes, and then began her evening adventure. Using what little money her parents gave her as a monthly allowance she struggled at first against the more experienced players, many of them professionals who were seldom reluctant to take the young girl's money. Some of them, being the southern gentlemen they were, believed that if they beat her badly enough, if they took all her money, she would give up gambling and pursue a career more appropriate to a young lady, or if not, she would pay her debts in a way they would enjoy more than card playing. They believed wrong.

After only a few weeks of gambling Lucinda's skills improved to the point that she began to consistently return to her room with more money in her purse than it had held when she left. By Christmas-time she was playing in bigger money games and consistently winning. Worried that her winnings, which she kept hidden under her mattress, would be discovered by the school mistress, she took the unprecedented and unladylike action of opening her own bank account. She did so over the objection of a bank manager who at first refused her request but was persuaded to change his mind by the large amount of money she offered to deposit. It also helped that he had an eye for beautiful young ladies, and Lucinda was as beautiful as any young lady New Orleans had to offer.

Lucinda's gambling forays ended when she was stopped late one night by a policeman on patrol. Her dark, lustrous hair, large glowing green-blue eyes, elegantly clad slender figure, and earthy manner led him to mistake her for a high-priced "woman of the night" returning from an evening of work. Refusing his request that she share a portion of her purse with him and let him sample her wares in return for his "protection," Lucinda was arrested, thrown into a paddy wagon with several drunks and prostitutes, and taken to jail. To her great disgust she was forced to spend the remainder of the night on a hard wooden bench in a cold cell with a floor covered in human waste.

The next morning, standing before a stern and totally unsympathetic judge, it didn't help Lucinda's case that the arresting officer was sporting a large purple bruise under his left eye. Her situation might have been worse, but encumbered by her long dress, her kick to his groin had missed its mark.

The arrest led to a hefty fine, her expulsion from school, and a forced return to Savannah. She left behind a bank account with a balance of over two thousand dollars, and an increased addiction to the gambling life, an addiction that would stay with her for many years to come.

Upon returning to Savannah it was only a week later that her parents insisted she enter into marriage with the son of a wealthy and powerful local family. They claimed it was the only way to save the family honor and ensure that she would be accepted by Savannah society after word spread of her New Orleans debacle. Still only seventeen and convinced she had little choice at the time, Lucinda acquiesced.

Her husband soon proved more of a boy than a man, someone who needed a mother more than a wife. This in no way proved an obstacle to Lucinda's enjoyment of life. She simply took several lovers, the first within two months of taking her wedding vows. Six months later, thanks to the jealous wife of a well known lawyer who had the grievous habit of talking in his sleep, her infidelity was uncovered.

Within days Lucinda's scandalous behavior was known throughout the city to anyone who could read a newspaper. When the judge overseeing the divorce proceedings called her as a witness and asked her what she thought of marriage, she described it, to an astounded audience, "as the perfect prelude to divorce." After her first and only marriage ended, a disgraced but totally unremorseful Lucinda left Savannah and returned to New Orleans with the intent to make her own way, knowing she could do so by entering full-time into the man's world of high-stakes gambling.

Her "seed" money was withdrawn from the New Orleans bank and for the next fifteen years she made a very comfortable living in gambling establishments and on board the many paddle boats plying the Mississippi River between the delta, St. Louis, Peoria, and points north. Always independent, she went where she wanted when she wished, living life with the same independence and fearlessness as when she was a child. Despite numerous proposals from an array of wealthy suitors she never remarried, preferring to take an occasional lover when she felt the need to be with a man.

During this time she also became recognized as one of the finest gamblers on the Mississippi, a player who could not be intimidated, never cheated, and never took an insult lightly. She was also noted for the unique motto she had adopted as her own, "any game you can name for any amount you can count," a motto she backed up with her card playing skills and unwavering willingness to play in high-stakes games. Dressed to the nines with perfect hair and make-up, always dripping with jewels, and never without the diamond stick pin she'd won with her first big pot, those men who accepted a challenge from the beautiful Lucinda usually left the table with less money than they started, but with a smile of admiration on their faces.

In the summer of 1855 Lucinda booked passage on the river boat steamer the *Delta Duchess* never suspecting as she did so that her career as one of the few women to succeed in the tough world of professional gambling was about to come to an end.

The *Duchess* was captained by Theron "Whitey" Varvil, a sometimes drinking companion, an occasional lover, and an ardent admirer of Lucinda as both a woman and a gambler. On the second night out he was present when one of the players at Lucinda's table accused her of cheating. The accuser, a pompous young man raised in a wealthy St. Louis home, was a poor card player filled with the false confidence of a sheltered youth which was compounded by his nightly consumption of large amounts of alcohol.

Not aware of Lucinda's reputation as an exceptional card player he was convinced when he took his chair at the table that he could easily beat the female gambler by pushing her into large pots, and that Lucinda, as was typical of women he'd known, would back down when faced by the strong and confident man he imagined himself to be. As a result of this miscalculation he lost heavily, not only out of his own pocket, but also from the large amount of cash entrusted to him by his father's business associates in New Orleans. Faced with certain humiliation upon returning to St. Louis without the money entrusted to him, and still believing he could bully Lucinda, he had suddenly risen out of his chair and demanded restitution from her.

"You, madam, have cheated me," he shouted in a whisky-slurred voice. "I demand you return my money or I shall see to it that when we arrive in St. Louis you will be arrested and sent to prison as deserving of any common thief."

Lucinda, only mildly annoyed by the words of a man she had already judged a fool of the first magnitude, calmly placed her ivory cigarette holder in the ashtray provided for her. Looking up at the young dandy she told him, "I have not cheated you, and I am deeply insulted that you called me a thief but doubly insulted that you would call me 'common'. As such, I would appreciate your immediate apology."

"Apologize?" blurted the irate young man, "to a slut like you?"

He was not aware of Lucinda's formidable temper, but Captain Varvil was. Not sure whether he was protecting Lucinda or the young gambler, Captain Varvil, with the assistance of two crew members, acted quickly to escort the still threatening and heavily inebriated young man to his quarters. Without informing Lucinda, the captain then instructed one of his Negro deck hands to see to Lucinda's safety for the duration of the trip to St. Louis.

At the end of the night, as Lucinda returned to her stateroom on the third deck, she was accosted by the same drunken, disgruntled young man. Faced by an unstable man holding a knife and threatening to maim her, she calmly shot him in the stomach with the single shot Derringer she always carried concealed in her clothing.

Having witnessed the affront and reacting to the gunshot, the ship's hand appointed by Captain Varvil to defend Lucinda quickly intervened, in perhaps a more grievous manner than the situation warranted. As easily as he would pick up a piece of luggage, he simply, and without a word, picked up the wounded knife wielder and tossed him over the railing into the brown waters of the Mississippi. To the young man's misfortune he was even less a swimmer than he was a card player. To the regret of few, save his family, he was never seen again.

"I am Phillip," whispered Lucinda's unsolicited accomplice in an educated voice, "and I was never here."

"No you were not," Lucinda replied to the large black man, "but I will always be grateful to you."

Seconds later the Negro disappeared below deck, only a moment before other passengers, alerted by the gunshot, joined Lucinda.

After the *Duchess* landed in St. Louis and the unfortunate gambler could not be located, an investigation by the St. Louis police ensued. When the investigation got around to Lucinda she readily admitted to playing a part in the tragic disappearance of the young man, but stated that after she shot him in self-defense, he unfortunately flipped backwards over the railing of the boat and disappeared. She revealed nothing about Phillip's role, knowing that to do so would most certainly result in his hanging.

Subsequently Lucinda was arrested by the St. Louis police, charged with second degree murder and brought swiftly to trial. The prosecutor attempted to portray her as a "painted lady" and questioned how a single shot from a small Derringer would cause the victim to "flip" over the ship's high railing. Fortunately for Lucinda the all male jury was less impressed by his arguments than by the dazzling beauty of the woman they were duty bound to judge. At the conclusion of the trial the sympathetic jury declared Lucinda to be innocent by reason of self-defense even though a few were still a bit dubious about the convenience of the body going over the boat's railing.

The trial that lasted for over two weeks was followed by all of the major southern newspapers. Thanks to the news reports Lucinda's infamy spread from New Orleans eastward to all the major cities throughout the Deep South, including Savannah. After the trial, a despondent Lucinda never again took a seat at a gaming table.

One evening, months after the trial, she was visited in New Orleans by a grateful Phillip. He encouraged her to consider using the skills she'd developed as a card player in a very different role.

"He told me about the *B and C*, and that Beau Carroll and Uriah could use a psychic," she recounted to Caleb, "and you know the rest of the story."

Feeling very close to Lucinda after hearing her story, Caleb was eager to learn all he could from her. It was at her unyielding insistence that Caleb grudgingly improved his reading and writing skills. In return for his attention to academics, she spent many enjoyable hours teaching Caleb the card skills she had learned from those years spent as one of the most successful gamblers to have worked on the Mississippi.

Caleb quickly learned how to handle cards, the mathematics of them, the odds on certain cards coming up, and when it is better to raise, call, or fold. Like Lucinda, Caleb soon became adept at stacking a deck so that he could deal out any hand he wished.

One day Caleb's curiosity got the better of him, and he asked Lucinda, "Are you really psychic?"

His question was prompted by his recollection of the people in Ireland thought to have 'the sight.'

"Caleb, as much as I hate to offend your Irish beliefs in mystical things, nobody is psychic, and certainly not me. Some of us have simply trained ourselves to better understand what we see and hear." Seeing the tinge of disbelief in his eyes, she thought for a moment before continuing, "The ability to accurately read card players and the ability to read people and make general predictions about them are much the same. I study the way people hold themselves, their facial expressions, nervous habits, their appearance, who accompanies them to a reading, whether they look happy or sad, and what conversation passes between them while they are waiting to avail themselves of my skills. All these observations allow me to make an educated guess as to what they do, who they are, and, most importantly, what they want to hear. That may seem psychic to superstitious people, or people wanting to hear something good about themselves, but it's truly based upon careful observation."

"Speaking of keen observation," she said, "cheating is another aspect of card playing that can be detected if you know how to look for it."

She admonished Caleb, repeating the first lesson she'd taught him regarding card playing, "Never, never, cheat at cards. It takes the fun out of the game, and worse, can be a dangerous thing when done in the wrong company, and gaming establishments are where you will more than likely find that wrong company. Always remember, the better card players don't need to cheat to be successful, but they must be able to recognize cheating when they see it."

With that said Lucinda shuffled the deck of cards she'd been holding, asked Caleb to cut the deck, and then dealt out fours aces. Before Caleb could comment she then dealt out a fifth ace. Caleb was amazed.

"Don't look so shocked," Lucinda said. "Before I'm through with you you'll be able to do that and a lot more."

Putting the cards back together, she continued her lesson with the now extra attentive student.

"Just as a psychic does when working a client, as you're playing, you need to study the players' faces, their body movements, betting patterns, facial expressions, and anything else that might tell you the strengths or weaknesses of their hands. At the same time you must teach yourself to conceal those things from whomever you're playing against.

Gambling is like war. If you can 'read' your opponent better than he can 'read' you, you'll usually win."

"Also," she said, speaking in her most earnest voice, "no matter what I teach you or how good a card player you think you've become, if you want to keep your money, don't play either mahjongg or poker with Hung Fat. I don't know how the little man does it, but he always wins. I have tried for years to figure out how the little Chinaman does it. After all this time I can only conclude he has the ability to read me, and I never thought that to be possible. Try as I might, I just can't figure it out."

Neither could Caleb, who shortly thereafter ignoring Lucinda's sage advice, lost over two weeks in pay playing penny ante stud poker with a seemingly exceedingly lucky and absolutely gleeful Hung Fat.

Chapter 14 The Runaways

Of all the jobs assigned to Caleb by Uriah, the one he enjoyed most was going out in front of the circus troop to scout out the next camping site. Caleb enjoyed the responsibility this job placed on him, along with the few hours of solitude it offered as he went out in advance of the troupe. He became adept at finding places with clean, running water, enough room to hold all the wagons, animals, and people, and above all, places where they could camp without raising the ire of either local property owners or the town law.

In early August Caleb had found just such a place along the banks of the Delaware River a few miles south of the sleepy town of Port Jervis, New York. They had made camp early and Caleb, Lucinda, and Jean were finishing their dinner and relaxing around a small fire while watching a color-filled sunset, when a large wagon with a man on horseback trailing behind it approached them.

When the wagon pulled to a halt in front of them, the three circus people could see the man on horseback was well-armed with a knife and a pistol in his belt and a rifle casually held across his saddle. His companion on the wagon seat had no rifle, but he did have a pistol in his belt and a large bull whip draped over his right shoulder. Both men, who appeared to be brothers, were large, wore filthy clothes, had full unkempt dark black beards, and appeared to be thirty years old or more. Caleb took an instant dislike to them, thinking they seemed as cruel-looking as any men he could remember.

Proof of the accuracy of his thinking was the human cargo they were carrying. Sitting in the bed of the sturdy wagon was a metal cage about six feet long, four feet wide, and four feet high. Crammed inside it and shackled in chains attached to their legs were a black man and woman. They appeared to have no food or water and were covered in dust and dried sweat which gave them a deathlike chalky appearance. Even in the dimming light Caleb could make out the reddish lash marks on the man's bare back.

Pulling the wagon to a stop a few arm lengths from their fire, the wagon driver gave Caleb, Lucinda and Jean a large smile, displaying his rotten, tobacco-stained teeth.

"We been looking for a good place to camp and was hoping you folks wouldn't mind us sharin' your fire and maybe a bite or two of food," he said, sounding as if an invitation would be forthcoming. He was wrong. Before either Caleb or Jean could reply, Lucinda stood up. Crossing her arms under her ample bosom and looking hard into the eyes of the man doing the speaking, she said in a voice far from friendly, "We're pretty much full up and about to get some sleep, so you and your partner should look further down river. In fact we'd appreciate it if you'd move a lot farther on, and hopefully down wind."

The driver, either slow-witted or stubborn, replied, "If'n you don't like the smell of darkies in your camp, maybe we could..."

Before he could finish, Lucinda pointed a finger at him and said in a voice filled with complete disdain, "It isn't them. It's you and your bounty-hunting partner back there. We don't like the looks of you or the smell of you, and we don't abide scum like you treating anyone, black or white, like an animal."

"I got the right to treat them runaways any way I want," said the man on the wagon as he gestured with his hand toward the prisoners "And I got the law on my side, but I bet you already know that."

As he spoke Caleb could see spittle gathering on the sides of the wagon driver's mouth.

"We know the law," said Jean, standing up and joining Lucinda in her rejection of the bounty hunters, "but the Fugitive Slave Act doesn't make what you're doing right and it damn sure doesn't make you welcome here, so start moving. Now!"

"I don't like being talked down to by nobody," said the driver, now visibly angry. "Maybe what you circus trash need is a taste of ol' Matilda."

He was moving his hand toward his whip as he spoke. His fingers had barely touched the whip's handle when a shot rang out, grazing the man's coat sleeve and hitting the whip's handle, sending it falling to the wagon's floorboard. The shot had been fired by Jean, who hadn't even taken the time to aim before making what Caleb recognized as a very difficult shot.

The startled driver jerked his head to the rear and shouted, "Charlie!"

Hearing the shot followed by his name, the bounty hunter on horseback began to raise his rifle in Jean's direction but before he could pull the trigger he was struck in the back of the head by the butt of a rifle. Without a sound he slowly slid out of the saddle and landed headfirst on the ground, dangling by a foot hung in the stirrup. Uriah stepped out from behind the downed rider's horse carrying his long rifle over his shoulder.

"Seems to me somebody had an accident," he said as he looked down at the unconscious bounty hunter.

With a grin on his face he looked at Jean and added, "Nice shot you made on the driver. Saved me the trouble of killin' 'im."

Jean, still holding his gun on the bounty hunter sitting on the wagon replied, "Well, it was either shoot the whip or shoot him, and if I shot him we'd have to go to the trouble of burying him or nursing him, and I didn't fancy either."

Replacing his Colt revolver in his shoulder holster, Jean looked at the man on the wagon, "You can make another try for 'Ole Matilda' if you like, or you can try for the pistol in your belt. If you don't feel like trying, I suggest you toss both the whip and that pistol stuck in your pants to the ground."

After only a slight hesitation and with no further protest, but giving Jean a look that was murderous, the driver did both.

During the next few minutes, and despite the angry objections of the bounty hunter on the wagon, the shackled man and woman were given an abundance of food and water. Between mouthfuls of food the famished prisoners begged to be released, but despite having sympathy for their plight, Uriah and the others were forced to do nothing. They knew that releasing the prisoners would have meant breaking the law, and that could lead to everyone involved going to jail, and trouble the *B and C* didn't need. Moments later Uriah sent the bounty hunters on their way, the slaves still in their cage, the horse tied to the back of the wagon with the still unconscious Charlie draped over the saddle.

An hour after sunset, Caleb watched as Uriah, who had been sitting silently by the fire, went over to the rope corral holding the troupe's horses, saddled his black, put rope halters on two other horses, and led them back to his wagon. He then disappeared inside it. Curious as to what Uriah was doing at that late hour and why he was taking two extra horses, horses he hadn't bothered to saddle, Caleb walked over to Uriah's wagon. He had just reached it and was about to knock on the door when Uriah emerged from the wagon holding a travel bag in one hand and his Sharps rifle in the other. In his belt was a revolver and a long knife sheathed in an ornate deerskin scabbard, one Caleb hadn't seen before. Seeing the long knife Caleb knew at once that Uriah, armed as he was, and with a hard and solemn look on his face, was about to alter the plight of the two runaway slaves.

"You want some company?" asked Caleb, not exactly sure what good he could do, but still wanting to be part of whatever his friend was about to do.

"Nope, not this time," answered Uriah, "what I got to do, I can do alone, but thank ya anyway."

Mounting the black and leading the other two horses, Uriah turned south. That he took the same direction as that taken by the bounty hunters only confirmed Caleb's suspicions.

"Somebody," Caleb thought as Uriah rode away, "is about to get an unwelcome visit from a very dangerous man."

Just before noon the following day, the bounty hunters, accompanied by a badge-wearing deputy, caught up with the troupe several miles north of Port Jervis.

Caleb was walking at the rear of the wagons checking to see if trouble followed, but also in the hopes of being the first one to spot Uriah when he caught up.

Riding up to Caleb, the deputy, in a voice tinged with a mixture of authority and boredom, said "Son, I'm Deputy Noah Bartlett. I hate to bother you folks, but I'm duty-bound to try and help these two upstanding citizens from North Carolina find their missing property. Now, you folks wouldn't know anything about two missing slaves, would you?"

The deputy had a nice look about him and it was clear to Caleb from the indifferent tone he used that his heart was not in aiding the bounty hunters. His body language left little doubt that he would not have been there except for his duty to the law.

Stepping in front of the deputy's horse, and rubbing its muzzle, Caleb replied, "If you mean do we know anything about those scum bags riding with you, the answer is yes. Last night we had the pleasure of throwing them out of our camp. As for missing slaves, we don't know a blessed thing about that, but wherever they are we wish them well."

Caleb then stared coolly at the two bounty hunters, silently challenging either one of them to call him a liar.

"That so," said the man who had been driving the wagon, "and just where's the old man what was here last night? The one what sneak-attacked poor Charlie here when his back was turned."

"I think you may have just called me a liar," said Caleb, "and, if it wasn't for my respect for Deputy Bartlett and the law, I'd drag you off that wagon and beat you in the way a man like you deserves."

Waiting for a response and receiving none from the bounty hunters, he addressed the bemused deputy, "As for the 'old man', he rode out at first light with a pocketful of cash. Said he was heading for Baltimore. I doubt he'll be back until he's spent it all on drinking and whoring."

Caleb was enjoying the lie when it occurred to him that maybe it wasn't much of a lie after all because Uriah actually did make a lot of trips to Baltimore.

Noticing the activity at the back of the line of wagons, Jean, who was leading the troupe north, stopped and trotted his horse back to where the men where talking to Caleb. Hung Fat and Mai Li, driving the last wagon in the caravan, looked on.

"Well, I guess that about covers it," said the deputy as he turned his horse to face the bounty hunters. "You fellas can look elsewhere, but even money says those runaways are probably half-way to Canada by now."

Starting to turn his horse back to the south he added, "I'd appreciate it if, in the future, you two wouldn't bother me or these good folks again."

"But he's lying," said the bounty hunter who had been hit on the head by Uriah.

"I doubt he'd lie, 'cause he ain't got no reason to help the Negroes. Besides, these people look honest," said the deputy. "Now, I suggest you ride out, and keep riding until you get out of my jurisdiction, unless you want to be arrested for harassing these folks."

Seeing the deputy leaving and knowing better than to remain behind without him the bounty hunters turned their wagon around and headed south looking back hard at Caleb as they did.

Caleb, not to be intimidated in any way, hollered after them, "You girls come back anytime. Bring Matilda with you."

At high noon four days later Uriah caught up with the troupe about forty miles north of the town of Monticello. He rode into camp looking tired and gaunt and without the two extra horses he'd left with.

The next day when Caleb casually asked about the missing horses all Uriah would say was he loaned them to some "friends." Other than that he offered no information about where he'd been or what he'd done. The

84

others in the troupe who had known Uriah for quite a few years already knew the answer.

Not long after Uriah's return Caleb was pleased to receive a letter from Matthew and Samantha courtesy of Phillip, who usually visited them at least once a month with messages and mail. Eagerly opening the letter, Caleb read

Dear Caleb,

We hope this letter finds you doing well and in good health. The year we spent near Baltimore was difficult. There was too little work to be had, and too many people, mostly immigrants like us, looking for it. Matthew was often forced to work as a common laborer, breaking his back for pennies a day. He never complained, but I hated the unhappiness it caused him.

We heard from people moving west that there were many Scots and Irish living in the Appalachian Mountains of Georgia and North Carolina, which is why Matthew, Eryn Gracie, and I are now living in the mountains of northern Georgia, not far from the town of Mineral Bluff. I love it here because it's still wild country. We see something new almost every day. The mountains, the rivers, and the weather often remind me of my home in the Highlands.

What cash money we need Matthew earns by clearing trees for pasture land or farming. He then cuts the trees for the lumber he needs to build houses or log cabins most of which he sells to new settlers. Anything else we need we either grow or take from nature. Matthew's happy as long as he can stay busy and work with his hands. I keep the house, have a large garden, and try to keep up with Eryn. We are happy and feel blessed by God.

Please visit us when you can. We would love to see you again.

Your friends,

Matthew, Samantha and little Eryn Grace

Thinking about the Moores and their new home, Caleb resolved that one day he would do his best to join them in the mountains of Georgia, wherever that might be.

Chapter 15 Tersha

It was a chilly but sun-filled day at the farm just two years after Caleb had joined the circus troupe; years that brought considerable changes in Caleb both intellectually and physically. Traveling with the circus from city to city, town to town, meeting a variety of people and facing various challenges had greatly increased the scope of Caleb's overall knowledge.

Most of Caleb's pure academic knowledge could be attributed to Lucinda's insistence that he read a wide variety of books such as those authored by Franklin, Paine, Chaucer, and Shakespeare borrowed from her personal library. Lucinda and other members of the troupe also engaged Caleb in countless hours of discussion and debate covering philosophy, religion, and politics. Those who proved to have extensive knowledge of the history, medicine, culture, and geography of lands within and outside the United States endeavored to share their knowledge with him. Much of their knowledge was passed on to the receptive Caleb who now, better than most men his age, could hold his own during almost any conversation with anyone. He was no longer the under-educated naïve young man who had stepped so uncertainly off the *Osprey*.

Although traveling with the circus had greatly enhanced Caleb's store of knowledge, it was his physical appearance that had undergone the most visible and dramatic change. He had grown another two inches in height and developed long well-muscled arms and legs. His muscular neck and shoulders led to a broad chest which fell to a flat, lean, rippled stomach. His face showed strength with its tight jaw muscles, straight white teeth, a strong square chin, deep-set intelligent eyes, and a nose with a slight hawkish bridge. His black, shoulder-length hair worn in a style copied from Uriah made him somewhat dashing in appearance. He had become an exceptional-looking man, and by even the most stringent standards, far above average in looks. His physical appearance, strong voice, and still boyish demeanor were well appreciated by many of the town women who saw him, an appreciation that invariably passed unnoticed by the unsuspecting young Irishman who was still sorely lacking in some areas of his education.

This same Caleb was back at the farm sitting on a wooden bench by the horse barn, enjoying the warmth of the afternoon sun, watching Uriah whittle on a stick, while listening to one of his endless and oft repeated stories of his time spent in the western mountains. Hearing the persistent squeaking of an ungreased wagon wheel, Caleb glanced up and saw an old weather-worn, rickety black and red circus wagon entering the farm from the north road. The unfamiliar wagon was being slowly drawn in their direction by a sway-backed roan horse. A good looking and obviously pregnant mare was tied to the rear of the wagon.

Caleb reached over and tapped Uriah on the arm, "That anybody you know?"

Stopping his whittling, Uriah's eyes followed Caleb's pointing finger, and getting to his feet with an incredulous look on his face announced, "Well, I'll be damned. Unless I've lost my mind that there is Tersha Barova, and a sight for an ol' man's sore eyes."

Jamming his knife into the bench and tossing aside the whittling stick, Uriah added, "Come on, boy, this is someone ya'll want to meet."

Before Caleb could stand up, the usually slow moving Uriah headed at a fast trot toward the oncoming wagon, led by the barking Al, and followed closely by the curious Caleb who knew only something or somebody important could cause Uriah to move that fast.

As they approached the wagon the driver brought it to a stop, dropped the reins, stood up, and called, "Uriah, you'd better slow down before you bust a gut or break one of those boney legs of yours."

"My legs will still be a'movin' when ya're an old lady with ornery grandchildren," replied Uriah, "but it's good to see ya even if ya are as sassy as ever."

Caleb could see that Uriah was more than just happy to see the driver. In all the time he'd known him Caleb didn't think he had ever seen Uriah smiling as big or looking so pleased.

"Not too sassy to give an old friend a big hug," said the driver as she tossed off the large floppy man's hat she was wearing, jumped down from the wagon and threw her arms around the neck of the bent over and beaming mountain man.

After a lengthy hug Uriah stepped back from Tersha and turned his head toward Caleb.

"This here," he said to Tersha, "is my Irishman friend who calls himself Caleb Quinn."

Caleb hardly heard Uriah's playful introduction because from the moment he saw Tersha throw off the hat he felt like he'd been kicked in the chest by a mule.

The girl now standing only a few feet away from him was the most dazzling creature he'd ever seen. She was slim and tall, the top of her head easily reaching to Uriah's chin. Her complexion was perfect, her skin a light olive in color, as if she were born with a slight tan. She had sky blue eyes beneath an immense crown of shiny black hair that fell in soft curls below her shoulders. Her nose was small and delicate and dotted with the faintest of freckles, some of which seem to have fallen onto her cheeks. All of these things were almost forgotten by Caleb when he looked at her mouth, a mouth like no other he had ever seen. Her full lips curled slightly upward at the corners, were a natural strawberry red in color, and framed small but perfectly shaped white teeth.

Caleb, his heart pounding in his chest and his mouth suddenly dry, could only utter a strangled, "Hello."

"Hello to you, Caleb Quinn," said Tersha, extending a delicate hand to him.

To Caleb, her voice sounded like the ringing of tiny porcelain bells. The two young people, their hands now clasped together stared into each other's eyes until several long seconds had passed.

"Enough of the introductions," said Uriah, breaking the brief silence while also observing the long look exchanged between the two youngsters.

Placing a hand on Tersha's shoulder, Uriah added, "Tersha, I sure hope ya're back here to stay 'cause we missed ya', gal."

Recalling the intense pride Tersha displayed even as a young girl, he added, "And if ya're looking for work young lady, ya' sure come to the right place."

Tersha slowly slipped her hand from Caleb's and swung her body around toward Uriah, allowing Caleb to see the outline of the full breasts pressing on her blouse. He struggled for a moment to move his gaze away from her body and back to her face, and in that instance Caleb could see the slightest beginning of tears in Tersha's eyes. In that split second she looked so tired and sad, so hurt on the inside, it took all the restraint he had to keep from reaching out and wiping away the wetness gathering at the corners of her eyes.

"Thank you, Uriah, and I do need work," Caleb heard her reply as once again he heard the ringing of bells.

"Good, but we'll get to that tomorry," said Uriah, "right now ya look a bit tired and I've got a hunch ya could use some good hot food."

Waving his arm toward the wagons set up nearby, he added, "Ya know the place as good as most so why don't ya just set up anywhere ya like. In the meantime Caleb and me will git ya some food and somethin' cool to drink."

An hour later, with help from Uriah and Caleb, Tersha had her horses pastured, her wagon set up near that of Lucinda, and was finishing a hot meal provided by Hung Fat and Mai Li. Since Tersha didn't seem to need any more help and had retired within her wagon, Caleb and Uriah returned to the bench, once again enjoying the sunny day, but also keeping a close eye on Tersha's wagon.

After allowing a few minutes for Uriah to start telling him about Tersha, Caleb lost his patience, and trying to sound as if he were only casually interested, asked, "Who is she?"

Uriah was fully aware that the young man next to him had been instantly smitten by Tersha and the question asked was more than casual. Remembering a time many years ago when a young Shoshone girl had captured his heart at their first meeting, Uriah leaned back against the barn wall, yawned and took a long stretch of his arms and legs, deliberately delaying his response to his eager young listener. Taking his time, he retrieved the stick he'd dropped earlier, pulled his knife out of the bench, and returned to his whittling.

"Well, are you going to tell me or not?"

Seeing Caleb was about to burst from curiosity, Uriah finally began to answer his question.

"About six or seven seasons back we hired her daddy, who claimed to be a Russian gypsy, to take care of the horses and wagons. He brought Tersha, who was twelve or thirteen years old at the time, with him, but there weren't no wife or mother. It only took a few weeks for all of us to figur' out he was a man as easy to dislike as Tersha was a pleasure to be around. He just didn't know how to be friendly, or even be half-way nice to folks. He was mean when he was sober, and even meaner when he was liquored up, and that was often enough. I also 'spect by the bruises Tersha sometimes failed to hide that he beat her on occasion. That made all of us madder than wet hens 'cause no child could have ever been sweeter, better behaved, or less deservin' of a whippin'."

After pausing to spit out a stream of tobacco into the dirt between his feet, he added, "I will say this…, despite the man's faults he was a wizard with horses. Best I ever seen and I've seen Sioux could teach horses to fix breakfast and clean up afterwards. Ride 'em, train 'em, cure 'em, birth 'em, Tersha's daddy could do it all. Within a year or maybe a bit more he had trained Tersha on how to trick ride on that same little mare ya seen behind her wagon. Tersha was as good as any rider I ever seen on that there Princess."

Again emptying his cheek of tobacco juice, he continued, "We was about to turn them into a full-fledged trick ridin' act when her daddy suddenly up and left, tellin' no one of his departure, and leaving a cryin' and broken-hearted Tersha behind. It spoke well for the child that despite the way he treated her, Tersha loved her daddy and his leavin' was hard on her. For the rest of us it was almost reason to celebrate. With her daddy gone and not knowin' any relatives she might have, we all sorta adopted her as our own. Tersha was a joy to all who knew her and soon became loved as if she were our own daughter. More'n once I wished she'd been mine, and I coulda' been the daddy she needed and deserved."

At that point Uriah stopped, wiped brown juice from his lips, and then sat silent for a moment. Caleb could see a touch of sadness in his eyes. To Caleb it seemed he was thinking back to another time, perhaps to a time when he had a family, maybe even children.

Not looking Caleb in the eye, Uriah continued his story, "Some of us, curious about where she come from and whether she might have folks somewhere, tried to ask her about her past, but Tersha would never speak even one word about it, not even to those who knowed her best. She kept any serious thoughts to herself and was always somethin' of a mystery. She stayed with us for over three years, but as I remember, it was about two months before ya joined us when her daddy showed up in Syracuse, loaded her up in the same wagon she came here in, and without no thanky or explanation at all to any of us disappeared down the road."

"What kind of work will you find for her?" asked Caleb, now more curious than ever and needing to know more about this stranger, this beautiful Tersha Barova who had so suddenly and completely shaken his world.

"As I remember it, Tersha's not someone ya tell what to do, so I'll let her choose whatever she wants, but it's my guess that as soon as her mare is able she'll get back to trick ridin' or the such. If not, I can tell ya she's a natural actress and able to become whatever character she wants to be. Just before her pa took her away, she was smart 'nuf to take advantage of her looks, all that black hair and honey-colored skin. With very little effort she could turn herself into whatever she figured out the townies wanted. She dressed up in the costumes Lucinda made her and then she became either an Indian princess, or maybe an Arabian dancin' girl. Several times she even worked with Lucinda as a crystal ball readin' gypsy girl."

Taking another spit and then slowly shaking his head, Uriah continued, "She sure was somethin' and could fool people and make some good money doin' it. I reckon' maybe that's why her daddy came back for her and took her away. I figur' he musta wanted her money or such."

"Now," he said while putting away his whittling, "if that answers your questions, I reckon' both of us got work to do while there's still a little daylight."

That night, Caleb dreamed of an Indian princess standing close to him, looking up at him with a smile on her face, the sweetest smile he'd ever seen.

Chapter 16 Angel

Several weeks passed during which time Caleb watched Tersha every chance he got but never got up the courage to speak to her other than a polite "hello" or "nice day" as they met in passing. Time and time again he deliberately passed her way hoping she might stop and speak to him, but nothing of the sort happened until late one night when he was awakened by a loud pounding on his door. The pounding was followed by a voice he recognized as Tersha's.

"Quinn, get out here 'cause I need your help," she shouted.

As quickly as he could, a puzzled Caleb, pulled on his clothes and boots and stepped out of the wagon. Tersha was standing there barefoot in a long cotton nightgown, a glowing lantern in hand.

"Come with me," she said turning toward the stables without waiting to see if he was following.

"Princess is about to foal, and I need your help," she repeated as Caleb caught up to her.

Side by side the two of them moved toward the stable, hearing the mare's neighing as they neared it. Caleb held back as they entered, watching Tersha go to the mare lying on the ground. As she knelt down beside what Caleb could see was a very pregnant Princess, she said, "You'll have to hold her head and try to keep her still while I pull out the baby."

Caleb moved to the mare's head, knelt down, and following Tersha's instructions, put one arm over the mare's neck and with his left hand pushed down on her nose. Tersha had moved to the mare's rear and immediately grabbed the two small hooves of the suddenly emerging foal.

"We're just in time," she told him, and then ignoring the mare's slightly jerking hind legs began to gently pull with both hands on the foal.

As Tersha pulled, the foal continued to slowly come forth, first its front legs, then the head, neck, and much of its belly.

"Come on baby, come on," Caleb heard her plead as she continued to pull out the baby. He was fascinated by her determination and the caring in her voice, but he was also acutely aware that her exertions had caused her cheeks to turn a light red in color. Even more tantalizing were the glistening beads of sweat running down her chest and disappearing beneath the front of her nightgown. Ashamed of his thoughts, Caleb returned his attention to Tersha's efforts to pull the foal from its mother.

He could see she was now tugging as hard as she could, but for some reason the foal seemed to be stuck halfway out of its mother.

"Can I help?" he asked.

"Yes, but hurry, I think the baby's rear legs are catching on something, and I'm not strong enough to pull them free."

"Hold on," said Caleb, as he moved to take Tersha's place behind the mare.

Nudging Tersha aside he grabbed the foal high up under its front legs and began pulling, not pulling with all his strength but with a good deal more than Tersha. Slowly, the foal's hips and then the hind legs began to appear. Catching Caleb by surprise the foal suddenly slipped completely out of its mother and landed with a wet splash across his lap. The foal, a filly, lay there motionless and covered in wet sticky mucus and some of the stringy-looking afterbirth that had emerged with it.

Suddenly feeling goose bumps on his arms and legs along with the beginning of a cold sweat covering his upper body, Caleb asked, "Tersha, what do we do now?"

Tersha's answer was to shove him out of the way and grasp the motionless filly by the head.

"She's not breathing," said Tersha, and began to clear away the mucus from the filly's nostrils.

Once the mucus was cleared away she repeated, "She's still not breathing."

To Caleb's amazement Tersha then pressed one hand over the filly's muzzle, put her other hand over one of its nostrils, and pressing her mouth against the other nostril began to blow big breaths into the motionless foal.

After about six such efforts, Tersha, breathing in large gulps of air, looked at Caleb and in a pleading voice said, "Caleb, I can't do it anymore, you've got to do this for me."

With no hesitation, Caleb grasped the foal's head as Tersha had done and began to repeat her actions.

After several unsuccessful attempts he heard Tersha's voice, "Blow harder," she cried. Caleb could almost feel the desperation in her voice.

Once more Caleb filled his lungs with all the air they could hold, and then blew as hard as he could into the foal's nostril. For a second there was no response, but then, with a muffled snort, the foal jerked its head up and blew out a small cloud of air and mucus, covering much of Caleb's face and arms with a thin wet spray.

"You did it!" exclaimed Tersha jubilantly, as, still kneeling, she put her arms around Caleb's neck, brought her cheek next to his, and gave him a huge hug.

As the seconds melted away Caleb could feel the heat coming from Tersha's cheek and breast, could feel the softness of her hair on his face, her hands pressing firmly into the muscles of his back. He returned her embrace for as long as he dared, but then fearing his body might betray the passion gathering inside him, placed his hands on her shoulders and gently pushed her back at arm's length. At that distance she looked more beautiful than anything he could have imagined.

"You did it," Tersha said again, looking into Caleb's face, staring at him with those remarkable blue eyes that seemed to see inside him.

Caleb could hear the joy in her voice while also noticing a flush of pink coming to her neck and then spreading toward the cleavage revealed by her loose-fitting nightgown. His heart now pounding furiously, his manhood almost fully aroused, Caleb turned away from Tersha and toward the foal, desperate to hide his arousal and the embarrassment it would bring him if she noticed.

Unable to think clearly because of his condition, he was barely able to reply, "Me and an angel."

"That's it, that's what we'll call her," said Tersha breaking into a smile, "she'll be our Angel."

Then gazing softly at Caleb she said in a whisper, "Let's move over there, out of their way," and without waiting took his hand in hers and led him to a small pile of hay next to the stall wall.

As they sat down a tail-wagging Al entered the barn and immediately trotted over to Tersha. Ignoring Caleb, he sat down in front of her, his mouth open and making loud panting noises.

"Hey there, Al," said Tersha, placing a hand on either side of Al's neck and vigorously rubbing him. "What's a good boy been up to?"

Caleb, first looking at Tersha's smiling face, and then at Al, could have sworn the dog had a grin of happiness on its face.

In response to Tersha's shaking, Al leaned forward and licked her twice on the face. He then carefully edged his way between Caleb and Tersha and lay down between them, never taking his eyes off her.

"I've seen you playing with him before," said Caleb. "And now I've seen what you did for Angel."

Looking at Tersha until she moved her eyes to his, he continued, "You must really like animals."

Placing a hand on Al's head, Tersha waited for several moments before replying, "I must admit I like animals more than I do most people."

As her eyes turned away from Caleb to look at Al she added, "Animals aren't like people. They have no deceit in them. They don't lie, and they don't hurt you for no reason."

Turning her gaze back to Caleb as she moved her hand to rub Al under his chin, she continued, "All they really want is for you to love them and let them love you. That's why I can't understand how anyone could deliberately be mean to an animal. It's even worse when people hurt people who love them. That's why I don't trust some people."

Studying Tersha's face and seeing the sadness that had crept into her eyes, Caleb could only think, "What or who could have hurt her so badly that she no longer trusts people?"

At that moment he became determined he would somehow change that, somehow make her trust him as she had never trusted anyone in her life.

They spent the next half hour watching silently as the mare, after rising to her feet, gently licked away the mucus and remains of the afterbirth covering her baby. Caleb and Tersha then watched the little foal that, after many attempts which left them laughing, managed to stand up, wobble on her long legs for a few moments, and then walk around her mother in search of one of her teats. Finally, after a few misses and some assistance from both her mother and Tersha, Angel began to nurse. Several times as they watched the little foal and her mother, Tersha broke out into what Caleb could only think of as "musical laughter." He knew as long as he lived this night would never leave his memory.

"I don't know how to thank you for what you did," she told him.

Looking at him with eyes full of happiness, eyes that seemed to sparkle, she continued, "That filly is half thoroughbred, like her father, and half Morgan like her mother. Someday I plan to have a horse ranch and through Princess and Angel and a good stud raise the best saddle horses in the country."

Noting the look of determination on her face, Caleb replied,

"My bet is you'll manage to do just that."

Then, searching his mind for something to say that would keep her close to him during the days to come, Caleb had a sudden inspiration, "I know how you can thank me. You can teach me to ride trick-style like I've heard you do."

With a mischievous smile on her face Tersha slowly reached out, put a hand on Caleb's arm and looked teasingly into his dark bright eyes, once again seeing the same boyish innocence which had attracted her to him when they first met.

"I would love to teach you about trick riding, anytime and anywhere you like," she said.

Her subtle message was lost on the uninitiated Caleb.

Only later, when Caleb was lying in bed and thinking about the night's events, did he wonder why Tersha had come to him for help. She could have chosen almost anyone else and certainly someone with more experience at birthing foals. Did she pick him because she likes him? He was still pondering these questions when he fell asleep.

During the following days, the people on the farm watched with smiles of approval as the two young people spent most of their time together. To no one's surprise but Caleb's, after less than a month he and Tersha became lovers.

Chapter 17 On the Road Again

On the first day of May, Caleb and Tersha joined the rest of the troupe making the various preparations for the upcoming tour. Wagons were cleaned and tents were carefully rolled up or folded. Wagon wheels and axles were greased, food was stored, beds and blankets aired out in the sunlight, harnesses repaired or replaced, and all the animals examined for any problems that would make them unfit for the road.

Two days later with everyone in the troupe looking forward to the beginning a new tour, the loaded wagons set out in a long single file line. After a successful trial run in Baltimore, attended by Beau, Phillip, and many of their friends, they spent the next two weeks putting on shows in small towns in Maryland and Pennsylvania: places with names like Hagerstown, Chester, Broomall, and Norristown. During this time Caleb was assigned many duties among them the heavy work of getting the tents erected and taken down before and after the shows. He was often joined in these tasks by Sven Knudson, a balding red-headed man who didn't live at the farm during the winter, but joined the troupe in Baltimore after spending the winter months with his family. Despite being of medium height and weight, and looking about forty years of age, Sven, who used the professional name the *Norwegian Nightmare*, earned his living by challenging townies to no holds barred wrestling or boxing matches. Those who were bold enough to accept Sven's challenges were charged two dollars to step into the ring with him, with the guarantee they would win three times that amount if they could last through five rounds without being pinned, submitting, or being knocked out. Many of the townies, after looking at the not so big and ordinary appearing Sven standing quietly in the ring, were more than eager to wager the two dollars. To their astonishment and misfortune, none but the strongest and toughest of them lasted barely two minutes, much less five rounds, and no one collected any winnings unless Sven wanted them to.

When Caleb asked Sven why he sometimes allowed himself to lose a fight Sven only acknowledged that he could sometimes make more money by betting against himself. Once again Caleb was getting an education on a subject not found in normal schooling.

Caleb was amazed at the holds, tricks, and power of the punches Sven used to defeat the challengers. As a boy he had learned a few wrestling holds from his father, for the Irish loved to wrestle, but Sven knew not only those holds, but a good deal more that he had learned from other wrestlers, some of them from other lands. Wanting to be better at wrestling, but also thinking it would impress Tersha, Caleb asked Sven if he would teach him how to wrestle and box, a request Sven readily consented to.

During the rest of the tour, Sven taught Caleb many of the finer points of each sport, explaining that his enhanced ability to fight might prove very beneficial because at some time during the tour it wouldn't be unusual for the men of the troupe to be called upon to defend themselves and the others from irate or drunken townies. Sven, at one time a professional boxer, also taught Caleb the finer points of boxing. How to throw a jab, how to move, how to block punches, and how and when to go for a knockout. Caleb also learned how, when necessary, to fight dirty; to use his fingers, teeth, feet and elbows to defend himself in any way when faced with a stronger man or by many men. More than once he impressed on Caleb, that when threatened by uneven odds the best tactic was to strike first, strike fast, and strike hard, not stopping until his foe was totally beaten and unable to mount an attack.

Sven once told Caleb, "The good feeling that comes with winning only lasts for a short time but losing can hurt like hell for days and days, or worse if you're unlucky or careless enough, it can get you maimed or killed."

In the middle of a scorching summer day, after an hour of boxing and another hour of wrestling with each other, a sweating and panting Sven stopped their sparring and led Caleb to a nearby creek they used to wash the sweat from their bodies. Standing in the creek and dousing himself Sven looked over at Caleb and noticed that his young protégé wasn't even breathing hard despite the hours of heavy exertion.

"Caleb, you've learned about everything this old has-been can teach you," he said as if talking to a son.

Then after taking a drink of water from his cupped hands, he grinned and continued, "If I show you anything else you're liable to take my job, or worse yet start jumping into the ring, betting against me, and then taking my hard-earned six dollars!"

Caleb, grateful to have earned the weathered fighter's respect, and remembering the numerous bumps and bruises given to him by Sven, replied, "Thank you for the compliment, but it'll be a cold day in hell before I'm stupid enough to try to take your money."

Until early August everything went well for the people of the *B & C Circus*. According to Cordell, the attendance was higher than the previous year, and the people coming to the show were spending more money than ever before. Caleb didn't bother asking Uriah why because he knew beyond any doubt the reason was Tersha. Uriah had been right when he said she knew how to attract a crowd, and at every town attract them she did.

In whatever character she assumed, her dazzling looks and sensuality easily made her the main attraction of the show, a fact that did little to ease Caleb's sense of jealousy when he saw so many men, young and old alike, watching her with fixed stares, unable to hide the lust in their eyes. Although he didn't like what he saw in the eyes of other men, at the same time it made him a bit proud and grateful for having such a beautiful and admired creature in his life.

By tradition, the circus rarely performed or traveled on Sundays. Many of the troupe attended the outdoor service conducted by Uriah, but mainly Sunday was the day used to fix what might be broken, to rest, to resupply the troupe, and most importantly to avoid any confrontations with the local church leaders who might deem their performing on Sunday an affront to the Lord. It was on such a Sunday that Caleb and Tersha volunteered to get supplies in Schenectady, a town in upper New York, about three miles from their camp. They had performed there the day before, thought the town was worth seeing again, and were more than willing to say yes when Uriah asked for volunteers to go back to town for supplies.

The wagon ride to town was pleasant and without incident. Arriving there Caleb and Tersha spent several hours walking hand in hand looking into the windows of the town stores, most of which were closed. Only the general store and livery were open. They made the general store their last stop.

Caleb was almost finished loading the wagon with the supplies they'd just purchased when Tersha, sitting on the driver's seat and holding the reins, spoke to him in a hushed whisper, "Caleb, you'd better get those things stowed fast because I think trouble's coming."

Following Tersha's worried gaze down the street, Caleb saw a crowd of twenty or more men and women approaching them. In front of them was a short fat man dressed in black waving a Bible over his balding head. They did not look like they were on their way to a Sunday social.

"There you are, you devil's agents," the fat man shouted while pointing the Bible at Tersha and Caleb.

"I think you're right," Caleb said hastily throwing the last of the supplies into the wagon, "they do look like they're mad at someone, and that someone seems to be us."

Raising his voice louder, holding the Bible even higher, and supported by several of his followers hollering, "Get them," the fat man, breathing hard and with spittle flying from his mouth shouted, "Punish them in the name of Jesus! Show them how God fearing people treat blasphemers and Jezebels."

"Uh oh, time to go," Caleb said to Tersha as, what was now clearly a mob, surged forward.

With the mob less than twenty feet away from the front of the wagon Tersha grabbed the buggy whip out of the holder at her side and hit the half-asleep, unsuspecting horse sharply on the rump. The horse, totally unaccustomed to the sting of the whip, reared its front legs about a foot off the ground and then charged forward into the oncoming people, leaving Caleb hanging precariously by his fingers to the rear of the wagon. Unable to gather his feet under him, feeling he was about to loose his hold, and thinking if he did Tersha might stop, he shouted to her, "Don't stop for anything!"

Caleb tried desperately to hang on, but when the wagon hit a bump he fell, hitting the packed dirt hard with his side and arm. Calling on some of the acrobatic lessons taught him by Hung Fat he was able to roll into a ball and then spring to his feet. Standing in the middle of the street, he watched as the wagon broke through the crowd, scattering men and women to either side. With a sense of admiration he saw Tersha, now standing up in the wagon, take a deliberate swipe with her whip at the fat preacher as the wagon passed him, barely missing his head but knocking the Bible from his upraised hand.

"Good girl," he thought to himself as the wagon broke through the mob.

The townspeople, after dodging the wagon, stopped and watched angrily as Tersha raced away. With Tersha and the wagon now out of their reach they turned their attention to the imposing figure left standing in front of them. Several of the men closest to Caleb, including the preacher, moved rapidly forward, confident they could overpower him before he could run. What they didn't know and wouldn't have understood if they did was that Caleb, as was his nature and that of his father, when attacked had no intention of running. With his temper up and thinking of the danger Tersha had barely escaped, his only thought was to attack.

Maddened by the threat to Tersha, he had lost any fear, and oblivious of the odds against him was determined to take the fight to the mob. Picking up a hand-sized rock he let out a yell and charged the mob, his eyes blazing with an anger and fury that would have sent any member of the mob into retreat if they had been close enough to see them. The first man Caleb reached was knocked cold by a rock to the forehead. The second man went down from a hard and fast fist to the middle of his face, causing a torrent of blood to stream from a deep cut on the bridge of his nose. The preacher was next. Within seconds and to his abject horror the little fat man found himself flat on his back with what to him was undoubtedly a crazy man standing above him holding a bloody rock.

Stunned by Caleb's unexpected and brutal attack upon their leaders, the mob stopped in its tracks, not sure what to do now that their once brave preacher was at the mercy of a madman. A man they believed was surely an instrument of the devil himself.

Looking at the town people gathered only a few feet away, Caleb pointed the bloody rock at them and said in a voice filled with rage, "Step back or I'll send this sanctimonious son-of-a-bitch to meet Jesus."

The crowd had only to look at Caleb's dark eyes, cold as ice, and at the two injured men lying on the ground to realize the man standing over the preacher meant every word he said.

The hushed silence was suddenly broken by a shrill female voice coming from the back of the mob, "It's not him that sinned against the Lord, it's the Godless woman we want," she shouted, "her that filled my man with lust and turned him against the word of the Lord."

A tall man standing in front of the mob then raised his arms and added, "Folks, I think we've done enough of God's work for today."

Within a minute the crowd, thoroughly cowed, slowly turned away and headed back down the street, leaving their preacher helplessly pinned beneath Caleb's boot which was being pressed firmly down on the terrified man's throat.

With the mob retreating Caleb turned his attention back to the man now sobbing under his booted foot.

"This is the man who wanted to harm Tersha," he thought.

Then reaching down he gripped the preacher's cheek in his left hand and forced open his ugly, round mouth.

"Chew on this," he said, and stuffed the small end of the rock into the man's open mouth, chipping several of the preacher's teeth in the process.

Not saying another word, Caleb straightened up, looked about for any other signs of trouble, carefully brushed the dirt from his clothes, and headed at a slow walk in the direction Tersha had driven the wagon.

After walking to the outskirts of town he was elated to see the wagon pulled onto the side of the road with an unharmed Tersha standing beside it. Approaching her he was surprised to see she was casually leaning against the wagon looking as if nothing had happened. He found her attitude a bit perplexing, as if neither of them had been in any danger at all.

"Well," she said, placing her hands on her hips and throwing her head back, "if you'd taken any longer to get here I might have left without you."

For a brief moment Caleb was hurt by her seemingly calloused attitude, but as he got nearer to her he could see she had been crying. Her eyes were red and a trace of tears could still be seen on her cheeks. The look on her face nearly broke his heart.

When they were only a few feet apart, Caleb was forced to catch her as she suddenly ran to him, leaped into his arms, gripped him hard about the neck, and with a choked sob in her voice cried softly into his ear, "Caleb Quinn, never ever scare me like that again. Never!"

Caleb, filled with emotion at the wonder of her in his arms, overpowered by his desire to protect her from any danger, felt as if his whole life and happiness was wrapped up in this bewitchingly beautiful young woman. He would not have had it any other way.

Chapter 18 Fire and Smoke

It was mid-morning, two days before Thanksgiving when a tired and hungry Caleb emerged from the dense woods bordering the eastern edge of the farm, a field-dressed doe draped over his shoulders. He carried a game bag stuffed with two snow geese, both killed by a single shot to the head.

Caleb had been hunting since just after dawn and was looking forward to leaving the Thanksgiving dinner meat in the capable hands of Hung Fat and Mai Li. After doing that, he wanted a warm meal to quell the rumbling in his stomach, but most of all, he wanted to spend the rest of the day with Tersha.

He was thinking of her as he always did when he was away from her. Almost as if he conjured her up he saw her in the distance, riding Princess toward him at a full gallop with Princess' two-year-old daughter running loose behind them. Stopping, he put the bag and the doe down at his feet and gazed with immense pleasure at the rider and horse racing across the open pasture, girl, horse, and colt framed by the blue sky behind them.

"Now that is a beautiful sight," he thought, very glad to be welcomed back to camp in such a heart-warming way. It was one of those rare sights he hoped he'd never forget.

Tersha, riding bareback, had her skirt hitched up so high Caleb could see all of her long slender and beautifully tanned legs. This was something he knew she did intentionally both to please and tease him. The wind was blowing her waist-length hair behind her while also pressing her thin white blouse against her rounded breasts. It was a chilly day, too chilly to be riding without a coat, so Caleb knew her wearing the thin blouse was also done intentionally.

"She is something special," he thought, happy that she would go to this effort just for him.

A minute later Tersha reined in Princess, stopping her so that Caleb was now standing next to her bare right leg. Angel raced past them, joyfully kicking her hind legs into the air as she went by.

"So, you've been wasting ammunition again," she said feigning a stern tone but unable to keep her eyes from revealing how happy being with him made her feel.

"Well, don't blame me," Caleb replied, enjoying their game of words but also aware she truly disliked seeing any animals killed for any reason.

He then casually placed his hand several inches above her bare knee, saying, "They attacked me so what could I do but defend myself?"

Tersha broke into her musical laughter at the image of her beautiful Caleb being "attacked" by a doe and a pair of geese. She was still laughing when she took the hand on her leg, slid off Princess, and stood with her lips only inches away from his. With her upturned face so close to his, and her body even closer, Caleb swore he could feel the heat coming from her.

"If the big bad hunter will promise not to shoot a cow on the way, I'll let him walk me back."

"I guess I can do that," said Caleb, "if that's what it takes to stop you from showing those bird legs of yours to everyone in the county."

Then he slowly kissed her. Breaking the kiss, he reached down to retrieve the doe and the sack and slung them over Princess' saddleless back.

Putting her arm snugly in his Tersha stood on the tips of her bare toes, giving the bemused Caleb a warm kiss first on his chin and then solidly on his mouth.

"You certainly drive a hard bargain, Mr. Quinn," she said, "and you know damn good and well you love looking at my legs."

"For some strange reason I do seem to find them rather attractive," he answered, smiling in agreement and giving her a kiss on her nose followed by a light pat to her bottom. With arms around each other's waist, and the horses following behind them, they headed back to the farm, both as happy as any two people could be.

After an hour of leisurely walking they arrived at the still mostly sleeping farm. While Tersha took the horses to one of the far pastures to graze, Caleb dropped off the game he had killed at Hung Fat's wagon. Leaving there with a handful of stolen oatmeal cookies he was on his way to join Tersha when Phillip, driving the same familiar carriage he had used for years, drove up to him.

"Good day," said Phillip, casting an envious eye at Caleb's handful of cookies, "you're certainly looking good and all pleased with yourself."

"So are you," said Caleb, graciously handing several of the cookies to Phillip. "I hope you're not here to try to get me to take a bath."

"No, no," Phillip replied shaking his head and laughing aloud. "I've got matters to discuss with Uriah, but I do have a letter for you." Reaching into his coat pocket, Phillip removed a crumpled envelop and handed it to Caleb. At first glance Caleb thought the letter was from Beau because they had exchanged correspondence on several past occasions, but after examining the front of the envelope he was surprised and greatly pleased to see it was from Joshua Webster.

"See you later at dinner," said Phillip, not at all offended when Caleb, focusing his attention on the letter, barely acknowledged his departure. Moving to the bench under a nearby tree Caleb sat down, opened the letter, and read

August, 1860

Dear Caleb,

For the past two weeks I have had the pleasure to act as host to Beau Carroll, who was kind enough to stay with me here in Belfast prior to continuing his trip to England and France. He tells me you are in good health and doing well in your new country.

I, myself, am feeling my age, but not so much that I am prevented from engaging in efforts to secure humane treatment by the British for the good people of Ireland. As of late the tide of justice seems to have turned slightly in favor of such actions. I, myself, can only hope to live long enough to see an end to the hardships and cruelties imposed on your countrymen for so many years.

You may be interested to know your friend Simon survived the fire that destroyed his home, but sad to say, the poor dear was terribly burned and now must contend with horrible scars about his face and head. He also suffered a severely broken leg when he was forced to escape the flames by jumping out a bedroom window. Worse still, the leg failed to heal properly leaving him with a permanent limp. He is now very reclusive, seldom venturing out, and only then with the aid of a cane.

Should you ever be in need of my assistance, please do not hesitate to ask. I will help in any way I am able. I would like very much to one day see you in person, but until that day, may the road rise to meet

105

you, may the wind be always at your back, may the sun shine warm upon your face, may the rains fall soft upon your fields, and until we meet again, may God hold you in the palm of his hand.

Your friend,

Joshua

Caleb had almost finished reading Joshua's letter for the second time when a soft hand on his shoulder and a warm kiss on the back of his neck brought an abrupt end to his reading.

"Forgot about me?" Tersha asked teasingly, while noticing that, as she intended, her kisses caused the hair on the back of Caleb's neck to stand up.

"How wonderfully easy it is to please him," she thought, grateful that he was part of her life.

Folding the letter and putting it in his pocket Caleb stood up, turned Tersha toward the troupe's kitchen, kissed her on her nose and forehead, and then hugging her lovingly around the waist as they walked, said, "At the risk of hurting your delicate feelings, I must say that after battling two geese and a doe to the death just so you'll have Thanksgiving dinner, the only thing on my mind is a good hot meal and a nap."

Tersha laughed and hugged him harder. She knew his appetite would change that night.

Moments later they joined Phillip, Uriah, and many of the others in the troupe for an early lunch. After eating their fill, Caleb and Tersha went for a long walk accompanied by the ever faithful Al. On the way back they noticed the wind picking up and a light rain starting to fall. Looking at the dark grey and black clouds gathering to the west they both agreed a storm was on the way.

In the middle of the night Caleb, now alone in his wagon, was jarred awake by a slap of thunder which seemed to have broken only feet above his wagon. Comfortable and warm under his blankets, he rolled over on his back to better hear the sound of the thunder and the light rain falling on the roof above him. After several minutes Caleb had almost slipped back into sleep when he detected the slight but unmistakable smell of smoke. Knowing neither fire nor smoke belonged in camp at this hour of the night, he hurriedly kicked off the blankets and pulled on

106

his pants and boots. Pausing first to slip on a coat over his bare torso, he stepped out of the wagon into a cold wind-blown rain and a sky being filled by repeated bursts of lightning.

Seeing no sign of a fire in front of him he moved to the side of the wagon and looked back toward the horse barn, shocked to see it partially engulfed in flames and smoke.

Breaking into a run, Caleb shouted, "Fire, fire, fire!", all the while thinking of the helpless horses trapped inside, especially Princess and Angel. He knew how deeply Tersha loved them, and if anything happened to them, she'd be totally devastated.

As he got closer to the burning barn he saw several horses running wildly from it. He could also see silhouetted against the light from the flames, what appeared to be a small figure inside the barn being showered by wind tossed embers while desperately trying to lead two rearing horses out of the flames.

"Get out of there you fool," he thought to himself, and then to his horror realized the figure about to be trapped in the burning barn was Tersha.

It was apparent to him she was no match for Princess and Angel who were violently rearing up, tossing their heads, screaming in fear, and struggling against the reins she held. Tersha had her back to him, the heels of her bare feet digging into the soft ground, pulling on the horses with all her strength, seemingly oblivious to the smoke and flames swirling about her.

Reaching her side Caleb jerked the reins out of her hands and hollered at her over the sound of the fire and the screaming of the terrified horses, "I've got them. Now get out of here!"

Looking at him with eyes teary from smoke and eyebrows singed by the fire, she hollered back, "You've got to save …," her last word lost in a fit of coughing and the sound of a burning timber crashing to the ground and narrowly missing her and the horses.

Leaving the reins to Caleb and holding her hands over her face she staggered outside and collapsed on the ground about twenty feet from the open barn doors.

Fighting to breathe and pulling on the reins of the horses Caleb, tugging with all his strength, dragged the reluctant animals out of the blazing barn and to the gate of the nearest pasture. Opening the gate, he led them in, dropped their halters, and gave Princess a hard swat on her rump, watching carefully as she and Angel ran into the darkness.

Turning back toward the barn he noticed a small group of people running to it with buckets and blankets in hand. Realizing Tersha was not among them he looked back toward the fire and saw her lying in a puddle of rainwater, not moving, with tiny wisps of smoke rising from her hair and the edges of her nightgown.

Racing back and sliding to his knees beside her, Caleb began to splash water on Tersha's face, hair, and clothing, at the same time sending his gaze down the length of her body looking for any sign she had been burned. Relieved to see only smudged soot and mud on her face and clothes, but no burnt skin, he placed his head against her chest, afraid he would not hear the sound of a beating heart. After detecting a strong heartbeat he lifted her to a sitting position, and wrapping his arms around her said, "Tersha, Tersha, talk to me. Please talk to me."

She slowly drew her knees up to her stomach, coughed several times, and to Caleb's relief, drew in several deep breaths of air.

Struggling to say the words she asked, "Did you... did you get them out?"

"I got them out and they're both fine," he replied, "and are probably stuffing their fat bellies with grass."

Before anything else could be said, Uriah was standing over them. "Better if you two get farther away from the fire," he said in a voice filled with compassion but was still more command than comment.

"The barn's lost and I wouldn't like losin' ya two with it."

"Caleb," he continued, "you might help get Tersha back to her wagon. She looks like she's had a rough time of it."

Noticing Caleb's blackened face and ash-covered hair and coat, Uriah added, "Ya don't look all that good your own self. Me, I got a fire to see to."

Then, leaving Caleb and Tersha sitting in the mud and rain he went to join in the fight to put out the fire before it had a chance to spread.

Caleb looked at Tersha's face, not sure whether the wetness below her eyes was caused by tears or the falling drops of rain. On an impulse he couldn't overcome, not even after such a close call with disaster, he kissed her on the lips, pleased the tip of her full soft tongue immediately met his, and then pushed passed it, filling his mouth with an incredible pleasure.

Pulling his head back to look at her he could barely hear her whisper through slightly opened lips that seemed to have suddenly grown puffy, "Again."

He kissed her again, this time holding the kiss much longer than the first, firmly pressing his lips down on hers, trying to drown in the sweetness of her mouth, the taste of her. He could feel her body stir as her tongue once again filled his mouth, and knew without a doubt her arousal matched his own. Caleb wanted the kiss to go on and on, but Tersha finally pulled her face away from his.

Looking at Caleb through smoky eyes not caused by the fire, and pressing her body even closer to his she said, "Make love to me, Quinnie."

As gently as he could Caleb picked her up and carried her to her wagon feeling the delicious warmth of her mouth as she pressed her lips into the curve of his neck. Entering the wagon after her, he began to remove his wet clothes while at the same time watching Tersha pull her nightgown slowly over her head, exposing her entire cream-colored body to his view. His eyes were uncontrollably drawn to her wet breasts and fully distended nipples. As the light from bolts of lightning came through the wagon's windows it sent rays of light racing across her body, making her appear like a living goddess, his goddess.

Seeing Caleb in the brightness from the lightning, Tersha moved next to him, and kissed him, a long hard and almost desperate kiss that she continued as her hands began exploring his manhood. Satisfied he was ready for her she pushed him backward on the bed, mounted his body, and began to slowly undulate her hips, straining to work him further and further into her. Within minutes she was lost in a world of passion, her eyes open but not seeing anything, not even Caleb. Her mind and body caught up in an overpowering need to possess him, to blend their bodies into one. Caleb was looking at her, enthralled by her beautiful body and the passion gripping her when she suddenly stared softly down at him and began to move her hips faster and faster, silently signaling him that it was time to thrust into her as powerfully as he could. With his hands pressing down on her hips he pushed upward into her again and again, matching his thrusts to her undulating hips, each time bringing her closer to a climax.

With a cry of pleasure escaping from her open mouth, Tersha collapsed on him, her sweat-drenched breasts coming to rest gently against his chest, her lips finding his and softly smothering them. Her hair, smelling strongly of smoke, hung down like a black curtain, enclosing both their faces in a veil of silky smooth darkness. Caleb's sense of time and place was totally lost in the wonder and passion he felt for her.

After lying silently together for only a few minutes, he could feel Tersha as she began to slide down his body, rubbing her body slowly and sensually against his, kissing his body over and over as she moved slowly lower. With every kiss, with every sound and touch of her warm mouth on his skin, Caleb felt a renewed passion stirring within his body.

Entwining his fingers in thick strands of her hair, he closed his eyes, totally captured by the pleasure she was giving him. After too brief a moment, Caleb opened his eyes, seeing nothing but the outline of her body, once more mounted on him.

"Again," he heard her whisper in the dark.

Reaching up and grasping a breast in each hand he began to gently squeeze them while pushing her away from him so that she was bent slightly backwards. He was mesmerized by the soft beauty of her skin; the stomach stretched flat, the erectness of her nipples pointing upwards, the view of her neck and face as she turned her head to the ceiling. With a strong thrust he drove deeper into her, loving the sensation of being in control of her, loving the pleasure he was giving this beautiful creature. With a final thrust upward he forced another cry of pleasure from Tersha's swollen lips, as they met together in an uncontrollable explosion of pure pleasure.

Overhead the thunder rolled and the lightning played across the night sky like children dancing between heaven and earth.

Chapter 19 The Separation

After several hours of watching the barn burn down to nothing but a pile of charred wood and ashes and knowing the constant downpour would erase any threat of fire spreading to other buildings, Uriah returned to his travel wagon for a few hours sleep. Waking just after sunrise, he returned to the burned-out barn looking for anything he could salvage, but also keeping an eye out for the cause of the fire. Most of the others who had fought the fire and seen the damage done believed the cause was a lightning strike, but Uriah thought otherwise.

Uriah had seen the fire and was convinced that if lightning started it the barn would have most likely burned from the roof down. From everything he saw the fire burned from the bottom up, meaning there was a strong likelihood the fire was started by accident or foul play, perhaps, he thought, "Maybe after all this time those bounty hunters decided to get even for the way we treated them."

Stepping over the remains of the front door, Uriah worked his way to the back of the barn, using the toe of his boot to move aside some burnt planking. He soon uncovered a smashed lantern lying on the ground next to a heavily burned stable wall. To Uriah this, not the lightning, was the logical cause and origin of the fire.

Moving around a burnt timber he could see the heel of a charred boot protruding from underneath a pile of collapsed beams and what had been part of the barn wall. Bending low he pushed aside some debris and exposed a man's leg, then his torso, and finally the arms and head, all totally burned beyond recognition.

The burned body would have been unrecognizable to most people but not to him. He had known this man years ago, known him as Ari Barova, Tersha's father. Even if he couldn't have identified him by looks alone, the gold medallion Barova always wore about his neck was proof enough. He was standing over the body, trying to think of why Barova would have turned arsonist when he heard several people approaching.

"Looks like we lost the whole barn," said Lucinda as she stepped over a burnt timber and stood despondently next to Uriah.

She then followed Uriah's downward gaze and saw the body on the ground, "But it looks like someone else lost a lot more."

After looking at the body for a moment Uriah bent down and turned the dead man's face slightly upwards, as if trying to identify it.

"Can't say for sure, but I think one of 'em bounty hunters decided to get even for what we done to 'em," said Uriah in a voice filled with false sincerity. Snorting strongly to blow the lingering smoke from his nostrils, he added, "Some fool people just never learn to leave well enough alone."

"Guess not," replied Lucinda nodding her head in agreement but not at all fooled by Uriah's words.

She too had recognized the medallion.

As they continued to stare at the body several others joined them, and hearing Uriah's explanation that the fire was most likely started by the bounty hunters, they quickly accepted what he said as fact.

To Uriah's way of thinking the discovery of Barova's burned body also explained another mystery that had to do with Tersha. Early that morning as he stepped out of his wagon, he had seen a lone rider leaving the farm and heading southwest. He only got a quick glance at the rider and horse before they disappeared behind the trees bordering the curve in the road, but he was sure it was Tersha on Princess. Because she rode Princess almost every morning it wasn't a surprise to see her riding that early, but he did wonder why her natural curiosity wouldn't have drawn her first to the burned out barn.

"Maybe," he'd thought at the time, "she looked at it before she went riding."

Now he figured that without a doubt Tersha was aware the dead man in the barn was her father, and that she must have played a role in his dying. It now worried him that he hadn't seen Tersha or Princess since he spotted them that morning.

Caleb woke up later than he'd wanted to. The night before, after returning from Tersha's wagon, he'd taken a "rain bath," using it to wash most of the soot from his face, hands, and hair. Now he stepped to his basin of water and washed off what the rain missed. After drying, he quickly dressed and left his wagon in search of Tersha, anxious to see her after their hours of love making and to make sure she hadn't suffered any serious injuries that had gone unnoticed the night before. He found her wagon empty and silent. Seeing the small crowd gathered at the barn, he walked toward them, thinking he would see her among the group.

He did not, and remembering how much smoke she had inhaled he became slightly alarmed at her absence, calling out to the crowd in a voice louder than necessary, "Has anyone seen Tersha?"

Several people turned in his direction and shook their heads. Their denial only increased Caleb's anxiety.

Uriah, standing in the crowd furthest away from Caleb, heard his question but remained silent. He understood Caleb's worry and indeed felt a deep concern of his own, but Tersha had chosen to leave as she did, silent and alone, and until he could find a reason to do otherwise he decided to respect her decision, even if it meant concealing what he knew of the truth from Caleb.

During that day and for several weeks afterwards Caleb scoured the countryside looking for Tersha and growing more distraught with each day. His only relief came from the fact that Princess was also missing, meaning there was a distinct possibility Tersha had left the farm of her own accord and not by force. He had searched his mind a thousand times for a reason she would have left but could think of nothing that made sense. She had simply vanished without any reason he could fathom.

As the days and the weeks and then the months passed, Caleb slipped into a deep depression, a condition that did not go unnoticed by Uriah. Somewhat regretting his decision to keep the truth of Tersha's departure from the young man he had grown to think of as a son, he sent a letter to Beau Carroll. It was not the first letter he'd sent to Beau explaining his suspicions about the fire and Tersha's departure, but in this letter he explained Caleb's heartache and asked Beau to do whatever he could to find Tersha, and if she approved, to inform him of her whereabouts.

Three weeks later, in early April of 1861, Uriah received a telegram from Beau informing him that Tersha had entered the Sisters of Charity convent located in Emmitsburg, Maryland. He had made confidential contact with the convent's Mother Superior and was assured by her that Tersha, now known as Novice Sister Veronica Barova, was well and receptive to guests, but only one at a time, and on a restricted basis.

Finding Caleb working alone in the new barn making preparations for the next tour due to begin in two weeks, Uriah handed the telegram to him and watched as Caleb read it twice. After the second reading a visibly shaken Caleb slowly folded the telegram, put it in his pocket and then turned to Uriah.

"I'll be leaving for a few days," he said quietly, but matter of factly.

"I thought ya might be," replied Uriah, "and I want ya to take my horse. He'll get ya there in a hurry.

Caleb weighed the offer for a few seconds before replying, "Thanks for the offer, but I'll take Angel, I'm sure Tersha would like to see her."

Within the hour Caleb had bathed, changed clothes, packed a few things he would need for the trip, and rode southwest on Angel. Uriah watched him go, wishing him luck as he did, and saddened to think what he could be riding into.

"I know how ya feel," the old man said to himself, and gripped by the memory of the love he had lost when little older than Caleb, wiped a watery haze from his eyes.

Chapter 20 The Parting

Emmitsburg proved to be a five day ride for Caleb. On any other horse he might have cut the trip to four days, but Angel, being young and standing just over fourteen hands and still slight of build, was accustomed to Tersha's weight, but not that of a rider Caleb's size. Out of consideration for the horse, Caleb kept Angel to nothing more than a slow trot, stopping often to rest the game little mare.

Caleb rode into Emmitsburg just as a brilliant orange-red sunset was casting its last rays over the town. Finding a tavern that had a room for him and a small pasture for Angel, he ate a meal that had no taste and then retired to his room. He managed to fall asleep only after several hours of seeing the image of Tersha's face floating in his mind.

The next morning, after waiting patiently for the sun to rise halfway into the sky, a nervous Caleb rode Angel the short distance to the convent. Stopping a few feet from the stone wall surrounding it, he dismounted, tied Angel's reins to a hitching post, and walked on unsteady legs to the heavy wooden door built into the wall. Using the metal clapper he knocked on the door and waited. A few minutes passed before the door was opened by an elderly woman dressed in a grey habit.

"I'm Sister Marian Kathleen. How may I help you?"

Caleb, suddenly aware of his early Catholic upbringing, felt small in the presence of a high-ranking member of the Church, but despite the feeling managed to stammer out,

"I am Caleb…Caleb Quinn. If possible I would like to speak to Sister Veronica."

Knowing full well who the young man must be, she still asked, "Are you a relative?"

As Sister Mirian Kathleen spoke she gave serious study to the face of the young man in front of her, looking carefully for any sign he might be a threat to the young Novice. She could see no threat, only a somber looking young man with an honest face.

"No," replied Caleb, "I'm just an old friend from her past."

"You don't look all that old," said the Sister, well aware that Caleb had been far more than a friend.

"Please wait here and I'll see if she's available to visit with you."

Nearly a half hour passed before Sister Marian Kathleen returned, opened the door, and indicated with a wave of her hand that Caleb could enter.

"Please follow me," she said, and then led him to a small outdoor enclave, partially covered in midmorning shadows, and holding the smell of roses and fresh-turned earth.

After bending his head to avoid hitting an overhanging trellis, Caleb straightened up and could see Tersha dressed in the same grey habit as worn by Sister Marian Kathleen, sitting on a backless wooden bench her hands in her lap, and looking up at him. Caleb stopped in his tracks his eyes fixed on her, hardly noticing when Sister Marian Kathleen made a silent exit.

Rising from the bench with a small smile of welcome but showing no other emotion on her face, Tersha stepped toward Caleb and in the softest of voices said, "It's good to see you again, Caleb Quinn."

Caleb had rehearsed in his mind what he would say to her when they met, but now all those words were erased by the sight of the face he loved so much and had missed for so long a time.

Wiping his tongue over dried lips, all he could say in reply was, "Thank you, you look well."

"So do you," said Tersha, and not surprisingly asked, "and how is my Angel?"

"If you'd like to see her, your Angel is outside," said Caleb, gesturing in the direction of the door and hoping Tersha was allowed to go outside the walls.

"Yes, I'd love to," and to Caleb's great pleasure took his arm in hers and slowly led him out the wooden gate until they were standing together in front of Angel.

"Hello pretty girl," Tersha said taking the filly's head in her hands and giving her a kiss on the nose.

Caleb could have sworn Angel's neigh was a sign of recognizing Tersha.

"Thank you for bringing her," said Tersha, and with her face turning serious, she looked directly into Caleb's eyes and said, "I know you want an explanation for my leaving as I did. Why I didn't say good-bye to you."

"Yes," said Caleb, "I didn't know if it was something I did, or…"

Before Caleb could finish his sentence Tersha turned toward him.

"It was not you," she said. "You were never anything but wonderful."

With her head down and in a voice he could barely hear, she continued, "The night of the fire my father came to my wagon after you left. He was mean drunk and demanding money. After giving him all I had, he began insisting I return with him to Philadelphia. I refused, but he was hopelessly drunk and wouldn't listen to anything I said. He tried to pull me outside. When I fought him he pulled out a gun and threatened to kill me. I cursed him. Then he told me if he couldn't have me, I couldn't have Princess and threatened to go to the barn and kill her. I could see that he was serious, but when I attempted to stop him he hit me with his fist, knocking me out for a few minutes. After I woke up I intended to go to you for help, but when I opened the door I could see the light from the fire burning in the barn. Still groggy, I ran to the barn and saw my father with a lantern in his hand. He was shouting, "I'll show that bitch," while at the same time trying to keep Princess from kicking down her stall door. I knew then he was crazy drunk and intended to kill all of the animals inside the barn."

"All I could think about was saving Princess. I picked up a shovel and hit Poppa on the head as hard as I could. When he fell to the ground, the lantern broke spreading even more oil on the fire. I tried my best to put out the flames with the shovel, but they spread too quickly, so I ran to the stalls and set all the horses free, including Princess and Angel, but when I tried to pull my father away from the barn he was so heavy I couldn't move him. I started to go for help but Princess and Angel got spooked and, for some reason, came back into the barn to me. I had to choose between saving my horses or saving my father. You found me trying to save the horses."

As she finished telling the story she tearfully turned her back on Caleb.

Moving in front of her so that he faced her, Caleb held her hands in his, "Why didn't you tell me. I could have helped. I could have gone away with you"

"How could I ask you to help someone who let her own father die? Besides, I couldn't let you live your life with someone who has had unspeakable things done to her, things she could never tell anyone about...except God."

Before Caleb could interrupt her she continued, "Caleb, I love you, and you're the only man I ever willingly gave myself to. When I was caught in the fire and thought I would die and never see you again, I promised God that if I could be with you just once more I would give my life to Him and Jesus. As difficult as it was to do, I have kept that promise."

Stopping to wipe tear-filled eyes, she added, "And that's why I'm here and why I must stay here. Please Caleb, try to understand what I'm saying."

"I don't want to understand. You can still come with me," pleaded Caleb, his heart starting to break with the realization of what Tersha had endured the night of the fire.

"No," she replied. "I will always love you, but if my staying here hurts you, I can only beg your forgiveness. As much as I love you, I also love God and have started taking my vows."

Pausing to look at Angel, she went on, "I would ask a favor of you. I've managed to keep Princess boarded in the convent's small barn, but she isn't happy there. She needs to be outside where she can run with other horses. Would you take her back to the farm with you? I know you love her and Angel and I'd like you to have them."

"I'll take Princess and Angel if you want me to have them, but what I really want is you," replied Caleb.

Looking with sad eyes into his, she said, "As much as it hurts me to ask this of you, if you truly love me, you will leave here and never return."

Struck into silence by the intensity of her demand and feeling a mixture of anger and despair, Caleb could only stare into her eyes seeing nothing there but a firm resolve and an end to their love affair. Accepting what he could not change, Caleb loosened the reins from the metal ring and swung into the saddle.

"If you ride around the convent wall to the back, I'll meet you at the barn," said Tersha.

She must have run to get there before him because by the time Caleb reached the barn Tersha was already leading Princess out of the door toward him.

Speaking not a word he took the lead rein from Tersha and turned Angel toward town. After Angel had taken only a few steps, Caleb turned in the saddle and looked back, hoping to catch a last glimpse of Tersha.

She was gone.

Part 3

A house divided against itself cannot stand.
~Abraham Lincoln, a statesman

Chapter 21 War

On his second day out of Emmitsburg, Caleb, riding Princess and leading Angel behind, was deep in thoughts of Tersha when three men, about his age, and all of them looking like thugs, stepped out from behind a line of dense tall bushes growing close to the road. Without any words they moved in front of Princess deliberately blocking the way.

Bringing Princess to a halt, Caleb watched warily, remembering that highwaymen often attacked people on the road, especially those traveling alone. Seeing the three men and suspecting they meant him harm, he felt no fear. With thoughts of losing Tersha still on his mind, he felt only the urge to violently meet whatever threat they, or anyone else, presented. He could feel a dark anger growing in him, an anger that could only be appeased through violence.

"Good afternoon," said the largest of the three, showing a gapped-tooth smile. "Nice horses you've got there."

"It's kind of you to say so," replied a stone-faced Caleb, "now get out of my way."

For only the briefest of moments the highwayman was unsettled by Caleb's response, enough so that he shot a glance at his companions, assuring himself they were there to support him.

Now reassured they'd come to his aid, Gap Tooth took a step forward and looked up at Caleb, "Boys this here fella' don't sound like much of a gentleman least ways not enough to be ridin' such a fine horse."

Caleb, already in a dark mood and not caring what happened to him, remembered Sven's words about striking first and striking hard when faced with tough odds. He struck first and struck hard. With a sharp kick of his heels to Princess' belly, he sent her forward, straight into the would-be robber. Removing his left foot from the stirrup Caleb kicked Gap Tooth in the face sending him stumbling backwards but not knocking him off his feet. His friends immediately stepped forward, drawing knives as they did so. That was their mistake.

Caleb, fully enraged and not caring about the consequences of facing three armed men, lifted his right leg over the saddle, slid to the ground, and drew his knife from his belt. Choosing the smaller of the men to deal with first, he faked a swipe of the knife at the man's stomach. When the man lowered his hands to defend himself from a cut to the gut,

Caleb, ignoring the knife in the man's hand, drove a straight left jab into his face, followed by a kick to the groin. Not waiting for the man to fall Caleb turned toward the third man. What he saw was not an armed assailant ready to face him, but the back of a man running desperately into the same bushes he had emerged from only moments before.

Turning his attention back to the first of the assailants, the one now holding his hands to his bloody face, Caleb grabbed him by the hair, pulled his head back and placed the edge of his knife to the man's throat.

"Didn't your momma teach you to never mess with a man you don't know?" Caleb asked, his face only inches from the man's ear. "And next time don't threaten a man who doesn't give a damn about living. And if you can't remember that," he said through clenched teeth, "remember this."

Hardly caring that the man was helpless, Caleb struck him on the jaw with a hard-thrown right elbow. The man fell into the dirt with blood gathering in a pool about his face. Ignoring the man he'd kicked in the groin, he returned to the nervously prancing Princess and Angel, stepped into the saddle, picked up the lead rope which he'd dropped during the altercation, and rode off, scarcely noticing the blood stains on the sleeve of his coat.

On April 13,1861, a tired, hungry, and haggard Caleb returned to the farm from Emmitsburg, aware as he rode in that something had changed. Not only were some wagons and people missing, but those people he could see seemed to be gathered in small groups speaking animatedly to each other. After removing the saddle and giving Princess a quick brushing down, he turned her and Angel loose in the pasture and went in search of Uriah. He found him in his wagon hunched over and writing a letter.

"What's happening?" asked Caleb as he stuck his head through the open door.

"Good to see you back," replied Cordell looking up from his writing. "Did you find Tersha?"

"I found her and she's fine, but she's staying in the convent."

"That so?" replied Uriah, knowing Caleb was stating the obvious.

Not yet ready to discuss his visit with Tersha, Caleb changed the subject by once again asking, "What's happened? Why are some of the wagons and people missing?"

Uriah slowly put down his pen and looked at Caleb, "I guess you haven't heard," he said, "some of the southern states, starting with South

Carolina, have left the Union. Fort Sumter at Charleston has been attacked by Brigadier General Beauregard and his provisional Confederate forces."

Thinking on that for a moment, he went on, "Beau Carroll sent a telegram tellin' me about the secessions, and as best I can figur' from what he said the North and the South are about to git into a full fledged war."

Uriah continued, "I passed the word along to everyone as best I could. That's why some of our people decided they needed a change of location. I hated to see 'em go, but I guess a lot of people are goin' to do some heavy thinkin' about what side they want to stand with."

Pausing for a moment, he added, "Son, I think our world is about to change and not for the better."

Chapter 22 The Decision

Because of the war the season of 1861 was proving to be disastrous to the *B & C Circus*. They were smaller due to the performers they lost when the war started. With so many men joining the Union army families had less money to spend and attendance was shrinking, not to mention losing the crowds that Tersha had attracted. Money the townies and the farmers had once spent at the circus had dried up. No longer were families seeking its entertainment. People in the northeast were using what extra money they had to support the Union cause. Roads were clogged with men and supplies going to and from the front so the time needed to move from town to town nearly doubled, cutting the number of shows that could be put on nearly in half. Provisions needed by the circus were in short supply and when they were available it was often at double or triple last year's prices. The *B & C* was going broke and Uriah had to make a decision.

For three days the troupe had been camped along the western bank of the Delaware River near the small town of New Hope, in very nearly the same spot, once called Coryell's Ferry, where, during another war, the Continental Army in 1776 kept the British from crossing the Delaware and moving into Pennsylvania. Keeping the British holed up in Trenton, across the river, General Washington and his troops were able to man a surprise attack and defeat them with the capture of Trenton.

The circus people were waiting for Uriah to tell them what they dreaded to hear. On the last day of June, after receiving a telegram from Beau Carroll, Uriah had made the decision he'd put off for two weeks. Waiting until after the evening meal to call everyone together, he made his announcement to the troupe.

"My guess is all of ya know why we're here so I'll make it short."

Pausing to look at the people he had known for years, loved like family, and felt responsible for, he continued in a voice that was suddenly shaky, "This season is over. In the mornin' we're headin' back to the farm. It don't make sense to keep tryin' to put on shows when ain't nobody comin' to see them."

"Any questions?" he added, knowing it unlikely there would be any questions or complaints from these circus people, most of whom were all too familiar with hard times.

As the troupe began to disband to prepare for the morning departure, Uriah caught Caleb's eye and with a hand gesture signaled him over to his side.

"Son," he said as Caleb approached, "after everyone clears the tent we need to talk but not here."

Several minutes later the two of them walked down to a nearby creek and sat down under the spreading boughs of a large maple tree.

"Caleb," Uriah said, plucking a blade of grass and putting it between his teeth, "I can't see a youngster such as yurself rottin' away at the farm for the next year, maybe more, so I been workin' on a few thoughts about yur future."

"I've had a few thoughts about that myself," said Caleb, "but before I tell you about them, I'd like to hear yours."

"First off ya could get work with Mr. Carroll in Baltimore," said Uriah.

As expected, Caleb answered with a quick, "No. Beau's done enough for me already, and I want to go out on my own."

"Good," said Uriah, "I believe yur'in one of those men destined to be a far travelin' man, a man the west would agree with. Maybe ya should head there, see the Rockies and the Tetons, maybe make a life in the biggest and best country God ever laid a hand on. Ya might even find that like me ya take to the Injun way of livin'; outdoors, free, and beholdin' to nobody but God."

"That sounds good, and maybe someday that's where I'll go, but not now."

"Well, that don't leave much," said Uriah, "so just what do ya figur' on doin'?"

Turning his head sideways toward Uriah, Caleb replied, "Once we get back to the farm I'm putting some stuff together and joining the army."

"Which one?" asked Uriah, already knowing the answer.

"Which one do you think?" Caleb asked, hoping Uriah would pick the same one he'd already decided on.

"Personally, I wouldn't give ya spit for neither one."

Not waiting for a reply from Caleb, Uriah continued, "The South is plain wrong, and the North talks about stoppin' slavery, but all they really want to do is stop the South from gettin' rich sellin' all their cotton to England while the mills in the North sit there doin' nothin'."

"Caleb," he continued, "when ya want to know the reason for folks goin' to war with each other all ya got to do is look to see who profits the most. The South profits from slavery, and the North profits from controllin' where the South can sell their cotton. The way I see it ain't neither one of 'em worth a good piss."

"I didn't know your thinking went so deep," said Caleb, grinning as he spoke, "and it all sounds sensible, but when I heard about a fella in New York City who's putting together a regiment of nothing but sharpshooters I made up my mind that it was time to fight for President Lincoln and the Union."

"Well, Caleb, ya do what ya think best, and whatever ya decide I wish ya luck. I can tell ya I've seen a touch of fightin' here and there, and it ain't never pretty. I just hope ya don't get yurself killed fightin' someone else's war."

The two of them walked back to their wagons, shaking hands and patting each other on the shoulder as they parted.

Days later the troupe arrived back at the farm, all of them relieved to find it hadn't been ransacked by either of the armies which had been fighting nearby. Caleb immediately set about packing his things for the trip to New York City.

The rising sun found Caleb sitting outside on the steps of his wagon, one hour before Uriah was to take him to the train station. He had been there since before dawn, having wanted to spend some time alone to take a last look at this peaceful place he had called home for over five years. The quiet serenity of the morning made it almost impossible for him to believe a war was being fought on nearby soil. Caleb hoped that the fighting would never find its way to this small corner of Pennsylvania. An hour after sunrise, and right on schedule, Uriah brought a wagon to a halt in front of him. Caleb was mildly surprised to see Jean Duval sitting beside him on the wagon seat.

As Caleb tossed his traveling bag into the back of the wagon and climbed in after it, he asked, "You're coming to see me off, too?"

"Not exactly," said Jean. "I'll be with you as far as the station. Then I'll take the train to Baltimore where I'll be getting off and going to work for Mr. Carroll."

Before Caleb could settle himself down in the back of the wagon Uriah reached under the wagon's seat and pulled out a long rolled up blanket.

"I know ya still ain't much of a shot and I blame Jean for that, but in case ya got to shoot somebody I want ya to have this here gun."

Caleb took the rolled up blanket and immediately rolled it open. Inside was a shiny, new 1853 model Sharps rifle, same as the one used by Uriah. Attached to it was a telescope.

"I tried her out and she shoots true," said Uriah, "I've also got a little somethin' else that might come in handy."

Reaching under the seat again he withdrew a box of cartridges. Handing them to Caleb he said, "I hand loaded these myself. Gave 'em a little extra powder so's, if ya feel the need to, ya can tickle a Johnny Reb at over 400 yards shootin' into the wind. I think it'll do ya a sight better than those old muzzle loaders the army's passing out."

"Thank you, Uriah. I'll be sure to put them to good use."

"Take good care of this while you're at it," said Jean as he removed a holstered revolver from under the wagon seat.

Caleb could see the revolver was an 1860 model Colt, capable of firing six shots before it needed to be reloaded, and as Caleb also knew, was very expensive. The holster holding it was identical to the one Jean had made Caleb practice with for many hours. He started to reject Jean's gift, but realized at a time like this, and with a man like Jean, it would do no good.

"Thank you," said Caleb as he placed the holster and the Sharps together in the blanket and rolled it back up.

Uriah, sitting on the wagon seat, had taken it all in, and was satisfied he and Jean had done all they could to keep Caleb alive. The rest would be up to Caleb and the fortunes of war.

"Now that that's over let's git to the railroad station before they leave ya behind and people start blamin' me and Jean for losin' the war 'cause ya showed up late."

Three days later, September 14, 1861, an excited Caleb stepped off the train in New York City. He had never felt so alone since before he boarded the *Osprey*.

Chapter 23 Enlistment

Caleb spent his first day and night slowly walking about the city, looking at the sights. In some ways it was more than he expected and in some ways less. Signs of great wealth were everywhere. Row after row of expensive homes stood as mute testimony to the prosperity and success of their owners. Shiny ornate carriages moved about the streets carrying passengers dressed in the finest of clothing. Huge buildings made of marble and granite blocked out the sun. Elaborate stores and restaurants were filled with patrons spending in minutes what would have taken Caleb months to acquire.

As much as the grandeur of the city impressed him, even more impressive to him were the appalling living conditions most of the city's inhabitants endured. He saw tenement buildings overflowing with people, most of them immigrants forced to live in utterly squalid conditions.

Along many streets garbage was piled up to the height of a tall man. The stench of human waste filled his nostrils with almost every breath he took. By the end of the day, Caleb grew increasingly thankful that Beau had sent him to the farm and not a big city.

Waking up later than usual on the following morning, Caleb enjoyed a long hot bath and a shave, followed by a breakfast of oatmeal, bacon, hard-boiled eggs, butter-drenched biscuits filled with strawberry preserves, and several cups of dark coffee provided to the boarders at Mrs. Sheer's Rooming House.

Returning to his room he gathered up his travel bag and Sharps rifle. Using the instructions provided by Mrs. Sheer, he set off in search of the 1st Regimental Sharpshooters' headquarters.

An hour's hard walk brought him to his Wall Street destination where he was greeted by a hard-looking Sergeant Glass. Within minutes Caleb found himself standing in line with forty or so other volunteers, most of them carrying their own weapons, and all anxious to get into the war 'before it gets won without us.'

After a quick medical examination, Caleb and the others found themselves standing in a large room empty of furniture, with only a single American flag attached to a wall.

Several minutes passed before a tall, distinguished-looking officer entered the room from an adjoining office. After looking over the men standing before him, he addressed them in a voice brimming with a combination of confidence and culture.

"Gentlemen, I am Colonel Hiram C. Berdan. You are here because you want to be snipers in the Union army. In order to achieve this goal you will have to take a test of marksmanship which only the best of you will succeed in passing. Those of you who fail will be encouraged to find duties in other regiments more in keeping with what other talents you may possess. Those who succeed in passing my simple test of marksmanship will become part of my *1st Regiment Sharpshooters*. As such you will be engaged in an area of this war which only a few of you, the very best and the very luckiest, will survive."

"The test I speak of is very simple. You will be required to put two consecutive shots into each ten-inch target starting at two hundred yards and increasing in one hundred yard increments to five hundred yards. If you think that is beyond your ability, please leave now so that you waste neither my time nor yours."

None of the men moved. Looking into the eyes of several of the recruits for any sign of indecision, and seeing none, he continued, "You will have the rest of the day to review the provisions of your enlistment and prepare your weapons. If you have no weapon one will be provided for you. Tomorrow morning at 7:00 a.m. sharp we will meet at the regimental shooting range to determine who will fail and who will succeed. Good luck to each of you."

The next morning the recruits were standing in the middle of a large field bordered on two sides by tall fir trees and covered in high grass and scrub brush. In the distance they could see an array of targets ranging from one hundred to one thousand yards. All the targets looked like Jefferson Davis, the President of the Confederacy. They would be setting their sights on the two hundred yard target.

Standing before the recruits, Colonel Berdan, the sun at his back and a brisk wind blowing from his right, once again addressed the recruits. No one noticed Caleb was not among them.

"I need a volunteer. Who will be the first to step forward and take the test?" asked Berdan.

The last word was hardly out of his mouth when a shot rang out. Instantly several of the recruits dropped to the ground while those that kept their feet were bent low, as if they could duck a shot already fired.

Colonel Berdan, an experienced marksman and accustomed to the sounds of rifle shots, had slightly hunched his shoulders in reaction to the shot, but other than that looked calm and unfazed. Straightening up and looking first to the left and then to the right, but not seeing or smelling any evidence of the shooter, he asked in an angry but controlled voice, "Who fired that shot."

His question was met with total silence.

"Speak up," Berdan said, "One of you had to have fired that shot, and even if it was accidental I want to know who."

Again, no one spoke, but several of the men did turn their heads and look at each other, searching for any sign of guilt on the faces of their fellow volunteers, while knowing at the same time it would have been almost impossible for any of them to have fired a shot without the smoke from the discharged shot being detected.

"If some of you ...," before Berdan could finish a second shot rang out.

This time Berdan had been looking closely at the assembled men. He knew none of the men in front of him could possibly have fired a weapon. To Berdan, the second shot sounded as if it came from a Sharps rifle some distance to the rear of the formation. Looking in that direction he saw a faint wisp of white smoke floating just above the tall grass over 100 yards away.

He calmly addressed his men, some of them just getting off the ground, "Someone is playing a game with me, and I mean to have the man's head."

Within a minute he had the men spread out in a line, much as a group of hunters would spread out to flush game birds.

"Now," he said, "we will find our mysterious shooter."

Seconds later he watched as the line of men, led by Sergeant Glass, walking at intervals of about twelve yards, began to carefully move out from the center of the field. Some of the more nervous recruits were carrying cocked rifles. Fifteen minutes later the line of slow walking men had crossed the field beyond where Colonel Berdan had seen the rifle smoke, reaching the line of trees at the edge of the shooting range. After thoroughly searching through the area and finding no sign of a shooter, Sergeant Glass ran back to Berdan.

"Ain't nobody there, Sir. Looks like he musta' snuck off when he saw us coming."

"Sergeant," said Berdan, "I don't believe in ghosts. Are you telling me there's no one in the area you searched?"

"Yes Sir. If anybody would have been there, we would have found him."

"Very well, Sergeant," said an exasperated Berdan, "reassemble your men on me."

Minutes later all the men were once again standing in loose formation in front of the Colonel. Speaking calmly he said, "Now that we've finished with that little exercise, we shall continue with the test."

"Mind if I join you?" asked a voice coming from the rear of the group in the same area that had just been searched.

The heads of all the men jerked in the direction of the voice. To their astonishment they saw nothing but grass where the voice had come from.

Berdan, staring intently in the direction of the voice, but unable to see a sign of the speaker replied, "Please do so. It would be a pleasure to make your acquaintance, whoever you are, and wherever you are."

Slowly the grass about 50 yards away started to rise, at first resembling the shape of a mound, then that of a man covered head to toe in grass, moss, leaves, and weeds. He looked like an apparition from a child's nightmare. Everyone watched this strange figure, carrying a scoped rifle covered with the same materials as he wore, walking toward them at a steady pace until he was standing silently before the Colonel. Removing the covering he wore in front of his face, he looked straight into Berdan's eyes, but said nothing.

"And you are?" asked Berdan.

"Caleb Quinn, sir, at your service."

Colonel Berdan waited several moments while he composed himself, not sure whether the man deserved to be hanged or complimented, but certain the young man standing before him had a talent not only for camouflage, but for doing the unexpected, the kind of talent he knew could be very useful in wartime. It might also be useful in solving the problem of how and who might train his recruits.

"You've proven you can hide," he said to Caleb, "but in order to be a part of this regiment you also need to show me you can shoot just as well."

"Sir," said Caleb, "if you'll use your glass to look at the target out there, the one at the 300 yard marker, you'll see I've already done that."

"Very well," said Berdan, "but I find it hard to believe anyone could hit that target. At the distance you fired it would be at least 350 yards away. With this wind and shooting with the sun in your eyes, I find it highly unlikely you could make such a shot."

Pulling out a glass from his waist Berdan extended it to its full length and placed it to his right eye. Focusing on the target he was amazed to find there were two holes in it, both in the space between Jeff Davis' eyes.

"Would you like me to finish taking the other eight shots?" asked Caleb.

Curious as to whether what he saw was a result of skill or a stupendous amount of luck, he said, "Yes, Mr. Quinn, but I ask that you fire only one more shot at a target of my choosing, and I choose the one at the eight hundred yard mark."

"Yes, Sir, Colonel," and with that Caleb brought his rifle to his shoulder.

Sighting carefully through the scope, he took aim, fired, and then returned the Sharps to his side.

"Sir," said Caleb, "if you'll examine the target, I believe you'll see that I fired true."

Colonel Berdan once again raised his glass and looked to the indicated target. On the upper left hand edge he could see the single hole made by Caleb's shot.

"Absolutely unbelievable," he thought. It was a shot only the rarest of marksmen could accomplish.

Lowering his eye glass and trying to hide his amazement, he said, "Young man, you've certainly proven yourself to my satisfaction, even if you did so in a most unusual and non-military way."

Several hours later Caleb and the thirty-seven other recruits who had passed the test were sworn into the *1ˢᵗ Regiment Sharpshooters*.

When the swearing-in ceremony was concluded, Colonel Berdan asked Caleb to join him in his office. Entering, Caleb noticed an abundance of plaques and trophies attesting to the marksmanship of Colonel Berdan hanging on the walls and placed on shelves. Following the officer's order, an apprehensive Caleb took a seat.

"Young man," said the Colonel, "let me explain to you how things are with the regiment. Many of the generals running this war have little faith in sharpshooters, preferring to stick to the antiquated belief that battles are won by marching men shoulder to shoulder into a wall of enemy fire using frontal attacks. This tactic results in trading man for man, as if playing a giant chess game with nothing but pawns. These leaders are absolutely mad. I am one of a growing number of officers in this army who believes Napoleonic methods must be done away with, but I'd be a fool to believe these same leaders won't place obstacles in the way of this regiment's success. Already my repeated requests that the regiment, after a short period of training, be ordered to the front lines have been put on indefinite hold. In fact, there are those in positions of command who insist my sharpshooters should be shipped to the front and used as any other infantry soldier, to be nothing more than cannon fodder for the Confederates. They refuse to accept my argument, my firm belief that after training the men of the 1st should be broken up into small units with each unit assigned to different infantry regiments or companies. This would be much more advantageous to the war effort and much more likely to add to the survival rate of men such as yourself."

"In order to change their minds and put my regiment, and all other sharpshooter regiments, into position to be effective I need men of forward thinking, men who are leaders, men who teach others how to fight, how to kill, and how to survive."

Leaning forward and placing his palms on his desk, he added, "If what I have seen from you is any indication, I believe you to be that kind of man."

"Sir," said Caleb, "I'm ready to do whatever you request."

"Good," said the Colonel, "because I've already selected you and Sergeant Glass to handle the training. I'll start out by telling you that as of now you are Corporal Quinn. You'll need the promotion if your fellow sharpshooters are to follow your orders."

"Thank you," said Caleb, not exactly sure what a corporal was, but figuring it was good to be one.

"Next," said Berdan, "I want you to teach every man in this regiment how to make and use whatever that camouflage outfit was that you used during your little demonstration. I also want you to teach the men your stealth techniques. Other than that, I need you and the others to complete your training within two months, and to be patient until I can persuade some army commander to properly use us. It may be some time before that happens, but when that time comes I want you and your men to be more than ready."

"We will be, Sir. You have my word on it."

"You've met Sergeant Glass," said the Colonel. "It will be his job to turn the men into soldiers. Quinn, it will be your job to turn them into snipers and camouflage experts, the best this army has ever seen."

Rising from his feet the Colonel said, "If you have no questions you are dismissed."

Caleb, after giving Colonel Berdan the best salute he could, left the room anxious to begin the training, while at the same time pondering the best way to go about it.

"I know," he said, thinking aloud, "I'll teach the men the same way Da taught Sean and me. Aside from the fact that animals can't shoot back, there's not that much difference between poaching and being a sniper. I'll teach them that all they've got to do is find the prey, kill it, and try not to get killed in the process."

That night as Caleb lay on his cot thinking about the day's events he formed a mental picture of his men fighting the enemy, killing, and getting killed. With sudden insight he realized he was not only responsible for the men's training; he was also responsible for their lives. As a cold, slight shiver ran through his body he looked down at his arms and saw they were covered in small bumps.

Chapter 24 Training

Six hard weeks had passed since the beginning of training. Of the original men who enlisted the same day as Caleb, only three were no longer with the regiment. One of the three, an Irishman, thought it acceptable to drink whiskey while on guard duty; the second man, a slightly-built former miner, had a persistent cough that would have made any prolonged concealment on his part impossible; the third man was caught stealing. The Irishman and the thief were assigned to the very front line of an infantry unit while the miner was assigned to a duty that would keep him away from the front lines.

Despite being hampered by unduly cold and wet weather, the training went well. The men did little complaining about crawling through cold mud, lying motionless in the rain for hours on end, and enduring days and nights of unrelentless training, all in addition to the two hours per day they spent marching under the watchful eye of Sergeant Glass. To Caleb's satisfaction the men made considerable improvements in their physical conditioning and their ability to move undetected through any terrain. As the days and nights of training progressed, Caleb felt satisfied that all of his men had a good start at becoming excellent snipers.

With the need for stealth in mind, Caleb began his "sniper school" by insisting the men make their own camouflage coverings. To that end, each man was given two body-sized squares of canvas, one a light tan color and the other dark green. A piece of netting completely covered each square. The two squares were then sewn together on three sides with an opening large enough for a man's head to fit through on the corner opposite the open end, and an open slit for an armhole in each of the other two sewn sides. One color showed on each side allowing the wearer to easily switch sides from tan to green, matching the background of whatever the terrain dictated. Separate hoods were made in the same way. The men then wove rags or strips of earth-tone cloth to their capes and hoods. Next, leaves, grass, brush, and anything else that might help to conceal them was stuffed into or tied to the netting. When all this was complete, each man had a poncho-like garment that would make him virtually disappear in most terrain while at the same time protect him from the rain and cold.

From day one Caleb impressed on his men the absolute need to be able to operate invisibly and in total silence, day or night. Whether in camp or training in the field, he did not allow them to carry anything that would cause any noise. Canteens were wrapped in cloth. Knives carried in soft scabbards. Ammunition was carried in cotton-filled ammunition bags. Telescopes and rifles were wrapped in camouflage material. To further impress upon them the need for both silence and preparation, the trainees carried all their field gear, including their rifles, with them at all times.

"Once you've gained your position and hidden yourself," he told them, "don't move. Don't talk. Don't so much as brush away a fly. Make no movement that might give away your position. It's a lot easier for the enemy to spot you if you move even slightly. If you're lying absolutely motionless they may step on you without knowing you're there."

"Your goal, once you have sighted on your target, is to take one shot, get one kill, and then get away alive and undetected. After you make that shot, change position or get away at once, whichever of the two options offers you the best chance of survival. Never forget that one shot will create a lot of interest in you, interest that can get you killed."

Like his father before him, Caleb lectured his troops at length, constantly telling them, "You must, at all times, be aware of your surroundings, both near and far. Look hard for anything that seems unnatural. Look twice as hard at what appears natural, for that may be where the greatest danger to you will be found. Never forget, as you hunt you may also be the hunted because the Confederates also use snipers, and from what I hear they're good, real good."

He urged them when selecting a target to have as their first priority the killing of officers, the higher the rank the better; after that they were to take out any target they could put their sights on.

Caleb put special emphasis on the importance of being patient, stressing the need to stay still for hours, even days, if necessary.

He cautioned, "Wait for a time when your chances of a successful shot and a successful undetected departure is most likely. If you don't, if you plan poorly, there's a good chance you'll end up dead."

He taught them the importance of using the cover of darkness and rough weather to move to positions of concealment; to make every effort to be in place when the morning sunrise revealed the enemy.

"Unlike the rest of the Union infantry who are conditioned to fight in daylight," he told his men, "you must be masters of the night. Learn to think of the night as a time of safety, a time you can move without being seen. Like it or not, most of your work will come at night when the rest of the army is sleeping."

In order to survive a conflict, especially when they were outnumbered or operating behind enemy lines, he warned his men to have a planned egress, a way of getting back to, or at least near, the Union lines, bearing in mind that these lines often shift during battle.

Caleb trained the men to hunt and kill the enemy much as his father trained him to hunt and capture animals. Although most of the army's generals still believed battles should be fought from trenches or across open ground, Caleb knew this type of fighting was not for his men or for himself. He also knew the greatest dangers to his men would be either a concentrated assault on their positions by a large number of men, or perhaps even worse, not detecting Confederate snipers before they detected the Union snipers. Because many of his men were superstitious, he didn't mention that some of them would probably die simply because of bad luck.

Marksmanship training proved to be a special concern for Caleb. Although all of his men were above average shots, he constantly impressed upon them need to fully understand the factors that affected accuracy. Bullets don't go straight in flight, they drop from the pull of gravity, or get pushed to the left or right by wind. His men had to learn to calculate rate of drop for various distances and circumstances they might find themselves in. Most of the men had never used a scoped rifle.

"Be careful that once scopes are sighted not to knock them out of alignment," he cautioned them. "You will usually have only one shot and no way to make a correction if your scopes are off even slightly."

It was soon apparent to Caleb and Sergeant Glass that some men were simply better than others at the different skills he was teaching. Some men, they came to quickly realize, excelled at shooting, some at stealth, while others were better leaders who thought more clearly under stress. Seeing these differences in his men gave Caleb the idea that he could maximize the strengths of the men and minimize their weaknesses by combining them into two-man teams. Breaking with military tradition and without informing Colonel Berdan, wanting him to see the end results rather than object to his radical idea before it could be implemented. He trained them not as a squad or solitary snipers, but as two-man teams, with each man serving to compliment the other.

With the aid and advice of Sergeant Glass, Caleb broke the thirty-four men, including himself, into seventeen teams. His and the

Sergeant's team selections were based on the men's personal compatibility along with the individual skills of each man. Both team members would be fully armed, but the better shot of the two would always be the primary shooter. For his partner Caleb chose a New Yorker named Jack Remza, the oldest member of the regiment, and a man who seemingly made no attempt to be a close friend of anyone. Remza was tall, gruff, burly, and often unnecessarily quarrelsome. Within minutes of learning he had been teamed with Caleb, an angry Remza, hands on hips, stood in front of Caleb.

"I know you can disappear like smoke on a windy day, and you're a good shot," Remza told Caleb, "but other than that I don't see you as nothing but a boot-licking, apple polishing, sissy boy that ain't never been in a real fight and couldn't whip my grandma."

Looking at the men who had gathered about them he added, "When I'm in a fight, I want someone tough at my back, someone I know I can depend on."

With that said he stuck his face right in Caleb's.

Knowing he had to instantly stifle any insubordination, Caleb calmly replied, "Mr. Remza, I think I know a place where you can find out if I'm a fighter or not."

Minutes later the two men found themselves several hundred yards deep in the woods, surrounded by the others in the regiment, but out of sight or sound of the camp's officers. Without speaking, the two men removed their coats and shirts, hung them over the branches of a tree and turned to face each other. Caleb was somewhat surprised to see that despite his age Remza looked as solid as a rock; the upper half of his body exceedingly well-muscled with a neck as thick as a horse's. His hands and arms were equally thick and muscled. All of it was covered by a dense growth of curly black hair that seemed to run unimpeded from Remza's jaw to his knuckles.

"Caleb," he said to himself, "do not let this man get his hands on you."

Before he could think another thought, Remza struck out with a vicious left hook that grazed Caleb's right shoulder and glanced hard off the side of his jaw. Caleb, slightly dazed, staggered backward, lucky to get his arms up in time to ward off a flurry of right and left hooks which landed mostly on his arms and shoulders, doing little damage, but still effective enough to send Caleb several more steps backward.

"Not so ready for a real fight, are you, sissy boy?"

"Ready enough," replied Caleb, "and now it's my turn."
Faking a step to the left, while moving his upper body slightly to the right, he shot a lightning-fast, straight left jab into Remza's face followed by two more. All three landed solidly, one on the nose and the other two on Remza's mouth and forehead. Caleb followed them up with a hard right upper cut to Remza's rib cage.

"Is this the kind of fight you were talking about?" asked Caleb as he stepped back from his adversary and took a deep breath.

"Fight? You call this a fight? I been in better fights than this at a tea party," replied Remza as he wiped away blood from a cut lip.

"Have it your way," Caleb said, and shot another left jab at Remza's face.

Remza, moving quicker than a man of his size should be able to, ducked the jab, and struck Caleb in the right elbow with another brutal left hook. Caleb felt his elbow go numb, and for several seconds could just barely lift his arm to defend himself from the blows that followed. For the next several minutes, both men continued to beat each other about the head, face and body. Caleb used the boxing skills taught to him by Sven Knudsen to inflict damage, while Remza, showing the strength of an ox, simply lowered his head and bored in blindly, letting loose blow after blow. After several minutes of furious fighting neither man had given an inch, or gained any advantage over the other. They were as evenly matched as any two fighters could be.

Then communicating silently as fighting men can sometimes do, they stepped back and looked at each other. What each saw was a man covered in blood, cuts, bruises, and gasping heavily for breath. Each also saw a man that was all grit and not quit.

"Corporal Quinn," said Remza in a gasping voice, but one that could be heard by the onlookers "as far as I'm concerned you'll more than do in a fight, and I'll whip any man who says otherwise."

"I can certainly say the same for you, Mr. Remza," replied Caleb, more than glad to see the end of the fight.

The two men then shook hands and staggered side by side back to camp, both of them feeling very pleased to know they had the kind of partner who could be relied on when the true fighting began.

During the final three weeks of training, Caleb pushed each team to live, eat, and breathe as one. They learned to use finger and hand signals and small gestures to silently communicate with each other. Stealth and camouflage were now second nature to every man in the regiment. When the training period came to an end, Caleb knew his men had become efficient, close knit fighting teams that would have little or no equal in either the Union or Confederate armies. They were ready to join the war.

Although the men claimed to be more comfortable using their own weapons, the lack of standardization of rifles and ammunition was of huge concern to both Colonel Berdan and Caleb. Without using the same rifles, scopes, and ammunition many of the men might die needlessly. Colonel Berdan had repeatedly requested enough Sharps rifles for his entire regiment, but the requests had been repeatedly denied by the upper brass who still doubted the effectiveness of a sniper regiment. To many of those generals the more manly way to fight a war was to have the men march shoulder to shoulder into gunfire.

At mail call on the last day of training, Caleb received a second letter from Joshua Webster. Letting his men wait for him, he took the time to open the letter and read it.

Early Autumn, 1861

Dear Caleb,

Over the past few years our friend Beau has written me several times speaking at length of your life with the circus and informing me of the military service you are now bravely rendering to your adopted country in its efforts to end slavery. As I fully expected from a son of Michael O'Connell, you have proven to be a man of courage, dedication, and honor. I pray you stay well until the war's end and for many years thereafter.

It is with some regret that I must inform you this letter will, in all likelihood, be my last correspondence. I am in sudden ill health and hope to join my beloved Moira within the month, or two months, if I am so unfortunate as to live that long.

My estate is rather modest, but having no heirs I am leaving half of it to a trust dedicated to the continuance of the struggle to free your people and mine, if I may be so presumptive as to think of myself as Irish, if not by birth, then certainly by choice.

The remainder of my estate, valued at approximately 10,000 pounds, I leave to you, to be used as you wish. I have no doubt you will put it to the greatest good. Upon my demise all the funds held in my

bank will be transferred to an account Beau has set up in your name at a bank of his choosing in Washington, D.C.
    I pray that God looks after you, and that we might someday meet again.

Your proud friend,
J W

    After reading the letter from Joshua, Caleb could only think of how fortunate he was to have shared those few days with a man of such exceptional character and courage.

    Not long afterward, on an evening during the first week of November, Colonel Berdan returned from a recruiting trip to Vermont. He immediately summoned Caleb and Sergeant Glass to his quarters.

    "Are your men fully prepared to fight?" he asked them.

    "As ready as we can get them," said Sergeant Glass, suspecting that at last, after sitting on their backsides while other regiments did the fighting, the 1st was being called to action.

    "That's good," said Berdan, "because the morning next we're finally going to join the war."

    Before either man could reply he added, "I do have a special something I want to give to you and the rest of the men tomorrow morning," a smile of triumph covered his face as he spoke.

    "I knew months ago we couldn't depend on those gold-braided SOBs in Washington to deliver on their promise of new Sharps rifles. So, using what resources were available to me, I've bought enough new rifles and ammunition for every mother's son wearing the 1st Regiment Sharpshooters insignia to have one. I hope I can trust the two of you to see to it that they're issued to the men after morning roll call."

    "Yes, Sir," both men replied simultaneously. They knew the rifles and ammunition must have been bought out of Colonel Berdan's own pocket, or worse, with money he was able to borrow.

    "That man is a true leader," Caleb told Sergeant Glass.

    "He is that," came the reply. "If only this army had ten more like him."

    Caleb was both pleased and relieved by Berdan's announcement. He felt certain the last obstacle to the regiment's success had been eliminated. Tomorrow, he knew with certainty, would be his best day in the army.

"Gentleman, get a good night's sleep," he heard Berdan say as the commander walked away. "You'll have one day to train those of your men not familiar with the Sharps."

Caleb started to tell Colonel Berdan that every man in the regiment, even those in love with their own rifles, had been forced by him to fire a minimum of thirty rounds from both his Sharps and the Sharps owned by several other men in the regiment.

"No," he thought, "in the morning that will be a surprise I present to our good Colonel."

The following morning, using their new Sharps, the men of the regiment put on a shooting display that even Colonel Berdan found hard to believe.

Chapter 25 Union Woes

Late fall, 1861 found the once proud and confident Union army suffering from a series of devastating defeats. The Union army led by sometimes incompetent and often inexperienced officers waffled in indecision and antiquated military thinking, while the Confederate forces under Robert E. Lee had just narrowly missed taking Washington D.C. itself. From South Carolina north to Virginia, and as far west as Oklahoma, the Confederates had the Union forces reeling. The few Union victories, and none that could be described as major, did little to counterbalance the Confederate victories at Fort Sumter, Bull Run, Kessler's Cross Lanes, Dry Wood Creek, Lexington, Blue Mills, and Barboursville.

A dozen of Berdan's sharpshooters, including Caleb and Jack Remza had unfortunately been assigned to one of the Union's smaller reserve armies, commanded by one of their lesser experienced generals, J. T. Nelson. Against the advice of several of his experienced officers, General Nelson chose to set up his latest camp in a poor defensive position at the Little Bethel River, on open ground surrounded on three sides by several small hills. Once more, another Union force with a poor leader in charge had been primed for defeat.

Two days after Nelson's army made camp, the Confederates, under cover of darkness and using the hills to hide their approach, hit the Union army at daybreak.

A spirited and outnumbered Confederate force of less than four hundred infantry, with little cavalry and no cannon support, and outnumbered more than two to one, had caught Nelson by complete surprise. Barely able to maintain even a semblance of an organized retreat, Nelson pulled his forces back five miles, stopping only after they had found and secured a high ground. Minutes later they linked up with a small cavalry regiment that had been heading for another battle front, but upon hearing the sounds of heavy fighting, rode to aid Nelson forces.

The successful early morning charge by the Confederates left Caleb and Remza hidden in enemy territory. Rather than run with the rest of the Union troops, they chose to stay back and remain hidden, figuring that after the Confederate troops passed by they could wreak havoc on the enemy's rear. To some it might have seemed a suicidal decision, but Caleb and Remza were fully confident that during the confusion of battle, they could find a suitable place of concealment, and then do all they could to damage the Confederates. When that was done, they would worry about finding a way back to their own lines.

The two men, now waiting for dark, had concealed themselves beneath a large pile of decomposed leaves and logs that had fallen across a small but fairly deep ravine. Their hiding place was about half a mile from the only good road in the area and less than three hundred yards from where the Confederates had set up their headquarters.

An hour after midnight, the rumbling of wagons along with Remza's gentle poking at him with the butt end of his Sharps rifle woke Caleb from a damp but comfortable sleep. Pushing aside the leaves covering his face, Caleb watched with Remza as a dozen or more cannon wagons led by a number of men carrying torches, passed slowly in front of them, moving in the direction of the Confederate line.

They were about to crawl from their hiding place and investigate further when the nearby sound of twigs crunching under boots alerted them to the approach of several men. Ever so slowly, Caleb and Remza lowered their heads until they were once again totally immersed under the bed of leaves and broken branches.

Seconds later they heard the sound of several men urinating and a twangy southern voice saying, "Most people might think movin' cannon wagons at night is plum crazy, but I'll bet when them bluebellies start their counterattack they'll think all hell has landed on them."

"'Spec so," said a second voice, "them not knowin' we got those big guns means Ol' Colonel Williams can blow them poor Yankee infantry boys into kingdom come when they start coming at us in their pretty straight lines. It'll be like shooting ducks on a pond."

"Yeah," said the first voice, "once they start their attack and get about half way, they'll be pissin' their pants when we roll them guns out of the trees and start blastin' away."

Ten minutes after the Rebs had hitched up their pants and left, the two snipers, armed with the knowledge unknowingly given them by the two Johnny Rebs, left their hiding place and cautiously headed north in search of the new Union line. Three hours later, after reaching the Union camp, Caleb found Colonel Berdan sleeping with his back against a wagon wheel.

"Colonel Berdan, Sir, excuse me Sir."

Slowly Berdan opened his eyes and saw Caleb standing before him.

"Quinn. Good to see you alive," said Berdan, staring into the darkness.

"I'm sort of enjoying it myself," replied Caleb.

"Since you see fit to wake me at this hour, I take it you've got something of importance to tell me."

"Yes sir. When and if Nelson makes his counterattack the Rebs will be waiting with a dozen or more cannon they moved up last night and hid back in the woods."

"Are you sure? The last intelligence report I got said they had no cannon."

"I'm sure. Remza and I have seen and heard the cannon being moved. We also overheard two Rebs talking about how they're going to be used. Once we start our advance they plan to wait until we get about halfway to their lines, then they'll pull the hidden cannon out of the woods and blast our boys to bits."

"I have to get this information to General Nelson so that he can cancel the counterattack," said Berdan. You're absolutely correct when you say that with no cannon of our own and crossing open ground under Confederate cannon fire we could be wiped out. I just hope our esteemed General Nelson can come up with a plan that doesn't get us all killed. So far all he's done is stay to the rear and give orders to protect our flank."

"'Excuse me, Colonel, but on the way here I had time to think on it and may have a plan General Nelson might like, especially if you present it to him in such a way that he can call the plan his own."

"I'm listening," said Berdan, knowing full well Quinn's ability to improvise an unusual course of action.

"Well sir, I noticed coming into camp a cavalry unit has joined us, so here's what I propose. Before the counterattack starts, myself and your other eleven sharpshooters will move into position to pick off the Confederate gun crews the minute they start to bring their cannon out of the woods. There's a position about five hundred yards to the right of their lines which would be ideal for us to set up in. It's got good coverage and good elevation. In the morning we'll have the sun at our backs and with any luck we can stay undetected long enough to not only disrupt their cannon fire but also long enough for our cavalry to hit the Confederate line of cannon."

"That sounds like a decent plan," said Berdan, "but when the Rebs do find you, they'll either turn their cannons on you or send a squad or two of infantry at you. Either way you won't have much of a chance to come out of this alive."

Getting only a shrug of his shoulders from Caleb, Berdan continued, "I'm fairly sure that by my endorsing your plan, General Nelson will at least consider it. I also know of a cavalry commander who's itching to get into a fight. However, I do see one flaw. If the Confederate guns are spread out in their usual manner, several of the guns farthest to your west will be out of range of your men to the east."

"Yes sir, they most likely will, but I'm thinking that just one team positioned to the west could handle those three or four guns. Also, if the cavalry, instead of attacking across the entire line, concentrates on the far right, nearest our sniper teams, the nearest of those cannon to the west and center of the line will have hell lining up on our cavalry. As soon as we start firing, send the cavalry at a dead run toward the right of the enemy line. Once they've broken past the cannons, send them hard to the left. Have them sweep down the enemy line and then have them keep hitting it. In the meantime, after the cavalry charges, get Nelson to move up his infantry as fast as he can. No marching in line but charging on the full run. With both surprise and numbers on our side even Nelson might find a way to win a battle."

"Your plan sounds good as far as the cavalry and infantry goes," said Berdan, but I still don't like the idea of your men being on such open ground and so close to the Reb infantry lines. They won't have much of a chance if the Reb infantry goes after them, as I'm sure they will."

"I understand the risk," said Caleb, "but if you'll take care of General Nelson and the cavalry, I'm sure my men will do their part regardless of the danger to their lives."

Berdan sat for several minutes re-running Quinn's plan through his mind. It was daring and would require not only perfect timing on the part of the cavalry and infantry, but also the absolute need for his sharpshooters to keep the Reb gun crews from firing their cannon before the cavalry could get inside the Confederate line.

"I'll get your plan to Nelson," said Berdan, "and convince him it's the best course of action. You get your men in position as fast as you can."

He immediately left at a run for the tent of General Nelson, knowing as he did so he might never again see Quinn or his men alive again.

Chapter 26 Counterattack

After assembling his men and explaining their role in the coming battle, Caleb moved them out into the pitch darkness of the surrounding countryside. He instructed three teams to concentrate on the cannon crews while the other two would focus on the nearest Confederate infantry. Just after 3:00 a.m. the sharpshooters had reached their objective, a thin cluster of trees running from the base of a small hill all the way to the top. Feeling by hand in the darkness, the men spent the next half hour carefully selecting the best places of concealment and protection, but places that would also allow them a clear field of fire toward the Confederate lines.

With the men now in position, Caleb crept up to each of the teams and whispered, "Good luck and good shooting."

He and Remza then began the long trip to a position near the guns farthest away, the ones to the west, the ones that would be out of effective range of the five sharpshooter teams they were leaving behind. He knew he and Remza would have to push hard to get there before the battle began.

Three hours later, having crossed back through the Union camp, Caleb and Remza reached a flattened area less than a quarter of a mile west of the Confederate lines. Carrying an extra Sharps each, they began the task of hiding themselves from the Confederates who they knew would soon be trying to find and kill them. With no trees or heavy brush to conceal them, they dug out two shallow trenches about twenty yards apart, put on their camouflage capes and hoods and settled down to wait.

Ten minutes after sunrise the Union infantry marched into position in the open field just under a mile away from the Confederate line. Behind them, hidden in the shadows of a thick stand of trees, the Union cavalry waited.

A bugle call sent the infantry moving slowly toward the Rebels. Minutes later, with the Union infantry closing to seven hundred yards the Confederate troops responded by starting to push their hidden cannon out of the woods. The five teams of Union snipers instantly opened fire. In seconds over a dozen men from the Reb gun crews lay sprawled out on the ground, dead or wounded.

On the other side of the Confederate lines, Caleb was picking off the gun crews of the three cannon located closest to him while Remza was sending killing shots into the enemy infantry. Those men who failed

146

to regain the cover of the trees or were brave enough to stand in the open and attempt to fire their cannon or firearms quickly became victims of his and Remza's devastatingly accurate fire.

Seconds after the firing began, a second bugle command blaring across the battlefield sent the Union cavalry surging forward out of the woods, their horses at a dead run. The Confederate gun crews and infantry were now faced with the choice of either dealing with the deadly fire coming from the Union snipers or leaving themselves exposed while they attempted to load, aim, and fire their cannon at the fast approaching Union cavalry and infantry. Before they could sufficiently act upon either choice, the Union cavalry broke through the Rebel infantry line on the right flank and hit hard at the now almost defenseless gun crews.

"They're inside the enemy line," hollered Caleb to Remza over the sound of battle.

"Yeah, they're in," yelled back Remza, "but if you haven't noticed there's a bunch of unhappy Rebs heading our way."

Rising to one knee for a better view, Caleb could see through the smoke floating over the battlefield a squad of Rebel infantry led by a saber-brandishing young officer, all of them charging in their direction. Bringing his Sharps up to sight on the officer, Caleb was about to pull the trigger when a cannon ball swooshed by his head, missing him by less than a foot. The cannon shot was immediately followed by what sounded like a hundred angry bees buzzing around his head. Almost simultaneously he felt a sharp sting to his neck just below his right ear. A second bullet then careened off a rock and struck him under his left armpit, spinning him sideways to the ground.

His left arm wounded, Caleb could only watch helplessly as his Sharps slipped slowly from his grasp. Turning to his right he could see two Rebs bearing down on Remza. Snatching his colt from its shoulder holster he fired two shots, both striking the soldier nearest Remza. The second soldier was stopped cold in his tracks when Remza, swinging his Sharps by the barrel, smashed the butt end into his attacker's face. A third Confederate soldier, bayonet waving in front of him, came out of the smoke and attempted to drive the bayonet into Remza's body. After deflecting the bayonet with his rifle barrel, Remza and the Reb became locked in a hand-to-hand fight to the death.

Unable to get a clear shot at the Reb who had attacked

Remza, Caleb swung his Colt back toward the charging enemy. As he did so he could see a large grey-clad figure bringing the barrel of a rifle directly in line with his chest.

With no time to aim, Caleb fired, as much out of instinct as intention. The Colt's bullet cut through the Reb soldier's hand holding the rifle and slammed into his chest. Mortally wounded the soldier slumped first to his knees, and then down on his side, his face toward Caleb. To Caleb, in those seconds before the young rebel soldier's life ended his eyes seemed to ask, "How and why?"

The Reb's questions went unanswered as one of his brothers in arms came out of the swirling smoke and charged at Caleb. Caleb aimed and fired two more shots. The Reb dropped his rifle but kept coming, forcing Caleb to fire once more. The soldier, now dying on his feet, made one more desperate effort to continue fighting. With his last bit of life he threw himself at Caleb, screaming as he did so.

Blood from the man's wounds spurted out covering Caleb's face. Half blinded by the blood, Caleb used his good arm to push away the now motionless soldier, then used his shirt sleeve to wipe away the blood blocking his vision. Still unable to see clearly, Caleb looked up in time to see the young Confederate officer, saber in hand, looming over him.

His colt now empty Caleb reached for his knife, knowing that even if he could get it out, it would do little good against the man about to strike him with the raised saber. Just when Caleb knew he would die, the Confederate officer was knocked violently forward by a fast moving grey horse and rider. Grazed in the head by the horse's left shoulder as it swept past him, Caleb, covered in blood and with the dead Reb infantry officer lying half across his body, was thrown to the ground, the back of his head hitting hard on the dried out earth, knocking him unconscious.

Caleb heard what sounded like a distant voice calling his name. Struggling through nausea and dizziness, he sought to make sense of his surroundings. Gone was the sound of battle, replaced by an eerie silence. The seemingly distant voice once more broke that silence.

"Caleb, wake up, you hear me. Wake up."

Caleb opened his eyes and saw Jack sitting beside him. Over Remza's shoulder he could a Union officer sitting calmly on a grey horse.

Leaning slightly toward Jack and pointing a saber at Caleb he said, "You'll need to get that man and yourself some medical attention. You can also tell your commander I said the two of you did a fine job. I, myself, have a war to win and must bid you adieu."

Caleb, hearing the sound of the horse moving away, lifted his head in time to see that the rider had captain's epaulets on his shoulders, a surprisingly youthful face and long yellow hair. Caleb thought he looked much as Sean might have looked were he alive. His view of the rider suddenly became blocked by Jack's face.

"Are you alright?" he asked, not realizing most of the blood covering Caleb was from the dead man lying only a few feet away.

"I could be better, how about you?"

"Yep, I'm fine," replied Remza, "one of them Rebs made me a present of his bayonet. Gave it to me in my shoulder, but being the sociable fella I am, I gave it back to him...in the heart.

Then moving to help Caleb to his feet, he added through teeth clenched in pain, "If you're finished with your little rest, I think both of us need to pay a visit to the hospital tent."

Caleb, looking at a deep cut on Remza's cheek and the blood running from his shoulder to his chest replied, "I'd feel a lot more rested if I hadn't had to do your share of the fighting for you."

"You call that a fight? Why I..." Remza was interrupted in mid-sentence by Caleb raising his good arm and pointing in the direction of the battlefield. Looking over the field, they could see that the Rebel army was now in full retreat.

"Well, I'd say it was whatever fighting caused these Rebs to be running back where they came from," Caleb responded.

Hours later Caleb and Remza, having received medical attention at the field hospital, stood at ease before Colonel Berdan and General Nelson.

"You and your fellow sharpshooters are to be commended for your role in helping me win this engagement," said General Nelson. "In the past I may have doubted the value of sharpshooters to the army, but after today I no longer have any reservations whatsoever. You've proven to me that one skilled sharpshooter can be as effective as ten regular infantrymen."

"Thank you, sir," said Caleb, "and the rest of the men, how did they fare?"

A moment of silence passed before Colonel Berdan, in a voice tinged with grief, answered Caleb's question.

"Three wounded and three dead," he said, "including Sergeant Glass. They gave a good accounting of themselves."

A tired looking Colonel Berdan then turned to General Nelson.

"With your permission Sir, I think my new sergeant and his corporal would like to be excused to get some much needed food and rest."

"Permission granted," said Nelson, and looking at Caleb and Remza said, "congratulations on your promotions...and thanks."

After Caleb and Remza left the tent Nelson said to Berdan, "Do you suppose that young Quinn might have an ancestor named Alexander, as in Alexander the Great?"

"Somehow," answered Berdan, "it wouldn't surprise me if he did."

Minutes later Caleb and Remza found an empty supply wagon, crawled into it, and immediately fell asleep. They didn't leave the wagon for over twelve hours. The food came later.

Chapter 27 Revelations

Seasons had passed and passed again, and still the war and the killing raged on. As the Union lost more and more battles and more and more men, Congress passed the first conscription act for the Union in March 1863. Called the Enrollment Act, it required all men between 20 and 45 years of age to enroll to fight.

Finally, in May, General Grant achieved a stunning victory over the South at Vicksburg, a victory that gave the Union control of the Mississippi River and effectively split the Confederacy in two. After the Battle of Gettysburg in July the tides changed in a war that had, to that point, primarily favored the South.

By the end of July, 1863, "Berdan's Sharpshooters," Caleb among them, had fought in every major battle of the Eastern campaign. Caleb was tired. Tired of killing other men and tired of losing friends he had made in the regiment. He and the others of the regiment had fought hard and with much valor, but they paid dearly for doing so. Of the original men who had enlisted with him, less than a handful had survived. Jack Remza was one of them, but only barely; he was now back home in upstate New York learning how to farm with one arm, and humorously demanding that he be addressed as "Hook."

In mid-November of 1863, because of his reputation as a superb shooter, Caleb had earned a reprieve from front-line duty by being temporarily loaned out to the security force assigned to protect the President. On this day the President was speaking at the dedication of a battlefield cemetery. A cemetery holding 7,500 soldiers, Union and Confederate alike.

"Four score and seven years ago..."

Caleb, having secluded himself several hundred yards away from the speaker's platform, could barely hear the President's words coming from the distance. Being back at Gettysburg was an almost surreal experience for him. Memories of the horrific battles fought there flashed before his eyes. This place was where Remza lost his arm, and it was where Berdan's Sharpshooters made one of their most significant contributions to the war when they routed Confederate snipers from their carefully built snipers' nests. He could see the "Devil's Den" more clearly in his mind than one could in the famous picture taken by Alexander Gardner that was titled *Death of a Rebel Sniper*; a rebel sniper whose demise may have come at Caleb's hands.

Returning his attention to the job assigned him, he used the telescope on his Sharps to scan the surrounding area within rifle distance of the President, looking for anything or anybody that might be a threat. Seeing no distant threat he moved the scope in the direction of the crowd gathered before the President. Starting at the back of the crowd he slowly panned the scope from side to side, his finger resting on the rifle's trigger guard. A moment later he stopped abruptly and locked his eyes on two men standing only a few rows back from the President's platform.

"I'll be damned," he whispered to himself.

In his scope he could see only the upper half of the two men, but it was enough. The man on the left had dark hair and was one of the few men in the crowd who was hatless. To his right, and wearing a high black stovepipe hat, was the imposing back and shoulders of a large black man.

Shortly after the President's departure from the Gettysburg Railroad Station, Caleb, released from duty, sat with the two men he'd had in his scope's sight at a small inn's outside table sharing a meal of fried chicken, cornbread, and a generous pitcher of beer.

Beau Carroll, the hatless man in the crowd, was the first to speak.

"It seems you have served your adopted country quite well, Mister Quinn" he began. "So much so you've even become a minor celebrity in the Eastern newspapers."

"That's not of my own choosing, and certainly no reason for you to call me Mister," said an almost apologetic but smiling Caleb.

"I'd much prefer that my name had never been mentioned, but there was nothing I could do to prevent it except try to get lost whenever one of those newspaper people came into camp."

"I understand," replied Beau, "but stories of your exploits have served a useful purpose by helping to recruit replacements for your regiment in particular and the army in general."

Beau then lifted his glass, "As a grateful citizen I salute your accomplishments, and as your friend, I am very pleased you are still alive."

"Thank you," said Caleb, "I owe much of what I've done to you and to a lot of good luck."

"Caleb, before we speak of anything else, I want to remind you that the money you inherited from Joshua is still in the Corcoran and Riggs Bank in Washington, D.C. Anytime you need money simply contact the bank or me by letter or telegraph and it will be sent to you post haste. You should also know the original amount has been nearly doubled due to some fortunate investments I've made on your behalf."

Pausing, and then raising his glass in Caleb's direction, Beau continued, "I must say with a bit of pride that you are now a man of considerable wealth."

"I appreciate what you've done for me and only wish I knew some way of returning the kindness you've shown me from the first day I arrived in this country."

"There is a possible way," said Beau, "but before we get to that, I have a confession to make. It wasn't by chance that you were assigned to the President's security guard. I pulled a few strings in Washington to make sure you would be here so that I could have this meeting with you...out of sight of any prying Washington eyes. I prefer, for reasons that may become evident in future years that our relationship become known to as few people as possible."

"Then I suppose I'm also compelled to thank you for the week of cooked meals, soft beds, and clean sheets I've had to endure," replied Caleb laughingly.

"You most certainly are," replied Beau, "but rather than having you graciously grovel at my feet, I wish to speak of an important matter, that matter being how you can repay me for the small services I've rendered to you."

Pushing his hair off his forehead he continued, "You know from your own experiences as a boy and as a man, that there are men in this world who have no caring or compassion for others, men who are willing to use any means, any device, including an unlimited degree of violence to achieve their goals."

"Yes," interrupted Caleb, "I'm more than familiar with such men."

"I'm sure you are," replied Beau, "but I want to make you aware that as there are men of evil, so too are there countries of a similar ilk. It is my fear, as well as that of others in high government positions, that one or more of these countries, thinking America will be weak and unwilling to fight, will make an attempt to overthrow or at least undermine our government after the war ends. If and when that happens, I want you to join me and others in doing whatever it takes to stop them."

Studying Caleb's reaction to his words, but seeing only a growing interest, Beau continued, "It will be dangerous work, work that will likely mean you risking your life."

"Sir, I can only tell you that whatever service you or this country chooses to ask of me, I will happily do."

"I felt certain that would be your response," replied Beau, "I think I knew when we first met that someday you and I would work together to do what we could to protect this country. I based those thoughts upon what I saw in you and what Joshua said about you in his letter of introduction. I suspected that you had the potential, that something special which sets some men apart from the average. That is why instead of finding you an ordinary job I sent you to live with the circus people. I felt confident they would teach you the skills that have made you the man you are today, a man ably equipped to join me in whatever endeavors lie ahead."

"It goes without saying that I would be honored to work with you," said Caleb.

"Good, and now, although our meeting has been brief, if you'll excuse me I must leave this pleasant company for urgent business in Washington. If you have any questions I'm sure Phillip would be pleased to answer them."

Beau then stood up, and after a warm handshake and "good luck" to Caleb turned toward the street. Seconds later he was picked up by a carriage that appeared as if on cue.

Phillip, who had managed to do away with most of the food at the table during Beau and Caleb's conversation, watched with Caleb as the carriage pulled away.

"There goes a very good and a very complicated man," he muttered while trying to swallow the last of the cornbread.

"That I don't doubt," said Caleb, "but tell me what I don't know about him and just how well you know him."

"Well, first of all, I know he's had some mighty pain in his life. One time, and just that one time, I saw Mr. Carroll with his shirt off. He had scars from shackles on his wrists and musta' had a hundred lashes across his back and chest. Somebody hurt that man a lot, and for a long time. Somehow I think the British had something to do with it 'cause he hates them body and soul."

Taking a swig of beer, Phillip went on, "I can also tell you I've been with Mr. Carroll for almost ten years and during that time he has helped a lot of people, some out of pure goodness, and others, such as some of the circus people you know, out of both goodness and for a purpose. We began working together when I was a young man with a chip on my shoulder, slaving as a deck hand on the *Delta Duchess*. That's where he recruited me, and for several years he and I worked with what some people referred to as the Underground Railroad. He and others working with us made it possible for hundreds of slaves to escape the south and get to freedom in Canada, especially in Nova Scotia. Beau had boarded the *Duchess* hoping to find a faster way to get groups of runaway slaves from New Orleans to Canada. After working out a plan with Captain Varvil to hide the runaways below deck, he asked me to be a contact between him and the runaways. As a result, over the next two years we helped dozens and dozens of my people escape. That alone makes him a hero in my eyes."

"Is he still in the runaway business?" asked Caleb.

"No, that ended after the war started, when he found another and even more dangerous way to help our country."

"What could be more dangerous than trying to get slaves past a bunch of shotgun toting slave owners and bounty hunters?" asked Caleb.

"You've heard of blockade runners," said Phillip.

"Sure. They're the Confederate and British ships trying to bring supplies to the South, but what do they have to do with Beau?"

"A lot. When the war started, Beau had his contacts in the south and the north spread the false rumor that he was sympathetic to the Confederacy and would be willing to use his shipping business to do whatever he could for their cause. The Confederates bought into it and within months Beau was in London organizing shipments of weapons and supplies to be exported to the Confederate ports in exchange for cotton from the South. To the Confederate's he was a hero, but what they didn't know was that most of the time when a blockade runner sailed from England, Beau sent the probable route and destination by faster ships to either Baltimore or Philadelphia. That information would then be relayed to the Union navy in time for them to be waiting to capture, sink, or turn back the blockade runners. My guess is Beau and the others working with him were responsible for stopping about half of the blockade runners that got caught before they could make port. What's really slick is that Beau, ever the businessman, was doing all this while collecting healthy commissions from both the English and the Confederates. Because of his role as a double agent, it's very likely that if exposed his life would be in danger from diehard Confederates ready to take their revenge on a traitor."

Reaching into his coat Phillip removed an envelope and handed it to Caleb, "If you have any doubt about what I just told you, read this letter Beau asked me to show you after he left our meeting today."

Caleb removed a letter written on fine parchment from the plain envelope and began reading

November, 1862

Dear Sir,

On behalf of myself and a grateful country, I thank you and your associates for the many contributions you have made to the winning of this war. I know of no braver or more valuable citizen of this great nation.

> *With deepest respect, your friend,*
> *Abraham Lincoln*

"I noticed that Beau's name isn't on the letter."

"No, it's not," replied Phillip. "Should a letter like this get into the wrong hands, and believe me there are still a lot of Southern sympathizers in Washington and thereabouts, it could end Beau's effectiveness, not to mention his life."

Caleb folded the letter and handed it back to Phillip saying, "Heroes do show up in the strangest places."

"Yes, they do," said Phillip, "in the strangest places, but men such as Beau and yourself, and perhaps even someone like myself, will always be there when needed."

Caleb let the compliment pass without comment but did feel warmed by it. Phillip was a man whose opinion mattered a great deal to him. Attempting to steer the conversation away from himself, he asked another question.

"You said something about some circus people being helped but with a purpose in mind. Can you tell me who you were talking about, or is that a secret too?"

"Well," replied Phillip, "I can tell you that if you wanted to find Lucinda you might start looking around Richmond. Jean Duval is roaming around Mexico, and Uriah is visiting friends in Colorado and Utah...supposedly for his health.... Each of them have underlying reasons for being where they are, reasons tied to aiding the Union cause. There are others, but none that you've met, but that could change before the war's over."

Caleb, aware from past encounters and the day's talk that Phillip was a lot more than just a man servant, said, "I'm curious how you came to work for Mr. Carroll."

"Not much to tell. My Pa and Ma and me were owned by Mr. Bowie who had a plantation just a few miles north of Opelousas, Louisiana. After Mr. Bowie didn't come back from Texas we were sold to Mr. John Farrow in the nearby town of Washington, just a few miles north. We worked on a plantation called Magnolia Ridge where we had it pretty good. Ma and Pa worked the kitchen and I became a houseboy. I mostly fetched this and fetched that, and sometimes carried Mr. Farrow's guns when he went hunting. That's how I learned a little about guns and how to shoot."

"About a year after we got there Mistress Farrow started using me as a playmate for their boy child, David, who was about my age. When they hired a live-in tutor for David, I stayed close during the lessons and by listening close figured out how to read, write, and do a few sums."

"I thought any slave who learned to read or write would be severely punished, even whipped to death."

"That's true enough," said Phillip, "and I for sure never told anybody, not even my folks. When nobody was around I practiced with a stick in the dirt 'cause if anyone got close I could wipe it out real fast. Anyway, I stayed as a houseboy until I was near about thirteen. That's when I got my growth and put on muscles, muscles that made me more valuable as a field worker. After that I spent two years working cotton in the summer and clearing land in the winter for more cotton fields."

Taking a breath, Phillip continued, "Then hard times and bad weather hit the plantation and Mr. Farrow had to auction off my Ma and Pa in New Orleans. A few weeks later I got sold to the captain of the *Duchess*. I spent two years as a stoker, and then Captain V. moved me up to cabin boy."

"Did you ever see your parents again?" asked Caleb.

"No. With Mr. Carroll's help I looked for them several times, but all we could find out is they got sold a couple more times and then disappeared."

"Anyway, it was during my time on the *Duchess* that I met Mr. Carroll. He was a frequent passenger and somehow figured out I could read and write. That's when he bought me from the Captain and used me as the go between I told you about before. I stayed on the *Duchess* and he promised me that my help would one day bring me freedom. Then, less than a year later he took me to the farm and gave me the papers making me a free man. That doesn't happen to many black men, so when I asked him why he was being so good to a slave he hardly knew, he told me he needed a loyal friend more than he needed a slave."

"Sounds like you got mighty lucky," said Caleb.

"I did, except for losing my mother and father."

"I'm sorry to hear about that, Phillip. I truly am. But I guess it makes you and me something alike because like you I lost all my family."

"More than you know," said Phillip, "'cause just like you I went to work on the farm and spent almost two years as a roustabout. Good years they were. Then Mr. Carroll asked me to work with him in Baltimore. I've been with him ever since."

"So just what is it you do for Beau?"

Phillip's reply was slightly evasive, "I do whatever he asks," said Phillip.

"I'm sure you do," replied Caleb. Then, looking Phillip directly in the eye he continued, "I have one last question. What does Beau want from me?"

"That's easy," said Phillip with a serious look in his eyes, "he wants you to be his assassin."

Chapter 28 War Continues

General Lee was losing the battle of attrition and he knew it. The continual pressure on him and his army was wearing down his troops and exhausting supplies. He knew his loss to Grant at Spotsylvania in May of 1864 was a reckoning of more lost battles to come. His last clear victory at Cold Harbor in June of 1864 had cost Grant 7,000 men in about twenty minutes due to the heavy fighting. The Union conscription allowed Grant to regroup while Lee's troops simply dwindled. Lee simply couldn't replace lost troops at the same rate as the Union was able to replace men they'd lost. The South's hopes rose when John Bell Hood scored a huge Confederate win on June 27 at Kennesaw Mountain, Georgia, costing Grant 3000 Union soldiers. However, Hood lost 1000 men he couldn't replace. The South's last desperate attempt at victory occurred in July when Confederate troops again attempted to take Washington D.C., to no avail. The blundered attempt was followed in August through December with Sherman's 'March to the Sea' devastating Georgia and then South and North Carolina as he approached the Confederate capital of Richmond.

After the battle at Kennesaw Mountain Caleb made his way back to the Union line just north of the Dallas Highway, thinking as he went of what could have been done to change the outcome of the battle, to avoid the carnage heaped upon the Union soldiers. All he could think was that too many old fools, still believing in their antiquated military tactics, were leading the Union army. Kennesaw Mountain should have fallen to the stronger Yankee forces, yet because of the mistakes of the Union generals the outnumbered and ill-supplied Confederates had managed to rout them.

Reaching camp, Caleb fell into a much needed deep sleep, a sleep which was shortly disturbed by someone shaking his shoulders.

"Sergeant Quinn, Sergeant Quinn."

He tried to ignore both the voice and the hand shaking him, but they would not go away.

"Wake up Sergeant, the general wants to see you at once."

"What about," muttered Caleb, still not ready to open his eyes.

"Don't rightly know, Sergeant. He just sent me here to get you. He had an urgency in his voice so I guess it's kinda important."

Five minutes later a slightly groggy and wholly disgruntled Caleb stepped out of his tent and started for the general's quarters. Halfway there he passed by a group of captured rebel prisoners huddled in a ditch and eating handfuls of bread and cheese being distributed from a bucket by their guards. He saw that many of the prisoners were wounded, their clothes were in tatters, and a few had no shoes, only strips of blankets they had tied around their feet. They looked like worn-out dogs, starved and beaten. Caleb wondered why, with all the dead men who no longer needed their clothes or shoes, these prisoners could not have been better taken care of.

He marveled in admiration at those bedraggled men who fought so well and with so little. "If we can't beat the likes of those poor souls," he thought, "is it any wonder we're losing so many battles?"

As he walked past the last of the prisoners, one of them briefly caught his eye. The man, who was larger than the other prisoners, had a ragged cloth covering a head wound. He also had mud-encrusted clothes and no shoes. Even in this miserable condition he was offering some of his cheese and bread to a fellow soldier who appeared wounded in both arms and unable to feed himself. Caleb continued walking, feeling good that a breath of humanity still lived on despite the horrors of war inflicted on so many men on both sides of the conflict.

"Despite the horror there can be a certain nobleness in war," he thought.

Then he stopped.

Something about the large man's back and the shape of his head triggered a distant but elusive memory. He hesitated, not sure if he should proceed to answer the general's summons or go back to satisfy his curiosity.

"By God, the general can wait," he decided, "I've got to know."

Approaching the man from behind, Caleb stood and watched, his presence not going unnoticed by the other prisoners. They knew any unsolicited attention they received usually resulted in something happening that made their imprisonment even more difficult. All their eyes were on Caleb when he tapped the kneeling man on the shoulder.

"Matthew Moore?" he asked.

The prisoner, who had noticed his comrades staring at him, stopped with a handful of bread mid-way to his friend's mouth then turned to look up at Caleb. Both men stared at each other, their eyes searching carefully over the features of the other man. The Rebel prisoner was the first to speak.

"You may know me but I...," he stopped, and then slowly got to his feet, his mouth breaking into a weak smile that was barely visible under his matted beard.

"Well I'll be damned. You're sure enough Caleb Quinn, but you look a lot different than the boy I knew on the *Osprey*."

"You look the same to me," said Caleb, "even though you look like you might have missed a year's worth of shaving and bathing."

Missed a few meals while I was at it," replied Matthew patting a stomach that was considerably smaller than Caleb remembered, "but I always did have too big an appetite."

It was clear to Caleb that Matthew had lost none of his love for being humorous.

"Matthew, how in hell's name did a peace-loving man such as yourself end up here instead of home with your family? I just can't figure a man like you fighting for the South."

The smile vanished from Matthew's face replaced by a hard look in his eyes. "Didn't have much choice. When the war broke out I wanted nothing to do with it so I stayed up in the mountains, kinda out of sight of the recruiters. That worked during the first couple of years when the recruiters were looking for true volunteers, but as the war wore on they got more demanding. It got rough when they started volunteering men whether they wanted to fight or not, which is why I moved the family further up in the mountains. Then about six months ago a bunch of Georgia militia caught up with us and told me that if I wasn't with 'em, I was against 'em, and if I was against 'em then I was a traitor. I'm sure you know what happens to traitors in war time."

Caleb could only nod his head as Matthew continued, "After they threatened my family, I banged a few of their heads, but it didn't do much good, so I became a volunteer. Now it looks like I'll be spending the rest of the war in one of your high-class prisoner-of-war camps I heard about."

"I believe your story," said Caleb, "and I may be able to do something to keep you from going to a prison camp, but first I've got to go see a general on other business. If you'll be good enough to stick around, I'll get back as soon as I can."

"Sticking around, that'll be easy to do," said Matthew as he gestured toward the armed guards.

"Good," replied Caleb. "I wouldn't want you to get hurt trying to escape."

He turned to leave but then turned back with a thoughtful look on his face.

"Forgive me, Matthew but I forgot to ask. How are Samantha and your daughter?"

"Daughters," said Matt, "got me two of them. The second one's name is Emmalou, and as best I know she, Sam, and Eryn Gracie are making it. I know from talking to one of the boys from Ducktown that they got through a rough winter. Still, I haven't heard from them in several months. Mail don't show up much where I been."

Only able to nod his head after getting his answer, Caleb headed at a fast walk to Sherman's tent.

Ten minutes later he was standing in front of General Sherman. The general was smoking an early morning cigar while sitting outside his tent, hatless and dressed in long handles covered by a blue coat. Caleb knew he was a short man, and even shorter on protocol. He expected their meeting to be short, too.

Without bothering to stand, Sherman waved his cigar at Caleb and announced, "Sergeant Quinn, I called you here because I'm having trouble with rebel snipers raising hell with our forward troops. One of them in particular has accounted for the killing of several of my best officers. He comes and goes without being detected, takes his shot and then disappears, kind of like I heard you do with the Rebs. He's got my officers so jumpy they started calling him 'the Ghost.' Well, this 'Ghost' is picking off my men to the point they won't risk wearing anything that marks them as officers. This situation presents a particularly bothersome problem for me because I have to get past Kennesaw Mountain in order to take Atlanta, and I don't need a bunch of jumpy officers ducking behind every tree or bush because they're worried about snipers. If you can get rid of those snipers, including the 'Ghost,' it might just make the difference between a quick campaign or one that might last a lot longer than necessary."

Caleb noted with a certain irony that both General Sherman and his aide were both wearing full length blue coats with no insignia that would identify them as officers. "It seems," thought Caleb, "the reputation of 'the Ghost' has extended all the way up to the high command."

Releasing a puff of smoke into the morning air the General continued, "The Confederate snipers, especially the 'Ghost,' have to be stopped, and because of your reputation as our best sniper, you're the man I've chosen to do the job."

"Yes, sir, thank you, sir." said Caleb, knowing he now had a possible means by which to secure Matt's release.

Sliding the cigar to the side of his mouth, the General added, "I want you to take care of the problem, regardless of what it takes. Do you understand?"

"Yes sir, completely sir," answered Caleb.

"Then that will be all, and good hunting," said Sherman, displaying his usual penchant for bringing conversations to a quick end.

Caleb, deciding this was the time to speak on Matthew's behalf, continued to stand in front of the General.

"Excuse me, General Sherman, sir. Before I go hunting this 'Ghost' I'd like to ask a special favor of you."

"Spit it out, soldier" said a somewhat puzzled Sherman, not accustomed to having an ordinary sergeant directly ask him for anything. Then again, he'd heard from several sources that this Sergeant seldom acted as expected, and that characteristic he suspected, probably accounted for his success as a sniper. If nothing else he was still alive, and that couldn't be said for most of the snipers who had come under his command.

"Sir, I have a friend from when I first came to this country. He's a prisoner on the other side of camp, and I would surely appreciate it if you would release him to my custody."

Sherman, with no hesitation, replied, "Well, if I did that for every prisoner, I wouldn't be much of a general, would I? So, I'm afraid that's not possible."

"Sir," said Caleb, "despite being a Rebel prisoner, he's not on the side of the South and has no wish to fight us or anyone else. After coming to America he moved to the northern Georgia mountains. When the war broke out he was forced, under threat of serious harm to his family, to fight on the side of the South. I give you my word he'll go home if he's released."

"I understand your concern for your friend," replied Sherman, "a lot of us have friends and relatives on the other side, but according to the rules of war I can't help him."

With a look of finality, Sherman said, "You're dismissed, Sergeant."

Ignoring the dismissal, Caleb shot back, "Sir, you want the snipers taken care of and I want my friend released. I wouldn't be alive today or fighting in this war if it weren't for him. My guess is if I couldn't secure his release it might seriously affect my concentration and aim when I encounter any enemy snipers. I never could shoot straight even a little straight when I was worried about my friends."

"That was an order, not a request, I gave you," said the general, now more carefully eying the young Irishman.

"Yes sir, but your order won't do anything to improve my aim. Releasing my friend would."

Sherman looked down at his boots and flicked an ash on the ground between them. Sherman's aide fidgeted. He'd never heard an enlisted man speak to the General in such an irreverent manner, and he was sure Sherman was about to come down hard on this rather stupid and stubborn as hell Sergeant. The General took another puff on his cigar.

His reply was far from what his aide expected. "Sergeant, here's what I'll do. If you take care of those snipers and get back here within three days with proof of your success, I'll grant your request...providing your friend also signs a pledge of allegiance to the Union. After three days me and this army are taking Atlanta and then moving into South Carolina. If you're not back by the time we move, then your friend will be treated as any other prisoner of war."

"Thank you, sir, and you have my word. I'll get your 'Ghost' for you, and I'll be back within three days or not at all."

"Good luck Sergeant Quinn, and if there are no other little requests on your part, you are dismissed."

As Caleb left them Sherman's aide could hardly believe the general was actually grinning. Now he'd seen it all.

An hour later, after informing Matthew of the situation, Caleb, his new sniper partner, Corporal Saville, and four other sniper teams were riding on a supply wagon heading for the front vanguard and a contest of survival with the best of the Confederate sharpshooters.

After five miles, Caleb spread the other four teams out in a line in front of the advancing Union army. He and Saville stayed on the wagon as it headed farther out in front of the troops. As the wagon followed a curve in the road on the crest of a hill Caleb looked out at the countryside in front of him, a look that brought a slight tingle to the hairs on his neck. If he could have picked the perfect place for a sniper to set up, this was it. The road ran through a wide open area with little or no cover for over two hundred yards to the left and right. On either side, just past the open fields, were hills covered with trees, rock, and heavy brush. A dozen snipers could easily hide in the surrounding terrain with an easy shot at anyone traveling the road, a road which would soon be busy with any number of wagons and troops, all of them prime targets for the Rebel snipers.

"We'd be sitting ducks," thought Caleb, "if a sniper starts shooting there is no place to take cover except for the wagons."

"Driver," he whispered, "when my partner and I roll out of this wagon you pretend you don't notice. Just keep going, and you might not want to be slow about it."

The words were barely out of his mouth when, as if on cue, a rifle shot rang out and Saville was knocked back into the rear of the wagon. The shot was fired from somewhere to the left and back in the shadows of the trees, just past the open land. It was the exact place Caleb would have chosen for an ambush.

Caleb instantly dove into the back of the wagon, noting Saville's shoulder wound as he did so. He started to tell the driver to "go," but the driver needed no encouragement. Lashing the horses, the driver turned the wagon, sending it hurtling back up the hill for almost a mile until it was well out of rifle range. Wasting no time, Caleb ordered the driver to get Saville to a doctor. A moment later, with his Sharps and cape in hand, Caleb jumped from the wagon and darted into the nearby woods.

After putting on his cape and hood, he lay behind a downed oak tree and started thinking out a plan, trying to get into the mind of the Confederate sniper.

"You're firing on a wagon on a road that will soon be filled with Union soldiers. To some people that may seem the act of someone with either a death wish or someone who is just plain stupid. But you're not stupid, and you have no intention of dying. You did it because you're smart and know the advantage of confusion, keeping your enemy off balance. Now you'll be moving, the question is, WHERE? Where will you go and who's your next target?"

"Retreating with the rest of the Confederate army back to Kennesaw or Atlanta would be the logical choice, but you don't work that way. You do the unexpected. So what does that leave?"

It suddenly hit Caleb, "You'll be moving in an unexpected direction, taking the obvious and reversing it. You'll be getting *closer* to the Union army front, closer to the target of highest value. SHERMAN! YOU WANT SHERMAN."

Caleb thought for a few more minutes.

"Where would I go if I wanted to get Sherman in my sights? Where? Where?"

Again, trying to think as his opponent would, an answer came to him.

"I'd watch and observe the Union camp and figure out for certain the next direction Sherman will move in, and that, as you surely know, is toward Atlanta. I'd know the Union forces need to get around Kennesaw Mountain and they'd do that by moving east and then coming into the city over Bald Hill. If I were you I wouldn't hunt where Sherman *is*, I'd hunt where he's *going*."

Almost breathing a sigh of relief, Caleb thought, "Now I know what you're going to do, and I'll be there to stop you."

By nightfall, Caleb had moved alone to the east of Sherman's troops and taken up a position he felt would be at least near to what 'the Ghost' would have chosen. Wrapping himself in his cape he went to sleep on an empty stomach.

Caleb woke a few minutes before sunrise and using his spyglass began to slowly traverse the surrounding area. He was looking at a dell about four hundred yards away when for a split second the vividly rising sun glinted off a piece of glass or metal.

Caleb instantly reacted by cautiously and deliberately taking aim and snapping off five carefully spaced shots in the general area of where he'd seen the reflection. Then, he was up and on the move, silently circling around the target area and using whatever cover he could find. When he was within fifty yards of the area, he stopped, remaining motionless for a half hour, his eyes and ears searching for any sign or sound of life.

Satisfied that no living presence existed, Caleb crept in and was rewarded by the sight of the sniper, dead on his back, shot through his chest and neck. Caleb knew the kill had been too easy. The Rebel sniper had made a very careless and stupid mistake by letting the sun shine off his glass.

"If you were the 'Ghost'," he said to the dead body, "and I doubt you were, you weren't nearly as good as I heard."

He headed back to Sherman's camp carrying the dead sniper's rifle and ammunition as proof his assignment had been successfully completed. He planned to keep his doubt about the identity of the sniper he killed to himself figuring Sherman didn't need to know the sniper probably wasn't "the Ghost." Reporting to the General, he found out that his men had taken out three other Confederate snipers and that a grateful Sherman was going to recommend medals for all of Berdan's Boys.

A day later a well-provisioned Matthew, with a personal note from General Sherman was headed home.

Three days after Matthew's release, Caleb sent a telegram to his bank in Washington, D.C. asking them to send $1,000.00 to Matthew Moore in Mineral Bluff, Georgia. He also sent a letter to the Moores explaining what he wanted done with the money.

Chapter 29 The End in Sight

January of 1865 saw the Confederate army facing increasing starvation and desertions. Desperate for more men, even slaves were conscripted and armed, but the tactic proved ineffective. And yet the Rebs fought on.

Caleb had never imagined such death and destruction as that perpetrated by Sherman's army as it crossed the south to the sea. He watched as the army moved through South Carolina and North Carolina. For twenty miles to either side of Sherman's march anything that could aid the South was destroyed. Crops, animals, plantations, small farms, and whole towns were wiped out. Caleb was well pleased when he and the other sharpshooters, because of their reputation, were reassigned to aid General Grant's army in Virginia. He wanted no more of this war against civilians.

In Virginia, Lee's army, what was left of it, was on the move, and so were the Union sharpshooters. General Grant gave them very specific orders. They were assigned to keep the Confederate troops of Anderson and Ewell from crossing Sailor's Creek as the Union forces waited for the VI Corp to arrive and crush the Rebels. Caleb knew his men would be in for a fierce fight against the die-hard Confederate troops. The Appomattox campaign would likely be the last hope for the Confederate forces, and they would do all they could to stave off a final defeat to their beloved Lee. Caleb had cautioned his teams to be extra wary, but not to forget their primary task of taking out as many high-ranking targets as possible.

Caleb sent four teams west toward Farmville where they could hold off the rebel troops before they reached Sailor's Creek, while Caleb and Saville, who had recovered nicely from his shoulder wound, moved east hoping by getting in front of the Union lines they could do some real damage to the boys in gray even before they reached Amelia Springs.

Caleb was confident his teams would do their part to keep the Johnny Rebs occupied until reinforcements arrived. He himself was out for bigger fish to fry. He wanted to eliminate any enemy snipers before they had a chance to do to the Union troops exactly what his own men were intent on doing to the Johnny Rebs.

Moving as rapidly and stealthy as possible, he and Corporal Saville made their way over the hilly countryside looking, as they moved, for the best possible shooting position. They finally selected a ridge covered with a strand of persimmon trees overlooking the only good road to Amelia Springs. Although the trees were only newly leafed, their thick growth provided a natural cover. Seville chose to take up a position high in the forked trunk of one of the larger persimmon trees, using the height to get a better view of the area. Caleb chose to position himself in a shallow leaf-filled depression about 50 paces away from and slightly behind Saville. With their capes and hoods pulled over them both men blended perfectly with their surroundings. Now the waiting game began.

After several hours Caleb found himself beginning to doze off when a sudden ruckus roused him. A pair of squawking ravens was dive bombing the tree where Saville hid. Apparently Saville was too close to a nest that had gone unseen by either of the Union snipers. The ravens' noisy behavior drew more than Caleb's attention. From what appeared to be out of nowhere, a single shot was fired and Caleb watched in horror as Saville fell from the tree and struck the ground as only a dead man would.

Forcing himself not to move a muscle, Caleb slowly shifted his eyes from left to right trying to discern exactly where the shot had come from. Carefully, he ever so slowly raised his camouflaged rifle, using the scope to scan the area on the other side of the road. He knew he was looking for an accomplished sniper because of the accuracy of the single shot. He also knew that for the first time since becoming a sniper he had failed to detect or sense a Confederate sharpshooter, and his failure had cost Saville his life and might well cost him his own. Caleb remained almost absolutely motionless, knowing any movement might be his last. After a long half hour had passed he thought he saw something moving back in the trees. It wasn't the movement of a man or animal, but the slight rise and fall of a piece of ground, as if it were breathing. The moving ground was about 250 yards away and set back about twenty yards in shadow-filled woods, woods that looked down on the road leading to Amelia Springs. The spot where the leaves moved was almost identical to his own hiding place.

Caleb stayed frozen in place, holding his fire, not wanting to shoot or expose his position until he was absolutely sure of his target. He knew beyond little doubt if he missed his first shot he could be dead before he could get off another one. Then the ground once again moved upwards ever so slightly.

Reconstruction. Custer and his troops were guest at the Bryson stagecoach stop in Liberty Hill during this time.

Pasavayio
In the Comanche language, the word means frog.

Horses and longhorns from the Spanish
The horse actually developed in North America and lived here 6 million years ago. However those ancestors of the present day horse died out between 6,000 and 10,000 years ago. Horses were reintroduced to North America by the Spanish in the 1500s.
The first cattle in North America were brought here by the Spanish in the late 1400s and early 1500s. Longhorn cattle are descendents of those cattle that were bred with other cattle imported from the Canary Islands by way of Portugal.

Mineral Bluff, Georgia
The home site of Caleb and Christine Quinn is an actual town in the mountains of northern Georgia abutting the border of North Carolina and ten miles from Tennessee. It is also the home of this novel's author.

casualties and three days later Robert E. Lee surrendered to Ulysses S. Grant at Appomattox Court House.

Terry's Rangers
Terry's Rangers was a regiment commanded by Benjamin Franklin Terry. The regiment was known as the 1st Texas Ranger Regiment and they fought for the Confederacy. Terry's Rangers saw action from Kentucky to North Carolina.

Comanche raids in Texas during the Civil War
When Texas joined the Confederacy its soldiers went east to do battle against the Union forces. The federal army posts in Texas were abandoned giving the Comanche carte blanche to begin raiding and regaining the territory they had lost to the Texas settlers. The Texas frontier retreated over 100 miles during the Civil War due to the raiding Comanche.

George Humphrey Tichenor George Tichenor was a physician who introduced antiseptic surgery as a physician for the Confederate States of America. After the war he patented an antiseptic made from alcohol, oil of peppermint, and arnica that was widely used to treat wounds.

Train from Galveston to Houston via causeway
A 10,000 foot railroad trestle "causeway" was built across Galveston Bay in 1860 providing service from Galveston to Texas City and then on to Houston. During the Civil War Fort Hebert was built to help protect the railway. The Galveston-Houston railroad carried Confederate troops and munitions to Galveston Island via the causeway to break a Union blockade of Galveston Island in 1861.

Train from Houston to Millican
The Houston and Texas Central Railroad Company made Millican (now Bryan, Texas) its northernmost terminus in 1860. It served as a vital distribution center for freight and Confederate troops throughout the Civil War.

Fanthrop Inn
The Fanthrop Inn located near Anderson, Texas was a stagecoach stop southeast of Millican. It became a stagecoach inn when the Fanthrop family opened their home to serve as a guest house for passengers riding the stagecoaches west from East Texas.

Liberty Hill as stage stop
The Liberty Hill stage coach stop was run by John and Amelia Bryson. It began as a stop for the military stage coach line from Austin, Texas. The military coaches would stop at the spring on the Bryson property to water their horses. The military drivers convinced Bryson of the need for a public stage coach stop at Liberty Hill.

Custer at Liberty Hills
After the Civil War, George Custer became commander of the cavalry in Texas. His duty was to assist with the transition of the Texas government during

"I'll be damned," said an amazed Caleb as he looked through his scope, "he's using a camouflage cape like we do."

Now Caleb stared even more intently through the scope and started to softly touch the rifle's trigger with his finger. At that moment another very small part of the ground shifted ever so slightly. That puzzled Caleb until he realized it was the barrel of a rifle and it was being pointed almost directly at him. Caleb immediately fired at the less than perfect target, knowing he himself had been detected and if he missed he'd be dead before he could get off a second shot.

A moment after he fired the single shot, the camouflaged Confederate rifle slipped slowly to the ground. Caleb, moving immediately to his left was tempted to fire a second shot, but held back, fearing he might be targeted if there was a second shooter. After a length of time, satisfied there was no second sniper, he crawled slowly through the stand of trees until he reached a gully which he followed to the bottom of a small rise lying between himself and the Confederate sniper.

After waiting for several minutes and detecting no movement, Caleb then circled around until he was about fifty yards from the Confederate's position. He was about to place a few more shots into the area when a voice spoke out of the shadows of the trees.

"That you sharpshooter?"

The voice sounded weak and had a distinctive accent. Caleb was surprised his presence and identity had been so accurately detected. Rolling behind a tree trunk he replied, "Yes, it's me."

After a brief silence the voice answered, "I reckoned it was you."

Pausing for a moment, the voice continued, "You may as well come on in, shooter. I'm done for and wouldn't mind some company before I go."

"Are you alone?" asked Caleb, not sure what this crazy talk was leading to, and wanting to stall for time to figure it out.

"I'm alone," came the reply.

For some strange reason Caleb believed the man's words were truthful. Maybe because he sounded tired, too tired to lie, the voice of a dying man.

"I'm coming in," said Caleb, not sure he wasn't heading into a trap, but forced by his curiosity and a grudging respect for a fellow soldier and sniper to find out one way or the other.

Moving from tree to tree he crossed the remaining distance to the Confederate sniper, walking instead of crawling but keeping low as possible. As he moved he could feel the hair rising on his arms and legs. "No need for you to be worried, young man" said the voice. "My part in this man's war is over."

A minute later Caleb was standing over the Confederate sniper who was sitting up against the trunk of a large sycamore tree. A telescope-mounted Sharps rifle lay over his lap. There was blood on the rifle.

"You with Berdan's boys?" asked the dying man.

Caleb could see that the wounded man was at least twice his age and in considerable pain. A few drops of frothy blood were on the man's lip and he was breathing in long slow breaths. His face, thin and pale, seemed serene, as if he was totally at peach with the situation.

"Yes," Caleb replied, "I'm Sergeant Quinn, 1st New York Regiment."

The wounded man looked up at Caleb, studying his face, "Heard about you. Some say you've got thirty kills. If that's true, I reckon I'm thirty-one."

"I don't count what I'm not proud of," replied Caleb, "I regret taking any life, but that's what we soldiers are bound by our duty to do."

It wasn't an apology, but Caleb felt the dying man would at least understand, if not appreciate, the truth of those words. It was not a time for men to lie.

"Don't be sorry, shooter," said the man seeing the regret on Caleb's face. With a little luck on my part it could have been you instead of me, but that's the price of war and always will be."

A sudden wracking cough interrupted his words. When it stopped, he wiped off his mouth and then continued, "By the way, I'm Joe Pokusa, from Texas."

"You the one they call the 'Ghost'?"

"I've heard that said, and now I guess it's about to be as much truth as made up."

A long moment of silence passed between the two men who were in some strange way forming a bond, a bond that fighting men sometimes feel even for those on the other side. Even for the very men who had just minutes before tried to kill them.

"Son," said Pokusa, "I'm going to make an unusual request of you. One you may not understand, but I'm hoping my best you will.

You've killed me, so I reckon that maybe you owe me, at least if you're the man of honor I think you are."

"I'll see that you're buried proper, if that's what you want. I'd do that for any man, especially a soldier."

"It's not that at all," said the "Ghost" now speaking with obvious effort. "When I'm gone, you can leave me here or have me carted off to some graveyard. I'd be proud to share the ground with other soldiers, blue or grey. What I do want from you will take you a long way from here, clear to Texas. I got a ranch and two daughters there, not too far from Liberty Hill, Texas. That's in the hill country. My older daughter's Ann, the younger, Christine. I think from what they wrote me some months back they got big troubles with outlaws and Indians and could use somebody like you to help them. I might wish it could be different, but I got nobody else to ask."

"So you think I'm the man for the job?" asked Caleb, wondering how someone who hardly knew him could place such trust in him.

"Call it a hunch," said Pokusa, "but I think the good Lord sent you here. You're a strong man, a good fighter, a man who'll fare well against long odds, if that's what he runs into. Isn't that what all us "shooters" are about, taking the long odds?"

Getting no quick reply from Caleb, he then shakily reached into his coat and removed a well-worn black leather wallet with brown rawhide stitching.

"There's a letter in here from my girls. That's how I know they got troubles. You can use it as an introduction when you meet them. They're something else, my daughters are. You'll like them, but try not to get them angry."

Reaching once again into his coat he removed a plain looking brass locket. Opening it and placing it in Caleb's hand, he said, "These are my girls. Ann's on the left and Christine is on the right. No man could ever be prouder of daughters than I am of them."

Taking the locket in his hand Caleb stared at the images of two young girls, perhaps sixteen and seventeen. Both seemed ladylike and beautiful. The younger one seemed to closely resemble her father.

"Now you know what they look like. Go there, find them, and, if they don't need help, you'll at least have gotten a good look at two of the prettiest girls in Texas."

Caleb gave the dying father a half smile before replying, "I believe you, and given that I've got no plans for after the war ends, I think I'd like to go to Texas."

The promise was in both Caleb's words and eyes.

Coughing heavily, Pokusa said, "Quinn, I don't hold all that much store in words, but if you'll give me your hand on it, I know you'll do your best to keep that promise."

Caleb reached for the hand Joe offered. It was when Joe reached for Caleb's hand that he noticed the revolver lying between Joe's legs. Joe saw the glace Caleb's gave the gun.

"Yes, it's loaded," he said, "and yes, I could have killed you."

"I'd ask why you didn't," replied Caleb, "but I already know the answer."

"And that would be...?" Joe's voice was now down to a whisper.

"You're tired of the senseless killing, tired of taking the life out of good men, and you believe no man should die alone. I also think you believe that sometimes in war there is a sense of honor between enemies as strong as that among friends.

As he spoke, Caleb realized his words were, in fact, a description of his own feelings.

Looking down, Caleb could only wonder if his new friend had died before he'd heard all the words just spoken.

After taking several hours to bury his friend and enemy in a shallow grave dug out with his knife and bare hands, Caleb left the woods and headed back toward Farmville and his men. He'd buried the Confederate's weapons with him but left his hat above ground as a marker.

As Caleb returned to the Union lines he saw an Army of the Potomac cavalry regiment moving quickly toward Anderson's Confederate forces. To his surprise they were led by the same yellow-haired officer who'd saved his life at Little Bethel. He was amazed that any cavalry officer who led first and led from the front as he seemed to do was still alive.

Arriving back at camp, Caleb learned that his men had done themselves proud. They successfully eliminated an unprecedented number of high ranking officers including an astounding eight Confederate generals. In the melee that followed thousands of confused and sometimes leaderless Rebels were wounded, killed, or captured, in part due to the damage his sharpshooters had inflicted on the Rebel's leadership. After two more days of fighting, the South had lost the last great battle of the war.

Three days later, on April 9, 1865, at Appomattox Courthouse General Robert E. Lee surrendered to General Ulysses S. Grant.

The war, now over for Caleb and Berdan's sharpshooters, left him with the question of what to do with the rest of his life. The answer was in the locket and wallet carried in his pants pocket.

Part 4

But I have promises to keep,
And miles to go before I sleep...
                    ~Robert Frost, a poet

Chapter 30 Texas

Several months later after the Holladay's Overland Express stagecoach rolled into Liberty Hill, a dusty Caleb and two other passengers were left standing in the street in front of a brown two-story building with a sign that read *Bryson's Saloon and Hotel*. The trip had been long and hard but had been beneficial in that it gave Caleb time to forget some of the horrors of war, horrors he hoped he'd left behind forever.

A week earlier, after arriving by steamer in Galveston, he took the Houston and Henderson Railroad train across the causeway to the mainland and then on to Houston where he boarded a Houston and Texas Central Railroad train to Millican in Brazos County. After crossing the Navasota River by ferry, he traveled on to the Fanthrop Inn at Anderson where he boarded the stagecoach to Liberty Hill. Having finally arrived at his destination, he took a minute to stretch out his cramped muscles before carrying his cloth bag and his poacher's cape through the building's swinging doors. The rifle stayed slung over his shoulder, ready for use if needed.

Giving his eyes a moment to adjust from the bright outdoor sun to the shadowy room, he moved to the bar and set his bag and cape on the rough cut planks that made up the floor.

"What can I get ya?" asked the bartender as he wiped his hands on a soiled apron.

"I'd like a room and a hot meal if you have them, and some directions to Joe Pokusa's ranch."

The bartender, giving the stranger an appraising and somewhat unfriendly look, replied "If you've got six bits, I've got a room now that the cavalry's gone off to Austin, and there's plenty of hot chili, cornbread and molasses in the back. As for the directions to the Pokusa ranch, let's see what we can do for you."

Placing both hand on his suspenders, the bartender looked toward the back of the room, and in a louder than necessary voice hollered, "Hey, can any of you hombres tell this here Yankee stranger how to get to Poke's place?"

For several moments a hushed silence fell across the room. Caleb could feel the sudden tension as if it were a cloak thrown over his shoulders. The few men sitting at the tables in the front of the room didn't move other than to turn their heads toward Caleb and the bartender.

Then, at the far back of the room, two men, moving at the same time, got out of their chairs and wordlessly approached Caleb. Caleb was not altogether surprised that their approach didn't look all that friendly. Both men looked to be in their early to mid twenties. The shorter of the two wore a single pistol on his right side, slung low and tied down. His boots were worn at the toe and his clothes had seen better days. A Mexican sombrero hung on his back. He had intelligent-looking green eyes set deep in a sunburned face topped by long light brown hair. To Caleb he looked all cowboy, tough and competent, but not particularly menacing.

Stopping less than six feet from Caleb, he announced, "I'm Tip Thomas, and if you've got business at Poke's maybe you should tell me what it is."

Now he looked menacing.

Caleb felt no need to hurry his reply, and took the time to look closely at the second man who had moved casually but with deliberation five feet to Caleb's right and close to the bar, effectively flanking him. He was dressed in a crisp white shirt and a black Mexican style suit with silver conchos running down the side of each pant leg. It was a suit which would have cost an ordinary working man a year's pay. He was armed with fancy crossed holsters holding twin Colts. His straight black hair and thin but handsome face revealed his Spanish ancestry. This hombre looked both tough and menacing. It was also evident from the position he'd taken next to the bar that he was a careful man.

"Yes, senor, tell us why you seek Poke's rancho," said the man in black.

Shifting his gaze back to the cowboy calling himself Tip, Caleb broke his silence.

"Unless you care to tell me why you want to know, my business at the Pokusa ranch is and will remain private."

"Then we have a problem," replied Tip, "because you got the look of trouble and unless you can prove you've got legitimate business there you ain't going to Poke's place any time soon."

Once again, Caleb hesitated before answering, glancing back to his right as he did so. The brief look revealed that the Spaniard was not looking at Caleb's face as most men would have done but at his hands.

"This man," thought Caleb, "has been here before and knows to watch the hands and not the eyes."

From the subtle body language he was giving off, Caleb knew the man was a gunfighter, and like a coiled snake, ready and wanting to strike at the first sign of a hostile move on his part.

"That is a dangerous man who knows his business and takes no chances," thought Caleb.

Not intimidated but wishing to avoid a confrontation that didn't need to happen, Caleb returned his gaze to the man named Tip.

"I can understand your concern. If you must know, I met Poke during the war. We were friends and I was there when he died. He had heard about Indians and outlaws raiding unchecked through the Texas hill country and he was worried about his daughters' safety. Before he died, he asked me to come out here after the war and make sure they're safe. That's what brought me to Liberty Hill, and I'll say nothing more on the subject until I've heard more from you."

"We're also friends of Poke and his family," said Tip, "and would like you to show some proof of what you say."

"I have this," said Caleb, reaching slowly with his left hand for the leather wallet in the inside pocket of his coat.

Opening the wallet he took out the letter Poke had given him and gave it to Tip, making no mention of the locket that was also kept in the same coat pocket. After taking several minutes to carefully read the letter, Tip handed it back.

"I know Ann's handwriting, and that's it," he added with a voice that had lost its hostility, "I don't figure you to have her letter unless Joe wanted you to. Sorry for the questions, but me and Dos kinda look out for the girls' safety."

Caleb could feel the tension between the three of them disappearing, as even the gunfighter to his right seemed to relax ever so slightly.

"In that case, my name is Caleb Quinn and I'm pleased to meet you."

Extending his hand to Caleb the cowboy said, "Pleased to meet you, and like I said, I'm Tip. I'm also the lucky fiancé of Ann."

A proud smile crossed Tip's face as he uttered the words.

Looking to his left, he added, "This here's Emilio Baca, but his friends call him Dos."

"Dos?" asked Caleb, knowing it meant two in Spanish and thinking he might be called that because of the twin guns he wore.

"Yeah, his daddy was Emilio Baca senior. Early on Dos didn't like being called Junior, like what happens to most boys around here named after their daddies, said it sounded too Anglo. So since we been kids, he's been Dos."

"Pleased to meet you," said Caleb glancing at Dos but not offering his hand. He somehow knew it wouldn't be accepted.

Unlike Tip, Dos continued to look hard at him and, as Caleb suspected, he did not offer to shake hands.

Looking almost apologetic for his friend's attitude, Tip said, "Me and Dos will be heading for Poke's ranch in the morning. You're certainly welcome to tag along if you want. In the meantime we'll be playing some draw poker at the back table later tonight. We found us a couple of greenhorns ready to be plucked, so if you got nothing better to do you're sure welcome to join in the plucking."

With a mischievous smile at Caleb, he added, "Taking money from three greenhorns is even more fun than taking it from two."

"This greenhorn just might give you that opportunity," said Caleb, aware that it was now probably too late to ride out to the Pokusa ranch, "but being the greenhorn I am, I'll need to clean up and get a bite to eat before I start turning my money over to you two card sharks."

"Good," said Tip, "see you then…and on second thought, I ain't quite sure about you being a greenhorn."

"We'll see," was Caleb reply. "Nice meeting you."

As Caleb approached the stairs leading to his room, he could hear the pleasant patter of rain hitting on the building's tin roof.

Two hours later, after changing into fresh clothes and eating a better than expected meal which included a very sweet slice of pecan pie, Caleb joined Tip, Emilio, and two other 'greenhorns' at the table. Both men were dressed in Eastern style clothes and had the pale faces of men unaccustomed to working outdoors. One, who was well-dressed and looked to be in his late forties, had a bulbous red nose, a thin wisp of hair hanging in his face, and smiling eyes. The other, a considerably larger well-muscled man, appeared to be about half the other man's age, was shabbily dressed in old pants and an overly large jacket. To some men they might have looked like sheep ready to be sheared, Caleb suspected differently.

During the first hour, Caleb stayed in only a few of the larger pots, content to win a little or lose a little while studying the players at the table. Looking at his money he was not surprised he had lost about twenty dollars. He knew Tip and Dos had each lost at least twice that amount.

Over the next hour Dos stayed silent as his money slowly dwindled away but not Tip.

After losing a modest pot to the older of the two men, he tossed his losing hand to the table and declared in a voice filled with disgust, "Just ain't my night. About all I seem to get are second-best hands and second-best hands get mighty expensive in a hurry."

It was true, Caleb knew. He also knew why Tip and Dos had lost slowly but consistently to the men sitting on either side of them. His turn to deal, Caleb reached for the loose cards.

"Tip, ol' pal, maybe I can deal you a winner," he said as he began to shuffle the cards.

Shuffling for longer than usual Caleb then dealt out five cards to each player.

Dos, sitting on his left, looked at his weak cards and passed.

The younger of the greenhorns on Dos' left said, "I'm in," and tossed two dollars on the table.

Tip, with a look of disgust, folded, and the older man on Caleb's right declared, "Your two and two more."

After taking a long moment to consider his hand, Caleb dropped four dollars on the table.

"Call," he said, sounding reluctant.

His call was followed by that of the younger man who was sitting directly across from Caleb. He then took two cards. The older gentleman examined his hand and smugly announced, "I'll play these."

Caleb merely glanced at him, "Three for me," and quickly dealt himself three cards.

"Your bet," he said to the younger man who now spent a long moment looking at his cards.

By most people's playing standards the man would almost certainly pass to a pat hand. Caleb was not at all surprised when instead two more of the younger man's dollars hit the center of the table.

The older man examined his cards and took a long look at the two other players, "I'll go your two and five more," he said putting seven dollars in the pot.

Without hesitation, Caleb reached for his stack of silver dollars, "I'll see that and raise ten dollars." He then added seventeen dollars to the money on the table.

The younger man studied his cards, then looking first at Caleb and then at the older man, he slowly turned his cards face down and slid them to the center of the table.

"Too rich for me," he said, looking disappointed.

The older man hardly able to hide a grin of triumph said, "And ten more to you, my friend."

Caleb leaned back in his chair and looked coldly at first the younger man and then the older, "I call," he said, "but before I show my cards I want to tell both of you gentlemen that I don't abide playing with cheaters."

Starting to object, the Easterners were hushed by Caleb's cold voice, "Before you start talking lies let me explain what you've been doing. You don't cheat by manipulating or marking the cards. What you do is use some very clever signals to let each other know who most likely has the stronger hand. Then the weaker hand folds, or if he knows his partner's hand is very strong, he works to build up the pot knowing any money he loses will simply go into his partner's pocket. Over a period of time, working together like you do, your little system invariably guarantees a nice profit. That, gentlemen, is cheating."

"See here, what evidence do you have to support these scurrilous accusations?" said the older man, sweat starting to accumulate at the top of his lip.

"You see here," replied Caleb, "this is how I know. I dealt your partner three aces, then a pair of threes. I gave you a straight flush, king high, the second best hand in poker. You then signaled your partner to raise. He did so, modestly building up the pot for you. When the bet next came around to him he folded a full house, aces over threes. Imagine that! He folded when by all the odds he was going up against a losing flush, a straight, or a weaker full house, along with my very chancy three card draw. That doesn't happen in an honest game."

"You," Caleb continued, looking at the older man, "were all too happy to raise into a three card draw. Easy money, you thought, knowing how very strong your hand was. Now, here's my proof."

Reaching across the table, Caleb turned over the younger player's folded hand. It was a full house, aces over threes, exactly as Caleb had described it.

Caleb looked at Dos and Tip, "Can you boys think of anybody, except a cheat working with a partner, who would fold such a strong full house?"

Reaching to his right, Caleb was about to take the cards out of the older man's hand, but before he could Tip slammed the man's hand on the table and turned the cards face up. They were all diamonds, nine through king.

"Nice hand," Caleb said, "but not good enough."

Slowly, one card at a time, Caleb flipped over his cards. He showed five spades, ten through ace, making a Royal Flush, the unquestioned best hand in poker.

Across from him the younger man leaned back in his chair and reached for the Derringer hidden in his waistband, but before he could withdraw it he found himself looking down the barrel of Caleb's colt. The barrel was only inches from the tip of the man's nose.

"Being as you won money by cheating, and people like Tip and Emilio here, who work hard for their money, and aren't all that fond of losing to cheaters, I suggest both of you be kind enough to return their money and mine. After that, I believe the two of you should walk over to the jail house, tell the sheriff you got caught cheating at cards, and then request he reward you for your new-found honesty by letting you spend the next week as paying guests in his jail."

"I like your idea," said Tip, "at least the part about them staying in jail for a while, but that first part you mentioned needs a bit of fixin'."

"What do you have in mind?" asked Caleb, certain from the look on Tip's face it would be interesting.

"You told them to walk to the jail," answered Tip, "men walk but snakes crawl. I say our cheating friends here should crawl all the way to the jail."

"I think my friend Tip has an excellent suggestion," said Dos, as he jerked the younger of the cheaters to his feet, relieved him of his Derringer, and led him not so gently out the front door.

Tip, following Dos' example, did the same to the older man. Both cheaters ended front side down, sprawled in the mud and not just a little of the horse droppings that had been deposited by the saloon's hitching rail.

A minute later, Caleb, Tip, and Emilio stood on the saloon porch watching the cheaters, encouraged by a shot from one of Dos' colts painstakingly crawl through the rain and mud toward the jail. The sheriff, hearing the shot, emerged from the jail house door gun in hand, ready for trouble. Only after hearing the story from Tip did he put his gun away and invite the mud-laden men into his "hotel cárcel," as he called it.

"Well gentlemen," said Caleb, "unless you can think of something better to do, and I don't imagine it could get any better than this, I'd like to get some sleep so I can be ready to head for the Pokusa ranch at first light."

"We'll join you at Webber's Livery just after sunrise," said Tip. "You'll need a horse and saddle, and he's got both."

"I'll be there," said Caleb, and with a good night wave headed for the stairs leading to his room.

After watching Caleb get to the landing and disappear to the right, Tip turned to Dos.

"Did you see what I saw?" he asked. "He pulled iron from that shoulder holster awfully fast. He just might even be as fast as you."

"I don't think so," said Dos, his voice revealing no emotion, "but, quién puede decir, maybe someday we'll find out."

Chapter 31 Poke's Place

The morning sun had just begun to burn away the previous night's rain when Tip, Dos, and Caleb entered the stables. They were greeted warmly by Rags Webber, the hunched over, toothless and ancient-appearing proprietor.

"Mornin' Tip, mornin' Dos, you two have a nice visit in Austin?"

"Not bad at that," replied Tip, "but it would have been a bit easier on us if ol' Dos here hadn't gotten into an argument with a fella who referred to Mexicans as 'pepper bellies.' Bein' as how Dos ended the argument with his fists and boots we were obligated to spend an extra day in Austin courtesy of the Travis County sheriff."

"I wondered why you two got back yesterday instead of the day before," said Rags. By the way, I heard what you did last night with them Easterners. To tell the truth it was a nice piece of work. I couldn't a done better my own self."

"Give Caleb here most of the credit for that," said Tip, with a nod toward Caleb.

Rags gave Caleb a quick look, much the same way a man would evaluate a horse he was looking to buy. He knew horses a lot better than he knew men, but he knew enough about men carrying Sharps rifles to believe the man standing in front of him was long way from being a greenhorn.

"Pleased to meet you and I suppose since you came in on the stage, you'll be needin' somethin' to put a saddle on?"

Instantly liking the man, but not enough to open himself up to a bad bargain, Caleb replied, "I need a good horse and a saddle with a rifle scabbard, but so far all I've seen are three broken down nags in your corral and some dried up saddles. I was hoping for better."

"Maybe I can do better," said Rags, who then turned and headed to the rear of the stable on two outrageously bowed legs.

A moment later he returned leading a good-looking buckskin mustang gelding that looked plenty big enough to carry a man of Caleb's size and tough enough to take any trail. On its back was a worn but quality-made saddle, such as Caleb had requested. The buckskin had been behind the stable and out of sight because as Tip explained, "Some of Rags' horses didn't always come his way with a legit bill of sale."

184

Ten minutes later, after Dos and Tip had saddled their horses which they'd kept at Rags' stable while they took the stage to Austin, Rags and Caleb had mutually agreed that forty dollars was a fair price for the gelding and another five for the saddle. Having completed the deal, all three men mounted up but were stopped by Rags before they could ride out.

"Thought I'd pass on somethin' before you leave. You fellas need to keep a sharp eye out ifin' you're headin' west of the Blanco toward Poke's place. Fella came in here a coupla days back and tol' me the Comanche been raidin' hard out toward Bandera and Kerrville."

"Thanks for the warning, Rags. We'll keep an eye out." replied Tip.

"From the talk the raiding party's bein' headed by Toad,"Rags shouted as the three men rode off.

Caleb looked at Tip whose face had suddenly taken on a more serious, concerned look, "He said Toad. Is that someone to look out for?"

"With both eyes scared and as wide open as you can get them," said Tip. "His name might not make him sound like much, but he is bad, real bad. I've seen his handy work and I don't ever want to see it again. Even before the war he was leading raids from Texas all the way up to the Oklahoma badlands. The only people he ever spares are women and sometimes young female children he either sells or ransoms. Anyone or anything else: men, boys, dogs, mules, he kills them all, and most are only too glad to die after he gets through playing 'skin the rabbit' with them. If we see him, and I hope we don't, you'll know him by the big Palomino stallion he rides. More than once that horse saved Toad's scalp because there ain't a horse in the whole of the state can stay with him. He's outrun and outlasted the horses of every Ranger or cavalryman ever tried to catch him, to the point that now when they see him, they just chase him for a while and then let him go."

Then pausing and looking at Caleb he added, "Besides, it ain't always smart to try to catch somethin' you might have trouble letting go of."

As Caleb listened to Tip's words he couldn't help but think back to Ireland, the Waringtons, and the unprovoked cruelty they dispensed.

"I guess purely evil men can be found just about anywhere."

"I don't know about that," replied Tip, "but from what I've heard from some old Ranger friends of mine, Pasavayio, which is Toad's

185

Comanche name and really means frog, might have had good reason for his hatred."

Dos, who had been silently sitting on his horse, suddenly cut into the conversation.

"I heard much the same story from my father," he told them, looking first at Tip and then settling his gaze on Caleb. It was back in 'forty-six and Toad's Quohadi tribe was camping peacefully on the southern end of the Pecos River when they got hit by a combined force that included Mexicans, Texans, Kiowas, and even a few Frenchmen and Apaches. The Quohadi had come to trade horses, but what they got was a massacre. Toad's people, including all of his family, were pretty much wiped out."

Looking at Caleb, Tip cut back in, "It was about a year or two later stories started coming out of Mexico and parts of west Texas and the New Mexico territory, stories of a lone Comanche boy making brutal raids on farms and ranches. Seems no one ever saw anything of him, but the boy-sized footprints he left behind after he butchered and burned anyone unlucky enough to get in his way told the tale. Over the years I guess his tracks got big enough."

"Sounds to me like he does have good reason to hate just about everybody," said Caleb thinking about the British and knowing him and Toad shared a similar history and a similar, but not exactly a like hatred. Toad hated just about every Texan, Mexican, and Indian, while he reserved his hatred for the English but not all of them.

Then with an urgency he hadn't felt before Rags' comments, Tip kicked his mount in the ribs and headed west at a fast pace. He knew that since the early part of the war Poke's place sat on the edge of what had become Comanche raiding grounds. The Comanche troubles really got serious when Terry's Texas Rangers went off to fight for Texas and Jeff Davis. Now the same area was being guarded by only a few Union troops who didn't know nothing about fighting Comanche, Kiowa, or even a fat squaw for that matter. He also knew Ann, Chris, and their grandma were alone at the *Circle P*.

Leaving Liberty Hill behind, the three men rode for two hours before stopping to rest and water their horses. The place they chose to stop was under a group of cypress trees growing along the bank of a clear running river.

After taking a long drink and splashing water from the river on his face, Caleb looked up at the worried face of Tip Thomas. He knew the cowboy was concerned about the safety of the Pokusa girls.

"How much further 'til we reach the ranch?" asked Caleb.

"My place is about an hour from here, and then it's another thirty minutes to Poke's place."

"Is the country between here and there as pretty as what we just passed?" asked Caleb, hoping to get Tip's mind off thoughts of raiding Comanche coming down on the Pokusa ranch.

"It is, and it doesn't change much for the next few miles," said Tip, "just more easy rolling hills, more wildflowers, a lot of clear streams and rivers, and most of the land filled with good grass being eaten up by a bunch of ornery longhorn cattle wanting to stick a horn in us cowboys. After that, out by Poke's place, it gets a lot flatter and drier and not what you'd call pretty, unless you're from Texas."

"You can thank my ancestors for those beautiful longhorns you'll see," said a smiling Dos, "as well as for the good horses you have under your flat Anglo butts."

"Well," said Tip jokingly, "at least the cows make for good dog meat and steaks a man can use to shingle a house with."

"True," said Dos, "and speaking of food, we need to make tracks if we want to reach Poke's rancho in time for some of Gram's cooking."

"Gram?" asked Caleb.

"You'll meet Gram," said Tip. "She's Poke's mother-in-law and the best person and cook in the whole of the hill country. After I lost my ma to the small pox, the same outbreak that killed the girls' ma, she practically raised me right along with Ann and Christine."

Within seconds all three men were back in the saddle, and an hour later they crested a hill overlooking Tip's ranch. Caleb could see what looked like a run down, one-room ranch house, a small corral, a dilapidated barn, and a few ramshackle outbuildings. The only sign of an animal was a red-tailed hawk looking down from the roof of the barn, hoping to spot an easy meal.

Pulling to a stop Tip said, "It ain't much but with luck and some plain ol' hard work I figure in a year or two I can shape it up into a place fit for me and Ann. What I'm really hoping for is with the war over somebody'll lay train tracks out this way. Someday, somebody's gonna make a lot of money if he can use the railroad to ship longhorn cattle to the eastern markets. That's why over the next two years I'm planning on puttin' my *Flying H* brand on every mangy longhorn I can get a rope on."

"Why the *Flying H*?" asked Caleb who would have expected a brand something more like the *Flying T*.

"My mother's name was Helen, so my pa just naturally called the place the *Flying H*."

Kicking their horses into a fast gallop, the three riders then continued their way west toward Poke's place, following what now could just barely be thought of as a trail.

Not far from their destination Caleb suddenly reined in the buckskin and said, "Hold up, I see something."

Dismounting, he walked several feet back down the trail and stepped into the high grass on his left.

"Unless your longhorns are prone to wearing horseshoes, I'd say a good size number of horses and men passed through here. They even tried to brush out the hoof marks after they crossed. My guess is they didn't want anyone to know they were here or where they're going."

Dos and Tip dismounted and looked over the area Caleb had inspected, surprised that they had missed what Caleb, a stranger to the land and presumably not familiar with looking for tracks, had spotted from horseback. After examining the area it was now also apparent to them that someone had tried hard to straighten out the grass where a line of riders and horses had passed. It was clear to all three men that the riders were up to no good.

Dos was the first to speak, "Twenty horses or more, some shod and some not. It's got to be a Comanche raiding party, and from the looks of the tracks one of the riders could be Toad."

"Seems for sure they're heading southwest," said Tip, "probably planning to cross the border somewhere south of Del Rio."

"How serious of a threat might they be?" asked Caleb of Tip.

"It could be just a few Comanche with a bunch of stolen horses, but it could be very serious if they've picked up any captives, especially if the captives are women or children. The captives, unless they're lucky enough to be rescued before they cross the border, will be in for a very rough time."

Heading for his horse Tip said, "Enough of my jabber. We need to get movin'."

They had been back on the trail for less than a minute when Dos spotted a large picnic basket just off the edge of the trail.

"I know that basket," he said, "it's Christine's."

Without another word being said the three riders kicked their horses into a dead run for the Pokusa ranch.

When they were within sight of the ranch they slowed their horses to a trot, worried they might ride into a Comanche ambush.

Caleb could see the ranch house only a few hundred yards away and quickly realized it had been carefully built with an eye for defense. The house was one-story high and made of square blocks of native stones which were about one foot in length and height. It was covered with a roof made of study logs chinked with straw-filled mud and covered by adobe shingles. The windows were about two feet high, but only inches wide, ideal gun ports for shooting through with a rifle or hand gun, but too small for an attacker to squeeze through. Several barrels of water stood to either side of the front door, undoubtedly to be used by the defenders in case of a fire or lengthy siege. The house was like a small fortress that could be adequately defended by only a few people. Caleb was impressed.

"Joe, you sure knew how and where to build a house," he said to himself, thinking of Pokusa.

As they came to a halt in front of the house a short and slightly overweight elderly lady emerged carrying a shotgun almost as long as she was tall.

"Gram," said Tip, trying not to unduly alarm the woman who had helped raise him, "good to see you."

Looking to the left and then to right and seeing no threat he nodded at Caleb, "This here is Caleb Quinn."

"Pleased to meet you, young man," said Gram. "Sorry about the shot gun but my eyes ain't what they used to be, and when I see riders coming toward the house I just naturally get itchy fingered."

Resting the butt of the shotgun on the ground she asked, "But why did you leave the girls behind?"

At her words Tip could feel his throat tighten and his stomach turn. "We didn't, I figured they was here," he answered.

"They ain't been here since yesterday afternoon," came the disheartening reply. "They wanted to be at your place, wanted to surprise you when you and Dos got back. They took a mess of food with them. I knew I shouldn't have let them go off on their own like that, but you know how stubborn they can be. When they didn't get back last night I figured you boys probably talked them into staying the night instead of riding back here at dark. I was hoping it was their horses I heard when you came riding in."

Looking up at Tip with worried eyes she said, "Tip, you figure the damned Comanche got my girls?"

Her words tore at the men because what she said and the girls' absence confirmed their worst fears.

Without waiting for Tip to tell Gram about the Comanche signs they had discovered, Caleb edged his horse over toward her.

"Ma'am, Tip and Dos know this country, and they know the Comanche. If the Indians do have them, we'll find them and get them back for you."

Addressing all three men in a stern tone of voice, Gram gave the kind of reply Caleb would have expected from a tough lady living in such an isolated and often dangerous land.

"Then shouldn't you be getting out looking for them instead of sitting here talking to a foolish old woman?"

"Don't you worry none, we'll be goin' soon enough," replied Tip, "but first we got to put together supplies to last a few days."

"Speaking of extra supplies," said Caleb, hitting on an idea, "I didn't see any as we rode in, but is there any way we can get three extra horses?"

"We got them," said Tip as he pointed toward the north, "you can't see it until you get up close but out there's a hundred or more acres of good grass and water inside a true box canyon. It's a mite unusual but it makes a good, safe, natural corral. What's left of Poke's horses are there. They ain't quite as good as what we're riding but they'll do for what I think you got in mind."

"What I'm thinking," replied Caleb, "is that we'll need to cover a lot of country in a short amount of time. I'm just thinking we can move faster if we go with two horses each and switch out when one gets tired. I believe it to be our best chance of catching up with the Comanche and rescuing the girls."

"I like your idea," replied Tip, "but catching up to them is only a small part of the problem. If the Comanche even think we're trailin' them they'll kill the girls and then split up, heading out in every direction they can. We've got to be extra careful because I promise you if we start chasin' them over open country and get spotted, the girls are as good as dead."

"Then," said Caleb, "it'll be up to you and Dos to figure where they're heading so we can get there first and put together some kind of ambush."

"I've been thinkin' on that," said Tip, "and unless I'm wrong they'd only head north if they intended to do more raidin', and with them already havin' at least two captives and a good sized string of horses I figure that won't happen. That leaves either west or south. To the west there's nothin' but hard country, little water, and a longer ride to Mexico or New Mexico. It's also Kiowa country, and the Comanche and the Kiowa ain't exactly on friendly terms, so it ain't likely they'll head that way. That leaves south or southwest like we saw back on the trail. It's the closest way to the border and for sure the way I'd go if I was them."

"Dos, I know you and some of your amigos have moved 'borrowed horses' through that country on your way to Mexico. Do you know the most likely route the Comanche would take and maybe a good place to cut them off?"

After thinking silently for a minute Dos answered, "I know for sure the route I'd take if for some reason I wanted to bring horses into Mexico without being seen. If they do take that route, I also know a good place we could set an ambush for them. It's a place not too many people know, but the Comanche definitely know it. It's a long deep canyon that's narrow on both ends but opens wider toward the middle. The canyon sits mostly below ground and is easy to pass right by without seeing if you don't know it's there. It makes for a good hidden camp during the day and has enough grass and water for the horses."

"How long to get there if we ride hard?" asked Caleb.

"Two days, maybe a bit more," answered Dos, "but if we ride to the northern end we'll leave signs the Comanche are sure to read. That would be the end of the girls and maybe us, too."

"Is there a way around, a good fast way to get to the other end without the Comanche figuring out we're on their trail?"

"We can cut straight south," said Dos, "and then turn west just south of the canyon and loop back to the southern entrance. It'll add more than twenty miles to the ride, but even at that if we're lucky we should be able to get there before the Comanche. They'll be moving the horses and their prisoners, and that should slow them up."

"Supposin' we do get there in time," said Tip, "how do the three of us manage to get the girls away from a Comanche raiding party without getting them and us killed? If it's Toad that's got them he won't just hand them over, at least not alive."

"You get me to the canyon in time," said Caleb, "and I'll take care of the Comanche."

"Big words, amigo," said Dos with a challenge in his eyes and voice, "but what do you know of such a fight?"

Looking straight into Dos' eyes Caleb shot back, "You'll just have to take my word for it, amigo, but it's the kind of fight I know best, the kind of fighting I've seen for the last four years."

"We shall see," said Dos, wondering if he might have underestimated this stone-eyed man who seemed to have so naturally put himself in command.

"Gram," said Tip to the old lady who had remained silent during their conversation, "if you'll put together food enough for us for a few days, me and Dos'll go get those horses we talked about. Caleb, if you don't mind, give Gram a hand getting' things packed up."

Two hours later, riding fresh horses and leading the others, the three grim-faced men headed south in a desperate race to find the Comanche and free the girls.

Chapter 32 Ambush

By the middle of the third day of hard riding Dos told them they were about twenty miles north and seven miles east of the southern tip of the hill country. South of that was nothing but a hundred or more miles of dry and barren country leading to an equally dry and barren Mexico on the other side of the Rio Grande.

After stopping briefly at a water hole to rest and feed the horses a few handfuls of grain, they decided to leave the spare horses there knowing that having fresh horses could come in handy...especially if they had Comanche hot on their tail. While gathering up brush for a make-shift corral, Caleb took the opportunity to ask Tip, "Do you think we've made up enough time?"

"Pretty sure," came the answer. The Comanche like to travel mostly at night so as not to be seen, and that slows them down, and like Dos said they're moving a lot of horses, and while I don't wish it on anybody, it would also help if they stopped to raid another ranch or two. That ain't likely though. 'Cause of Indian trouble there's damn few ranches left in this part of the country."

Pausing to look first to the north and then to the south he continued, "My guess is we'll be at the south end of the canyon a good five hours before they get there...if they get there."

"If they don't show up, I promise you I'll be going into Mexico after them," vowed Caleb.

Tip knew that neither he nor Dos would be going back unless they rescued the girls or at least found their bodies.

"Strong words," said Tip to the man he still knew so little about. "You and ol' Poke must have been pretty close for you to feel like that. Most men wouldn't risk so much, even for a friend."

"Let's just say I owe him, and let it go at that," said Caleb.

"Suits me," said Tip, but added, "it's still a lot to do for people you've never met and aren't kin to."

"Like I said," replied Caleb, "I owe him...and we need to get moving."

Three hours later arriving at their destination, they immediately entered the canyon and headed north.

The southern end of Bella Vista Canyon was about forty yards wide. The walls of the southern entrance started out at about twelve feet but rose to over eighty feet as the canyon wound its way north for about three miles where it opened up to a width of over three hundred yards. The floor of the canyon's opening was covered in either rock slabs or soft sand. Toward the middle and widest part the canyon the floor flourished from its stream's overflow and sprouted a fairly large area of thick green grasses. It was a perfect place for anybody moving horses to stop and make camp. It was also the place Caleb chose to spring his ambush.

Dismounting from the buckskin and bending down on one knee, Caleb used the loose sand to outline his plan to Tip and the skeptical Dos. The two Texans had figured on a surprise assault by all three of them with guns blazing. Neither of them imagined any one man would think he could ambush and then hold off a whole party of Comanche, but that was exactly the plan Caleb laid out.

"Run that plan by me one more time," said a doubting Tip, "I want to be sure I heard you right."

"Sure," said Caleb, "but we've only got time for one more go through. Then I've got some climbing to do, while you and Dos, after erasing any tracks we've left here, need to get into position."

"First of all, I think the Comanche, if they're as cautious and ambush wary as you've told me, will come through the canyon single file and with at least a twenty yard gap between riders. That would be their safest way to travel the gauntlet the cliff sides make. I don't know whether they'll have the horse herd up front or trailing, but I'm thinking trailing so they don't have to eat their dust."

Dos, looking up, asked in a voice almost dripping with sarcasm, "Then, according to your plan, you'll be up on the rim picking them off one by one as they come through? Is that right, amigo?"

"Something like that," replied Caleb, starting to get angry at his fellow rescuer.

"Quiet," said Tip, placing a hand on Dos' forearm, "let the man talk. We've got to get this right and we're wasting time."

Caleb continued, "When they come through, I'll take out whatever Indians are in front of the girls. Then I'll put shots to the rear of the girls' horses to start them running. Hopefully the girls'll be level-headed and quick enough to realize what's happening and get their horses moving toward you on a full run."

Then Caleb asked Tip and Dos, "Do you think the girls will have the sense to make a fast break for it once the shooting starts?"

"Both Ann and Christine were born and raised in this country," replied Tip. "They know near as much about horses and gunshots as you or me. When you start shootin', you can damn sure bet that if they can, they'll get their horses movin'."

"Good," said Caleb, "'cause that's when you and Dos break out of cover and go for the girls. Try to wait for them because I don't want you to have to ride back into that bunch of Comanche to get them."

Pausing to think, Caleb then added, "You'll need to wait out of sight about three hundred yards down from where I'm at on the rim. That should put you out of sight due to the bends in the canyon but still close enough to get to the girls before any Comanche catch up to them. When you hear the first shots, show yourselves, grab the girls, and head south out of the canyon. You'll also need to be ready to handle any Comanche that get past me. After that, ride hard to where we left the horses. Whatever you do, don't stay there long and don't turn back for me. Just stop long enough to water the horses and leave the buckskin out of sight so I've got something to ride when I get done here. I'll be taking the same way out of the canyon when I get through with the Comanche."

"Caleb," said Tip, "the easiest part of the trail, through the wide part of the canyon, will take the Comanche over toward the western wall. That's almost three hundred yards from where you'll be up on the rim. You think you're capable of makin' that kind of shot, hittin' movin' targets from an elevated position at three hundred yards or more?"

"I can and have done it," replied Caleb, "you just make sure you take care of the girls and I'll take care of the shooting."

"One thing you may have forgotten," said Dos, "there will still be an hour or more of daylight. We already told you the Comanche move at night."

"I remember what you said, but I'm betting that changes. It will be difficult even for them to get through the canyon at night. Besides, I'm thinking that by being down in the canyon they can go through it in daylight because they can move the captives and horses without being seen. Then, once they're through the canyon they'll plan on using the cover of the coming darkness to once again hide them as they move through open country."

"I hope you're right," said Dos. "It'll go hard for everyone if you're wrong."

Caleb did not miss the underlying threat in Dos' words, it was something to remember.

"Time to go," he said, slinging the Sharps over his back and heading to the canyon's steep eastern wall.

Caleb had removed the scope from the Sharps and put it in his saddle's rifle scabbard, confident he wouldn't need it for what he considered to be short-range shooting. He also felt certain he might need to fire at a very rapid rate, and that using the scope would take precious seconds longer to sight on his targets.

As Caleb studied the canyon wall looking for the best way to scale it, Tip walked over to him and shook his hand, certain beyond little doubt he'd never see Caleb alive again. Beyond a doubt this stranger who had so suddenly entered the life of him and his friends was about to die on the rim of Bella Vista Canyon.

"Whatever happens," Tip told himself, "if we rescue the girls it will be worth it, even if it costs all three of us our lives."

As Tip turned away to mount his horse, he told Caleb, "Good luck, my friend, shoot straight, and I'll see you back at the waterin' hole."

Looking down at Caleb he added, "Word of advice, if it's Toad we're chasin', and I'd bet on it, most likely he'll be ridin' up front. Get him first if you can 'cause the Comanche don't necessarily have a chief like most tribes, but he is their leader and killing'him first may slow them down until they find somebody else to take charge. Besides that, if Toad stays alive he'll most likely be after us all the way back to the Blanco.

"I'll make a special effort to see to it that he never leaves the canyon," said Caleb. "Now you two need to get moving…and good luck to you, too."

Turning to the high eastern wall he began climbing as Tip and Dos rode away slowly dragging sage brush behind them to cover their tracks.

For Caleb the climb proved less grueling than he had anticipated. The wall had any number of protruding rocks and cracks that he was able to use to get good hand and foot holds. It also helped that the wall's face was made up of hard rock and was dry and virtually crumble-free. Although he knew better than to let his concentration lapse while he was climbing, he couldn't stop from taking a few moments to think that Hung Fat had put him through climbing challenges that were just as difficult, if not more so.

Reaching the top and then standing up to survey the area Caleb was surprised by two things. The sun, which he hadn't been able to see from the canyon floor, was still an hour or more away from the horizon. The second surprise was that he could actually see all the way to the northern end of the canyon, and then another mile or so beyond it. If the Comanche approached in daylight there was a good chance he'd see them before they entered the canyon.

"Now I guess we find out if we chose the right route," he said to himself, knowing if they had guessed wrong they were unlikely to ever see the girls again, much less rescue them.

Putting his Sharps down near the edge of the rim, he took off his shirt and wrapped it around the field glasses hanging from his neck. He knew that by looking through the glasses in the direction of the sun beginning to sit low on the horizon he would run the risk of the Comanche seeing the sun's reflection off the lens. The shirt would cut the risk to almost zero.

For the next fifteen minutes Caleb scanned the country out past the canyon's northern end. He saw nothing. No movement anywhere except for two dust devils swirling across the dry land like dervishes and then vanishing almost as quickly as they formed. Still staring through the glasses ten minutes later he saw them. A long strung-out line of horses and riders, they emerged out of a hidden ravine and moved at a fast pace toward the canyon's north entrance which was still at least a mile away from them. As they got closer and out of the haze of heat waves rising from the ground, he could see the lead rider on a large palomino, followed by two other riders. Behind them he could just make out two figures in skirts, each riding their own horse. All told, he counted three riders in the lead, then two girls followed by two more riders, and five riders pushing the herd trailing up the rear.

"Good," he thought, "you riders in front just keep coming and stay in single file."

Bent low and returning to his rifle and the rolled up cape, he checked his ammunition in the Sharps and then carefully set aside a handful of cartridges within easy reach of where he intended to fire from. He then rolled out the cape and hood, leaving the lighter side out, and rubbed what little rock dust and dirt he could scrape together first on the cape and then on his face. When he was done, he was satisfied he and the cape were a very close color match to the walls of the canyon and the rock surface on the rim.

As he put on the cape he felt the first drops of rain starting to splatter the nearby rocks.

"May be good, may be bad," he thought. "It'll make shooting just a mite harder, but it might also make the Comanche keep their heads down as they ride. I just hope they get here while there's still enough light left in the canyon for me to clearly make them out."

Looking down at what would shortly be a shadow-covered floor he told himself, "No more looking toward the sun. Give your eyes every second you can to adjust to the low light down there."

As the minutes passed Caleb lay motionless underneath what had turned out to be a gentle rain, a rain that quickly turned to steam as it lay on the rocks heated by the day's scorching sun. Below him the water began to collect in small pools on the canyon's floor.

Then he heard it. Just the faintest sound of a walking horse splashing through a pool of water. A moment later a lone Indian rode into view and slowly walked his paint horse through the wide expanse of the canyon floor. Caleb sighted on him but let him go. He would do nothing until the girls entered the clearing. He watched unmoving as the rider and horse reached the end of the clearing, and after sitting still for a minute turned around and rode back, disappearing into the gateway from which he'd first emerged.

Caleb waited while trying to control his breathing, to become as relaxed and still as possible. He knew any movement, even a slight rise in the cape caused by an uncontrolled deep breath might give his presence away to a very sharp-eyed man, and any Comanche raised on the wide open plains would certainly be that.

Caleb was accustomed to using the cape amongst grass and trees, grass and trees that might be expected to move with a slight wind. Hiding, even camouflaged, among rocks demanded a greater degree of stillness simply because rocks did not move in the wind. Caleb knew that until the shooting started he had to blend perfectly into the unmoving rocky terrain.

Chapter 33 Toad

Long minutes passed before a palomino walked slowly into Caleb's view. Its rider looked to be short and stout with a rounded face covered in black and yellow stripes. The size of his head and the length of his well-muscled arms seemed as if they should have belonged to a man of much greater size, making him look as if he'd been put together from the parts of two or three men of different sizes. Stopping his horse after advancing only a few feet into the wide part of the canyon, the man he knew must be Toad sat motionless moving his oversized head neither left nor right.

"He's listening," thought Caleb, "he's cautious and smart, and he knows this is ambush country."

At that moment Caleb hoped Tip and Dos had muzzled their horses. The last thing he needed was for their horses to pick up the scent of the Comanche horses and then start talking to them.

Toad began turning his head very slowly from right to left, ignoring the light rain falling on his bronze-colored face. He then looked up and stared directly at the spot where Caleb was concealed.

Through his hood Caleb now had a full view of Toad's face. He had a thin slash-mark of a mouth, a short flat forehead, and what looked to be a severely hunched back. Caleb could not help but think back to the frightful gnomes and gargoyles his friends had talked about when he was a boy. Nothing they described was equal to the pure face and body of evil sitting on the palomino. Despite his reluctance to end a human life, Caleb imagined how good it would feel to send a bullet into that ugly face.

Then, without even looking to the western rim of the canyon, Toad casually turned his horse around and slowly made his way back toward the narrow entrance. Approaching it, he once again stopped and remained motionless, listening. Turning his head, he once more looked up in Caleb's direction.

"He can't know I'm here," thought Caleb, "nobody could, not at this distance, not with the naked eye."

But despite this certain knowledge, a cold chill still ran across his back.

"That man scares me," he told himself. "I can see how he has lived so long and has been impossible to catch or kill."

A second later Toad disappeared into the mist rising from the canyon floor as it warmed again after the rain.

Minutes passed before the Indian on the paint again rode into the open area. Seconds behind him a pinto carrying Ann appeared followed closely by Christine riding a blaze-faced sorrel. Wrapped around Christine's waist Caleb could see two skinny white arms.

"Jesus, Mary, and Joseph," he muttered, "she's got a third captive riding behind her. That could complicate things at a time when I damned sure don't need any complications."

Riding only a two horse-length behind Christine's horse was a Comanche on a brindled pony, followed closely by Toad.

Waiting until they were slightly more than halfway through the clearing, Caleb said to himself, "That's far enough."

Sighting carefully on the profile of the lead rider's body, he fired, sending a bullet just behind the Indian's left arm and into the deepest part of his chest.

Not waiting to see his target fall, Caleb next sighted on the canyon floor just past the hind legs of Christine's horse and fired two more quick shots. The sorrel reared up about a foot off the ground and then shot forward. Caleb could see the little girl behind the rider almost lose her grip. She would likely have fallen hard had not Christine reached back with her right arm and pulled the girl closer to her.

Ann's horse was almost as quick to move. With a yell and kick from the barefoot girl, her horse, after first prancing slightly sideways, took off, Ann's legs and feet frantically pounding against its sides.

The Indian on the brindle reacted at a speed that caught Caleb by surprise. He kicked his pony forward and to the right of the girls' racing horses, deliberately putting them between himself and the side of the rim where the shots were coming from. Caleb couldn't shoot at him or his horse without risking hitting the girls. All he could do was watch helplessly as all three horses, running almost side by side, raced to the end of the clearing and out of sight.

"He's yours now," said Caleb, thinking of Tip and Dos.

Caleb then shifted his sight to find Toad, but he was gone, vanished back into the canyon neck from where he'd emerged. For a split second Caleb kept the Sharps sighted only a few feet in front of the same neck from where the rest of the Indians would have to appear if they intended to pursue the girls, and of that happening he had little doubt.

"No," he told himself, "that's not how you lead a running horse, and they'll have their horses running full out when they emerge."

Making the correction, Caleb sighted his rifle so it would hit twenty feet to the left.

"Come on," he said, "come to me."

Down on the floor of the canyon the light was fast fading. Caleb knew the Indians had little time to wait unless they wanted to try to find the girls in the dark.

Suddenly the herd of horses, moving at a fast run as Caleb had anticipated, broke into the clearing. Caleb could see no riders, but he did see a rifle barrel appear from under one of the lead horse's neck. Before the hidden rider could find a target and fire, Caleb put a round into the horse's head. Horse and rider tumbled to the ground, throwing up a small cloud of sand, the rider crushed under his horse. Regretting what he had to do, Caleb was forced to shoot a second horse when he spotted another rifle barely peaking out from under its neck. The horse took several stumbling strides and then it, too, crashed to the ground, throwing off the rider. Caleb then took careful aim and put a bullet into the head of each downed Comanche.

To the south he could hear a series of shots coming from what he hoped were Tip's and Dos' pistols.

"So much for the one that got past," he told himself, hoping that Ann, Christine, and whoever the little girl was, were now being led to safety as fast as possible by Tip and Dos.

An eerie silence fell over the canyon while Caleb waited motionless under the cape, sweat beginning to gather on his face and neck.

"Patience," he told himself, wiping beads of sweat from his eyes, "three down and seven to go."

Two figures on foot suddenly darted for a group of large boulders lying at the base on the far side of the canyon. Caleb slowly swung the barrel of his rifle toward them, sighted on the lead figure and fired. The Indian jumped into the air and sent a loud scream echoing across the canyon even before he hit the ground.

"Four," counted Caleb.

Before Caleb could get off another shot the second runner dove behind a pile of dense high rocks. Caleb once again wiped the sweat from his eyes, wiggled slightly closer to the rim of the canyon, and sighted on the rocks where the Indian had disappeared. Between two of the larger rocks was an opening several inches wide. In that opening Caleb could see a bright red color, the same bright red color of the clothes worn by the Comanche. Taking his time he aimed between the rocks and fired. He saw the red between the rocks jerk, followed a moment later by a slow trickle of blood that seeped out of the crack between the rocks and ran into the ground.

"That should be five down, five to go," he thought.

Caught off guard by watching the flow of blood, Caleb was a fraction of a second late picking up on the rider that burst into the clearing. Swinging the Sharps he snapped off a shot but missed, the bullet chipping off a piece of the rock wall just beyond the rider. Now, taking his time he patiently sighted on the rider clinging to the side of his horse. Caleb was eighty feet above the Indian and from that height could see just enough of the rider's body clinging to the pony's side to give him a shot. When the Comanche was twenty feet from where the clearing closed in, he squeezed the trigger. The bullet nicked the back of the running horse, slammed into the rider's lower stomach, and burrowed upward into his body. The rider hit the ground headfirst and then lay squirming on his back, the blood from his wound quickly turning the grass around him from green to red. A second shot from Caleb's rifle then struck him in the mouth and exited out the back of his head.

"Six. Four left," Caleb registered in his mind as he sighted the Sharps back on the rocks sheltering the Indian he knew he'd wounded but wasn't sure he killed.

He waited, looking for any movement, but seeing only the small pool of blood. For ten minutes the canyon was still and quiet. Seeing nothing, Caleb was about to change his position on the rim when a shot rang out from below and a piece of rock flew up only inches from his head. Startled only slightly by the near miss Caleb slowly moved back away from the rim.

It was obvious from the shot that had just missed him, his place on the rim had finally been detected. Feeling even more sweat drenching his body Caleb thought, "Guess I don't have to worry any more about hiding," and removed the hood and cape. The touch of rain that had begun to fall again and the slight breeze spilling across the rim felt wonderful.

He then pushed the cape a few inches over the rim, just far enough he hoped, to let the Indian below see it, and think he was still in it. Scooting low on his belly, he took up another position, ten feet to the right of his original one. There he waited, hoping to do so for a long time, time enough to allow the girls to complete their escape. That hope vanished only seconds later.

The badly wounded Indian, the one wearing the red shirt, was still able to fight, but knowing he had little time before death took him, stood up and directed a rapid volley of shots toward Caleb's empty hood that was peeking over the rim.

"Got you," Caleb told himself and killed him with a shot to the chest.

"Three more to go," Caleb told the wind.

Caleb lay still for another ten minutes, his eyes fixed below waiting patiently for the remaining Comanche to show themselves when, for no explicit reason, words from the past entered his thinking.

"Boy," he heard Uriah's voice, "it ain't the Injuns you see that get ya killed, it's the ones ya don't see."

Shocked that he hadn't thought of it before, Caleb instantly realized the real danger was no longer in the canyon below but on the rim. Twisting his body quickly to the right and rolling onto his back so that he was now facing away from the rim, he was just able to get the Sharps pointed at the chest of an on-rushing Comanche no more than ten feet away. He pulled the trigger a split second before a lance tip was driven deep into his left leg, about six inches above the knee.

Caleb's shot hit the Indian squarely in the middle of his broad chest, a fatal shot, but not damaging enough to stop the Comanche's momentum from carrying him past Caleb and over the canyon's rim. He left his lance sticking out of Caleb's leg.

Silently wincing in pain, Caleb was staring at the lance when he saw the shadow-like figure of another Indian coming from his left. Again his Sharps spurted death, the bullet hitting the Indian just below the heart, tearing away muscle and bone, and stopping him dead in his tracks.

Fighting through the pain in his leg Caleb counted, "Eight and nine."

The tenth Comanche, Toad, suddenly rose off the ground twenty feet away, rifle in hand. Caleb pulled the trigger of the Sharps one more time. The expected blast from the rifle never came, only a click that told him the Sharps was out of shells.

Chapter 34 Mano a Mano

Caleb reacted instantly by dropping the Sharps and reaching for the Colt revolver in his shoulder holster. A bullet from Toad's rifle passed between Caleb's reaching fingers and slammed into the Colt as it was halfway out of the holster. The shattered pistol drove straight into Caleb's chest, knocking him back and driving the air out of his lungs. Even more damaging to Caleb, the bullet, after striking the gun, ricocheted into his upper chest, striking and fracturing his collar bone, and lodging itself in his chest. Blood from the wound quickly began to run down the front of his shirt.

Desperately he sought to sit up but could only manage to lift his head. In front of him stood Toad, feet set wide apart, gazing calmly down at what he now believed was a defenseless foe. Caleb looked back at him, finding it interesting that although he was about to die, he felt no fear, just the calm realization that having done what he could to set the girls free he had come to his end, an end that so many people in his life had already known.

Still, he wanted to live, but maybe even more than that he wanted to kill Toad before he died.

With his breath returning, a smile started to build on his face. Speaking in a voice as strong as he could muster Caleb shouted toward the Indian standing over him, "You are one ugly mother. Toad they call you, and a toad you are."

The squat man in front of him didn't reply, not in words. Slowly, he too began to grin, widening the scar running from the corner of his mouth back toward his ear, making him appear even more wide-mouthed and toad-like.

The Indian suddenly did something that Caleb could never have imagined. He bent down and still staring at Caleb, carefully placed his rifle on the ground.

For just an instant Caleb thought the Comanche was about to show some sense of being civilized, even merciful. That notion quickly vanished when Toad reached around his back and pulled out a large Bowie-like knife. He then extended his empty hand, palm up, toward Caleb. With his fingers he gestured for Caleb to get up and come forward.

"Come to me," said the hand gesture known to all people.

"That son of a bitch plans to kill me an inch at a time," thought Caleb. "Well, that may be, but I'll be the last person he ever puts a knife to."

Caleb reached forward and grabbed the lance about a hands-width away from where it was sticking into his leg and then, gritting his teeth in advance, jerked it out. Gushing bright red blood immediately burst out of the deep hole left behind. Ignoring the pain and the blood he then used the lance to pull himself upright. Out of the corner of his eye he could see Toad watching him, his grin now even wider. Caleb could not help but notice Toad was missing several front teeth. He half expected a forked tongue to come spilling out of the gap.

"He's enjoying this," he thought, "like a snake watching a wounded sparrow. What he doesn't know is this sparrow has teeth."

Caleb still had the Indian lance in his hand and for a brief moment thought about trying to use it as a spear, but then realized if he did Toad would simply pick up his rifle and finish him then and there.

Hoping to anger his adversary and cloud his thinking, Caleb raised the lance in front of his face, and then staring at Toad with all the contempt he could put on his face, spit on it and flung it down on the ground.

"Give yourself a chance," he thought, "work on his pride as a warrior. Let him choose to fight, man to man, knife to knife. The old way."

Then reaching behind his back he removed the Bowie knife Uriah had given him years ago and held it out in front of him for Toad to see. It was almost identical to the knife in Toad's hand.

Pointing his knife at Toad he said, "Come and get me, or are you a warrior who squats like a woman when he breaks water?"

Toad's eyes closed slightly, and then he spoke in English.

"I understand you. You must understand me. I will leave you with no skin on your body and no eyes to see. You will try to scream for the death you want but your mouth will be stuffed with your sickly white manhood."

Toad then spit on his knife, moved forward in a low crouch with his arms spread out to his sides, and began to slowly wave the knife back and forth, a look of purest evil in his eyes.

Caleb responded by taking one step forward with his injured leg, trying to leave most of his weight on the good one. He then moved his left arm as wide of his body as he could, pain rushing through him from the broken collarbone. He held his knife out in front of him to his full arm's length, hoping Toad would think his stance was that of someone who would stab rather then slice with a knife.

Toad was the first to attack with a swipe of his knife at the air in front of Caleb, and then a stab that fell far short of Caleb's body. Caleb recognized both moves for what they were: feints, a false attack to test Caleb's reaction. Caleb fell back, feigning a weakness of his wounded leg, a weakness that was only half false. He followed with a short stabbing feint of his own, noting that Toad only straightened his body very slightly to avoid the stab, and in doing so showed nothing but contempt for Caleb's thrust.

"He's been here before," thought Caleb.

A moment after that thought a strange sensation hit Caleb. Against all reason he was beginning to enjoy the fight, even though by all odds he wouldn't survive it. Wounded, almost helpless, he now felt more alive than he could ever remember, and for the second time in his life he truly wanted to kill. He wanted to kill, to not merely defeat an enemy but to take his life.

Snapping his thoughts back to the problem at hand, Caleb then circled to his left, hoping Toad would do likewise and end up with the glare from the setting sun in his eyes. Toad didn't cooperate. Instead he launched a second attack, this time coming in lower and slashing at Caleb's wounded leg, the one Caleb had deliberately left slightly in front, the one he hoped to bait Toad with. A burning pain told Caleb he had misjudged Toad's quickness and the length of his arms.

Before Caleb could fully react Toad's blade cut across the knee of his wounded leg, opening the knee cap to the bone and sending forth a fresh flow of blood. Caleb felt the pain, but knew his luck was still holding because had the cut been a few inches higher or lower he would have been seriously crippled and left to fight on one leg.

"So," he thought, "you want to whittle me down a cut a time. We'll see who does the whittling."

Still moving to his left as Uriah had taught him, he let his wounded leg collapse half way, once again inviting Toad to make another move toward it. Toad did make a move, but not for Caleb's leg. With a stabbing motion, Toad went for his gut, but when the knife was half-way there Caleb used his open left hand to bat Toad's knife blade to his right, trying to force it down and over to the Indian's left side, away from his own body.

The knife in Caleb's hand was a blur as it slashed down fast and hard, finding flesh, fingers, and bone. Toad jumped back, blood dripping from his knife hand. He then backed up another step and looked impassively at his bloody hand. His small finger was dangling from his right hand, held there by a fragile piece of skin. The finger next to it and Toad's knuckles had also suffered a deep gash.

Toad stepped back two steps, staring calmly at Caleb and then back to the wounded hand still holding the knife. As if to show Caleb his total disregard for pain or injury, he brought the dangling finger to his mouth, bit through the rest of the skin holding it on to his hand, and spit it out at Caleb's feet, all the while fixing Caleb with an icy stare that promised a horrible death. Caleb only stared back stoically, impressed, even amazed at the Indian's toughness.

Moving in again, Toad slashed rapidly back and forth keeping his knife moving and forcing Caleb into a stumbling retreat. As Caleb fell back, his wounded leg responded with a further lack of strength. He did not care, his only thought was to kill his enemy.

"This has to end soon," he told himself. "I must find a way to finish him while I can still stand and before I bleed out."

Toad, injured and realizing the white man had the courage and heart of a true warrior, was also looking for a quick end to the fight. Suddenly he made the mistake Caleb was waiting for.

Making two more long slashes from left to right, the Comanche suddenly lunged forward and stabbed with a fully extended arm at Caleb's stomach. Caleb came up slightly on his toes and twisted a few inches to the right as Toad's knife missed his stomach but found the flesh of his right hip. As Toad's knife sliced into Caleb's hipbone, it slowed Toad just enough to give Caleb the opening he needed.

Caleb, running out of strength from the loss of blood knew it was now or never, that he had one chance, a last chance to kill the Comanche. As Toad started to raise his knife again, Caleb completed the twist to the right by putting all his weight on the injured left leg and spinning in a complete circle, a pirouette, the same move Uriah had used on him years ago. Just as his right foot was about to touch the ground Caleb brought his knife above his shoulder and chopped down blindly and as hard as he could where he judged Toad's head or neck would be.

Toad, still holding his blood-covered knife close to Caleb's hip, attempted to avoid the blow by raising his shoulder, but it did him no good. Caleb's knife passed over the raised shoulder and sliced halfway through Toad's short neck, a blow that severed an artery and cut halfway through his windpipe.

The knife in Toad's hand fell to his feet as he stood motionless for just a moment, then slumped to his knees and crashed face-first at Caleb's feet, his mouth and eyes wide open in anguish, his hands reaching up and around grasping his throat in a vain effort to hold the huge wound closed. Moments later he made a gurgling sound as his lungs pushed his last breath through the gash in his neck and between his bloody fingers.

Caleb stood over him, his knife now dangling at his side, Toad's blood dripping down the knife blade onto the ground. For just a moment he thought back to the knife fighting lesson given to him by an old man using a burnt stick.

"Thank you, Uriah, you taught me better than you know."

Barely able to move, Caleb spent the next few minutes cutting up the straps of his shoulder holster and using the strips of leather as a tourniquet to stop the flow of blood from his leg wound. Satisfied he had done all his strength allowed him to do to stop the bleeding, he then fashioned a sling from a piece of his cape and used it to support his left arm. He painfully gathered up the Sharps along with Toad's rifle. Using strips of the cape he tied them together and slung the weapons over his back. Retrieving the lance, and using it as a walking stick, he hobbled over to Toad's body.

Looking down at the Comanche who would never again steal another horse or take another captive, he said out loud, "Your pride got you killed, but it kept me alive, so some folks would say that not killing me when you could was real stupid, but nobody can say you weren't a first-rate fighting man."

Then turning away, Caleb followed the rim of the canyon north, the direction from which the three Comanche on the rim had come. As he hobbled along he had to squint his eyes against the brilliant mix of red, orange, and gold colors making up the fast fading sunset. It was a sunset as beautiful as any he'd ever seen. It was a good day to be alive, a good day to have killed his enemy.

Overhead the ever opportunist buzzards began their slow circling down to the body of Toad and his band of Comanche.

Chapter 35 Struggle to Survive

A little over a half mile of walking brought him to what he was looking for, what he knew had to be there. Caleb believed Toad and the other Comanche must have had an easier way to climb up to the rim because that would be the only explanation for them reaching the top as fast as they did. Now he could see where the canyon rim dipped until it was less than forty feet above the canyon floor. Peering over the side he could see several natural footpaths just wide enough to allow a careful man to work his way up or down. After sitting down and dangling his legs over the rim's edge, he threw his Sharps, Toad's rifle, and the lance over the rim. He knew that by doing so he might lose or break them, but he also knew that in his weakened condition they could seriously impede his descent. If they didn't break apart, they would be easy enough to retrieve when he reached the canyon floor. Easing his way and stopping several times to rest, Caleb hobbled and slid down the now darkened ledges. His descent was hindered by a few jutting rocks that caused him to trip and often poked at his wounds no matter how hard he tried to keep the rock from contacting the injured parts of his body. He was just too beat up to do more than try. He tumbled blindly down the last few feet to the canyon floor, a fall that landed him in darkness and reopened his leg wound.

He wanted to lie there and rest but knew he had to stop the blood he felt seeping out of his leg and through the makeshift bandages. Cutting off his bloody pants leg he pressed pieces of it to the wound until he felt the bleeding had stopped.

For several minutes he sat with his back against the canyon wall, his ears straining to hear any sound, his eyes hopelessly searching in the darkness for any movement. Hearing and seeing nothing he decided he had to get moving while he could still stand upright. Again using the retrieved lance for support he started north, forgetting to retrieve the two rifles. His desiccated cape had long been forgotten remaining on the canyon's rim.

In the now utter darkness of the canyon floor Caleb could see nothing, not even the hand he held before his face. After several minutes of feeling with his hand as he moved down the rock wall, Caleb froze in place as he heard a scraping sound coming from only a few feet away. Unable to see a potential enemy in the darkness, he was about to thrust the lance out in front of him when what he recognized as the soft muzzle of a horse touched his arm. Touching the horse's head and then moving his hand along its neck, he realized he was standing next to an animal far above average in height. Remembering the smaller-sized mustangs he'd seen the other Comanche riding he knew the giant horse standing next to him had to be Toad's palomino stallion.

"Easy now big horse, easy," he whispered while continuing to gently stroke the horse's neck. He felt the horse shiver and then relax. Moving his hand over the horse's head his fingers felt for and found a thin braided leather bridle.

"Good," he said, talking into the darkness, "now I've got something I can use to ride you...if you'll let me."

Holding the bridle loosely in his hand he eased his way along the palomino's side, hoping to find a saddle. There was none.

"So I'll have to get on the hard way," he told himself, not sure he had the strength to do so, but sure if he didn't, he might die in the canyon along with the Comanche he'd killed.

Using the last reserve of strength in his uninjured leg, he grabbed the horse's mane, leaped up off his good leg, and pulled himself onto its back. Lying motionless, he half expected to be thrown off, but the palomino stood as still as a statue. After struggling to get his right leg over the stallion's back, an exhausted Caleb slowly leaned forward and wrapped his arms around the horse's massive neck.

"Good boy, good boy," he said in a whisper, grateful the palomino was so tolerant of a strange rider, especially one smelling of blood.

"Seems like you've smelled blood before, huh, boy?"

The palomino responded with a soft snort through his nostrils. Caleb's answer was to close his eyes and relax his tortured body even more on the palomino's neck. He then gave the horse a gentle tap on the side with the heel of his good leg.

"Take us out of here," he whispered. Then, unable to prevent it, he closed his eyes and fell into a deep stupor, his head resting on the horse's neck.

Caleb woke to the echoes of hooves striking the rock floor as the palomino walked slowly through the narrow canyon walls now bathed in light from the full moon overhead. As the horse moved, he could feel a deep throb from his wounded leg and shoulder, a throb that seemed to beat in unison with the rolling motion of the horse. Too tired and weak to sit up without calling on a strength he needed to conserve, he continued to rest over the horse's neck, glad for the warmth it gave off.

"I guess you'll find a way out," Caleb told the surprisingly gentle stallion, not knowing whether the palomino was taking them south or north but thankful that Toad's horse had continued to at least keep moving.

An hour later Caleb felt the palomino stop and lower its head. Perhaps calling on what he had learned as a young wild horse, the stallion had found a small pool of water trapped in a depression on the canyon floor. Hearing the slurping sound of the horse drinking, Caleb, desperate for water, slid off the right side of the horse so that he would land on his good leg. Then he crouched down and began to share the cool and quenching liquid with the horse.

After several minutes, feeling refreshed and slightly stronger Caleb once again climbed on the stallion's back and continued riding in what the stars told him was north. Two hours later, well out of the canyon and barely able to keep his eyes open, he stopped the palomino underneath a lone mesquite tree, dismounted, tied the reins to an overhanging branch and was sleeping soundly within a minute.

Awakened by the sound of the stallion's nickering and prancing feet, Caleb was at first blinded by the glare from a rising sun. Squinting in the direction the horse faced he could barely make out through the glare a party of horsemen heading his way at a fast gallop.

Weaponless, except for his knife, and with no place to hide, he could only struggle to his feet and stand to meet them, hoping they weren't more marauding Comanche. As they got closer he was relieved to see they were a troupe of army cavalrymen. To the front of them rode Tip Thomas.

Chapter 36 To the Rescue

Coming to a halt only a few feet away from where Caleb stood, Tip jumped from the saddle and exclaimed, "I'll be damned. When we looked through the binoculars and saw the palomino under the tree we thought we'd found Toad, but instead we've found ourselves a miracle."

"No miracle, just a busted up fool of an Irishman who's damned happy to see you," replied Caleb.

"You sure look like you've been in a hellava fight," said Tip noting that Caleb was covered in blood and seemingly close to death's door. Tip found it incredible that Caleb was not only alive but standing in front of him.

"Fight?" asked Caleb, remembering the long ago words Jack Remza had spoken, "what fight was that?"

Tip chuckled, amazed this bloody and half dead man could still make a small joke. "You Irishmen got to be crazy," he replied.

"Did you get the girls out safely?" Caleb asked.

"We got them out and they're in good shape. A mite bruised up and awful tired, but otherwise just fine and undamaged."

Tip then paused to look Caleb up and down, and satisfied the man would live at least a few minutes longer he said, "Your plan worked almost exactly as you laid it out. When you started shooting, me and Dos headed your way and almost collided head on with the girls and the one Indian you were kind enough to leave for us. I don't know who was the most surprised, me and Dos, the girls, or that poor Comanche. Anyway, I latched onto the girls and Dos put two rounds into the Comanche. Then we all lit out of there at a dead run and didn't hardly slow down until we got back to Outlaw Creek. We stopped just long enough to switch over to the fresh horses, give the girls a few minutes rest, and then got the hell out of there, leaving the buckskin just in case you managed to stay alive. I got to tell you, Dos and me didn't give you a snowball's chance in hell of getting' out alive, you being a tender greenhorn and all."

A full blown smile now covered the cowboy's face.

"Thanks for the vote of confidence," said Caleb.

"You're welcome," said Tip.

"Anyway," Tip continued, "that's when we got mighty lucky. We was headin' for the Camino Real, figuring the road would be safer and a lot easier on the girls when, after little more than an hour's ridin', we spotted the camp fires from a cavalry detachment out of Austin. It was led by the same officer we met in Liberty Hill before you arrived there. I didn't know at the time that he was the commander of the troops in Texas. When we saw it was the cavalry we'd run into, Dos lit out to the south. He's got good reason for not wantin' to keep company with any army boys."

As the curious men in the cavalry squad dismounted and started to gather around them, Tip went on, "After makin' sure the girls were taken care of and tellin' the story about leavin' you behind with all those Comanche, I joined up with Sergeant Kitchens here and his squad and headed for the north end of the canyon, while another squad headed for the south end. We figured, aside from findin' your body, there was a slight chance of trappin' Toad and his bunch between us. Good thing we came to the north like we did, otherwise we might never have found you."

"You won't have to worry about Toad or any of the other Comanche," said Caleb, "they've made their last raid."

"You got them all?" asked an incredulous Tip. "I'd call you the biggest storyteller in Texas if I wasn't standin' here lookin' at you and that big Palomino, a Palomino like Toad was said to ride."

From the circle of enlisted men now surrounding them a voice blurted out, "What happened back in that canyon with you and Toad?"

For the next few minutes, while Tip washed out Caleb's wounds and applied makeshift bandages, Caleb gave his account of the fight as every man in the troop listened in absolute silence. Most of them, although having limited experience with Indian fighting, hardly believed one man, by himself, had ambushed and killed so many Comanche, including the legendary Toad. Tip was not among those who doubted Caleb's story.

"When the Comanche came into the canyon I saw a girl riding behind Christine. Who was she?" asked Caleb.

"All we know is her name's Shannon Edwards," replied Tip. She was captured up north by the Kiowa and then traded to the Comanche. Best guess is her folks were killed in a raid, but we're not sure 'cause she's not talkin' much. Ann said she talked so much after the trade Toad threatened to cut out her tongue unless she was quiet. He probably would have, too, except it would lower the price he could get for her in Mexico. Anyway, I guess she's probably still too scared to say much but you can still see some spunk in her eyes so it's my guess she'll be okay. Knowin' Ann and Christine, Gram's going to have another mouth to feed until we can find her kin. That is, if she has any."

With the storytelling ended, Tip asked, "Do you think you're up to riding back to camp?"

He knew Caleb was seriously injured and had had little sleep for the past three days, but he also knew they needed to get him back to camp so someone who knew doctoring could treat his wounds.

"Not bareback 'cause I'll need something to hand on to, but if you can get a saddle on the palomino, I'm good to go, but it'll have to be a slow pace. Don't want to wear out you and the rest of these boys trying to keep up with a greenhorn like me."

Caleb would have laughed at his own joke, but knew it would hurt too much. Minutes later, Tip was riding bareback and Caleb was hanging on to the saddled palomino.

The ride back was uneventful but not their arrival at camp. The group of troopers left behind had expected the men in the scouting party to return either empty-handed or at best with a few Comanche horses or maybe the body of Caleb Quinn. Caleb, weak and hurting throughout his entire body, was little prepared for the barrage of questions thrown at him by the troopers who gathered around them.

Tip, seeing the fatigue on Caleb's face and knowing Caleb needed urgent medical attention, told them, "I've got the whole story and I'll answer your questions in a few minutes, but right now this man needs rest and some patchin' up."

Then he and one of the troopers helped Caleb into a tent and placed him on a cot. Within seconds Caleb was asleep, a sleep filled with bloody images and the face of Toad.

Chapter 37 The Meeting

It was pitch dark in the tent when Caleb, compelled by thirst, the pain from his wounds, and the need to relieve himself slowly fought his way back to consciousness. As he started to sit up he was stopped by two hands on his shoulders. The hands then gently pushed him back.

"You need to stay where you are," said a soft feminine voice in the dark. You're badly wounded in several places and any movement could get those wounds to bleeding again."

Caleb knew the army didn't usually travel with women, which meant the voice speaking to him most likely belonged to one of the Pokusa sisters.

"Which one are you?" he asked, the words barely able to escape his dry throat and parched lips.

"I'm Christine," came the soft answer.

An instant later a match was struck and held to a candle sitting on the small camp table next to the cot. As the light spread throughout the tent Caleb was able to see her face.

The voice he'd heard had been soft, and a bit husky, that of a grown woman. But the face before him was that of a girl, an extraordinarily beautiful girl, the younger girl in the locket. Her teeth were small and bright, captured between large pink lips. She had a deeply tanned face but not so tanned as to hide her rose-colored cheeks, giving her an almost doll-like appearance. Her long hair was straight, the color of corn silk, and shown brightly even in the dim light of the single candle. Her deep set eyes were the lightest of blue and topped by the palest of eyebrows. She glowed with an innocence that denied what Tip had said about her toughness. She had a look of freshness which made it almost impossible to believe that only few days earlier she had been the captive of the Comanche.

Ignoring her command to stay still, Caleb rose to place his weight on the elbow of his right arm, and then took a moment to etch the face before him into his memory. Christine did not try to stop him.

"Why are you here?" he asked.

With a smile that seemed to erase much of his pain, and a look of tenderness a mother would give a hurt child, Christine bent forward until her face was only inches away from him. She explained in a low, almost whispering, voice, "I'm here because a brave someone who I'd never met helped rescue me from the Comanche, and that someone now needs some nursing until the army doctor can get here."

The closeness of her lips as she spoke reminded Caleb that wounded or not, he was still a man.

"I need...,"

Before he could finish Christine stopped him with a slender finger placed over his lips, "Hush. We'll get along better if you don't start arguing or trying to do anything on your own. Now, if you don't mind, I need to look at your leg and your shoulder."

She did not tell him she'd noticed the effect her closeness had on him, or that while he was unconscious, she and Tip had cut away his bloody clothes, allowing her to briefly study his muscle-filled body for any wounds that may have been hidden under the clothing. The sight of Caleb's nearly naked body, the first such she had ever seen, had jolted her. He was wonderful to look at.

The tone of her voice told Caleb she was not one to be argued with, not that he wanted to argue. His thirst and his bladder could wait until later.

"First comes this," she told him, and then reached into a bag at her feet and removed a large bottle marked 'Alcohol.'

"This," said Christine, "contains a new type of medicine the army uses against infection."

Caleb, having seen Dr. Tichenor's treatment used during the war and knowing what she was about to do, cringed in mock fright.

"Would you like it a little at a time or all at once?"

"I don't want it at all," replied Caleb, "but if you must do it, please, just a little at a time."

Her nursing him was something he wanted to stretch out as long as possible.

"Your choice," she said as she removed the cap from the bottle and pulled back the blanket covering his legs. After removing the bloody bandage, she then tilted the bottle all the way over and poured half of its contents on Caleb's open leg wound.

The burning sensation which followed instantly ripped through his entire leg. Had it been a man breaking his word as she did, Caleb might have either grimaced in pain or put a fist in his face, but with a beautiful young woman doing the pouring he managed to hold his response to a puckering of his lips like a man sucking on a sour lemon.

"Jesus, damn," he finally found the breath to utter, "is that your idea of a little at a time?"

"I only did it fast because it works best that way," she replied with a slight hint of a smile, "and now that we're done with the tough part the rest won't be nearly so bad, not for a big tough fella like you." Her face remained only a short arm's reach away.

Still feeling the pain from the alcohol flooding his wound Caleb didn't feel so tough, but neither did he care if the army doctor took a couple of days to get there.

For the next half hour, using the materials in her bag, Christine continued to tend Caleb's wounds. She was slow, careful, and tender, stopping several times to smile at him as she worked. With each smile they took a moment to look at each other.

Finally finished, she returned the alcohol and bandages to her bag, and then patting him on his arm said, "Now that you're all fixed up, did I remember to thank you for saving me, my sister, and little Shannon, from the Comanche? You must know you are now our official and forever hero."

"I had some good help and more than my share of luck," said Caleb, trying to hide the pleasure her words gave him.

"Luck," came a voice from the entrance to the tent. "According to the patrol that just got back with your buckskin and several other Indian ponies, the canyon was filled top to bottom with dead Comanche, including Toad. I'd say what you did was a cut or two above lucky.

The speaker was Tip, and Caleb knew the woman standing next to him was Ann. She too was beautiful, but in a different way than Christine. She looked regal, almost aristocratic. She was taller, slimmer, and her hair was darker in color. Only the color and shape of her eyes matched Christine's. Caleb could only look at her and Tip and think that they looked so comfortable and familiar with each other, like they were made to fit together.

"Look what the cat's drug in," said Christine, letting Caleb hear for the first time a bit of her laughter. It was a perfect match to her looks.

Ann stepped around Tip and displayed a large iron skillet covered by a handkerchief.

"This cat's brought your patient a plate of warm beans, fresh pan biscuits, and a cup of hot coffee with lots of sugar."

"Also," she added reaching into her skirt pocket and taking out a tin can, "can't forget the peaches I brought for dessert."

"I can't imagine where you managed to dig up such wonderful food," said Christine. In fact, she was not at all surprised Ann had manufactured another of her miraculous, out of nowhere, meals, "I'm sure my patient won't turn it down, or perhaps mind sharing a few of the peaches with his nurse."

"That, my dear greedy sister, is up to your Mr. Quinn."

Then Ann, looking squarely at Caleb, added, "And thank you, Caleb, for what you did for my sister and myself."

"You're welcome," replied Caleb as he looked at Ann, marveling at how quickly these two sisters had seemingly recovered from their ordeal with the Comanche.

He decided that later on he would ask either Tip or Sergeant Kitchens if this country always produced such beautiful, incredibly tough, and resilient women, or was it just these two.

Tip, taking a few steps forward and placing an arm around Ann's petite waist, told Caleb, "We've decided we'll all stay here until the doctor arrives to patch you up. After that, when you get stronger, we'll head back to the ranch."

"Speaking of getting stronger," said Christine, "you two need to skedaddle so my patient can get some rest."

Before Caleb could get out a protest Tip and Ann excused themselves, leaving Caleb and Christine alone to share the dinner Ann had brought to the tent. As he ate Caleb saw no reason to complain about being left alone with Christine.

When they finished the meal, Christine checked his wounds once more, then gathered up her bag and the empty skillet, and started to leave.

"I wouldn't mind if you stayed just a little while longer to talk," Caleb said, hoping to prolong her visit and learn more about her.

"Not in your weakened condition, Mr. Caleb Quinn," she answered, giving him a grin, "but I'll be back first thing in the morning after you've had more time to rest up."

She left the tent with a smile on her face, thinking, "I didn't know heroes came in such beautiful packages."

Caleb watched her go thinking, "That's the best looking nurse any man ever had."

The next morning Caleb was anxiously waiting for Christine's return when a tall figure with flowing blonde hair and an impressive mustache pushed his way past the tent flaps and stood in front of Caleb. Although dressed only in an undershirt and pants held up by suspenders,

Caleb recognized from the man's bearing that he was an officer. For some reason he couldn't explain Caleb thought he'd seen the man before, many years ago.

"It appears," said the officer, "that for the second time I have the privilege of commending you for a job well done...and, oddly enough, much like the first time, I find you wounded and on your back, looking up at me. Maybe history does repeat itself."

Caleb suddenly remembered a cavalry officer coming out of the smoke of battle, and riding down a saber-carrying Confederate officer as he was about to bring an end to a young sharpshooter's life. He also remembered during the final days of the war seeing a Union cavalry charge led by an officer with long blonde hair. This had to be the same man.

"Thank you, sir, and thank you for what you did for me that day on the battlefield at the Little Bethel."

"It was a privilege and a pleasure," replied the visitor, raising his clenched fists before his face, "and wasn't it a glorious day for the Union?"

Before Caleb could reply the tent flap was pushed open.

"Excuse me," came Christine's voice as she entered the tent, "if you gentlemen are done talking about how wonderful war is, I've got a patient I'd like to take care of."

"It seems, Mr. Quinn, that I've been outranked by true beauty," said the officer, "but before I go I want you to know I fully expect to spend the next several years taking the fight to the Indians. I've heard said Lee told Grant if it hadn't been for all the Irish in the Union Army, the South would have won the war. I tend to agree, especially based on what I know you accomplished during the war and now with the Comanche. With this in mind I would certainly like to have you back in uniform and under my command."

"Thank you for the offer," said Caleb, barely looking the officer in the eye, "but I've had my fill of fighting and killing. This Irishman never wants to know war again, not against anyone, including Indians."

"That's a shame. For myself, I can't think of anything so good in life as to engage and then defeat one's enemy."

"The dying of men," Caleb instantly decided, "would not diminish this man's love of war."

After the officer left, Christine moved toward Caleb and sat on the edge of the cot. When her hip came into contact with his leg Caleb

219

was astounded by the effect of having her touching him. Not since the last night he spent with Tersha had he been touched in even a slightly intimate way. It was like a wave of longing was washing over him. Trying to stave off the feeling, he asked, "Now that he's left, can you tell me who that was?" hoping not to reveal the pleasure she gave him by simply being so close.

"Certainly. His name is Custer and he's the commander of the cavalry battalion stationed in Austin. He's here in case any diehard Rebels want to keep the war going by trying to join up with Maximilian in Mexico, but right now he seems far more interested in fighting Comanche. I might add he also seems to think very highly of himself but from what I've heard, despite all his fancy ways and oversized opinion of himself, his men would follow him through the gates of hell."

Glancing toward Caleb's wounded leg under the blanket, she then asked, "How is my hero feeling this morning?"

Aware that he still looked haggard as a mange-covered mongrel, and hadn't shaved in almost a week, with what he hoped was an attractive grin on his face, Caleb answered, "I'm not ready to take you dancing just yet, but I do feel a lot better thanks to your nursing and to Ann's cooking."

"Sergeant Kitchens tells me the doc should be here by noon tomorrow at the latest. You'll feel even better when he takes care of your cuts and removes the bullet you've got up there under your collarbone," she told him.

"I hope so," said Caleb, "the sooner I get off this cot the better I'll like it."

Placing her hand on Caleb's, Christine gave his hand a soft squeeze and then said, "Before that happens I have some questions I'd like to ask you."

Chapter 38 Confession

As she spoke she was still holding his hand in hers.

"Go ahead and ask," said Caleb.

Her voice and the look on her face suddenly turned serious. "Tip told me you were with my father when he died. Is that true?"

"Yes," replied Caleb, feeling a sudden knot in his stomach.

"Yesterday when Ann and I were cleaning your clothes, we found the letter you showed Tip and the locket Pop always carried. Did he give them to you?"

"Yes."

"Why?"

"He was dying and wanted me to return them to you. He also wanted me to use them as a way of introduction."

Now placing both her hands on his, she continued, "This morning I overheard some of the soldiers talking. They said Caleb Quinn was a Union sharpshooter and something of a legend. That he'd killed dozens of men. Is that true? Are you that Caleb Quinn?"

"Yes, I was a sharpshooter in the Union Army."

As he answered her question he could see the start of tears gathering in her eyes.

Caleb lowered his head and closed his eyes, sickened by what he knew would come next.

"I have to ask," she said, "You say you were my father's friend and you were with him when he died?"

"Yes, I was there when he died," said Caleb, "and yes, I will always think of him as my friend."

Tears had begun to spill down Christine's cheeks. Choking back a sob and lowering her head she asked without looking at him, "Were you responsible for my father's death?"

Caleb opened his eyes and stared into hers.

"It was war," he answered, "but yes, it was my bullet that killed your father. I wish it had never happened, but it did, and I can't change it."

At that moment, looking at the suffering on her face, he almost wished he'd never come out of Bella Vista Canyon.

Christine did not move for several long moments, just continuing to sit there next to him with her eyes closed, her hands still holding his, while choking back several sobs.

Finally opening her eyes, she looked into his, "Please," she whispered, "tell me how it happened. I need to know."

Caleb told her, omitting nothing. He started with General Grant's order and ended with the grave he had placed her father in. He also told her of her father's dying request that he go to Texas to look out for his daughters.

When Caleb was finished he could only wait for her response, a response he was sure would include words which would forever come between them.

Straightening up and looking calmly at him she began to speak through trembling lips, "My father told me he was fighting for the South not because he wanted to defend slavery, but because Texas was a part of the Confederacy. He felt the need to repay Texas for what it had given him...the chance to live and raise a family in a free land, a land he was not born to, but a land he loved. When he came from Poland the only people he knew were his mother's cousins, the Szeliga's, who had come from Germany and settled near Fredericksburg. That's why he came to Texas."

Pausing a moment to brush away the tears running down her reddened cheeks, she continued, "Pop was an excellent judge of people and he must have seen something good and true in you, something more than just a skilled sharpshooter. Perhaps even something of himself because you were also fighting for a country you weren't born to."

Caleb had no reply, and could only stare in wonder at this girl who had so much of her father's strength, and hopefully, much of his forgiveness.

"He's gone now, and you're here," she continued, "and despite what happened, I'm glad you're here. I'm glad you're alive."

"I wish there was..." his words were cut off by the hand she placed over his lips.

She then lowered her head until her cheek was touching his. Caleb could feel the warm wetness of her tears as she whispered in his ear, "Caleb Quinn, I don't want you to apologize for what happened, not now, not ever. I want nothing to stand between us. From this moment on what happened during the war will be forever buried where it belongs, in the past."

Several minutes later, after tending to his wounds, she was almost out of the tent when she turned back to him.

"By coming here you kept your word to my father, and that I understand. Still, other men might not have done so, so I have to ask, was there any other reason you made such a long trip, and then risked your life for me and my sister?"

Caleb hesitated, not sure how he could answer her question without sounding too soft, too sentimental, too weak.

"I owed your father," was his reply.

"I understand that. What I want to know is was there any other reason, any something that made you face an almost certain death to save people you didn't even know?"

Again Caleb hesitated, not sure he wanted her to understand him, not sure she could.

He finally answered, the words spilling out in a torrent, "Sometimes people make an instant connection with someone they've just met. It was that way with your father and myself. I felt a connection like I had with my own father and my brother. Because of that connection, I had to keep my word to protect you and your sister. Besides, I had no place else to go, no place to belong to."

He couldn't bring himself to tell her the other reason, that her picture in the locket had stirred something inside of him. It was another instant connection, but different...deeper.

Christine looked at him, seeing for the first time not a hero, or a killer, only a man filled with hurt and sorrow, a man who seemed lost and terribly alone.

"Thank you for telling me," she said, and turned away to hide the fresh tears in her eyes.

"My poor Caleb," she thought as she closed the tent flaps behind her, "my poor Caleb."

Chapter 39 Healing

The next morning the army doctor arrived and after removing the bullet, using a number of stitches to close Caleb's leg wound, and potent ointments to treat the wounds, he declared Caleb well on the mend and that after another three or four days of rest he would be fit for travel.

For the next several days Caleb and Christine grew steadily closer as they engaged in hours of conversation while she continued nursing his wounds. Late in the evening of the fourth day Caleb declared that he was ready to travel.

"In that case, I must go tell Tip to see to our travel arrangements," said Christine. He's already procured a wagon for us.

As she started to leave, he stopped her. "Christine, before you go there is one more thing I would like you to do."

"What is that?" she asked, hoping Caleb would ask for what she, herself, had been constantly thinking about.

"As your official hero, do you think it's possible that I might be deserving of a small good night kiss? Nothing serious you understand, just a small one."

"It's not something a proper nurse would do, not even to a hero, but I think it can be arranged," replied a happy Christine.

With a sultry smile on her lips she moved back to the cot, her hips swaying and her eyes fixed on him, teasing him, exciting him. Then using the wetted tips of her fingers she extinguished the burning candle.

A day later, the two couples, along with the other former captive, Shannon Edwards, headed for the ranch. Shannon, they'd learned once she again began to talk, was the lone survivor of a raid on the way station her parents had operated on a desolate section of the Camino Real. She was thirteen, tall, thin as a reed, and seemed to have completely recovered from her experiences with the Kiowa and the Comanche. Christine and Ann had taken an instant liking to her when being held together by the Indians

The slow moving wagon, borrowed from the army and carrying Caleb, Ann, and Christine left the camp shortly after sunrise followed by a string of horses which included the palomino.

Tip and Shannon, who turned out to be an excellent rider and didn't want to ride on "a bumpy wagon that hurts my butt," led the way, with Shannon on the buckskin and Tip on a paint pony he had declared to be "spoils of war."

Colonel Custer had insisted that they have a cavalry escort for the first day of the trip to provide them extra security until they reached a more traveled section of the great road.

As the wagon slowly made its way east, Caleb, who was now being cared for by both sisters and despite being bounced around by the bumpy road, began to feel better. Much better!

On the third day of travel Caleb was lying back on a pile of army blankets while Christine once again changed his bandages and treated the wounds with her never-ending bottle of alcohol along with the ointment provided by the doctor. She had just completed her latest round of treatment when Tip rode up to the side of the wagon and looked down at Caleb.

"If I'd known all it took to get pampered by two beautiful women was to get a few scratches here and there," he said, trying to sound and look serious but losing the fight to his own laughter, "I'd have picked myself a fight with some real tough Comanche, not those poor little blanket Indians you picked on."

"I'll tell you what," said Caleb, immensely enjoying another of the back and forth taunting he and Tip often exchanged, "when I get to feeling better I'll go out and round up a few of those nice 'little blanket Indians' for you to play with."

Bringing the wagon to a halt, Ann turned to Tip.

"Mr. Thomas, if you have nothing better to do than poke fun at our poor Caleb I suggest that you and I ride out ahead of the wagon and find a suitable place for us to stop for lunch."

Tip, never one to pass up an invitation to be alone with Ann, readily agreed to her suggestion and within minutes the two of them had ridden out of sight. Ann was on Shannon's horse while a slightly disgruntled Shannon was left holding the reins to the wagon.

With Shannon now driving the wagon, Caleb and Christine watched quietly as Tip and Ann rode out. As the wagon continued to roll along through the hill country, Shannon kept her two passengers occupied with her incessant chatter; chatter that hadn't let up since she once again found her voice.

"Shannon, my dear," said Caleb, "if you would refrain from flapping your gums for just a few minutes, I have something important I want to ask Christine."

"All I wanted to…"

"Shannon," said Christine, "hush!"

Shannon hushed, but from the look on her face she was none too pleased about it.

Caleb turned to Christine and asked a question that had tested his curiosity since first meeting Tip and Dos, "How is it that Tip managed to stay out of the war. Most men his age either volunteered or were conscripted."

Not wanting her to think he was asking the question as an insult to Tip, he added, "He's a long way from being afraid of a fight so I know that didn't hold him back."

"No," she replied, "he's got no coward in him, and by not joining up when the war broke out he made a few enemies. At the time making an enemy of anyone who was all pumped up with Confederate pride could be rather dangerous. Now, if you ask him once he might tell you that someone needed to stay behind and protect me and my sister, and everyone else from the Indians."

"I think that's the same decision I would have made," said Caleb, fully understanding how difficult it was to lose someone you love.

"If you ask him a second time he might tell you he didn't believe in slavery and wasn't about to fight for it just to keep a lot of slave owners happy. However, if you ask me the truth of it, I say he couldn't stand the prospect of being away from Ann, which also happens to be how she feels about him."

From what he had seen of Ann, Caleb could easily understand why Tip didn't want to be away from her. He knew he was now feeling much the same way about her sister.

"It's a special thing when two people have that deep a feeling about each other," replied Caleb.

Then. wishing to change the subject before it got too personal, he continued with a second question, "How does Dos fit into your family?"

"As far as we all feel about Dos, he doesn't just fit into our family, he is family and has been since he was thirteen. His family and mine had been friends for years, and as little girls we often visited at the Baca ranch just north of us, up on the Colorado. Their ranch had been in the family for at least a hundred years, long before the Alamo, and they had a land grant to prove it. When some big money Anglo ranchers decided they wanted the land, they had lawyers in Austin challenge the title. The Bacas lost in court to a judge whose only son was killed at Goliad with Fannin, and who had an unabiding hatred for any and all Mexicans. In his decision he even described Mexicans as 'intruders' in the great state of Texas. Dos' family appealed the judgment for over a year, but the ranch was put up for public auction anyway. When it was all over, the ranchers who started the whole thing got the Baca's place for next to nothing, while the Baca's were homeless."

"I'd say some of the Mexicans in Texas have something in common with the Irish," said Caleb.

Caleb's comment made Christine take a moment to look closely into his eyes, hoping to find more clues as to what made him the person he was. All she saw were eyes that were intelligent and caring, eyes she believed would never lie to her, eyes that were losing their sadness. Her thoughts about Caleb were rudely interrupted.

"Go on," said an impatient voice coming from the front of the wagon, "go on, tell me more about Dos."

For once Shannon was more interested in what someone else was saying than what she, herself, had to say.

"Whatever you say, Miss Shannon," said Christine, aware that since her rescue the young girl had taken an unexpected interest in the dashing Mexican, even though their time together had been very brief. Christine knew Shannon was not the first young girl to fall under the spell of Dos' dashing good looks and brooding eyes.

"Anyway," Christine continued, "Dos' mother and sister went south to Monterey, while Dos and his father stayed behind, inflicting their own idea of justice. We saw them once in a while during the next year, but they never stayed for more than a few days. Pop told me they had turned into night riders, rustling horses and maybe even holding up a few banks and stagecoaches. When the Rangers finally caught up with them, Dos got away, but his father didn't and was hanged on the spot. After months of running from the law, Dos came to live with us and has been with us ever since. Since he's been grown he spends some time with us, some time with Tip, and at other times he just disappears for weeks or even longer. He's like a leaf that can't stop blowing in the wind. I do know he's traveled as far away as New Orleans because he brought Ann and me Limoges jewelry boxes from there."

"I'd say he's been down a rough road," Caleb replied, but also thinking Dos had plenty of reasons for his dislike of Anglos. Dos had his Texans and he had the British.

"It sounds like he's an orphan...just like me," said Shannon in a voice that sounded somewhat pleased with the possibility. "Tell me more about him," she pleaded.

"Shannon," replied Christine, "I'm sure we'll see Dos when we get back to the ranch, so if you want to know more about him you can ask him yourself. In the meantime, if you don't get those horses going just a little faster we may starve before we ever get to where Tip and Ann are setting up lunch."

With a look of quiet determination on her young face that indicated she'd do exactly as Christine suggested about Dos, Shannon gently slapped the reins against the hindquarters of the horses.

For two weeks after returning to the *Circle P*, except for an hour or so of sitting on the porch each day, Caleb had been confined by the ever vigilant Christine and Gram to a room at the back of the house. Of the two, Gram may have been the harsher warden, but Caleb knew of no prisoners who ever had a more enjoyable or caring jail keeper.

"Young man," she was telling him after catching him trying to sneak out of his room, "unless you do what you're supposed to do to get well, I'll have to take a switch to you, and don't think I won't."

Her threats were usually followed by her turning away from him and swallowing her laughter in her cupped hands.

Aside from staying in bed on an almost continual basis, Caleb had learned the other things he was "supposed to do" as part of his recuperation. First and foremost was never refusing a second helping of Gram's apple pie and always laughing with her at her sometimes ribald jokes.

"You'd better do what she says," said a voice coming from the doorway, "'cause Gram can swing a pretty mean switch."

Caleb turned his head to see Christine standing in the doorway, and to Caleb's eyes no person or painting could have been more beautiful. Always one to set her own fashion style, she was wearing snug fitting men's pants and a tucked in Mexican-style blouse which rendered bare her suntanned shoulders, very soft-looking shoulders that were partially covered by sun-bleached blonde hair. The drops of sweat dripping from her neck into her blouse sent an instant surge of desire washing over Caleb's entire body.

"You've got to get me out of here before I bust a gut on all the food she's forcing me to eat," begged a somewhat serious Caleb.

He wasn't used to inactivity and even with his leg wound and collar bone not completely healed was anxious to get outdoors where he felt he belonged, where he had spent most of his life. The confines of a house and the constant mothering he had received for the past weeks were tolerable for only so long.

"As your nurse I would advise against it," said Christine, "but as a young lady who deserves to take an occasional ride with a certain stubborn and ungrateful young man, you might be interested in knowing there are two saddled horses waiting outside for someone to ride them."

Within minutes, with Caleb on the buckskin and Christine on a dappled gray, they were riding slowly side by side away from the house.

"We won't have time to see the entire ranch, but take my word for it it's about ten square miles of mostly brush and rock, with barely enough sparse grass and water to handle a few hundred ornery longhorns and some wild burros."

To Caleb's way of thinking the area near the house seemed more like a farm than a ranch. The house itself faced west which allowed the residents to sit on the porch each evening with an unobstructed view of the often spectacular Texas sunsets. The other three sides of the house were enclosed by dozens of live oak trees which served to protect it from both wind and sun. Between the house and the trees on one side was a large vegetable garden, and on the other side a chicken coop. Past the trees and well away from the house were a bunkhouse, a barn with an overhanging shelter, several corrals, and an outhouse. The bunkhouse, barn, and corrals were all empty except for two milk cows munching hay under the overhang. An empty buckboard wagon shared the overhang with the cows while chickens were everywhere peeking at the sparse grass for insects or seeds.

"If this is a ranch," wondered Caleb to himself, "where's the livestock?"

What Caleb didn't know and what Christine was about to show him were the wonders of the family's box canyon to the north, and the answer to his question.

Chapter 40 The Secret

Caleb and Christine continued riding north for over two miles, slowly covering flat ground that seemed to Caleb to stretch forever to the distant horizon. As Christine had said, it was a dry and barren land, land Caleb found little to his liking, much preferring the green hills of Ireland, or just about anywhere he'd traveled with the circus or the army.

Just as he was about to question Christine as to why she or anyone would want to live in such a desolate place, she said, "Get ready for a big surprise and a little rougher riding."

She then moved her gray to the front.

A moment later the flat terrain started to gradually drop until they found themselves riding down into a winding ravine which had been hidden until they were right on top of it.

"No wonder it's hard to catch someone in this country," he thought.

After a ride of about five minutes and what Caleb estimated to be a descent of at least twenty-five feet, the ravine opened up until it was about forty feet wide. Caleb could see that the forty feet were closed off by a pole fence with a center gate.

When they reached the gate, Christine leaned down and removed a wire loop holding it closed. Caleb followed her through the opening and waited as she closed the gate and replaced the wire loop.

"A minute from now you're going to see something you won't see in any other place but here," she told him.

"I don't want to disappoint my favorite nurse and riding companion but I've got to tell you that I have seen holes in the ground before."

"Maybe so, Mr. Smarty, but not like this one," Christine replied, "and now I want you to lead the way so I can watch your face."

"Will do," said Caleb, and using his knees and with a soft tap of the reins urged the buckskin forward.

True to Christine's word, in less than a minute Caleb rounded a sharp curve in the ravine and found himself looking at a sight he could never have imagined possible in this otherwise flat and nearly barren country.

Looming before him was the box canyon where Tip and Dos had rounded up the extra horses they used to pursue the Comanche. The canyon widened out until it was at least a good half-mile across, and then stretched out for least another two miles or so, ending at a wall that looked to be about fifty feet high. The entire floor was covered in a carpet of tall grasses, grasses that were far higher and greener than any outside the canyon. The grasses were sprinkled with patches of pink, white, and blue flowers, all of them apparently watered year round by not one, but two small waterfalls that came together to create a small lake. In turn, the lake supplied the water to a sparkling creek that bubbled through the canyon and disappeared into a series of small, almost marshy ponds not too far from where Christine and Caleb were sitting on their horses.

Now Caleb understood why only a few horses were kept at the ranch house. Throughout the canyon and grazing its full length was a mixed herd of blooded horses and some hardy looking mustangs, altogether maybe forty-five or fifty in number. Grazing among the herd were dozens of longhorns, some of them nursing calves, and more than a dozen fat sheep desperately in need of a good shearing. Caleb could imagine no place more suited for grazing animals.

"My God," said Caleb to a grinning Christine, "how did your father or anyone else get lucky enough to find a place like this? It's like a hidden paradise. Grass, water, shelter, it's got everything!"

"Pop didn't find it," she answered. "When he first came to Texas he took a job driving freight wagons between Galveston, San Antonio, and Waco. That's how he met Dos' family and it was Dos' dad who told him about this property and its hidden canyon. You've got to remember the Spanish were in Texas two hundred years before the Anglos arrived, and they learned the secrets of the land through exploration and by listening to the Indians. Anyway, Pop took one look at this place, filed a claim the next day, and then for over two years spent every dollar he had and most of his waking hours fixing it up. When he had a decent house and the start of a successful horse ranch, he went back to New Jersey where he had spent his first few months after arriving in this country; the place where he had previously met the woman who would become my mother. Days after he arrived they were married and a month or so later they were here at the ranch. It was one of those love at first sight stories that happens only once in a blue moon.

Caleb was still sitting on his horse wondering what a blue moon was and admiring the view while stealing an occasional glance at the woman he had learned to love when a gold horse burst out of a stand of trees in the distance and headed at a full gallop toward them. Its tail and mane were flying and it seemed to have wings on its feet.

"There's the palomino," exclaimed an excited Caleb, "the way he's running toward us I think he remembers me."

"I don't know what about you he would find worth remembering," Christine said teasingly, "but he certainly remembers that every time I've come here during the past two weeks I've had a saddle bag full of grain and sugar cookies just for him."

A minute later, as proof of her words, the stallion, totally ignoring Caleb, came to a dirt-throwing stop next to Christine's gray. He then shook his head a few times and began to nuzzle the saddlebag draped behind Christine's saddle.

"When I first tried to grain-feed him the poor thing didn't know what grain was. Now he's a big spoiled baby, and won't go away until he's been fed and petted."

Sliding out of the saddle Christine then removed her saddlebag and dumped the grain in it onto the grass. The palomino instantly began to chomp greedily on the mixture of oats and corn.

"He probably needs all the grain he can get," said Christine while patting the palomino's neck, "considering all the mares he's been forced to service since he got here."

"Aside from his questionable moral ethics he's a fantastic horse," said Christine, "and smarter than most people, which begs the question, 'What do you intend to do with him?"

"Me?" asked Caleb, "I wasn't aware he was mine to do with."

"Tip says he is," replied Christine. "He said you were the last man to ride him, and with no brand on him, and no Toad to argue ownership, that makes him yours. At least that's the argument Tip used to convince Custer to let us take the palomino with us when we left the cavalry camp. Believe me, Custer wanted him badly and wasn't all that happy he didn't get his way."

"I sure won't argue with Tip's thinking, but I really don't know what I'll do with him. Maybe I'll take him to Georgia with me and put him to stud, or maybe I'll just sell him to the first person that makes me a good offer."

"Sell him," Christine scolded, "go to Georgia!"

It was the first time he had mentioned his plan to go to Georgia and as he said it he was looking inquisitively into Christine's eyes, wondering how his words might affect her. What he saw was a sweet, almost impish face that was suddenly starting to turn a bright pink with anger.

"Caleb Quinn," she retorted as she stared with now blazing eyes straight into his, "you're not going to sell him and you're not going anywhere with the palomino unless you take me with him, and that means if the palomino goes to Georgia with you, then so do I."

Finished with her statement, she placed her hands on her hips and raised her chin as if daring him to challenge her.

"All of which I suppose means I'll have to marry you before I can leave with the palomino?"

As Caleb asked the question, Christine had slowly lowered her chin until she was looking down at her clasped hands.

"Yes," came the barely audible reply through lips that barely moved.

Her cheeks seemed suddenly drained of color.

"You drive a hard bargain," said Caleb, excited by her "yes," "and I surely don't want to loose the palomino, so I guess it is Christine Quinn you'll have to become."

Now looking up at Caleb through sparkling bright eyes Christine demanded, "Caleb Quinn, if you don't get off that horse, bad leg or not, and kiss me I'll...I'll..."

She never completed the sentence because Caleb was suddenly off the buckskin and lifting her off her feet with his good arm, then kissing her, a hard bruising kiss that went on and on and on. Finally breaking the kiss but keeping her face next to his she pressed her body firmly against his and in the husky voice that sometimes overcame him whispered in his ear, "Mr. Quinn, if you think proposing to me means you can have your way with me, you're absolutely correct."

"Who did the proposing?" asked Caleb, acting like he hadn't heard the last part of what she had said, when in fact her words had come closer than she knew to bringing him to his knees.

"We can argue about that for the rest of our lives if you wish," said Christine, "but right now I want to take you to my special place and the main reason I brought you here. You are going to see something few men have ever seen, so be ready for another surprise."

She then remounted and led a bemused and curious Caleb toward the far end of the canyon, bringing her horse to a stop about fifty yards from the end of it. A still puzzled Caleb could see nothing out of the ordinary. In fact, the only thing he could see in front of him was a high wall; the same kind of wall that made up the rest of the canyon.

"Wait here until I call for you," she told him. Then she rode about thirty yards further, turned the gray to the right, and disappeared behind where the wall of the canyon jutted out in such a manner that it blended in almost perfectly with the background. To Caleb it seemed as if horse and rider had been absorbed into the canyon wall.

"Christine," he called, not sure he was enjoying this mystery.

"Just wait a minute and don't you move 'til I call you," came her laughing, teasing reply.

Several minutes passed before he again heard her voice. It sounded far away and had a distinctively echoing quality to it.

"Now," she shouted, "come and find me if you can, and I hope you can swim."

Puzzled even more by her reference to swimming, something he had never learned to do, Caleb moved the buckskin forward and turned where Christine had turned. Before him stood Christine's gray, about thirty feet away on totally open ground that offered absolutely no place of concealment. Despite this Christine was not to be seen. After overcoming his initial surprise at her disappearance he set his mind to solving this mystery. A quick look at the canyon's sheer wall convinced him it would have been impossible for anyone to climb it. Still, the only thing Caleb could see of her was her clothes, all of them, hanging on the gray's saddle.

"Damn," he thought as his practiced eye sought a clue to her disappearance. Somehow he knew there had to be an opening somewhere, even if the wall did appear to be solid rock. He was about to call out to her, hoping the sound of her voice would give him a clue to her hiding place, but before he could open his mouth HE SAW IT. It was an upright cylinder of rock that came out about three feet from the wall and was almost indistinguishable from the wall itself. It was like a camouflaged chimney hidden against a perfectly matched background.

Caleb dismounted and following Christine's example removed all his clothes and hung them over his saddle.

Stepping gingerly on his bare feet he walked first to the right of the cylinder and found nothing but an impenetrable rock face. He then moved to the left of the rock formation and was rewarded by the sight of a dimly lit, three foot wide crevice that extended into the wall and then curled out of sight. The crack in the wall was wide enough for a man or woman to pass through but too narrow for a horse.

Caleb entered the crevice and found himself following what seemed to be fifty or more worn hand-carved steps leading downward for over twenty feet. The smoothness and uniformity of the steps intrigued him.

"Somebody must have carved these steps years ago, even centuries ago," marveled Caleb.

He had heard this area of the country might have been populated for thousands of years by peoples who left their marks on the land and then mysteriously disappeared. He could easily understand why this canyon, protected as it was from the weather and prying eyes, would have been where some of them might have lived. Moving ahead his next few steps brought him out of the crevice and into an open area slightly larger than the *Circle P*'s barn floor. An array of crack-like openings in the roof of the enclosure, allowed in enough light to bathe the grotto-like room in soft rays of light and shadow. Along one wall he could see hundreds of white butterflies gathered together to form a moving, breathing wall. A dozen or so butterflies fluttered about the room lending it even more of a magical quality. Caleb realized what Christine had led him to was a hidden miniature box canyon within the larger box canyon, a freak of geography, a secret hidden within a secret.

The floor of the room was half covered by a deep looking pool of blue created by rivulets of water seeping slowly from the canyon's walls. Sitting on a large rock with her long white legs dangling in the pool was Christine.

"Come on in," she invited him, deliberately allowing him to view her entire breathtakingly beautiful body for the first time, "I think you'll love the water."

As Caleb walked around the edge of the pool and approached her he was not exactly sure how to reply to such an offer, so instead he asked, "What's a blue moon?"

Her laughter went ringing through the room.

It was almost dark when the famished couple returned to the ranch house. Watching from the kitchen window was Gram.

As she observed Christine's still wet hair, she murmured to herself, "Guess they've been to the 'secret place,'" and with a smile of understanding she hurried to fix the two lovers their supper.

Chapter 41 Plans

The next morning as Caleb was about to take a seat at the kitchen table he was greeted by Christine who was carrying a tray piled high with eggs, fat back, and a mountain of biscuits covered with butter and honey. After Christine set the food in front of him she filled his cup with hot steaming coffee.

Eying the food Caleb jokingly asked a question he was confident he knew the answer to.

"What have I done to deserve having such a beautiful young lady, such as yourself, serving me such a bountiful breakfast?"

"Well," whispered Christine as she bent close to his ear, "after making me shame myself by proposing to you, and then letting you ravage my innocent young body for hours on end, I thought I would do my best to punish you by serving you a meal almost guaranteed to burst your poor little stomach…or would you prefer wind pudding and hot rabbit tracks?"

"I did not ravage your innocent young body," said Caleb, "I only sought to show you my friendly nature and love of the outdoors. As to the proposal that you claim for your own, if you must know, I already had it in my mind before we got to the canyon that there was no way I was leaving for anywhere without you accepting my proposal. You just beat me to it, and for that I will be eternally grateful because it will give me something to tease you about even when we're old and toothless."

"Is that your way of saying you love me?" asked Christine, while still cherishing the words he'd said over and over the day before.

Adopting a more serious tone, Caleb replied, "I do love you, and I think it started the first time I saw your picture in the locket. I thought then I wanted you for a wife and the mother of my children. I looked at your picture and knew I wanted to have children with you who are good and strong and will make a mark on this land."

Then placing a hand on her cheek added, "And when I lay down for the last time I want you there with me."

"Well, my fine licentious Caleb, if you must know, those are the same thoughts I've had since the first time I saw you lying there wounded in the tent. It broke my heart to see you so badly hurt. To see such a lovely body all cut up and bloody."

Moving together they then shared a deep and passionate kiss that was interrupted by the sound of Tip coming through the door hauling a half-full pail of fresh milk. Ann and Shannon followed him, Ann carrying an apron full of fresh eggs and Shannon holding a handful of fresh flowers.

Looking at the food on the table, Tip asked, "Is this…what is known as the condemned man getting the proverbial last meal?"

"No," said Caleb, realizing news of his and Christine's engagement must already have traveled from Gram to Ann and then Tip, "this is just an example of how I'll expect to be treated as a married man."

"Speaking of marriage," replied Tip, "Ann and I had previously discussed the possibility of you two lovebirds getting married, and now that everyone in the household knows it's a definite fact, we think it would be great if we had a double wedding."

Caleb looked at Christine and could see from the silent approval in her eyes that a double wedding would suit her just fine. He also suspected she and Ann probably had talked about it prior to yesterday's ride to the canyon.

"Yes," he said, speaking for the two of them, "I think a double wedding would be perfect."

"Good," said Ann, "as long as my dear younger sister understands that I, being the older and the prettier, should be the first to say 'I do.'"

"I will certainly defer to your advanced age and beauty," replied Christine. "I also think its time you and I and Shannon go into town to do some shopping if we're going to look like the beautiful brides these two fine gentlemen deserve."

An hour later the wagon was hitched and the three girls were on their way to town. After debating it for about two minutes, Caleb and Tip decided that any work around the ranch that needed doing would have to wait. They caught up with the wagon before it was half-way to town, explaining that they decided to come along as protection for the girls.

It was a typically hot day in the middle of September that found Caleb and Tip outside the Liberty Hill General Store drinking a cool beer and waiting for Christine and Ann to finish buying the cloth and other items they needed to make their wedding finery.

"What prompted you to get yourself a side gun instead of another shoulder rig like you had?" asked Tip, eyeing the new holster and Colt revolver Caleb had strapped around his waist. Caleb had purchased it only minutes before.

"A few reasons," replied Caleb, "most of the time in this part of the country it's too damned hot to wear even a vest, much less a coat, and a shoulder holster is best worn out of sight under coat or vest so that when it's pulled it comes out as a surprise."

"Besides," he added, "I can always wear both if I feel it necessary."

"Yeah," replied Tip, "I recall how you surprised a certain four-flusher when you first came to town."

He didn't mention how surprised he and Dos were at the speed of Caleb's quick draw.

"Secondly," continued Caleb, "I'm thinking a side gun just might be faster when it comes to clearing leather, and given the toughness of this country and the hard cases like you in it, being even slightly faster might mean living instead of dying, and I prefer to do what I can to stay among the living."

Caleb was about to reveal his third reason when the girls exited the store, their arms filled with packages and their eyes sparkling with happiness. Shannon was carrying the largest load.

"I guess we should have brought two wagons instead of just one," joked Tip, but he knew this was a special occasion, the first time in years the cash-strapped girls had spent any of the precious money they'd saved from selling horses to the army.

Ann was quick to fire back at him, "Don't be making fun of what are soon to be the two most beautifully dressed brides in all of Texas," she proudly announced.

"Besides," chimed in Christine, "if you must know, most of these packages are clothes and such for Shannon. It's about time she had clothes of her own and not just our threadbare hand-me-downs."

Caleb was about to reach out and help the girls load their packages into the wagon when he noticed two men approaching, one of them gesturing toward them. Both men wore store-bought suits, Derby hats, and no visible firearms, but they looked like trouble.

"Yankee Carpetbaggers," he heard Tip mutter, "Wonder what they want with us?"

"Excuse me," said the larger of the two men as they approached, "would you ladies be the Pokusa sisters and the current owners of the *Circle P* ranch?"

His voice was both prissy and malicious sounding, something that didn't go unnoticed by Ann who instinctively knew low-lives when she met them.

"Whatever you're selling we don't want any," replied Ann as she looked at the men with obvious disdain.

"I'm not selling, I'm giving," came the reply, and with that he rudely stuffed a piece of folded paper in between two of the packages Ann was holding.

He slowly stepped back, crossed his arms over his chest, and gave all of them a contemptuous look, as if to say, "You don't dare mess with me."

He then continued, "What I've delivered to you, Miss Pokusa, is a fair notice of foreclosure due to the nonpayment of back taxes in the amount of $649.59. You have twenty-eight days to make payment in full to the county tax office. After that your ranch will be foreclosed on and everything on it will become the property of this county and the state of Texas."

Caleb could see that Tip was about to explode, but it was Ann who acted quickly to prevent an incident.

"Gentlemen," said Ann, looking at the two men, "you have served your papers and you should leave...now. Also, should you set one foot on our property before you have a legal right, you will not be treated as officers of the state of Texas but as the common criminals you are."

The second man, smaller and slimmer than the other, then made the mistake of stepping forward and speaking only a few feet from Ann's face, "You'll learn to speak more respectful of us when we take over the ranch," he said arrogantly.

"That," thought Caleb, "makes it personal."

Caleb's temper, which had remained dormant for so long, suddenly flashed. Stepping forward he grabbed the man with one hand and pushing with his other hand shoved him over the hitching rail into the dusty street. The second of the notice servers followed shortly after, courtesy of Tip's booted right foot.

Minutes later the wagon carrying the girls, followed by Tip and Caleb on horseback, headed back to the *Circle P*. From a saloon window across the street from the general store a pair of cold dark Spanish eyes watched them as the buckboard made its way down the road.

Looking back at the men who had been tossed into the street Christine called to Caleb, "Can they do what they said?"

"Yes, they can, but they won't," replied Caleb, already adding to a plan he'd been formulating for several weeks.

They rode slowly on in silence until Ann finally said, "We don't have that kind of money, not anywhere near it, not even if we could sell all the horses and cattle we've been holding in the box. Nobody around here has that kind of money. And we sure won't be able to secure another loan from the bank. The taxes are only delinquent because with everyone off fighting the war or staving off Comanche attacks, the state never even bothered trying to collect land taxes."

"Let's stop for a minute," Caleb said.

Ann pulled the wagon off the road and Caleb and Tip climbed into it.

"I've been wanting to talk to all of you about something, and I think now's the time," said Caleb calmly and reassuringly.

"Have you been keeping some dark and dangerous secrets from me?" asked Christine, using her most playful voice in an attempt to lighten the sober mood brought about by the tax collectors.

"In a way," replied Caleb, "and as I see it, this is as good a time as any for this lucky fiancé of yours to fess up to a serious character flaw."

"Just one?" chided Christine.

"I may have more than one, but just one that I'll admit to. You'll have to find the others out on your own."

"Well, Mr. Quinn, just what is the big flaw you've been keeping from us?"

After clearing his throat Caleb began, "What I'd like all of you to know is that I am far from penniless. I have a good deal of money in a bank back east."

"I'm not rich," Caleb added before his listeners could respond, "but I certainly have enough money to pay the past due taxes on the ranch and then some. I also own a good deal of property in northern Georgia which is partially why I want Christine and me to live there after we're married."

Looking at Tip and then at Ann he added, "When Christine and I go to Georgia I think it's best that we leave you two as the sole owners of the *Circle P*, that is, if Christine agrees."

"Certainly I agree," said Christine, pleased that under circumstances that would put her and Caleb so far away from Texas, he was making the same suggestion she would have.

"That's settled then," said Caleb.

"But I can't...," Ann's words were cut off by Caleb.

"You can, and you will, and you must," said Caleb, "nothing could please me more. Furthermore, it is my intention to provide enough money to you and Tip to not only pay the taxes, but to get the ranch firmly on its feet. Other ranchers are starting to drive cattle to the markets in the north, up in Kansas and Missouri. You use the money to hire some hands and round up enough of the free-ranging longhorns hereabout and do the same. You can also use the money to add more blooded stock to your horse herd."

Tip retorted, "But I don't know how long it will be before we can repay the loan."

"Never think of it as a loan because I neither expect nor want repayment," said Caleb. We're family now. Call it a bride price if you want to, but considering what a wonderful person it is I'm taking away from you I feel I'm paying far too low a price."

Tip and Ann could hear the sincerity in his voice.

Without consulting Tip, Ann said, "We agree to your generous proposal but only if you promise you'll bring my sister back here to visit whenever you can."

"Fair enough," agreed Caleb, "but only if you do your best to visit us whenever possible."

The next day Caleb returned to town and sent an urgent telegram to the Corcoran and Riggs Bank in Washington, D.C. He then sent a second telegram to Mineral Bluff, Georgia. He also stopped by the stage line office to pick up a small package; wedding rings, one for each of the soon-to-be brides.

Chapter 42 Trouble

Caleb spent the next three weeks going back into the canyon, both alone and with Christine, practicing with his new side gun for hour after hour. He realized by the end of the first day's practice that there were two conventional rules for using a handgun that he would ignore. With a shoulder holster you drew, then, with the weapon coming out at nearly eye level, took a split second to line up the target on the revolver's sight. The motion allowed for a quick aim before pulling the trigger. This movement was fairly fast, faster he believed than the sidearm that needed to be lifted to the eye level before aiming and firing. What Caleb realized was that if when using the side gun, he broke with the conventional teachings of draw, aim, and fire and instead simply drew and fired, relying on his own innate ability to aim from the hip, he could draw and shoot faster without losing vital accuracy, especially at close ranges.

The second change was the sight at the end of the revolver's barrel. He realized that with no need to aim along the sight then the only possible function of the sight was to slow down the barrel when it was withdrawn from the holster. Without the sight he could draw just a fraction faster than with it. Caleb wanted that split second. The sight was now completely filed off.

Within days, and after firing hundreds of rounds, Caleb felt he was approaching a degree of proficiency that even Jean Duval might have admired. He was also better prepared for what he thought might soon follow. The third reason he had bought the side arm and wanted to become as proficient with it as possible.

Days later Caleb was under the barn overhang trying to squeeze milk from a reluctant cow when he noticed Dos riding toward him. Because Dos hadn't paid a visit to the ranch since early in Caleb's convalescence, his arrival came as something of a surprise. As Caleb studied Dos a feeling of apprehension passed through him. Something was not right. Dos had ridden past the ranch house without stopping or even looking in that direction and seemed far too focused on him.

Dos stopped his horse about twenty feet from Caleb and then, bringing his right leg over the saddle-horn, slid his lithe body slowly to the ground. Staring straight ahead at Caleb, he firmly swatted his horse on the rump, sending it trotting away.

In a voice barely above a whisper, Dos said, "I understand you intend to marry Christine."

As Caleb suspected by Dos' body language, this visit would not be a friendly one. Dos' tone of voice sounded almost casual, but Caleb knew there was nothing casual about it. Dos, the third reason Caleb had bought the Colt and holster he was now wearing, had come to kill.

"That's correct," replied Caleb, "I suppose you're here because you have some objection to our marriage?"

"I thought you would understand," said Dos, "but instead you could leave and never return, nobody would blame you, and nobody would have to die."

Dos' threatening words started to push Caleb's temper to the brink of becoming a curtain of anger that would not be lifted until a final confrontation occurred. Still, Caleb tried to hold back his temper, knowing such a reaction could lead to a mistake, a fatal mistake. He also had no wish to end the life of a man who was so close to Christine, Ann, and Tip.

"You know I can't do that," shot back Caleb in an unyielding voice, "not now, not ever."

"Then unfortunately someone will have to die," said Dos.

"Yes, someone will die if you force the issue, if that's what it comes to," replied Caleb, now staring not into Dos' half-closed eyes but at his hands with their thumbs hooked into his gun belts. Caleb's own hands hung motionless at his side.

Caleb was looking for any twitch, any movement, even the slightest opening or closing of Dos' fingers. If he saw any of those signs he would start his draw.

The silence between the two men was suddenly shattered by the blast of a shotgun, followed by the ground between them exploding in a sudden shower of rocks and dirt. Unnoticed by either man Christine had emerged from the house, crossed around behind the barn, and now stood under the barn's overhang, Gram's smoking double-barreled shotgun in her hands. She had seen Dos riding up, and she too had read his body language.

"Dos Baca," she told the startled gunman in a firm as rock voice, "I've got one more load of buckshot left in this gun, and I'll use it if I have to."

Dos, who hadn't taken his eyes off Caleb despite the shotgun's blast, slowly turned his head toward her. A quick study of her anger-filled face let him know beyond any doubt she was not making an idle threat.

"I can't let you marry this gringo just because he helped us save you," Dos said, "and besides, I know you have loved me since we were children. If I have to, I'll kill him to stop you from marrying him."

"Hear me clear, Dos," replied Christine. "I do love you, but for the good man you are and as the brother I never had, but not in a marrying way, and not in the way I love Caleb. You've got to understand that."

Dos hesitated for several moments before replying, "Are you sure, Christine, absolutely sure?"

"I am sure I will never marry anyone but Caleb, and I will use this shotgun if you try to stop it from happening," came her reply. Her teeth were clenched and her eyes were turning as cold as stone.

The gunman's shoulders slumped ever so slightly as he focused his eyes intently on Christine's face. Dos then stared at her in silence as a look of resignation grew on his face.

Caleb stood motionless, recognizing that Dos was now deciding on a course of action that could mean life or death. Whether to back off or draw and fire, unmindful of the fact it would most likely cost him his life. Love, Caleb knew, could drive a man, even a man like himself, to do strange and unreasonable things.

Finally reaching a decision Dos spoke to Caleb.

"Amigo," he said, "if not me, I'm glad it is a man such as yourself that Christine has chosen…, and that I don't have to kill you."

Then smiling the charming smile that only he could, Dos added, "Besides, a man like me never knows when he'll need a friend."

"I feel the same way," said Caleb, moving his hands from his side while stepping toward Christine, "and besides, we can't have a double wedding without a certain 'brother' and friend to give away the brides."

Dos now broke into a truly friendly grin. "I will expect the invitation, and also the honor of being the first to give the traditional kiss to the new brides."

"Tip and I will be honored for you to do so."

Hearing those words Dos suddenly went from looking like a stone-cold killer to someone happy to be part of the group.

Without another word Dos then walked over to where his horse had stopped and swung gracefully into the saddle. Turning his horse away from them he headed back toward Tip's ranch.

Caleb and Christine, now standing side by side, watched as Shannon scurried out the front door of the house, shouting, "Wait! Wait!"

Dos pulled his horse to a stop while Shannon, wearing her prettiest new dress and suddenly looking very grown up, stopped next to him. With one hand gripping the toe of his boot she used the other hand to reach up and offer him a handful of wildflowers. Accepting the flowers Dos then bent down out of the saddle and gave Shannon a brief kiss on each cheek.

"Gracias, little one," they heard him say, then he rode out.

Caleb turned to Christine and gently placed his arm around her shoulders. He could see tears of happiness and relief in her eyes.

"You'd better show up on time for the wedding," yelled Christine to Dos as he rode off waving his sombrero.

To the best of anyone's knowledge, a starry-eyed Shannon did not wash her face for the next three days.

Chapter 43 The Homecoming

It was late April, 1866, when Caleb and Christine turned their horses off the main road running between Chattanooga and Knoxville, then headed east out of Cleveland, Tennessee toward North Carolina. It had been a long and arduous trip, filled with memories neither would forget, but their minds were now focused on the new home and the new life that lay ahead. Behind them trailed four fully loaded mud-colored, Percheron mules they'd purchased in Chattanooga. Late that day they picked up the old copper trail at Ocoee Lake and followed it up-river, making camp just before sunset along the eastern shore of the lake.

After unloading the mules and then hobbling them so they wouldn't wander away during the night, Caleb let loose the palomino, now named Prince, and the buckskin which Christine named Tawny, to graze on the foot high mountain grass. Caleb knew the mules, if not hobbled, were more than likely to be gone by morning, but Prince and Tawny, now addicted to the treats Christine invariably carried in her saddlebag, would stay within the sound of her voice. With the animals cared for, Caleb then helped Christine set up camp.

They worked together gathering wood needed for the cooking fire that would also keep them warm in what they had discovered could be chilly nights despite the time of year.

With the fire blazing, Christine took Caleb by the hand and turned him toward the west. They spent several quiet minutes with arms around each other, gazing at the surrounding mountains covered in spring green and back dropped by the setting sun, all of it being reflected in the clear still water of the lake.

"Caleb, this country is even more beautiful than you told me. I'm glad you brought me here to make our home."

"I can't argue with that," replied Caleb while thinking that nothing in this country or anywhere he'd ever been could match the beauty of the girl standing beside him. Thinking back to what had brought them together he found himself still amazed that he was married to a woman such as her.

After eating, they took a brief swim in the lake to wash off days of accumulated sweat and dust, leaving the water only after their lips turned blue. They made love as the sky above them turned brilliant shades of orange, red, and pink. Falling asleep in each other's arms, they both agreed it was the perfect end to a perfect day.

Two days later they turned south at a stone marker with *Atlanta 100 miles* painted on it. An hour later they waded the horses and mules across a small river and into Georgia.

"We should be there any time now," Caleb told Christine as the horses climbed out of the river.

True to his word, little time passed before they were looking at a square Appalachian-designed log cabin sitting on the edge of a clearing that extended down a valley surrounded by high, densely wooded hills. Several acres of the property were enclosed by a three tiered split-rail fence that held within it several cows, a pair of mules, and two horses.

As they approached within fifty yards of the cabin Caleb shouted, "Hello the house," after a moment hearing his words echoing off the nearby mountains.

Samantha, wearing flour on both her face and apron, walked out on the cabin porch and hollered back, "Caleb Quinn, if that's you and your new bride, you are a week late."

Caleb and Christine could see a small child, also covered in flour, peeking out from behind Samantha's skirt.

"It's us," replied Caleb, "...and mighty glad we are to finally be here."

"I don't mean to sound inhospitable," a smiling Samantha replied, "but me and Emmalou are the only ones here and unless you two are starving I'd like to take you to where Matt is just finishing up your new home. That is unless some hunting or fishing got him off track."

"That suits us, and then some," replied Caleb.

He knew that like himself Christine was very anxious to see their new land the house being built on it. They remained on horseback watching as Samantha removed her apron and placed it on the porch rail. She then grabbed a halter from where it hung over a rocking chair and headed for the horses. A few minutes later she was sitting bareback on a black stud horse with Emmy sitting in front of her. With Caleb and Christine following she led them down through the valley for about half a mile amidst winding wagon tracks, then up to the crest of a hill overlooking a scene nearly identical to what they saw as they'd approached the Moore's cabin.

Below them was another, but larger cabin, surrounded by another split-rail fence. Three men could be seen working on the barn set to the north of the house, but what caught Caleb's attention were the two horses in the pasture enclosed by a split rail fence. A small girl of about six or seven was riding bareback on one of the horses. As the horse galloped through the pasture the rider was holding the horse's mane in one hand, laughing out loud, and shouting, "Mama, look at me, Mama!" as she waved and rode toward them.

Caleb looked at Sam not sure he could believe his eyes. It wasn't the sight of a child riding so fearlessly toward them, but the horse she was riding on that left him nearly speechless.

"Those horses," he said, "they're Princess and Angel."

As he turned to look again at the horses and rider his thoughts quickly went back to a dark-haired girl and the horse breeding dynasty she had dreamed of. Just as quickly he dismissed the thoughts. "This," he gratefully told himself, "was a new time and a new place."

He had indeed come home.

"That's them, all right" replied Samantha, "and the little girl with the big mouth is my Eryn Gracie. About a month ago an old man named Cordell showed up here with the horses. Said he was a friend of yours and that you'd know what to do with them."

"Uriah's here?" asked an incredulous Caleb.

"He was," answered Samantha. "He stayed for a week. Spent most of it fishing and hunting with Matthew and telling a bunch of whoppers to anyone who would listen. Lordy, that man could tell stories."

"That would be Uriah," said Caleb, wishing just once more he could have heard his old friend tell another of his tall tales.

"Anyway, we tried to talk him into staying longer 'cause we knew you were on your way, but he said he was anxious to get home to his Rocky Mountains while he still had the eyes to see them. Twice he mentioned wanting to breathe the high mountain air of the Rockies. He had a strangely sad look when he said it. It seemed that in his own way, he was saying his last good-byes to you through us. I got the feeling he really cared a lot about you."

Seeing a touch of sadness on Caleb's face, Samantha placed a sympathetic hand on Caleb's arm and continued, "Anyway, we have hardly been able to get Eryn off of Angel since he left."

Then turning to Christine, she pointed to where the men were working, "There's your new home. I hope you'll like it."

"It looks wonderful, more than wonderful," replied the excited Christine, "I can't thank you enough."

"Don't thank me. Thank Matthew, my brother Mikey who joined us here from Scotland after the war, and our neighbor friend we call Uncle Harrell. They built it and I think it's a house second to none, including my own."

In her haste to see her new home Christine made the mistake of being the first to reach the house, an oversight that allowed a giant of a bearded man to pull her off her horse, swing her in a big circle, and then give her a hug that threatened to break her bones.

"Matthew, put that poor girl down," scolded Samantha, "that's no way to treat a lady, especially before you've even been introduced."

Without so much as a slight strain to his extended arms, Matthew obediently plopped Christine on the ground and turned to Caleb.

"I don't know how we deserved it, but you and me, we got us the two best looking women in these mountains," he said.

"You won't get an argument from me," replied Caleb, "but one of them sure settled for a no account husband."

"You shouldn't talk about yourself like that," Matthew retorted as he walked toward Caleb and extended his hand in welcome.

Behind him Mikey and Uncle Harrell stood silent but smiling. They knew what was coming next.

"It's good to see you too," said Caleb as he looked first at Matthew and then at Samantha. "It took a while to get here, but now we're finally home.

As he was speaking his hand was slowly being squeezed harder and harder. Caleb squeezed back, knowing he was still outmatched by Matthew, but not nearly as badly as he once was.

For the next ten seconds or so the contest went on, much to everyone's enjoyment. Then, to Caleb's relief, Matthew pounded him on the shoulder with his free hand, and announced, "Yes, now you're finally home."

Chapter 44 New Beginnings

It was thirteen days after the new year, 1867, and a steady snowfall of several days had the house and ground blanketed in fluffy white. Caleb and Matthew had spent the last four hours huddled around the fireplace waiting for Samantha and Ma Flowers to do what they had come to the Quinn's cabin to do.

Twice Samantha had emerged from the bedroom, once to fix the men a quick meal and again to let Caleb know everything was going "just fine." All the men needed to do was "be patient, and bring in some more firewood."

Matthew looked at Caleb and could tell he was as nervous as only a first time expectant father can be.

"Don't you worry none," Matthew told Caleb. "Christine is in good hands. Milly Flowers is the best around these parts at midwifing and doctoring. According to some she's brought dozens of babies into this world and not a one worse for the trip."

With a smile he added, "However, I understand she lost at least six or seven first-time fathers."

Caleb was not all that amused.

Toward midnight a drowsy Caleb heard the strong cry of a baby coming from the bedroom. He instantly left his chair and headed for the bedroom door, but before he could open it a quicker moving Matthew grabbed him by the shoulder.

"Better hold off going in there until they call you. They'll need a few minutes to clean things up."

Grudgingly accepting the wisdom of Matthew's words, Caleb returned to his chair. Twenty long minutes later the door opened and Samantha stuck her head out.

"Your family is ready for you," she told Caleb.

Not even remembering to say thank you, Caleb, his stomach churning, hurried into the room as Samantha and Ma Flowers left it.

The first thing he saw by the firelight was Christine, propped up in a sitting position by several pillows. In her arms he could see what looked like a small bundle of clothes.

With little sign on her face of the long ordeal she had just endured, Christine looked down at the bundle in her arms, "Sean Michael Quinn, I'd like to introduce you to your father."

She then lifted a corner of the blanket to reveal a small red face with a full head of dark black hair.

"He's beautiful," said Caleb, reaching out to touch the baby's tiny fingers which closed over his larger one.

Then looking at Christine, he gently touched her cheek with his free hand, "I can't believe something this small could give out such a loud cry."

"He's strong and lusty all right, just like his Papa," Christine replied, pride from their accomplishment beaming from her face.

"Caleb," Christine continued as she looked up at him with a smile, "now that we've got us a Sean Michael, have you thought up a name for our children to come?"

"I can think of one or two," commented Caleb, his thoughts going back to the many friends he'd made since leaving his home in Ballycastle.

Christine, fully aware of the love and intense passion she and Caleb had for each other, replied with a knowing smile on her lips, "I don't think one or two names will be nearly enough."

As Caleb reached out to enfold his wife and son in his arms, the lilting call of a night bird could be heard in the distance.

Coming Soon
The Saga Continues...

The Promise

Beauregard Carroll left the White House by the same secret tunnel he had used when summoned by President Lincoln. President Johnson's last words still burned into his mind.

"We must stop them at all cost."

The light from the single lantern lit his way as he traveled through the five-hundred yard long tunnel. The tunnel, built as a safeguard after the White House had been burned and ransacked by the British in 1814, was damp and lit only by the lantern carried by Beau. It was after 10:00 p.m. when he emerged onto 15th Street and took a seat in the waiting carriage.

"Hurry," he told the driver.

"Yes Sir," answered Phillip as he gave the two black horses in front of him a flick of the buggy whip.

"We've been compromised," Phillip said matter-of-factly as the carriage started to pull away.

He then handed a yellow envelope to Beau.

Beau opened the unsealed envelope paying no visible attention to the spot of blood on it. Inside was a half-inch thick stack of one hundred dollar bills. It looked to be about three thousand dollars. Beau flipped through three on top, noting they all had the same serial number.

Beau glanced at Phillip's dark face.

"You got these courtesy of...?"

"Pigeons."

As he said it, Phillip couldn't hide the small grin on his face.

"You did say pigeons?" questioned Beau.

He knew this wasn't a time for puzzles, but he also knew Phillip had his own way of telling a story.

"Yes Sir," said Phillip noting the anxious look on Beau's face. "It was pigeons that let me know someone was across the street on the Hotel Monaco's roof. Two hours ago I parked the carriage over on F Street so that I didn't draw attention to the great house when I noticed a flock of pigeons fly off the roof. Pigeons don't take to the air at night unless they're disturbed or threatened."

Beau sat silently, suspecting how Phillip's story would unfold.

"So I drove off and circled back behind the hotel and made my way up the back fire escape to the roof. That's where I found a shooter with a scoped rifle beading in on 15ᵗʰ Street."

Beau knew Phillip was a natural hunter of both men and animals and unsurpassed at silently stalking prey, particularly at night. Knowing what would have transpired, he only asked, "Any identification on the shooter?"

"Nothing. No papers, nothing but a red fleur-de-lis tattooed on his wrist. The money was in his coat pocket."

Three hours later the carriage pulled to a stop in front of the Carroll mansion. Beau quickly entered and went to the basement where he spent the next hour tapping out a message on his personal telegraph. When he finished, he checked the spring-loaded Derringer attached to his left forearm, picked up the leather travel bag containing clothes, cash, weapons, and several different identification papers. Moving to the front entrance vestibule he spent several minutes peering through the one-way glass, searching the mansion's grounds for any sign of a threat, anything out of the ordinary. It was an exercise in caution that had served him well for many years, and was now even more necessary if, as Phillip stated, "We've been compromised."

Seeing the approach of the carriage, Beau took one more long look about the grounds and then left the house. The carriage, now being pulled by a fresh pair of horses, had hardly come to a stop when he handed his bag to Phillip.

"Where to?" Phillip asked.

"The train station," answered Beau.

As Beau took his seat in the carriage he noticed the gleaming handle of a small revolver sticking out of his companion's boot. He knew this was only one of several concealed weapons Phillip carried.

"Where we going to catch a train to?" asked Phillip.

Beau casually leaned back in the seat and lit a small cigar and smiled.

"I hear the mountains of Georgia are very nice this time of year."

Novel Facts

While this novel is a work of fiction, it is based upon many actual happenings. Some of the facts are detailed below.

English control of Ireland
The English gained control of Ireland in 1169. They retained control of the island nation for over 800 years and in Northern Island even in the 21st century.

English law repressing the Irish
English laws beginning with the Statutes of Killarney in 1367 were imposed for the purpose of repressing the Irish people. The Penal Laws, enacted in 1695 , were especially harsh.

"Most scholars agree that the Penal Laws helped set the stage for the injustices that occurred during The Great Famine and fueled the fires of racism that were directed against the Irish by the British. Lecky outlined the Penal Laws as follows:

The Catholic Church forbidden to keep church registers.
The Irish Catholic was forbidden the exercise of his religion.
He was forbidden to receive education.
He was forbidden to enter a profession.
He was forbidden to hold public office.
He was forbidden to engage in trade or commerce.
He was forbidden to live in a corporate town or within five miles thereof.
He was forbidden to own a horse of greater value than five pounds."
He was forbidden to own land.
He was forbidden to lease land.
He was forbidden to accept a mortgage on land in security for a loan.
He was forbidden to vote.
He was forbidden to keep any arms for his protection.
He was forbidden to hold a life annuity.
He was forbidden to buy land from a Protestant.
He was forbidden to receive a gift of land from a Protestant.
He was forbidden to inherit land from a Protestant.
He was forbidden to inherit anything from a Protestant.
He was forbidden to rent any land that was worth more than 30 shillings a year.
He was forbidden to reap from his land any profit exceeding a third of the rent.
He could not be guardian to a child.
He could not, when dying, leave his infant children under Catholic guardianship.
He could not attend Catholic worship.
He was compelled by law to attend Protestant worship.
He could not himself educate his child.
He could not send his child to a Catholic teacher.
He could not employ a Catholic teacher to come to his child.

He could not send his child abroad to receive education.
(From: MacManus "The story of the Irish Race" 1921.Devin-Adair Publishing Co., New York).

Hedgerow schools

Being forbidden by law to educate their children, the Irish devised an innovative way for them to receive schooling. A willing teacher would gather the children in a hidden place, often among dense foliage, and teach the children clandestinely.

Potato famine

A devastating potato famine occurred in Ireland from 1845 – 1852 causing one million deaths and forcing emigration of one million Irishman. The plague wiped out the potato crop leaving the Irish without the staple crop of their diet.

Charles Trevelyan

Charles Trevelyan, Assistant Secretary of the British Treasury, during the Irish potato famine was responsible for distributing the grains the English stored in the event of a shortage of food among their people. He refused to release the stores that could have been shipped to Ireland claiming the Irish were not really starving. On an ironic note, most of the grain that was stored had been sent to England from Irish farms.

The Giant's Causeway

The Giant's Causeway is a geologic oddity that exists on the northeast coast of Ireland. It is composed of columnar and massive basalt at the edge of the Antrim Plateau and extends into the water of the Irish Sea that separates Ireland from Scotland.

County Antrim

County Antrim in Northern Ireland spans the upper east coast of the island with Belfast, the capital of Northern Ireland, within its confines. It is bordered on the south by the Republic of Ireland and in the west by County Derry and Lough Neagh. It contains the small villages and towns of Ballycastle, Torr, Cushendun and Carnlough, Carncast, Ballygally, and Carrickfergus,

Death ships

Death ships, many of them converted slavers, were the vehicles by which over a million Irish immigrated to the Americas beginning with the potato famine. During the long journey, which could last several months, the woeful conditions on board often led to the loss of many lives, hence the designation "death ships."

Patapsco River Valley, Fells Point and Fort McHenry

The Patapsco River Valley is the natural inlet from the Atlantic Ocean to the city of Baltimore, Maryland. It flows past Fort McHenry. A battle at the fort during the War of 1812 witnessed by Francis Scott Key inspired him to write the *Stars Spangled Banner*, the National Anthem of the United States..

Help Wanted Irish Need Not Apply

Irish immigrants in the United States often faced the same discrimination they had suffered in their homeland. If they could find work at all it was usually as menial laborers with low paying jobs. The advertisement below from the New York Times in 1854 is an example of the problems the Irish faced.

Circus in the U.S.

The circus in the United States in the mid 1800s was not the circus of Barnum and Bailey but more akin to rolling sideshows, offering juggling, sword swallowers, trick shot artists, horsemen, fortune tellers and snake oil. For many American towns and cities the sideshows were a looked-forward to annual event. At one time in the 19th century there were over a hundred such sideshows operating in the United States, most of them east of the Mississippi.

Coryell's Landing

Coryell's Landing was the location of Coryell's Ferry north of Trenton, NJ on the Delaware River. It was a pivotal position during the Revolutionary War, especially in the Battle of Trenton.

Scots and Irish in the Appalachians

In the 18th century when the British colonies were being formed European migration into Appalachia began. Immigrants from Ireland and Scotland, particularly the Ulster Scots or Scot-Irish, began emigrating from Pennsylvania to the mountain areas to the south. These emigrants moved deeper and deeper into the mountainous terrain from what is now West Virginia as far south as northern Georgia.

Fugitive Slave Act

The Fugitive Slave Act was passed by Congress as part of the Compromise of 1850. The act stated that all runaway slaves must be returned to their masters. The act led to "bounty hunters" tracking runaways into the north as they tried to escape to freedom because of the bounty they would receive from the owners of the slaves.

Civil War

Fort Sumter attack and General Beauregard

When South Carolina became the first state to secede from the Union, General Beauregard became commander of the Confederate forces in Charleston. He was ordered by the Confederate Secretary of War to offer General Anderson, the commander of Fort Sumter, the opportunity to surrender by evacuating the fort leaving it in Confederate hands. Anderson refused and the Battle of Fort Sumter became the first battle of the Civil War.

Berdan's Sharpshooters

During the Civil War snipers were used by both sides. They proved to be effective and lethal fighting forces. There were reports of soldiers, usually officers, being killed at a range of over 800 yards, and one supposed wounding of a Confederate officer at about 1500 years. These snipers were usually marksmen of the highest order and used the best of rifles, including the legendary Sharps with a scope. The most famous of these sharpshooter groups was commanded by Colonel Hiram Berdan and that 1st Regiment became known as Berdan's Sharpshooters.

Enrollment Act
Passed in 1863 the Enrollment Act, passed by Congress said that all men between 20 and 45 had to enroll in the Union army.

Battle of Gettysburg
The Battle of Gettysburg was fought at Gettysburg, Pennsylvania on July 1, 2, and 3, 1863. It was the bloodiest battle of the Civil War. More than 46,000 Americans were casualties of the three day battle. While the Union was considered the victor at Gettysburg, it is easy to say that no one won the battle.

Devil's Den
During the Battle of Gettysburg, Confederate sharpshooters in Devil's Den were captured by Berdan's sharpshooters, an event memorialized in a picture taken by Alexander Gardner that was titled *Death of a Rebel Sniper.*

Planned Assassinations of President Lincoln
There were at least six planned assassinations of Abraham Lincoln during his tenure as president thus justifying the need for the protection that Caleb provided during the Gettysburg Address.

Battle of Spotsylvania
The Battle of Spotsylvania was fought near Spotsylvania Court House in central Virginia on May 8 – 21, 1864. The battle was a Confederate victory with great loss on both sides. Grant's Union forces had 18,000 casualties and Lee's Confederate forces 10,000-13,000 casualties.

Battle of Kennesaw Mountain
The Battle of Kennesaw Mountain was fought in Georgia, just north of the city of Atlanta on June 27 and 28, 1864. The battle resulted in 4,000 casualties. The Confederates won the battle.

Battle of Sailor's Creek
The Battle of Sailor's Creek was the last major battle of the Civil War and was fought on April 6, 1865.. During the battle 8 Confederate generals were killed, probably by sharpshooters. A cavalry troop led by General Custer was one of the many Union cavalry troops that took part in the battle. Lee's Army of Northern Virginia suffered 7,700